Stardust Souls

Gabriela Lavarello

This book is a work of fiction. Names, characters, businesses, organizations, places, events, and incidents are the product of the author's imagination and are used fictitiously. Any resemblance to actual persons, living or dead, events, or locales is entirely coincidental. All quotes retrieved from other works are public domain.

For more information contact:

Gabriela Lavarello:

authorgabrielalavarello@gmail.com

ISBN Paperback: 979-8-9931501-2-3

ISBN eBook: 979-8-9931501-0-9

ISBN Hardcover: 979-8-9931501-1-6

First Edition: October 2025

Also by the Author

The Raymara Chronicles (High Fantasy)

Book 1: *Of Liars and Thieves*

Book 2: *Of Secrets and Serpents*

Book 3: *Of Shadows and Flames*

Short Story Anthologies

Gone by Morning: *The Night Game*

The Fabric of Festivity: *The Christmas Party*

Sweet Bitter Love: *Dear Me*

Romance

The Holiday Proposal

Happy Ending Holiday

To the hearts that ache, and the ones that still dare to love anyway.

Stardust Souls

"LIFE COULD DO NOTHING FOR HER, BEYOND GIVING TIME FOR A BETTER PREPARATION FOR DEATH."

- Jane Austen, *Sense and Sensibility*

Prologue

July 11, 1860

Wails broke through the silent night.

Blood, water, and sweat pooled around the woman, her back and legs quivering with strain.

"You're doing wonderful, Madam Hale. Keep pushing."

And so, the woman did, listening to the quiet yet reassuring instructions of the midwife seated between her open legs. A tear broke through the temporary silence, followed by a whimper that fell from the woman's pale lips.

"One more, Madam. I can see the babe's head."

The midwife whispered words of encouragement to the woman, who, with a groan and final scream, pushed.

A second scream pierced through the air, singing in harmony with the new mother. The babe was blue but wailing, and the woman gasped, the edges of her vision blurring as relief and residual pain flushed through her skin. She let her head knock back against the thin pillow and closed her eyes as a flood of warmth entered her heart, washing away any sense of pain she experienced before.

White light burst across her closed eyelids, and the woman cracked them open to see a ball of white fire streak across the night sky in a magnificent arc. The woman turned away from the comet, knowing very well that her husband was outside, excitedly watching the phenomenon and writing his observations.

It was why he was not with her for the greeting of their first child.

"It's a boy," the midwife sang with a laugh that lightened her delicate features.

The woman sobbed, and a sudden sense of protectiveness flooded through her bones.

"May I hold him?"

The woman's voice was raspy and worn, and her throat burned from both lack of water and incessant screaming. But the silence bothered her more than a sore throat.

"Give me my child," she commanded more strongly now, and mustered the rest of her tattered strength to lift her head.

A gasp whooshed from the woman's body, and horror blanched her soul. The midwife was seated, petrified as she looked down at the babe. He was no longer wailing, but peering up at the midwife with clarity in his silver eyes.

"Those are no human eyes," the midwife quavered and pressed the baby toward the woman.

She nearly recoiled at the sight but forced her fingers to take hold of the baby boy who now stared at her.

"Most babes are born with light eyes," the woman said, forcing logic into her tired mind as she gazed down at the boy. "They will turn into a beautiful blue, or perhaps hazel, just like his father."

"Of course, Madam," the midwife said quickly. "We must finish your birthing."

The woman grunted, pain flowing through her body once again as the midwife relieved her of the afterbirth and cut the umbilical cord. A cooing sound made the woman look down at her baby once more, and mixed emotions of love and fear coursed through her heart. She knew that he was in no way anything other than human, as something otherwise didn't exist.

And yet a glimmer of doubt crawled its way into her chest as she gazed at her baby.

He was already beautiful, even minutes after birth. She could see the man he would be, with sharp cheekbones and full lips that were open slightly as he gazed up at her. Dark lashes framed those strange silver eyes that seemed to peer into her very soul. His skin was dark in contrast to hers, and she knew that his father would be proud of the evidence of his heritage. Fear of how the other children would treat him constricted at her chest already, for he had both his eyes and skin to differentiate him from the rest of Scotland.

"Have you a name for the babe?" the midwife asked, though her clipped tone made it evident that she didn't honestly care to know.

"Matthew," the woman replied softly. "But he will be Milo to those closest to him."

A loud bang upon the bedroom door made the woman jump, and the midwife scurried to the edge of the bed, pulling a thick woolen blanket over the woman's naked body before hurrying to the door. The woman held her breath, wondering if it could perhaps be Duncan, though she knew it wasn't. Her husband would still be out gazing at the great comet, and besides, he would never knock at his own home.

Bright light pooled onto the floor as the door opened, and the fire of the comet's tale was evident. A melodic voice sounded from outside the threshold, and both mother and baby went quiet. The midwife returned shortly, accompanied by an unfamiliar woman. She was fair and short, with hair of flaming red cascading down to her waist. Her face was smattered in freckles, and kind brown eyes gleamed with knowing as she regarded the mother and babe.

"Please forgive me for the abrupt entrance, Madam Hale," the stranger said, and the mother recoiled at the posh British accent that undulated from her tongue.

"Who are you?" the mother asked. "I already have a midwife."

The stranger gestured toward the hall, to where the midwife was now scurrying from sight. "It seems as though you used to have a midwife."

The mother closed her mouth, and a sudden wave of dizziness made her close her eyes with a groan.

"I apologize for my intrusion. You must be exhausted," the stranger spoke again, and she forced her eyes to open again.

"What is your name?" she was able to rasp out.

The stranger took a step closer, and the mother pressed her now sleeping babe closer to her chest. The stranger sensed her tension and stilled; the kindness on her face waned as a sudden seriousness replaced it.

"My name is Lennora Devonne, and I have come to take you and your family away."

The mother recoiled. "We do not need to leave Edinburgh. My family is perfectly safe."

"You are not, I'm afraid," Lennora said, shaking her head. "The birth of your son has put your family in grave danger."

The mother's stomach gave a terrible flop. "And why is that?"

"Because," Lennora said. "Your baby isn't human."

"Whosoever is delighted in solitude, is either a wild beast or a god."

- Aristotle

Chapter 1

Milo

August 16, 1880

Milo's spirit escaped from his body twice in one night.

His dreams had been fitful and strange, and it was common for his spirit to seek solace in a calmer place when the nightmares took over. Pulling away from the sea of stars that his spirit continuously fell into, and returning to his prison of flesh and bone, was difficult, and he found it most unpleasant every time.

A familiar deep ache returned, and his finger twitched, followed by the entire hand. A hard gasp cracked through his chest, and he lurched upright, finding himself on a large bed in an even larger room.

"Mornin', Yer Highness."

A gravelly male voice sounded from the far side of the room, and blinding light sent the prince gasping in tandem with flinging silk sheets over himself. Milo blinked the dancing lights from his vision, and his manservant, Penn, came into focus. He was short and squat, with wisps of greying hair floating around his head like sea grass caught in an invisible tide.

"Penn, what time is it?" Milo groaned, falling back onto the pillows.

"Nearly nine-thirty in the morn', and later than yer royal arse is allowed to be in bed," Penn replied, his thick Liathic brogue making Milo smirk nonetheless at the flippant comment.

Penn tossed a robe over his face, then breezed away to finish opening the heavy satin drapes.

"Today is the dreaded meeting my mother has been talking about all month." Milo grunted as he stood, wrapping the forest-green robe around himself.

"I'm sure there's a reason behind Her Majesty's constant reminding. Yer most forgetful when it comes to your duties as prince, Matthew."

He rolled his eyes, hating the way his full name rolled off Penn's tongue and instantly soothed his nerves.

"Honestly, sometimes I think you forget yer supposed to take over this kingdom one day," Penn continued.

"I do not wish to be king," Milo whispered under his breath as he began rummaging through an old oak dresser in search of a fresh tunic.

"Ye are to be king despite yer groaning, and a king doesn't dally in bed until luncheon," Penn replied, making Milo jump.

After all this time, he frequently forgot that Penn was a goblin, thus his sharp hearing. Milo had always laughed at the fairy tales from the Earth realm, better known as Elaria by the citizens of Astrum, that portrayed goblins as warted, green creatures. However, it wasn't entirely false. He had seen Penn transform into the rather unsavory monster before, but it was a rare occasion, and his manservant knew how to control his temper.

Milo shook his head and grabbed a midnight blue tunic, not bothering to close the dresser behind him.

"It happened again."

Penn faced him, concern flashing across the goblin's gray eyes, which were nearly hidden beneath bush-like eyebrows. The folds of light fatty skin around his thin lips shifted as the manservant frowned and crossed over to Milo.

"No wonder ye were still as a statue when I entered yer rooms," he replied, and Milo heard the hint of worry lacing his otherwise calm tone.

"It's getting easier to navigate back to my body," Milo lied. "I still find no reason to tell my parents."

Penn pursed his lips and helped Milo shrug into a crisp black coat after he had pulled on a pair of plain dark trousers.

"As ye wish, Yer Highness. But one day ye won't be able to swim through those stars as well as ye think, mark me on that."

"I can handle it," Milo ground out, grabbing the polished boots that Penn held out with perhaps a bit too much force.

"That's what ye always say. Now go, Her Majesty seemed ready to hang someone when I walked past her this morn'."

Milo snorted and turned away without answering, knowing just how correct Penn's statement likely was. Before his hand closed around the door handle, Milo paused by a mirror ensconced in gold filigree. He didn't look too disheveled today, though his mop of unruly curls seemed to be defying gravity, sticking up in strange angles around his head. Milo ran a hand through the dark brown strands, wincing as his finger caught on a tangle. His attention drifted down to his eyes, and he sighed.

Veins of white crisscrossed over silver eyes framed by dark lashes, for which many girls and boys had admonished Milo's luck. In truth, Milo was partial to his eyes. They were the only part that truly felt like him, though he'd been seasoned to fear them since the dawn of his first memory.

His eyes made him different.

Dangerous.

Unnatural.

"Yer going to be late for breakfast, Lad," Penn's rough voice called, breaking Milo from his anxious thoughts.

He shook his head, barely glancing at his long limbs and polished boots before yanking the door open and stepping out into the morning.

It was a bright day at Rightford Castle, and humid summer air filtered through open windows as Milo passed through a grand hallway lined with paintings of magical rulers long past. His stomach rumbled, and soon the thought of a large breakfast pushed away any worries of astral projecting and his worried mother.

"Matthew Rose Hale, watch where you're going!"

Milo stopped in his tracks and blinked, finding himself almost nose-to-nose with Esther Hale, his mother. Esther was a stunning woman, or at least as stunning as women could be, in Milo's opinion.

Her mid-age was far from evident on her smooth ivory skin, and intelligent blue eyes scrutinized him in a way that never failed to make him feel sorry, even if he hadn't done anything wrong. Her thin lips were almost rendered invisible from being pressed together in a frown, and her long, straw-colored hair was twisted into an expert updo pinned to the top of her head, leaving a few strands out to frame her heart-shaped face.

"Don't be silly, Milo. The dining room is in the opposite direction."

"I thought of going down to the city for breakfast today." Milo shrugged and knew immediately that his mother would be close to fainting at the thought of him leaving Rightford Castle without an escort.

"Don't worry, Your Majesty, he's coming with me."

Milo turned, and a grin instinctively bloomed on his lips at the sight of his closest friend, Jeremy Nightingale. The warlock was tall and powerfully built, with a shock of flame-red hair that always seemed to lie in perfect waves around his head. Freckles peppered his fair skin and sharp jaw, accentuating long lashes and full brows that framed his midnight blue eyes. His lips were curved into a sensuous smile that made Milo's knees wobble, though he had never allowed himself to entertain anything other than simply admiring his dashing friend.

Milo cleared his throat and took a step closer to Jeremy before turning to his mother. Her gaze was stern, though Milo sensed genuine concern radiating from her otherwise harsh expression.

"Very well," Esther relented. "I suppose it's only right, as you have the day off from your studies."

Relief made Milo smile. "Thank you, Mother."

"Just remember to return to the castle before sunset," Esther said with a tinge of excitement. "The meeting is finally upon us."

"Of course, Mother."

With a final look between the two boys, Esther swept away, her exit punctuated by the click of her heeled boots.

"What was that about?" Jeremy asked.

"Breakfast," Milo grunted.

"You still haven't been able to learn what this blasted meeting is about?" Jeremy asked.

"She said something about visiting the vampire clan from Red City last week. I didn't ask further questions about it."

Jeremy tensed, and rage flashed across his features.

"I don't see why she'd want to be in the same room with those monsters."

The subject of vampires was never a welcome one around Jeremy, as the very thought of the blood-sucking monsters made his friend's past make an unwelcome return. Milo quickly blinked away the image of the young warlock standing in the threshold of Rightford Castle, covered in blood and shivering like a kitten.

"Gods, I'm sorry, Jeremy," Milo mumbled. "I always say the wrong thing."

Jeremy shook his head, and an easy grin returned to his lips. "Don't apologize. Your painful honesty and lack of self-restraint are what I love about you most."

Milo's cheeks grew hot, and Jeremy punched him lightly on the shoulder. It wasn't that he didn't care about the feelings of others; it was that he forgot how to hold back when a thought came to his mind.

"Come on, Star Prince, let's get you some breakfast," Jeremy said and clapped his back.

Milo rolled his eyes again and fell into step beside his friend, their shoulders brushing occasionally as they moved down a flight of stone steps. He looked out of the old windows that lined the hallway, overlooking Itiltica, the capital city of Cathair Liath. The city sprawled out below the hill upon which Rightford Castle stood. The tall central clock tower was just visible through the misty morning, and the rest of the dark stone buildings were mere smudges within the sea of gray. Milo's father, Duncan Hale, had always told him about how similar Itiltica was to his home city of Edinburgh in Elaria, which had always made Milo feel as though the place wasn't so special after all. What was the point in having a beautiful city at your doorstep when its replica existed beyond a thin portal veil?

"Milo, you're doing it again."

Milo blinked twice and let out a small sigh.

"Sorry," he said, angling his head to find Jeremy watching him.

"You really are the only person who thinks so loud I can almost hear you."

Milo shrugged. "The world is vast and there's much to think about."

"That's your way of saying how insignificant you feel your life is in relation to all of existence."

Milo didn't answer, and Jeremy continued, "You're a prince, Matthew. Whatever notions you may have about Astrum not mattering are ridiculous."

Milo sighed. "I know. But is it that foolish of me to feel this is all a bit ridiculous if there is a twin of our entire world floating around somewhere?"

"Not floating around somewhere. Our reality is quite literally sitting on top of Elaria."

"Semantics," Milo replied with a dismissive wave.

"I understand that you want to experience more than your life in this castle, I really do," Jeremy said. "But you can't blame the placement of our realm for your lack of enthusiasm to become king."

Milo's chest constricted, and he nodded once. This was always how they were; Milo's mind took him to faraway places, and Jeremy was always there to anchor him back to reality.

"You called me Matthew," Milo said, raising his eyebrows. "I hate it when you call me that."

Jeremy chuckled deep and low, and he leaned into Milo as they reached the arched gates and stepped out into the gray morning that threatened rain.

"That's why it's my favorite thing to call you."

"LOCK UP YOUR LIBRARIES IF YOU LIKE; BUT THERE IS NO GATE, NO LOCK, NO BOLT THAT YOU CAN SET UPON THE FREEDOM OF MY MIND."

- Virginia Woolf, *A Room of One's Own*

Chapter 2

Frances

Frances Baudelaire was covered in blood.

Her fingers were sticky with it, and the tangy smell coated her nostrils. A curse flew from her tongue as she fumbled with a large shard of glass lying within the pool of crimson. The vial of blood had been intended to be her midnight snack, but her trailing thoughts made her slip. The blood was still warm, and she wondered which poor soul had been offered up as a sacrifice, only to be unceremoniously wasted on the black marble floors.

"Princesse!"

Frances shot to her feet at the shrill female voice and turned to find a plump maid with stark black eyes and hair to match, waddling closer. Frances took a step away from the broken vial and shot Cecile, the maid, an apologetic smile.

"I lost my grip," Frances said and wiped her palms across the fine, crushed silk of her violet gown.

Cecile clenched her jaw and shook her head. "Oh, Princesse, you are much too clumsy when your mind is occupied with those silly books from Elaria."

Frances pursed her lips and took another step back as the

maid bent down to clean the mess. Cecile was correct in her assumptions; Frances had dropped the vial because she was mulling over the last mystery novel she had just started.

"They are not silly, Cecile. They are teaching me."

Cecile snorted. "Teaching you what exactly?"

Frances bared her teeth, allowing her canines to lengthen and prick her lower lip. It was a warning for the maid to back off, but Frances knew she would do no such thing. Cecile was a vampire herself and had never followed correct etiquette toward Frances or the rest of the Baudelaire clan. It was something Frances admired, if not enjoyed most, about Cecile—only not when her harsh words targeted literature.

"Aah, *calme-toi*, Princesse," Cecile said with a wave of her pudgy hand. "I will clean your mess."

Frances tilted her head in silent thanks before gliding in the direction of her rooms. Pain sliced into her lower lip, and Frances cringed as she retracted her fangs and ran her tongue along the punctures now slick with blood. Her stomach let out a growl of hunger, and Frances silently reprimanded herself again for her clumsiness.

Château des Ténèbres was quiet at this late hour, and Frances relished the feeling of being alone and unwatched by her mother's servants. Her gaze traveled from the black marble floor to the gilded stone walls surrounding her, which were adorned with murals depicting angels and demons communing, fighting, and engaging in other animalistic activities. The castle had been home to Irdin, one of the first angels to come down to Astrum during the realm's creation, and the mighty battle where the angel had been slain was now written upon the walls of their home forever. Frances snorted and glanced out the stained-glass window at the end of the hall, though she saw nothing other than faint streaks of rain spattering against the red and blue panes.

A memory flashed across her mind; her and her father

standing amidst a storm, his smiling face turned toward the heavens as thunder cracked through the sky and rain pounded down on them. She blinked and turned away from the window. She took two long strides to her bedroom and stepped inside before firmly shutting the door, and the memory of her deceased father in the hallway beyond.

Parchment crunched underfoot, and Frances let out a curse as she stooped to grab a rogue page. She folded it without looking, moving through the mystery novels, science textbooks, and forensic journals stacked and crammed on every surface of the room. Some called her obsession with books and academic journals unhealthy, but it was the only way she could learn. If she had only known how to read the signs of struggle and causes of death one year ago, she would have caught her father's killer.

His death had been announced to the country as the result of a hunting accident, though how anyone had believed that story, Frances didn't know. It had been a cover-up, a way to hide any signs of weakness. Because though her father had died during a hunting trip, it had not been an accident—no.

A rogue vampire had murdered him.

Rogue vampires belonged to no clan, although they frequently formed groups with each other, and their addled minds had only one focus: to kill. It didn't matter that the assassin—his once sane mind overturned by toxic blood—had been captured and beheaded in secret on her mother's command nearly three months after the incident. If Frances had known sooner, she would have caught him that day, and she could have been the one to kill the worthless man.

Frances let out a shaky sigh and began undoing the laces of her blood-soaked dress. The fabric sighed and swooshed to pool at her feet as she stepped out of it, and she sat in her favorite red velvet chair, situated before a wooden desk stacked with more papers and books.

She caught her reflection in the small mirror perched upon the desk, finding sad blue eyes staring back at her. Frances tilted her head, wiping away a streak of blood that had smeared across her creamy cheek. Her skin was smooth and void of blemishes, much to Frances's distaste. She had always loved freckles and thought it was one of the grander crimes not to have been gifted with them.

Her lips tilted down in a frown, which was always the telltale sign that she was thinking too much. Long lashes and dark eyebrows framed her eyes, and her strong nose gave her a severe and intimidating appearance, yet she was beautiful, according to past lovers.

Frances's gaze fell to the desk, where an old piece of parchment depicting an autopsy of the human stomach lay before her. Frances pushed it aside with a groan, wishing for once that she was not interested in such horrific subjects.

"Frances, are you there?"

Frances jumped and turned toward the door, where a muffled male voice called her name. She stifled a wave of excitement and arousal at that voice and hastened to answer it. The man who waited in the hall never failed to make her knees buckle and heart race. Well, if she had a heart, she would think his presence would quicken it.

She opened the door and let out a short exhale as she met the sight of a man with wine-red eyes and sultry lips, framed by angular cheekbones and rich brown hair.

"Anton," Frances murmured, and the demon smiled.

"NOWADAYS PEOPLE KNOW THE PRICE OF EVERYTHING AND THE VALUE OF NOTHING."

- Oscar Wilde, *The Picture of Dorian Gray*

Chapter 3

Milo

Honey slid through Milo's fingers and dripped onto the cobbled street. The sticky bun burst with flavor against his tongue, sugary dough filling him with more satisfaction than he dared admit. Though he was a twenty-year-old prince, it was a rare occasion for his mother to let him find a bakery and eat such delectable treats, and an even rarer occasion at the castle cooks would dare defy her and send him sugary pastries in secret.

Jeremy let out a groan of pleasure at Milo's side as he bit into his sticky bun, and Milo chuckled at the sight of his friend's ecstasy.

"You need to find a girl soon. I fear for that sticky bun if you don't."

Jeremy narrowed his gaze and took the last bite, another more exaggerated moan flying from his lips and making a few passersby give him odd stares.

"Why would I need a woman to satisfy me when this bun did an excellent job?" Jeremy asked, licking the residual honey from his palms.

Milo tore his gaze from Jeremy's tongue and focused on

finishing his own food, though his own fingers suddenly felt much too sticky.

"Besides, Lyra would kill me if I were to bring a girl home without telling her," Jeremy continued, utterly oblivious to Milo's sudden lack of oxygen.

It wasn't that Milo had feelings for Jeremy, because he most certainly did *not*. But it was no use when his friend did things to other parts of his body. Damn the Gods, maybe it was he who needed to find someone soon. Milo tore his thoughts from his particular needs and focused on Jeremy's comment, the image of a light-haired girl floating into his mind.

"She is desperate for you to find love. I swear I can see her withering away each time you turn someone down."

Jeremy snorted and wiped his hands on his trousers. "That is because my cousin knows nothing of love or at least is unaware that it's not something one simply flings at another with the first sign of attraction."

Milo shrugged and finished off his sticky bun with a sinking feeling. It was likely the last time his mother would let him take a meal in the city for a long while.

"Come on." Milo sighed. "We might want to return to the castle before we overstay our welcome."

"Let's go to Lennora's first. You can ask Lyra if I'm as abstinent as a priestess." Jeremy winked, and they started down the cobbled road.

Large stone buildings with dirt-smeared windows intermingled with smaller, shabbier shops and homes. The city was disorganized and chaotic, which made Milo love it all the more. They passed vending carts manned by gnarled hags and proper gentlemen, though Milo knew their pristine attire and smooth skin were a glamour covering up whatever unsavory creatures lay beneath.

They turned down the main road until they reached a

large stone bridge that marked the city's entrance. Milo glanced over the edge and down to the river below. Large fish and water sprites danced in the water, and a lone toad croaked from the muddy riverbed.

"Hurry up, or I'll leave you behind," Jeremy called from ahead, and Milo tore his attention from the river to catch up with his friend.

They walked in silence for a few minutes, and soon the soft swish of tall grasses swept against Milo's legs as they walked through the field separating the city from Blackwood Forest, a sprawling place into which few ventured.

"Why haven't you found someone?" Milo asked. "It's not as though you receive little attention. Just the other day, that girl nearly fainted in your presence."

It was nearly a daily occurrence for a woman or man to throw themselves at Jeremy, even in Milo's company. But when Jeremy ignored each advance, it had become something close to a game: predicting how many suitors he would receive in one night. Milo knew he took some to his bed but never let another into the depths of his soul. Milo was positive he knew Jeremy best, and though it offered a strange sense of pride, he still yearned for his friend's happiness.

Jeremy sighed, his breath puffing out in a silver plume through the crisp, drizzling day. He was silent for some time, and Milo was almost sure he wouldn't respond. A duck quacked from a distant pond that glittered in the weak daylight. They entered a thicket of dense trees and foliage on the outskirts of the city before Jeremy finally spoke.

"I'm incapable of loving. Everything I have ever loved has either died or been ripped away from me. I find it pointless to soften my heart when it will all be for nought."

Milo's chest tightened, and he reached out to squeeze Jeremy's arm. "I'm still here. So are Lennora and Lyra."

Jeremy shook his head. "Not like that. I know you love

me, but I fear that it will be torn away from me every second of the day. After…"

"That night," Milo finished for his friend as he seemed to choke on the words.

Jeremy gave a curt nod. "After that night, I can't help but think that this has all been a dream and I might wake up at any moment."

"You were six years old," Milo murmured, and Jeremy shrugged again.

"It doesn't change what happened."

He had been there for his friend since Lennora had brought him to the castle fourteen years ago. Milo had been six years old as well, but all the time in the world and such a young age would never take away the memory of Jeremy covered in his family's blood.

A raven's cry flung Milo back to reality, and he blinked to find the gray outline of Lennora's cottage already in sight. The lush forest almost swallowed the stone building, though he was sure that the witch preferred it that way. Summer had a habit of doing odd things to Blackwood Forest, such as making even the smallest of wildflowers grow to impossible heights in the blink of an eye. The tall grass caressed Milo's legs as they pushed through the foliage, and Jeremy moved ahead as they neared the cloud of wings and claws.

"Shite, the little bastards never leave, do they?"

Milo knew what Jeremy was speaking about without having to ask, for the unkindness of ravens clustered around the cottage was obvious enough for a blind man to take notice. Jeremy waved and cursed at the big black birds, who cawed and flapped their wings in protest. The short stone wall lining a small flower garden on either side of the cottage was nearly obscured by the birds, and Milo reluctantly shooed away a smaller raven that started pecking at his boots.

"Why are there so many of them?" Milo asked, continuing

to stomp his way through the flurry of wings and loud caws in search of the red front door.

"They're attracted to the magic," Jeremy sputtered through a mouthful of feathers as a raven grazed his face and flapped away. "It gets worse each time Lennora casts a powerful spell."

The entrance finally came into view, and Milo lunged for the copper handle, nearly tearing it off the old painted wood in attempts to wrench it open. He and Jeremy stumbled inside, and Jeremy gave one last shout of indignation toward the crying birds before shutting them outside.

Milo surveyed the simple interior that had not changed since he could remember first visiting the witch's cottage. It was made entirely of stone, from the dark floors all the way to the tall walls. The only parts that were not stone were the two small windows on either long wall, and the thatched roof that constantly leaked during the rainy season, which was *always,* considering they were in the rainiest region of the realm. A rickety, dented wood table stood flush underneath one of the windows, and a bundle of rosemary burned within a shimmering shell bowl. A vase of wildflowers, no doubt Lyra's doing, sat next to the bowl in a myriad of warm colors. A dark velvet curtain was strung across the far wall to hide away Lyra and Lennora's bedchamber, which was two cots set against opposing walls.

A small counter and fireplace lined against the wall opposite the table, embers still glowing hot within the small hearth. But it was not the simple splendor of the place that made Milo's heart lurch every time he entered it. It was the books.

Textbooks and ancient scrolls of lore were stacked and piled on every spare surface of the place, and a stack of papers even covered the seat of the singular reading chair in the room, which pressed into a corner near a small table coated in dried wax. Milo ducked under a bundle of herbs that hung from the ceiling and moved toward the chair while Jeremy started rebuilding the small fire.

"Where have they gone off to?" Milo asked absentmindedly as he thumbed through the yellowing parchments.

"Not a clue, my guess is that Lennora had to pry Lyra from a new lover," Jeremy answered before muttering something under his breath, conjuring new flames to settle over the logs.

Before Milo could reply, the cottage entrance burst open, causing him to drop the delicate pages back to the chair. Milo could hardly tell who had just entered from the flurry of cloaks and hair that swirled about. The loud curses and arguments were not hard to understand, however, and it was obvious that Lyra and Lennora had arrived.

"I am not a child, Mother, I can do what I bloody want!"

Lyra Devonne stomped past Milo and disappeared behind the silk curtain, only to reemerge with a different dress already strewn halfway over her naked body. Milo turned away at the sight of her soft skin and grimaced, not ever understanding the girl's dismissal of even a bit of modesty. No, Milo had seen Lyra's nude body more times than he had ever seen any other woman nude, which was not saying much, because he was never inclined to see them in such a state of undress.

"You are only nineteen years old and still living under my roof!" Lennora bellowed back, not before she leaned over and placed a quick kiss against Jeremy's cheek.

Lyra huffed and put her hands on her hips. "It wasn't even a very dangerous spell; I had it under control."

Lennora scoffed and approached Milo, giving him a tired and slightly exasperated smile before planting a kiss on his cheek as well.

"What is this all about?" Jeremy asked, standing.

A streak of coal dust smudged across his cheek, and Milo ached to brush it away. Lyra rolled her eyes and moved to stand with her back to Jeremy. He instantly began lacing up the back of her new gown, the long periwinkle skirts brushing merrily upon the dusty floor.

"Mother walked in on Edward and me while we were—well, it doesn't matter now." Lyra shook her head. "The point is that I will never see him again, and it's all her fault."

Milo and Jeremy exchanged an incredulous look before Lennora replied. "Your cousin was trying to put a binding enchantment on the young man while they were engaged in a rather... private act."

"Mother, I'm surprised you conceived me if your way of saying I was fucking the man is that we were engaged in a 'private act'," she raised her fingers to make quotation marks in the air, a further punctuation that made Lennora's cheeks flush scarlet.

"Watch your tongue, young woman. I have no issue turning you into one of those ravens flocked outside the cottage."

Lyra made a face at her mother, knowing very well that Lennora would stand by her word. Jeremy finished tying off the laces and squeezed his cousin's shoulders.

"What kind of binding enchantment did you attempt?"

His question was curious, and Milo knew it was his way of making his cousin feel comfortable in telling the truth. Lyra breezed past Milo to plop down upon the chair, sending a physical cringe coursing through Milo's body at the soft crunch of papers under her weight—*ungrateful woman.*

"Edward has continued seeing other women when he told me that he was being faithful," Lyra huffed. "I wanted to bind his favorite part so that it would only work properly when he engaged with me."

That uncomfortable heat flew to Milo's cheeks again, and he watched the girl in horrified awe. She was pretty, with long golden hair that fell in loose waves to her waist and intelligent emerald eyes. Her cheeks were round in the way that most men would consider charming, but her sharp nose and shapely figure made her stunning. Or so he was told.

"Binding a man's bit to remain limp sounds like a grievous act indeed," Jeremy said with a grin. "Shame Lennora arrived so soon."

Milo stood outside the conversation, enjoying the banter between Jeremy and Lyra. They'd been this way since he could remember, and days spent in the cottage always brought back the best memories he had. He angled his head to watch Lennora, who muttered to herself and gathered books that had fallen across the floor in the tizzy of hers and Lyra's entrance. Milo moved to help, and she gave him a grateful look as he leaned to pick up a fallen tome, offering it to her.

"Thank you, dear," Lennora said, taking it.

"I'm guessing that Lyra was not successful in this binding ritual?" Milo asked, his voice cracking slightly at the mention of any binding.

"Of course I was successful." Lyra snorted, then shot a glare at her mother. "But it was undone within minutes."

"And with good reason, too," Lennora said. "That boy is trouble, and I didn't need him finding our home to get to you."

Lyra frowned and looked between Jeremy and Milo. "What are you two doing here anyway? Milo, don't you have that meeting to attend today?"

"We wanted to see you. Is that so hard to believe?" Jeremy replied.

"You chose the worst day possible to visit, I'm afraid. Mother has been in fits all day preparing for the queen's meeting, and now I'm in shambles because my life has been ruined."

"Lyra, I will have you clean the well if you don't shut your mouth," Lennora snapped, and Lyra's smug expression turned sour.

"That's not fair, mother, the well spirit always pulls at my hair and drops leeches on my arms."

Lennora gave her a stern look. "Exactly my point, dear."

Milo moved to stand next to Jeremy, and they exchanged a glance that begged for escape from the bickering witches.

"We must be going, but I will see you at the castle in the evening," Jeremy said, giving both his cousin and adoptive mother a dashing grin.

Lyra shrugged and disappeared behind the velvet curtain once more. Lennora gave them both a look that Milo could swear was worry.

"Be safe, boys. I will see you before the meeting, Jeremy. I believe your mother said we were to meet in her sitting room at eight o'clock tonight, Milo dear."

Milo and Jeremy turned to leave, and Milo couldn't sway the unease that churned in his gut. The ravens had scattered some since their arrival, but Milo still had to swat away a few rogue wings that brushed past his head.

"I'm not sure if I like the sound of this meeting after all," Milo grumbled after a bout of silence.

"I doubt that it will be anything to worry about," Jeremy replied. "I'm sure you're already overthinking it."

Milo didn't answer immediately. His head felt thick, and worry was already nagging at him. Jeremy was right, damn him. He overthought absolutely everything, and this was no exception. Milo supposed his friend was right, but it didn't help the sinking feeling and sense of foreboding that plagued him the rest of the way to Rightford Castle.

“WHERE THERE IS
NO IMAGINATION,
THERE IS NO HORROR.”

- Arthur Conan Doyle, *A Study in Scarlet*

Chapter 4

Frances

"Hello, Miss Baudelaire."

Anton Ferrazco, a demon prince and her current lover, stood at the threshold of her bedroom, his smile of dark honey making warmth pool in her stomach.

"What are you doing here?" Frances asked, stepping aside to let him pass.

The demon took two long strides inside before waiting for her to close the door with a soft click. Frances didn't want to hear his response; it did not matter. She wanted to be close to him, to feel their bodies pressed together most intimately. Anton flashed her another breathtaking smile and stepped closer.

His answer was cut off by Frances's lips crashing against his, her head tilted up, and palms braced against his broad chest to reach his height. He answered the kiss without hesitation, and heat pooled low in her abdomen as he nipped her bottom lip with a low growl.

"*Mi Reina*," he breathed, the foreign words nearly making her knees buckle.

One hand traveled down his chest to rest against the waistband of his trousers, all while their lips and tongues moved in a well-practiced dance. She had always enjoyed sleeping with the prince, his tastes and preferences in bed aligning with hers. It was one of the reasons she had returned to him for almost four months, his excitement for rougher kinds of intimacy setting her body ablaze.

Anton shook his head softly and caught her trailing hand in his, stopping it just shy of its intended destination. Frances let out a sound of disappointment, and he pulled back just enough to look down at her.

"I have come to pay my respects and to say goodbye."

Frances frowned, her hand still on his chest, now gripping his lapels.

"To say goodbye? Why?"

Anton pressed his swollen lips together and shook his head, a lock of dark hair falling over his brow. Frances instinctively reached up to brush it back, but he caught that hand too and gently pushed it away.

"Please. I cannot waste time here with you, no matter the lovely past we have shared."

Pain, slow and steady, began to creep into her chest.

"Why?" she asked again, and Anton let out a huff of frustration.

"*Mierda mujer*, do you not care that you are to be married in two months?"

Frances blinked, the sudden surprise nearly making her stumble. "What?"

Anton seemed to notice her shock, and his own expression softened, the anger that made his wine-colored eyes flare scarlet dying away. "You did not know. I apologize."

"I would know if I were getting married in two months, which I certainly am not," Frances snapped, confusion and growing concern flooding her senses.

Anton growled again, his gaze traveling the length of her

naked body, nostrils flaring. He seemed able to smell her lingering desire, too.

"Put something on, please," Anton said, his voice strained.

Frances placed her hands on her full hips and raised her eyebrows, ignoring his request for modesty. "I am not getting married. I don't know how you obtained this information, and I frankly don't care. If you want to end our affair, then say so; it would hurt much less than this."

The demon closed his eyes and let out a short, strangled breath.

"Your brother came to me this morning," he replied quietly. "He would not tell me the details, but it was clear that you are betrothed to another, and I must cease communicating with you."

The world spun slightly, and Frances thought she might faint. Anton seemed to notice her trembling knees and reached for her, gently settling her back onto the velvet chair. How could her brother have arranged a marriage for her without her knowledge?

Soft fabric whispered over her skin, and Frances blinked, her focus returning to Anton, who had swept a sheet over her body. His touch was gentle and steady as he tucked it around her shoulders and draped it over her chest. She had only seen this side of the demon prince once, after a particularly eventful night of lovemaking that had ended in a few bruises forming on her pale skin. It had been the first time she'd ever gotten a bruise, and before that moment, she had thought her undead state could not elicit such a human response to pain.

"Did he say whom I was to marry?" Frances asked.

Anton shook his head, and a bark of laughter escaped her lips. This was positively the worst joke her brother had ever played on her. Ridiculous and utterly impossible. She was not getting married in two months; she would not.

"*Putain,*" she spat, and Anton cringed.

Though he came from Solaria, one of the southern countries in Astrum that humans had called Spain during her travels in Elaria, he understood French perfectly.

"Please, watch your tongue, my dear. This does not grant license for such profane language," Anton said, placing his large hand over her trembling ones.

"You have come to me with life-changing news, Anton, if you are correct and my brother did commit this atrocious decision. I think this situation perfectly warrants profane language."

Anton sighed. "I understand, and I don't blame you. But my time here is short, and I wanted to give you something before we part ways."

Frances looked into Anton's eyes and ached to smooth away the crease in his brow. But she could not, and he did not wish her to. She kept her fists clasped tightly in her lap as Anton released his grip and reached into his coat.

He withdrew a rectangular box of dark, polished wood, and Frances frowned. "Anton, you know I don't like jewelry."

"It's not jewelry, *Mi Amor*. It is something much better."

Anton pressed a small brass button at the base of the long side, and the lid sprang open. Two daggers gleamed up at her: one silvery white, the other pure obsidian. The hilts were bound with black leather, twin serpent heads etched into the pommels. Frances let out a squeal of glee she would otherwise have suppressed. She had never been allowed one, let alone two, as her family deemed their status and breed sufficient protection against any unsavory onslaughts. The image of her father's dead body flashed through her mind, and Frances blinked rapidly. Anton's smile faltered, and he began to close the box.

"Don't," Frances said quickly, placing her hand over his to stop him.

Anton's eyes flicked up to hers, and he offered the box, letting her take it into her lap.

"They are Tormenta and Infierno — Storm and Hell," Anton said, pointing to the black blade first, then the silver.

"They are beautiful," Frances said, frowning. "But I don't know how to wield a blade."

Anton's lip quirked, and he gently lifted the silver blade — Infierno.

"You do not need to know how to wield a weapon to wield these," he explained. "This one binds itself to a target and deals a killing blow, no matter how poorly it has been thrown."

"That's possible?"

"When a demon blacksmith forges it, yes."

"What does this one do?" Frances asked, pointing to the black blade as he gently replaced the silver in its spot.

"That one is a weapon of torture," Anton said. "It functions similarly in binding to its victim, but it targets the less deadly — yet far more painful — parts of the body."

Frances shivered, and Anton closed the box. He drew to his feet, gaze still locked on her, pain flickering in his eyes.

"I have cherished our time together. Remember that," Anton murmured.

Frances's heart sank, and she placed the box on the cluttered desk before standing, letting the sheet fall from her body. Anton let out a strangled curse and looked away.

"I am trying to keep this parting quick, but you are making it dreadfully hard," he growled.

Frances smirked knowingly, stepping closer, sashaying her hips and forcing his gaze back to hers with a flash of her magic. He tensed at the sensation, eyes widening slightly as she ran her tongue across her upper lip.

"You have already wasted too much time explaining my

bleak future," Frances replied. "And besides, what if I, too, wish to give you a parting gift?"

Anton's throat bobbed, and he remained still as Frances ran a finger down the buttons lining his trousers. The fabric under her touch was tight and straining, and her smile grew.

"Frances," Anton breathed.

"Anton," she echoed. "Do you not want me one last time?"

She ran her finger along him again with more pressure, and his soft groan was answer enough. A curse in Spanish flew from his lips, and he leaned down, crashing his lips against hers. She opened her mouth instantly, his tongue brushing teasingly against hers. She gasped as he trailed his hands over her curves, and she gripped his groin lightly, eliciting a growl from him in turn.

"Lock the door," Frances commanded against his lips, and he broke away just long enough to obey.

Her body ached, and she didn't hesitate as he turned back to her. She unbuttoned his trousers in one quick movement. The sight of his considerable length made desire thrum through her veins, but she had offered him a gift, and she would be damned if she didn't deliver. Anton's eyes clouded with lust as she wrapped her hand around him.

"I will make sure you miss me," Frances said, kneeling on the floor.

Anton groaned as she took him into her mouth. "I will never miss you, My Dear. I cannot miss someone who is already dead."

His words struck a stinging blow, but desire relented, and she continued. She used her teeth gently, drawing a ragged breath from him at the slight pain she inflicted. He would not miss her; perhaps that was true. But even if he did not care, she would bring the heavens down to ensure he remembered her.

"To learn is not to know; there are the learners and the learned. Memory makes the one, philosophy the others."

- Alexander Dumas, *The Count of Monte Cristo*

Chapter 5

Milo

Milo's feet dragged up the stairs.

He didn't want to attend this meeting; he wanted to go to bed. He doubted that sleep would come, however, even if he abandoned his duties and escaped to his enormous rooms. The knot of nerves and trepidation bouncing around in his stomach with each step was enough to make him dizzy.

The towering castle walls suddenly felt much too close, and he blinked quickly. A swipe of sweating palms against his navy coat and a curse helped his feet reach the main landing and golden door ahead.

It would be all right; it was only a conversation about the kingdoms to be invited to Rinnta, the equinox ball in one month. His mother always did get rather stressed around the occasion. Cool air carried the stifling scent of lotus perfume as Milo entered his mother's lavish sitting room. It was much too pink, and the many shades of the dreadful color seemed to swallow the space whole. White silk couches were arranged in a half-moon shape in the center of the room, and vases of flowers lined each window and small corner table.

The king, queen, and Lennora were waiting inside. A few members of the council that Milo didn't recognize stood silently along the pink wall, and his stomach gave a terrible lurch.

This meeting was most certainly not about Rinnta.

"My dear, how good of you to join us," Esther said with a warm smile.

She had changed into a modest gown of deep purple, the bodice doing nothing to accentuate her stick-like figure, though it did bring out the strands of gold in her light hair.

Like I had much choice in the matter. Milo gave a tight-lipped grimace and moved further into the room, though his feet yearned to rebel and run the other way.

"What's wrong?" Milo asked. The returning blinks of mingled surprise, confusion, and excitement made Milo frown. Would anyone start this conversation?

"Nothing is wrong, Matthew," Duncan replied, and Milo met his father's dark stare.

The king was a tall, dark-skinned man with tightly wound, cropped curls close to his head. Lean muscle rippled beneath Duncan's expertly tailored suit, and Milo saw himself in his father's thin build, though he knew that even he had more muscle on his bones.

The king ran a hand over his trimmed beard. "Your mother and the rest of the council have come forth with an exciting opportunity, and we wanted you to be the first to know of the changes coming to Cathair Liath. You are to be the king in two years, after all."

Milo gulped, the unease growing so strong that his fingers began to tingle. He clenched them behind his back, hoping that the sensation was just nerves and not another magical accident threatening to interrupt the meeting.

"What sort of opportunity?"

"It's not so much an opportunity as an arrangement,

which will do our kingdom some much needed good," Duncan replied, and Esther's expression flickered with hope.

The tingling in his fingers pulsed in time with his growing impatience.

"Well?" Milo asked. "Do I need to beg you on my knees to get it over with, or will you continue to draw it out?"

"Matthew, do not speak to your father in that way," Esther snapped, but Milo didn't flinch at his mother's reprimand.

"This is a big choice for all of us. We are only trying to ensure that you are told in the best way possible," Duncan replied, his expression turning apologetic.

"Then who can tell me in the best way possible? I swear I won't break," Milo ground out. Lennora took a step forward, the light of the candles catching upon her flame-red tresses as she moved.

"As we all know, your family's establishment upon the throne was something never seen before in Astrum history. You were born in Elaria, and your parents are human."

"I know," Milo said, dreading the story that Lennora was about to recount for what felt like the thousandth time.

"When the previous ruler, Queen Rinalta, fell ill, she and I both had visions of a stardust soul taking the throne in her stead," Lennora continued. "It was pure chance that your birth fell on the day of her death, and I knew that you were special the moment I laid eyes on you and brought your family to Astrum.

"You are a gift from the gods, Matthew, though few in the kingdom agree with the visions of a single witch and their deceased queen."

"Why are you telling me all of this again?" Milo asked, not liking the weight that her words carried.

"Because this decision was made to protect you, as well as your family," Lennora replied. "Though you were legally instated as prince through the signature of the late queen, it doesn't mean that the citizens of Cathair Liath believe your family is fit for the throne. Your parents have done an excellent job of ruling for the past twenty years, but the threat of attack from neighboring kingdoms has been constant. There is concern that some will consider that when the time comes, your rule alone will be a weakness."

The room was beginning to spin slightly, though Milo wasn't sure if it was due to the lotus perfume smothering his nostrils or the current conversation. A thin gasp of air slipped through his lungs, and Milo's heartbeat quickened at the words continuing to fall from Lennora's lips.

"There has been communication with the Baudelaire clan in Terre Rouge for a few months. Their king, Cesaire Baudelaire, was killed nearly one year ago in a hunting accident, leaving his son, Prince Malichi, in charge of running things."

"Okay." Milo shrugged, attempting to ignore the heat now emanating from his core.

"The country has been in turmoil since the king's death, and they need an alliance," Lennora said.

"What does that have to do with us?" Milo asked, hoping to whatever angels or gods still in existence, that this conversation wasn't going in the direction he feared it might.

"They want to ally with Cathair Liath, Milo. One that will unite our kingdoms and stave off threats currently looming over both of our heads," Lennora said evenly, though there was a note of tension in her melodic voice.

"We have spent weeks discussing the matter with the council, and they agree that it's a wise decision," Duncan said, and the old council members nodded silently.

Milo had no care for the damned council or how good an alliance they were about to enter. He was more concerned by the fact that his skin was burning and a metallic scent now mingled with the lotus perfume. His magic, or perhaps his entire person, was going to explode if they didn't tell him what on this dreary plane of the universe was going on. Lennora seemed to note the panic in his expression and took another step closer. He didn't like the look of pity so plain on her face. He didn't like it one bit.

"Get it over with, Mimmi," Milo whispered, speaking the name he and Jeremy called her as children. He didn't care that his parents and the rickety council members heard his childish plea.

Lennora smiled, though it didn't meet her eyes. "You are to marry Princess Frances Baudelaire in two months' time."

The words clanged in his brain, and he shook his head, as if doing so might make them go away.

"We looked into the safety of a union with the vampire clan, and I can assure you they are quite amicable," Lennora continued, though somewhat hurried this time. She could sense him retreating within, away from the sudden turn his life was about to take.

"It will be a wonderful union," Esther said brightly. "I heard that she is beautiful despite the fact that she is... well... dead."

He couldn't breathe.

"Milo, are you with us?" His mother's question pierced through the overwhelming flow of panic threatening to swallow him whole.

Milo shook his head and flexed his fingers, which proved to be a terrible idea. Stardust flew from his palms in a stream of silver light, and the pink floral rug beneath his feet erupted into flames. Mingled shouts of alarm and surprise bounced against the walls, but Milo only stared numbly at the fire licking at his boots.

Lennora swept forward and shot out a hand. "*Irot*!"

The flames died, as if doused with a bucket of water. Only a gaping hole with charred edges remained, and Milo gulped. His powers were just another thing that he couldn't control.

"Matthew! What on Astrum was that for?" Esther cried out. Milo shook his head again.

"Mother, I cannot do this." His voice was ragged, and he was sure his parents had noted the hint of panic in his words.

Duncan took a step toward him, his expression lined with frustration. "You will marry the Baudelaire princess, and you will apologize to your mother for setting her rug on fire."

"I'm afraid I can only do one of those things," Milo whispered, half to himself. He barely felt the brush of Esther's thumb across his cheek as she spoke.

"My Dear, I hope you will put more effort into controlling your abnormality."

The sting of her words was close to a physical slap, and Milo bit back his anger. He was trying every day to control his *abnormality*, but no amount of training could stop his magic from lashing out against intense emotions.

"I'm sorry, Mother," Milo ground out instead.

"I understand that this is a lot to take in, but please understand that I am trying to save our lives."

Milo clenched his jaw, making himself meet his mother's stare, so perfect and poised in her finery. It was as if she had been born for the role of queen. As if it were written in the stars. Her eyes were filled with nothing but worry, and he couldn't help but feel a pang of pity for her. How would she ever forgive him for not going through with the marriage and ruining her perfectly crafted plans?

"I'm sorry to all of you, but I will not marry Frances Baudelaire."

Before anyone could respond, Milo turned on his heels and bolted for the exit. The blasphemously improper act would have made Penn fall over dead, he was sure. But escaping the closing in walls and sickly-sweet air was the only thing that mattered now.

The slamming door muffled his parents' shouts, and Milo

took off at a sprint to the only place that would make him feel better and help him remember how to breathe. Dark splotches darted across his vision as he moved through the thickly draped halls and walkways, panic and anger making his body feel hot again. Familiar double doors of dark polished wood lay ahead, and Milo blinked against his blurring vision. There would be no one inside The Study at this hour, which he knew from countless experiences of sneaking into the grand space after nightfall. He fumbled for a gleaming brass handle and shoved into it with a desperate gasp.

Silence enveloped Milo as he stepped inside, and he let out a sigh as the comforting scent of books settled over him. He closed his eyes and took a calming breath, allowing the silence to envelop him.

"The Study is closed at this time, you know."

Milo jumped at the male voice that dripped through the walls, and he jerked his head to the left, finding a man seated upon the floor with ink-stained skin. He was unfamiliar, which was surprising given Milo's constant outings and social events.

The stranger was tall, at least as far as Milo could tell, his long legs stretched out upon the carpeted floor. Milo's throat caught at the man's face and the striking beauty he wore with such ease. Golden hair stuck out in all directions, and a lock hung over long, dark eyebrows and hazel eyes that looked straight at him.

"Who are you?" The man asked, making Milo jump again.

"I—" Milo stuttered, and the stranger's full lips curved upward.

"I didn't expect to cause you such a fright."

Milo shook himself and straightened, a habit drilled into him from the countless posture lessons he'd endured as a child.

"This is where I go to be alone. I didn't expect it to be... occupied."

The stranger's smile only widened, and Milo stood frozen as he rose smoothly to his feet and stepped over piles of discarded books and ink-blotched pages littering the floor. The top four buttons of his linen shirt were undone, revealing smooth olive skin and rippling muscle.

Milo forced himself to ignore the exposed chest and meet the stranger's stare, which was indeed a few inches taller than his own.

"What makes you entitled to decide when people must stay or go?" The man asked, crossing his arms.

"I-I didn't mean it like that," Milo stammered. "I just didn't expect someone else to be in here at this hour."

"I work here," The man replied, leaning casually against an overstuffed bookshelf. Milo furrowed his brow in confusion.

This strange man must have been appointed to The Study recently, for Milo knew everyone who worked in the grand space, caring for some of the most ancient and magical books in existence. Besides, he most certainly would have remembered him.

"That's not possible," Milo retorted. "I would know."

"Oh?" The man asked. "And how is that, are you the prince or something?"

Milo remained silent at this, and the stranger inclined his head in realization. "My apologies."

Milo cringed and shook his head. "Please, don't. I get it enough from everyone else."

"Prince Matthew, then, is it?"

"Everyone calls me Milo," he replied quickly, surprising himself for telling the man a name that only close friends and family called him.

"I'm Sage Astaseul, and everyone calls me Sage," The man said.

A smile fluttered to Milo's lips, and Sage returned it, his piercing gaze lowering to the floor with what Milo could only place as shyness. Silence engulfed the room, and the air grew thick. Milo leaned against the wall and closed his eyes against another wave of nerves and residual anger.

"Are you all right?" Sage's voice was soft and questioning, and Milo blinked. Sage had taken a step closer, and his foot now stood upon one of the ink-stained papers. Sage followed Milo's downward gaze and cursed, leaping back and snatching it.

"Damn," He hissed. "Professor Binks is going to kill me."

"Professor Binks?" Milo echoed the name of his very own mentor and head of the scholar guild. "I thought you worked in The Study."

"I do," Sage said importantly, then quickly deflated. "Or, I will, once I pass this bloody sympathy test."

Milo fought against the lightness in his chest, though he'd heard how difficult it was to pass the sympathy test. Joining the scholar guild, individuals who cared and worked with the ancient tombs in The Study, was one of Milo's passing fantasies in life. The desire had been squashed quickly, however. He doubted that his own fickle magic would be a good combination with, at times, highly dangerous materials. And besides, he was the prince after all.

"It sounds like it might be my turn to ask if you're all right," Milo said.

Sage grinned, and something deep inside of Milo's soul did an odd flip. The man was strange, yet so breathtakingly beautiful. Milo shook the thought away and pressed deeper against the wall, hoping that perhaps it would swallow him whole, sparing the eventual confrontation with his parents.

As if he had read Milo's thoughts, Sage folded the now ruined paper and looked up at him again. "I can't imagine your excitement of being betrothed to the Baudelaire clan."

Milo frowned. "How do you know about that?"

"We know everything in The Study. The very walls tell us everything that goes on in Astrum."

There was a slight pause, and Milo raised his eyebrows. Sage's serious expression molded into a grin.

"I also may have overheard the queen speaking to Professor Binks about it this morning."

Milo almost threw up in embarrassment at the small chuckle that fell from his mouth. This man was insufferable, yet he managed to make him laugh. Damn him.

"Well, I only found out a few minutes ago."

"Which I'm assuming is the reason behind your hasty entrance?" Sage asked, and Milo nodded. "Are you not excited about the union?"

Milo grimaced. "I'd rather be turned into a mouse."

"I'm sure that can be arranged. Though—"

"Matthew Rose Hale, get out of that study immediately!" Queen Esther's yell pierced through the thick walls, and Milo cringed.

"You've been summoned," Sage commented and stooped to gather the discarded papers strewn about the carpet.

"I had no idea." Milo braced himself for the torment he'd face in a few horrible moments. "You might want to leave before she spews her wrath at you, too."

"I was already on my way out."

Indeed, Sage had gathered up the mess he'd created, and the books and papers were now held precariously in his arms. Sage started toward a corridor at the far end of the room, and Milo watched with a slight sinking feeling, as if he'd been offered up one of his favorite books only for it to be snatched away again. He turned to leave when a voice stopped him in his tracks.

"Milo?" He whirled to find Sage watching him, his long, ink-stained fingers wrapped around papers. A lock of golden hair had fallen over his brow again, and Milo bit the inside of his cheek as he met Sage's gaze. "I do have a few questionable friends that I could employ, should you truly want to become a rodent."

Milo didn't stop his laughter, and Sage's grin widened.

"I will call upon you with haste, should I need to take you up on it." Milo dipped his head.

"Good," Sage murmured. "I will be anxious to receive your summons."

"Few sons are like their fathers—most are worse, few better."

- Homer, *The Odyssey*

Chapter 6

Frances

Searing cold and flaming rage were all that Frances knew as she stalked down the dark halls, barefoot and barely dressed, save a dark, silk robe that billowed behind her like a flag. Her brother would pay for his treachery, she would assure it.

The door burst open against her slamming palms, and she barely registered her stinging skin as she stormed into the lavish rooms. She scanned the familiar tidy spice, opposite to her own messy quarters, before locking on a dark-haired man whose back was turned to her. The muscles of his shoulders rippled as he leaned over a desk pressed against a window that overlooked the moonless night.

"How *dare* you!" Frances spat. The vampire straightened and turned to face her, and Frances nearly throttled him at the slow blink he gave in answer.

He leaned against the arm of his chair; the simple cream tunic having been rolled up at the sleeves to expose his pale skin. Malichi Baudelaire was a handsome man with wavy black hair and full lips, now pulled down into a frown. His long neck, high cheekbones, and intelligent blue eyes were the masculine image of Frances, as identical as twins could be.

"Hello, Frances," Malichi replied in a low tenor before turning back to his desk. "I assume Anton just paid you a visit."

"Indeed, he did," Frances seethed. "It was his very last, according to him."

"I'm pleased to hear it. You don't need any more distractions."

A muffled scream of annoyance tore from Frances's chest, and she stomped closer, skin crawling with the desire to slap the casual tone out of him.

"When were you going to tell me?"

Malichi turned to face her again and leaned back, languid as a cat. "Tell you what, exactly? That you are no longer allowed to sleep with Anton?"

"That I've been betrothed, you idiot!" Frances yelled, and the windowpane rattled from the force, though she took the happening as an agreement to her woes.

"I'm sorry that I didn't inform you earlier." Malichi sighed but said nothing further.

"You're sorry?" She scoffed. "This grants more than an apology, brother. I don't even know to whom I've been betrothed!"

Malichi wiped a hand over his face and considered her, fatigue looming over him like a shadow. "It wasn't entirely my choice. Mother proposed the idea first."

Every thought was wiped clean from Frances's mind. "Mother did this? Why?"

"Because our position on the societal food chain has been in danger ever since Father's death," Malichi replied. "Other kingdoms and even a few noble houses in Terre Rouge have started talking. There have been rumors."

"Rumors of what?"

"Taking the crown, if you must know."

The ground seemed to shift beneath Frances's feet, causing her to take a step back. She had no idea, not even an inkling of a thought, that her family could be in danger. She pasted on an easy smile and rolled her eyes, though the memory of her father made her muscles tense.

"Come now, Brother. We're vampires, and one of the oldest bloodlines in Astrum. We cannot be killed easily."

"But we can be killed," Malichi said quietly. "And there are many who are paid to do such things."

"Why would anyone want our family dead? Aside from any rogue idiots who try their luck."

Her brother shrugged. "Why does anyone want to kill, dear sister? It's for politics and power. Now that Father is dead, Mother and I are the only ones left to rule the kingdom. Most believe that a woman who was once a peasant, and her son, is not such a wise choice for the throne."

"I thought our people loved Mother despite that." Frances frowned. "And besides, we aren't weak with you running the kingdom. Our lands have flourished under your rule."

Malichi's lips quirked up a fraction, and it was the closest thing to a smile that Frances had seen in almost a year.

"I appreciate your confidence in my abilities, but unfortunately, you and Mother seem to be the only ones who think so. Our spies have informed me that multiple attempts on all our lives have been stopped in the past six months. I'm afraid to think of what would have happened if they hadn't intercepted the assassins in time."

Frances cursed softly. Her family's life was in danger. The image of her father's mangled body flashed through her mind for the second time that night, and she clenched her fists against her robe.

"And what esteemed kingdom will lead us out of this threat?"

Malichi watched her, as if calculating if she even deserved to know. Finally, he opened his mouth, and Frances nearly stumbled again as he said, "Cathair Liath."

Cathair Liath, one of the smallest kingdoms ruled by humans, was going to save them? Frances couldn't help laughing. Malichi remained impassive as he waited for her mirth to expire, and soon dread began to replace the disbelief settled in her soul.

"You're joking."

It was impossible that the little kingdom of Cathair Liath could drag them out of their impending doom, what with the endless threats that loomed over their own heads since the dawn of the Hale family's instatement on the throne.

"I'm afraid not." Malichi shook his head.

"So, you believe that in marrying into that disgraceful family, our safety will be restored?"

"It's not as simple as that, sister. Matthew Hale's family might remain human, but he is not," Malichi said with a meaningful look. A shiver caressed Frances's spine at that, and she shook her head.

She'd heard the rumors of Cathair Liath's prince being a stardust soul but never believed it to be true. Stardust souls were some of the rarest beings on Astrum, and she had hoped to perhaps one day meet one and see what they were like, what with having the essence of the Universe flowing through their veins.

Frances crossed her arms. "But the rumors of their own ever-present danger are as popular as most roadside gossip."

"And that's exactly what it is, gossip. They have ruled successfully for the past twenty years, and people do respect them, or at least they fear the stardust prince's powers enough not to revolt."

"If that is so, why would they want to agree to a union with us?" Frances asked, her head beginning to spin with confusion and fatigue. Her tongue still tasted of Anton, and the sting of his words lingered on her non-beating heart.

I cannot miss someone who is already dead.

"Mother arranged it somehow." Malichi pursed his lips. "They require a strong political alliance that will aid Prince Matthew when he takes the throne in two years. We were once one of the most respected countries on the continent, and both families are confident that this union will only strengthen our standing and security. Their army is one of the best in Astrum. It is why no one has tried to take the throne yet."

Frances sighed. She was no good at politics and even worse at understanding it. She knew Malichi and their mother knew better than she; she only wished she didn't have to be a pawn in their game.

"Do you truly believe this union will save us?" Frances asked, her voice a near whisper.

Her brother thought a moment before nodding. "I believe it will. My advisors and the council have all agreed that it is a wise course of action."

Frances bit back a curse and lifted her chin. If her marrying this mysterious man was the only way of ensuring her family's safety, then so be it. However, she would ensure that it happened on her terms. She would have a wedding that everyone would remember.

"Very well, I agree to marry Matthew Hale."

Malichi's gaze softened. "Dear sister, I'm afraid you never had a choice."

"I DO NOT WANT PEOPLE TO BE VERY AGREEABLE, AS IT SAVES ME THE TROUBLE OF LIKING THEM A GREAT DEAL."

- Jane Austen, *Jane Austen's Letters*

Chapter 7

Milo

August 17, 1880

The sound of silverware clinking against delicate China rattled through Milo's brain.

Sunset swept tendrils of orange and pink light across the thick stone floor, bathing the dining room in a warm glow. Yet Milo felt far from warm; in fact, he feared his lamb stew might make a reintroduction from his stomach.

His parents sat across from him, eating as though they hadn't dropped the most life-changing announcement of Milo's life just the day before. Duncan met Milo's stare and gave a fatherly nod. Milo dropped his gaze back to his food, now even less appealing than before.

"Matthew, dear, please don't pick at your food," Esther said sweetly.

Milo sighed and let his spoon clatter into the bowl. "I'm not hungry."

"We both understand how you might be feeling," Duncan

said slowly. "But it is for our own good, as well as for the good of our people."

"I didn't choose for them to be our people," Milo grumbled, feeling the frustration radiating from his father as if it were his own.

Esther let out a dramatic sigh and set down her utensils. "When you were born, I thought the biggest hardship our family would face was being accepted by society."

"And my eyes."

"It was a complete shock when Lennora arrived," Esther continued, ignoring her son. "I did fight against it, you know. I didn't choose for us to be here."

"The gods chose him," Duncan said.

"The gods are dead," Milo replied in a monotone voice. "Professor Binks makes it clear they disappeared long ago."

"Professor Binks doesn't know everything," Duncan said evenly. "And even if it is so, the previous queen of this land chose you as her heir."

"I still don't understand how Lennora and the queen having a vision could convince them I'm the true heir of Cathair Liath," Milo huffed.

It was a question he couldn't shake, one that had lingered in his mind since learning the truth. Lennora's vision could have been a simple premonition, yet the way she explained it always made it feel like something... more. Something that sent a shiver of stardust through his veins and made his body hum with secret knowledge not registered by his mind.

Something that felt like the gods speaking to him—even though, as he had said, the gods were dead.

"It is as hard for you as it is for us," Esther said, and Milo noticed the faintest flicker of tension in his father's jaw. "But we must persist, no matter the obstacles along the way."

"What if I don't want to persist?" Milo shot back. "If doing so means I must marry a woman—" He nearly stopped, then cleared his throat quickly. "A vampire—then I'm not sure it's worth it."

Esther gave a shaky smile, tendrils of her golden hair floating around her face like an angelic halo. "It will all work out in the end, Milo. I will ensure it."

"Eat your dinner," Duncan said gruffly.

And just like that, Milo's protests were shut down. A thick knot settled in the pit of his stomach, and he blinked against unshed tears. Being a prince had been portrayed as whimsical and enjoyable in every fairytale he had read, and now he wanted to find every one of those books and burn them. Or perhaps step into one of the stories and switch places with the smiling princes with perfect lives.

He needed air—certainly not more stew.

Milo pushed back from the table, flinging the napkin from his lap haphazardly over his bowl. "I said I'm not hungry."

"Matthew, sit down," Esther demanded, but Milo was already heading for the door, his fingers tingling with the threat of oblivion.

"Un sot trouve toujours
un plus sot qui l'admire."

"A fool always finds one still more foolish to admire him."

- Nicolas Boileau, *Épître IX*

Chapter 8

Frances

August 21, 1880

Pleasure coursed through Frances's body as she moaned, rolling away from the nameless woman brought to her for dinner. Frances licked a stray droplet of blood from her lower lip and let her gaze fall over the woman, whose fair skin glistened with sweat.

Crimson trails streaked from the punctures at her neck, and a familiar hunger still throbbed at Frances's core. She let out a feral growl, leaning down to trail soft kisses along the woman's skin before latching onto her throat once more. A gasp escaped her lips, and the woman's fingers knotted into Frances's raven-black hair.

Pleasure and life flooded Frances's body in a dizzying wave, and soon both satisfaction and completion pushed her over the edge. The woman let out a faint cry as she reached her own oblivion, and Frances finally pulled away from her throat.

"You tasted wonderful. I might ask my brother to keep

you," Frances purred, her thick French accent slurring with the ecstasy of her meal.

The woman blinked and sat up shakily, blonde hair sticking to her face and shoulders. She did not speak, and her soft brown eyes avoided Frances entirely. That blank, dazed stare was what Frances hated most about her meals—a reminder that these offerings had no idea who she was, or of the realm of Astrum. The hypnotizing enchantment would wear off soon enough, and the woman would remember nothing.

Frances wasn't concerned with where the seekers—servants tasked with finding meals for the royal household—found her subjects. She only cared that the humans were clean, healthy, and somewhat attractive. Malichi ensured the enchantments worked, and only a few offerings were ever kept for more extended periods. Frances had never been interested in keeping one; what was the point if she could taste them all?

She stood from the large bed and crossed the private dining room to retrieve her nightgown from a nearby chair. Pulling it over her head in one swift movement, she spared no glance at the woman now fast asleep, nor at the lavish room draped in red velvet. She could hardly blame her victim—humans were weak. Even a small taste of blood was enough to drain them for hours.

Frances opened the door and glided past two young maids waiting silently outside, then moved down the long, gilded hallway. She soon reached her bedroom and stepped inside, sighing as she sank onto her bed.

"That took longer than usual."

Malichi's low voice carried through the room. Frances rolled her eyes, turning to face him as he lounged across her favorite red velvet chair, his long legs draped over the corner of her desk, the tight trousers showcasing his powerful muscles.

Frances flashed her brother a wicked grin and flopped onto her four-poster bed in a decidedly unladylike manner.

"I decided to stay for dessert," she said. "She was very sweet."

"I'm sure she was," Malichi mused. "I do hope you aren't too intoxicated to talk politics."

Frances groaned. "At this late hour? Come off it, Malichi. We can speak of my bleak future when the sun rises."

Malichi's pointed look told her he most certainly would not come off it, and the conversation she'd been avoiding was imminent.

"You know that with each day you brush me off, our departure date draws closer," he said. "I will not have my sister act like a blundering fool when we meet your new family."

"You mean *our* new family," Frances shot back. "I remind you, brother, that by marrying that stardust prince, we're all being dragged into their messy lives."

"Just because his parents are human does not mean they're dirty," Malichi said. "Besides, aren't humans your favorite feeding source?"

Frances grinned mischievously, the taste of the woman still lingering on her tongue. "Oh, but you forget, brother. I like it dirty."

Malichi's lips twitched into a frown. "You will marry Matthew Hale whether you desire it or not, Frances."

"Why can't *you* marry him?" Frances pleaded. "You're older than me by five minutes and far more agreeable."

"Because, my dearest sister," Malichi said through clenched teeth, "I am the last male head of our clan and cannot tie myself personally to the Hale family. I can't leave our poor mother alone to clean up every mess in Terre Rouge."

"I should like to see her try. Perhaps it will take her mind off Papa."

Loss tore at her heart, and the flash of pain that crossed Malichi's face confirmed he felt the same hurt.

"You would do well to remember that his death is partially why you are to do this. They can offer us protection that another vampire clan cannot."

"I am aware, brother," Frances snapped. "And you would do well to remember it's the only reason I've agreed to marry that scrawny man."

Malichi smirked. "I hear there's a surprising amount of muscle beneath his baggy tunics. I'm sure you'll discover it soon enough."

Frances wrinkled her nose. "I typically prefer men bigger than me—or at least big enough to lift me."

"I care not for your preferences, sister. This is politics, and unfortunately, you are the moving piece in all of this."

"I am tired, brother," Frances sighed. "I don't want to talk about this."

"As you wish." Malichi rose from the velvet chair and stretched. "Just remember, we depart for Cathair Liath in ten days."

"Good night, Malichi," Frances said pointedly, flinging a pillow over her head as he left.

Heat welled behind her eyelids, though Frances knew she would not cry—she had never known the pleasure of weeping. The budding warmth in her tear ducts was a cruel mockery of what she would never experience. Emptiness crept into the gaping hole in her chest, nestling coldly against her heart. She was good at pretending everything was fine, at appearing strong and solitary. But her father's death had broken her and her family. She had coped and pieced herself together in the ways she could, as had Malichi and their mother.

She had always been good at being alone. She had dreamed of meeting the perfect man or woman and loving them for who they were—if they did the same for her. That would no longer happen, not with Malichi and her mother dictating her life.

Her life was bound to a man she had only ever seen in paintings, and perhaps it was as much as she deserved.

A strangled sound escaped her throat. Frances realized dully that it was a sob. Apathy flared through the pain, smoothing over the anger like a cold caress. She let it wash over her, singing her into a haze of sweet darkness.

"ALL THAT WE SEE OR SEEM IS BUT A DREAM WITHIN A DREAM."

- Edgar Allan Poe, *A Dream Within a Dream*

Chapter 9

Milo

August 22, 1880

"What can you tell me about *The Book of Silver*?"

Professor Binks, the old yet scathingly tall scholar, had a soft voice that echoed through the small nook in The Study where they sat. It was one of his favorite corners of the sprawling library, with a rounded wall of glass that offered a view of lush forests and rolling meadows. It would have been a beautiful day, with the sun making a rare appearance between thick clouds and setting the land aflame with emerald light. It was not beautiful, however, because Milo was barely taking any of it in. No, he was focused on the fact that a clan of vampires was about to walk through his doorstep in ten days.

Professor Binks cleared his throat, and Milo jumped. He gave the frowning professor an apologetic glance before looking down at the bound leather book containing years' worth of his scrawling handwriting, mostly academic notes.

He would not speak of the small sections of poetry that took up a few pages. Nor the drawings.

"Most believe that the stars created the first gods and goddesses, who were granted the knowledge of the universe. They joined together and created *The Book of Silver*, a tome that held a kernel of their knowledge within. It was used to create multiple dimensions, and at the moment of completion, the gods and goddesses joined together. The result of their love was that of the entire universe rejoicing, which became the first meteor shower.

"The Book of Silver was coveted for a millennium, when the gods decided to give it to their children to guard and protect. Angels and demons were deemed caretakers for the book, and the gods granted them the ability to use it—though it would only work when the blood of both heaven and hell touched it."

"Very good," Binks nodded. "And what did *The Book of Silver* do when the angels and demons first used it?"

Milo did his best not to sigh. This was material he had learned in nursery rhymes and bedtime stories. He didn't understand why they were reviewing it again in his final year of study. "It created Astrum, along with anything that comes from magic."

"But it did not only do those things," Binks said, and Milo frowned as he continued. "The Book of Silver has been used to create and destroy other dimensions, which caused many of our great wars. Angels and demons, along with their children, sought to use the book to create worlds where they could reside, and it was passed among many ill-fitting rulers.

"During the War of Asura—the war which killed most of our gods—Akiru created a stardust soul, god of luck and miracles, and Anuca, god of shadows. They molded the remnants of a comet's tail into a being resembling a human and sent it to save the book, then disappeared along with the remaining gods. Like calls to like, you see, and the stardust soul and *The Book of Silver* were the same. They were created with the power of the universe within them, and thus were harder to kill—and harder to create.

"The stardust soul used their magic to take the book and hide it. That was the last time it was seen. Demons were sent back down to hell, though some managed to hide and escape their demise. Angels returned to the universe as well, deciding they could do better by residing in the cosmos and relaying messages through the priestesses. The Book of Silver was lost forever, and the creatures of Astrum created their own systems."

A frown had formed on Milo's face at some point during Professor Binks's long monologue. He had heard this story many times before, but he had never heard of a stardust soul being the one to hide the book.

"If one of my kind saved the world," Milo asked, "then why does everyone in Astrum hate stardust souls?"

Professor Binks's face fell slightly. "It is not that they hate stardust souls. In fact, they are widely respected and worshipped on other continents. Even Asura is now ruled by a stardust soul who descends from the line of the original savior of the book."

Milo clenched his fists in his lap. "So, they only hate me because of my parents?"

The unnaturally tall professor did not answer for a few moments, and Milo took a shaky breath. If being stardust wasn't enough, having humans for parents and being born on the earth-realm had truly done him in.

"They don't hate you, Matthew," Professor Binks said at last. "Most fear what they do not know, and that fear manifests as wariness."

"But I don't even know myself!" Milo exclaimed. "I've never gotten a clear answer as to what stardust souls truly are."

I am afraid of myself.

The realization was nothing new, nor was the irony lost within his fitful and angry thoughts.

"You are nothing and everything, Milo," Professor Binks said. "You are a body created by gods in the heat of a moment. You are a protector and a reminder of what was."

Milo shrugged. "Lennora tries to tell me that I'm closer to a witch than anything."

"Your powers are similar to those of a witch," Professor Binks agreed. "But the emotions that cause your magical outbursts, as well as the kind of magic you produce, well..."

He trailed off, and Milo huffed. "Yes, and throwing myself into accidental comas is a lovely benefit as well."

"Your brashness is not lost on me," Professor Binks warned, though his expression softened. "We are trying our best to find a suitable instructor to help you understand and hone your abilities. But it takes time, and you seem to appear with a new ability every month."

"I'm fine teaching myself, thanks," Milo snapped—though both knew his words meant nothing.

He *did* want help, if he were being completely honest. But if there was something he wanted more than a teacher, it was some damned acceptance for being alive.

"I hate being different. Is it so impossible for the world to accept a single family of humans ruling a kingdom? It's not like we're the only humans to live in Astrum."

Professor Binks stepped toward the window, and Milo noted a faint blue sheen to his pale skin as the sun touched him. Milo had always wondered what sort of magical being the professor was, but no one would ever tell him.

"I am afraid that the topic of justice evades me, even in this grand space full of books," Professor Binks said. "One cannot determine or force the opinions of what is right or wrong onto others. We can only do our best to be kind and be the change we wish to see."

Anger coiled in Milo's gut, and he stood from his seat with a loud scrape.

"It isn't enough," he ground out. "Sitting by and being kind to someone won't do any good if they just turn around and spit at the next person they don't like."

"Being angry won't make people like you either, Matthew," Professor Binks said. "And it certainly won't make you an honored king."

Milo cursed and reached for his notebook with haste. He barely noticed the flash of silver particles that shot from his fingers and coated the gleaming table in shimmering dust before he turned and stalked off. Professor Binks didn't stop him; he had stopped trying some time ago.

The smell of dew and metal swallowed Milo's senses as he pushed through the stacks of books and headed for the sprawling staircase that led to the main castle, to freedom. A surprised yelp sounded from behind, and professors began swarming around and past him, their many heads and differing shades of magical creatures blending as he moved toward the exit.

Someone stopped him. Milo glanced sideways to find the familiar young face of the man, Sage, from the other night, watching him. There was no fear on his face, no alarm in his hazel eyes, only concern.

But Milo didn't stop. He turned his head and continued up the stairs, ignoring the strange weight in his heart that seemed to tug him backward toward Sage. Milo shook his head and clutched the book tighter to his chest as he burst into the castle and ran down the halls, to the only place he knew would bring him some much-needed peace.

"I BECAME INSANE, WITH LONG INTERVALS OF HORRIBLE SANITY."

- Edgar Allan Poe, *letter to G.W. Eveleth*
Jan 4, 1848

Chapter 10

Frances

Frances was positively intoxicated.

A giggle escaped from her lips before alcohol was pressed to them, drowning out the girlish sound. They were to depart for Cathair Liath in just over one week, and she had done nothing in the five days of knowing her fate besides read books, fuck, and drink both her needed meals and whiskey.

Tonight, however, she only drank whiskey.

It was her last night of freedom before she would be whisked away by her mother to get primed for their journey. She was to be presentable upon their arrival—whatever that might mean.

"We don't want you to meet your fiancé looking like a wild woman," Daithine, her lovely and ridiculously blunt mother, had said the night before.

She'd simply mussed her unruly curls and stuck out her tongue in reply before taking a swig of amber liquid straight from the bottle. Yes, perhaps she was being a bit overreactive about the whole thing, but these were her last days of freedom before being thrown into a life she didn't even want. No one could blame her for being a bit reckless.

Now, as she sat in her favorite lavish bar in the city of Ville Rouge, all she wanted to do was crawl into bed with a book and perhaps try to convince her brother one last time that this was all a terrible mistake.

Laughter filtered through her roaring ears, and the smell of fine scotch and incense filtered through her senses. If she were a normal woman, she would be there with friends, tipping her head back with laughter as one of her companions made a witty joke. But she was not normal, and the only company she had been graced with was a palace guard standing watch by the entrance. She let out a huff and picked up her nearly empty glass from the gleaming bar.

The liquid burned hot trails down her throat and sent a warm feeling through her stomach, but she didn't so much as blink. It tasted faint in her mouth. Her surroundings felt dull and shadowed, as though someone had draped a sheer—yet noticeable—curtain over everything.

"*Bonsoir, Madame. Tu as l'air seule ce soir.*"

Frances did her best not to scrunch her nose at the male voice that had spoken at her side. She swung around, and her mouth went dry at the sight of—

"Anton?"

The demon glanced at the empty glass in her grip, and she quickly placed it back onto the bar. She hadn't realized that it was the demon prince, for she had no idea that he was so fluent in French. Yet here he was, a fitted black trench coat buttoned down over his usual dark trousers and gleaming boots.

Her heart ached at the sight of him, but more out of pain this time than longing. She remembered his final decree as she had given him pleasure.

I will never miss you, my dear.

Forever was a long time to remember those words.

Anton sighed and leaned back in the high-legged chair as

his wine-colored eyes looked her up and down, eyebrows tilting downward as he took in her rugged appearance.

"What happened to you?" he asked bluntly, and Frances scoffed.

"Nothing since you last saw me. I am still betrothed to a man that I have never met, nor have the desire to meet."

Anton let out a low chuckle, and Frances's toes curled in absolute betrayal to her mind and heart. He still affected her, and she did not like that.

"You seem to have an abundance of witty comments at your disposal," Anton said, and Frances gave him a sarcastic smirk.

"It is my most redeeming quality."

Her glass was filled by a large man with wings like those of a bat protruding from his shoulders. She gave him an honest smile, and he gave her a tired once-over before turning away. Frances frowned and peered down at her red velvet dress, which she thought made her figure look lovely.

"He can smell how drunk you are," Anton said, seeming to notice her confusion.

"Well, he is technically the one who put me in this state," Frances mumbled before turning back to the demon. "Why have you come here? I thought that you were supposed to leave and never see me again."

Anton's eyes flashed scarlet, a clear sign that a nerve had been struck. He let out a deep breath and reached to take Frances's hand in his own. She forced herself not to shrink away from him and allowed his warmth to sweep over her.

"I know that I was not supposed to return, but I do not care."

Frances snorted. "And why is that? You believe that I would willingly come to your bed one more time after you used me and then walked out the door after finishing without so much as a goodbye?"

Anton's grip tightened on hers, and his angular jaw clenched in tandem with the motion. She was telling nothing but the truth, for he had left her still on her knees after she had given him his gift, with barely a glance over his shoulder as he finished redoing the buttons of his trousers.

It had made her feel dirty, discarded, and fully unvalued.

"That was a mistake, and I was trying to honor your brother's wishes," Anton said.

"You could have helped me to my feet at least, or perhaps helped me clean up your mess," Frances replied, if only slightly too loud.

"Frances, calm down. I did not come here to fight with you."

"No," Frances snapped and withdrew from his touch. "You came here to fuck me and then leave me again like you did every time before that. I am not simply a warm vessel for you to stick your cock into whenever the mood strikes."

"Frances," Anton growled, his eyes flashing again. "Do not push me."

Frances let out a bark of laughter that was decidedly unladylike and turned to her drink, gulping it down in one fell swallow. "And you would do well not to push me either, Mister Ferrazco. I am a princess, and I am tired of being used and discarded as though I mean nothing to people."

"Frances—"

"I do believe Princess Baudelaire would like you to leave, Mister Ferrazco."

Malichi's calm tone broke through Anton's reply like a sharp blade, and Frances turned her head much too quickly to find her brother standing by their seats. The room swam, and Frances instantly regretted her last drink. By the nausea rising in her throat, the drink seemed to regret entering her body as well.

"Mister Baudelaire," Anton stammered. "I was—"

"Just leaving, I expect," Malichi replied with a cold smile that did nothing to soften his sharp cheekbones or stare of ice.

Anton met Frances's gaze, and she dared not look away. She let him see the longing she felt for him, as well as the pain he had dealt. She didn't want him to go, if only so she could force him to apologize and take back what he had said.

I will never miss you, my dear.

Anton clenched his jaw and let out a sharp breath through his nose before gliding to his feet and straightening his coat. He didn't meet Malichi's cool gaze as he stepped around him and turned toward the exit. Frances's body felt sluggish and tense all at once, and she waited for him to step out of her life forever—or perhaps only for a few hundred years.

But he paused by her ear before he left, and the words he whispered sent a dreadful shiver down her spine.

"You did not mean anything to me—not ever. I'm afraid that only now I have truly learned what sort of monster you are."

And then he was gone, his breath nothing more than a whisper against her ear as the door slammed shut behind the demon prince. Laughter and loud music surged back into Frances's senses as she let out a shaking curse, and her brother sat down in Anton's vacated seat.

"Mother told me you left the castle in a hurry after she offered that you take a bath. You are not a child, Frances."

Frances sniffed and glared down at her pale hands, clenching them in a halfhearted hope it would staunch the terrible feelings surging through her. It was one of the more negative sides of being a vampire; emotions were heightened in an almost dizzying way.

"Perhaps I am a child," Frances grumbled, and looked up at Malichi, who shook his head.

"You are nearly twenty-two years old; it is beyond time that you learn to behave yourself."

Frances scowled. “Being in one’s early twenties, especially as a vampire, is arguably still a child. Besides, I only need to act like a lady to those who matter.”

“Your perception of those who matter is far different than mine,” Malichi said.

Silence stretched between them, and Frances’s mind drifted back to the dreadfully handsome prince who had just torn her silent heart to little pieces. Had she cared about him enough to be hurt by his abandonment so deeply? Their relationship hadn’t been anything past physical, though a small corner of her emotions had softened to his presence and grown to like it—perhaps a bit too much.

“It was for the best, Frances,” Malichi said softly.

He knew her too well, and she him. Perhaps it was because they had been born only minutes apart, though she felt that it was more than that. He had been her friend and companion through everything in life, from her first skinned knee to her first kill.

“I don’t know what is best anymore,” Frances replied, and Malichi gave her a pat on the shoulder.

“Beings like you and I are not granted the freedom to live and love who we choose. It is perhaps not a tasteful way of living, but it is for our survival.”

“I do not want to be a shell, brother,” Frances said hollowly. “I desire to live and do the things that make me happy. I want to find out which of those sorry souls murdered our father. I want—”

She didn’t know what she wanted anymore, not past that point. Her books and her father’s death had been the only things that mattered to her for the past year.

Malichi’s hand enveloped hers, cold skin against cold skin. She did not pull away, instead looking into eyes that mirrored her own sadness, though they were void of the lust for life that would never be granted to them.

"We are immortal, my dear sister. There is eternity to find out what exactly it is you want, though I'm afraid it can only just be that. Want."

"GOOD AND EVIL ARE SO CLOSE AS TO BE CHAINED TOGETHER IN THE SOUL."

- Robert Louis Stevenson, *Dr. Jekyll and Mr. Hyde*

Chapter 11

Milo

Wind whispered unheard secrets against Milo's face as he urged his horse onward into a gallop. Monty, his midnight black stallion, snorted as he pushed forward on powerful legs, and Milo leaned forward in the saddle as he maneuvered the horse toward a glittering lake just in sight.

He was going to be married to a vampire in two months, and they'd be in the castle in slightly over one week. He was alone and discarded every day of his life, and there were times when he felt his parents didn't even know he existed. And yet, now that he was one step closer to the throne, he was suddenly something important to them.

A pawn, nothing more.

Anger bit into Milo's heart, and he urged Monty to go faster, and the stallion obliged. They were soon in a flat-out gallop, racing along the open meadows that lay before his favorite spot in Astrum. He felt safest in the saddle or alone outside with a good book. It was the only two things, other than time spent with Jeremy and Lyra, that set him at ease, and that kept the volatile magic within at bay.

Milo swung from the saddle and landed on the ground

with a soft grunt. He removed Monty's bridle and gave the horse a pat on the neck, who sniffed him once before wandering off to find suitable grass to eat.

Milo slung the bridle over his shoulder and walked to the lone tree and the shade it provided on the late summer day. He sat and leaned against the trunk, glancing over at Monty, who was now a few feet away, grazing at his leisure.

Milo let out a sigh and looked back toward the lake. Water sprites danced across its glittering surface in celebration of a rare sunny day, which would have warmed his spirits in the past, but now it only made him feel worse.

How was he supposed to marry someone he didn't know? His parents' marriage had never been outwardly loving, and Milo always thought that they were only together for his sake, and now for the sake of the kingdom. But that didn't mean he lacked the desire for love.

His thoughts about the matter had always been muddled, as he could never make himself attracted to a woman, no matter how hard he tried. The inhabitants of Astrum were relaxed about sexuality and love, and most he'd met had been in affairs with every being in existence, aside from humans. Yet he couldn't understand the ability to desire everyone; he barely liked himself. But there had always been something about a man with a charming personality and witty mind that made him feel certain... things.

His mind strayed to the night of his betrothal and his strange encounter with Sage. A shiver ran up his arms at the memory of his golden skin and hazel eyes that seemed to pierce straight into his soul.

Gods, I am a dramatic bastard.

He couldn't deny the way that he had felt when he'd met Sage, nor the fact that he hadn't been able to sleep for most of the night, due to their interaction running on repeat through his mind. Milo let out a strangled sigh, remembering passing him in the study not even an hour ago, and the curious look Sage had given him.

He remembered me, Milo thought.

The thundering approach of hooves made Milo jump and glance over at Monty, who was still in the same spot but now turned toward the sound, his powerful neck arched and ears flicking in curiosity.

A gleaming cherry bay appeared on the top of the hill, and Milo let out a sigh of relief at the familiar horse. He wiped his sweating palms against his trousers and waited for Jeremy to swing off his mount and approach the tree.

"I thought I might find you here," Jeremy said in greeting, and Milo grimaced.

"Predictable, am I?"

Milo moved slightly, and Jeremy sat at his side. Their arms brushed together, and Milo savored the warmth that radiated from his friend's muscled body. They remained silent for a few minutes, and Milo allowed himself to relax into Jeremy's shoulder and let his comforting presence ease over him.

"I'm getting married," Milo said weakly.

"Don't I know that," Jeremy replied, and gave Milo a playful nudge, though Milo felt the pain slicing through his tone.

Jeremy had done his best to keep Milo's mind far from his impending marriage during the last few days, and had done surprisingly well at it, too. The topic was sensitive for both of them, and Milo didn't blame Jeremy for not wanting to talk about his fiancée. She was a vampire after all, the same sort of monster that had murdered his family.

"I just don't see a point in any of it," Milo grumbled. "Do they not see this will bring me less happiness than the lonesome life I already live? They could have at least given me the freedom with whom I love."

Milo could sense Jeremy watching him, but he dared not meet his friend's gaze.

"Do you think having a choice in the matter would have made it any easier?"

Milo shook his head. "I don't know, perhaps. But having this torn away makes my life feel even more gray than it was before."

"Gods, you are so dramatic, Milo." Jeremy chuckled, and now Milo did shoot him a glare.

Jeremy raised his eyebrows, and Milo wanted to slap that grin off his face, no matter how correct his friend might have been.

"You must be happy with your life and the decisions you make, no matter how hard it might be. It is not up to anyone else, or the freedoms that you have, to make you happy," Jeremy said.

Milo brought his attention back to the water, unsure that he could take looking into those midnight blue eyes for much longer. Jeremy belonged to a corner of his heart that he would dare not touch.

"I know, but gods do I wish for it to be otherwise," Milo replied.

"Agreed," Jeremy said, and Milo thought he noticed a flash of pain across his friend's face, but dared not mention it.

"I have this aching hole in my chest, and I've had it since I can remember," Milo blurted, and Jeremy stilled. He continued, unsure if he would ever be this honest with himself again. "I'm afraid, Jeremy."

"Of this marriage?" Jeremy asked, and Milo shook his head.

"Of all of it, I suppose. I don't know how to control my powers, and they are so slippery that sometimes it feels like I'm fighting with my own essence."

"That's where you've got it all wrong," Jeremy replied evenly. "You must befriend that part of yourself, not fight it."

Milo feared he was right, but it went well beyond that. He needed to befriend his entire self, for his magic wasn't the only thing that he feared. It was the insatiable anger that roared in his veins whenever he thought about the injustice of the world, and the overwhelming pain he felt at the distracted looks and dismissive comments his parents tossed at him. It was everything, and now there was another piece of kindling to add to the fire.

"I hate it when you're right." Milo scowled, not wishing to delve deeper into the well of pain he already resided within.

Jeremy nudged him again. "You have me by your side through it all, Milo. I won't leave you, not ever."

Milo nodded, knowing the truth behind Jeremy's words. He would stay with him even through his marriage to a vampire, and he would be with him through his countless trials and tribulations as king.

"I will be by your side through it all as well, I hope you know that," Milo murmured.

"I do."

Something close to contentment washed over Milo at that, and he let the silence, save the whispering wind between the falling leaves and rippling water, lull him into a much-needed state of calm.

He would be all right, he knew that. With Jeremy at his side and a teacher to guide him through his magic, he would be able to face the new world that was opening to him.

"Oh, I nearly forgot," Jeremy said, and Milo jumped.

"What?"

"It was the reason I came to find you, actually," Jeremy said and cursed under his breath. "Your mother is going to have my head."

Milo grimaced, and any traces of contentment and calm made their exit.

"That is never a good sign," he mumbled, and Jeremy gave him an apologetic smile that bordered on the side of... was it worry, or fear?

"What is it?" Milo asked again, and Jeremy ran a hand through his hair.

"Spit it out, Jeremy," Milo snapped.

"Fine. Your mother came to me in a state of distress and asked me to search for you. I told her that you were surely fine, but I went to find you anyway."

"Why did she want you to find me?" Milo asked. "I surely couldn't have caused that big of a tizzy by leaving class early."

"Well, it was partially that," Jeremy said, and excitement briefly replaced that strange negative emotion hiding there. "You opened a portal in your desk."

Milo's heart skipped a beat. "I did *what*?"

"It wasn't a very big one, it was just to your mother's sitting room, and one of the scholars fell through it after slipping in the stardust you flung everywhere."

Milo barely remembered the shower of dripping silver that had spilled from his hands in his haste to leave, but he hadn't known it would open a damned portal.

"Is everyone all right?"

"Yes, a new pupil managed to close it, and everything in the study is back to normal," Jeremy replied. "As I said, it was only partially the reason why I came to find you."

"And what was the other reason?" Milo asked, gripping his knees as tension made his skin tingle in a supremely unpleasant way.

Jeremy's face paled, and he wiped his palms on his trousers. Fear returned to Milo's gut. Jeremy was always good at acting calm in the face of danger, and only truly terrible things made his palms sweat.

"There was an assassin found in the castle, Milo." Jeremy's voice quavered slightly.

The world darkened a few shades, and Milo blinked away the sudden dizziness that threatened to take his spirit to the stars.

"Were they apprehended? What did they want?" Milo forced himself to speak, and Jeremy sighed.

"They got away before any identification was made, but we found a piece of fine leather on the floor in front of your rooms."

Milo blanched. "My rooms? Why would an assassin be loitering about there?"

Jeremy's returning look of fear was answer enough for Milo, and he let out a rattling breath and squeezed his eyes shut as the world began to spin.

"Someone was going to kill me."

"THE HEART IN HIS RUGGED CHEST WAS POUNDING, TORN."

- Homer, *The Iliad*

Chapter 12

Frances

August 29, 1880

A soft knock disrupted Frances's thoughts about death.

She had been reading a textbook on forensics and anatomy when the sound startled her, causing her to nearly drop the manuscript. She eyed the door, using her heightened senses to determine who stood on the other side. The familiar scent of cedar and musk infiltrated her nose, and she let out a sigh of relief. It was only Malichi.

"Come in," she called softly, and the door opened.

A disheveled and disgruntled-looking Malichi crossed the threshold, and Frances couldn't help the spark of glee she felt at both his frustration and his presence in her room. It could only mean that something had gone awry with the marriage arrangement.

"What's wrong?" Frances asked as she closed her book.

Malichi moved to the velvet chair and sat with a huff. It had been three days since the night at the bar, and neither of them had spoken about his unsavory, yet not unwanted, intrusion between her and Anton.

"There has been an attempt on Prince Hale's life," Malichi said in a low, tired voice.

Frances did her best not to sound as excited as she felt by the news. "Was the attempt successful?"

Malichi glared. "Don't sound too hopeful, dear sister. The prince is in good health, by the sound of the letter I received tonight."

Her spirits fell just as quickly as they had risen, and Frances let out a small humph of disappointment.

"Then why have you come if not to tell me that he is dead? His life being threatened means nothing to me."

"It should mean something to you," Malichi snapped. "As soon as you two are wed, your life will be tied to his, and whoever is a threat to him will be the same unto you."

Frances clenched her hands into fists and met her brother's stern gaze. "If the attempt just happened, then perhaps there's time for the assassin to try again."

Malichi's lips formed into a grim line, and she noted the tension in his shoulders as he leaned farther back into the chair.

"It was made nine days ago, and they were unable to find any suspects."

Frances frowned. "Nine days? One would think a more convenient messaging system would have been created with magic at our disposal."

"The messenger magpies were thrown off course with the summer storms."

She wished the silly birds had been thrown into a different dimension instead.

"That was not the main matter I came here to speak to you about, I'm afraid," Malichi said. "Queen Hale has decided that her son's life is in danger, and she has decreed it best that we relocate the engagement festivities and ceremony to safer territory. We will bring necessary members of each court and an officiant for the ceremony, but otherwise keep the company small."

"Where are we to go?" Frances asked, her interest piqued slightly by this.

Spending eternity in Rightford Castle would be dreadful, and perhaps this change would be an opportunity to spend her last months of freedom away from her future cage.

"Wisteria Manor," Malichi said, and Frances gasped.

"Wisteria Manor? Why there?"

"It is in a secluded part of Cathair Liath, far from prying eyes and potential threats. Besides, if the rumors are true, it is quite haunted and not very appealing for someone to follow us there."

"If someone wanted to kill the prince, don't you think they would overlook the fear of ghosts?" Frances asked.

"You would think so, but it seems that it is our best option. Queen Hale has decreed that we must proceed in a place far away from the public eye. The closest civilization to the manor is hardly a town, so it seems as though it is the perfect place."

"I do hope the rumors of rooms that appear and disappear on their own are true," Frances said, unable to help her excitement. "I would like to discover some hidden treasure while we are there."

Malichi stood and straightened his waistcoat, which had crinkled slightly during his momentary lounging.

"As long as you appear at gatherings and meetings that require your presence, you may do whatever you would like while we are there. It's not as though any of us could stop you from doing what you please at any point."

"It is a quality that I do enjoy about myself."

Malichi snorted and made to leave. "You enjoy any quality in yourself that breaks the rules of society."

Her grin widened, but she did not respond as she watched him, when a sudden curiosity swept over her.

"What ails you, brother? Truly?"

Malichi's hand paused not an inch above the door handle, and he turned halfway to give her a neutral look—though she knew it was a bluff. Some emotion she could not pinpoint clouded his eyes, but he would not reveal it.

"I am in good health, and you are to be married. There is nothing that ails me."

"That is not an answer, Malichi."

She had never seen him take an interest in anything other than his duty since their father's passing, and part of Frances thought that he truly did not care about anything beyond the kingdom and his many responsibilities. Yet there were instances where she caught a wild gleam in his eyes—something hungry for life beyond the existence he had been given.

"We leave in two days," Malichi said after a pause, and Frances wanted to scream at his complete change of subject.

He opened the door, and Frances did not speak as he began to shut it, though he paused one last time. She met his gaze and found a note of sadness there as he watched her.

"The security of our family is most important to me, Frances. It is the only thing that I want, and I daresay my own foolish desires are of little importance compared to the well-being of you and our mother."

"But I care about your well-being," Frances replied softly. "Is that so hard for you to believe?"

His stony expression cracked for only a second, and she thought she caught a twinge of pain there. "No, it is not hard for me to believe your love for me, dear sister."

Malichi gave her a nod and departed, leaving her alone with her muddled thoughts.

She did not think about her family in the way he did, and it hurt her to know that he was the one taking better care of their mother than she was. Not that Daithine Baudelaire, temptress and regality bound within a body of flesh and bone, needed much taking care of.

Even still, Frances had been too caught up in her own selfish hurt over their father's death to consider how deeply it might have affected both Malichi and their mother. Perhaps, during their time at Wisteria Manor—with its ghosts and her free moments between the looming wedding—she would be able to figure out what it was that truly made her brother happy.

"We penetrated deeper and deeper into the heart of darkness."

- Joseph Conrad, *Heart of Darkness*

Chapter 13

Milo

The dark spires of Wisteria Manor cut through the fog like a sharp blade, and Milo wished they would run him through.

The two-day trip to the manor had been long and uneventful, but he was grateful to have Jeremy and Lyra for company during the endless hours spent in the carriage. His mother hadn't allowed him to take Monty and had sequestered him with his friends for matters of security. A submissive wave had instantly tempered any objections that had escaped his mouth, and Milo had been shuffled into the gleaming box by Penn the very next second.

Now, as they bumped along the winding cliffside road toward the looming manor of dark stone and glinting glass, Milo was glad to be surrounded by four sturdy walls. Though his legs were stiff and the muscles in his back felt as though they had aged fifty years, he was grateful for the plush seats and protection from the elements.

He glanced out at the sea, and despite himself, his breath caught at the impressive sight. Foaming waves crashed against massive rocks standing some distance from the shore. The water was dark and roiling, as though Ghedenta, goddess of the seas and tide, was angry and preparing to lay siege to the land beyond. A flash of a glittering tail broke the surface, and Milo jumped, narrowing his eyes to see if it would return. He'd heard of sirens living in the ocean, staving off any human pirates who slipped through the cracks in the seams between Astrum and Elaria.

He turned his attention back to the carriage and the sudden lump of trepidation rising in his throat. They would arrive at the manor in less than an hour, and he would be meeting his bride-to-be the following day. The thought made him want to vomit, but a warm hand on his shoulder stopped him from doubling over.

"Don't get sick all over me. The coat is new," Jeremy said, though his tone was sweet beneath the mockery.

Milo leaned back in his seat and half-turned to his friend, who appeared as nonplussed and calm as ever—the bastard.

"It might do you some good to get dirty every once in a while," Milo retorted, and Jeremy grinned.

"I do enjoy getting my hands dirty—just not in a way acknowledged by the public eye."

Milo glared, though his cheeks burned.

"You're a devil."

"Better than a pig." Jeremy waggled his eyebrows, and they both chuckled.

"You might want to be careful about what you say in case Lyra wakes," Milo said, glancing at the folds of pale pink skirts covering Jeremy's cousin, whose dark lashes fluttered open at that very moment.

"Jeremy should be careful to say what, exactly, in case I wake?" Lyra asked, her sugary voice laced with curiosity.

Jeremy shot Milo a sidelong glare before sneering at his cousin. "Nothing that you haven't already done, I'm sure."

Lyra's red-stained lips curved upward as she patted a lock of curly golden hair into place across her shoulder.

"I would say yes, though it depends on the subject," she said prettily. "I'm confident I've done more things than the two of you combined."

"Why are we speaking of this?" Milo sputtered. "We're about to step into my bleak future, and the only thing you two can talk about is sex."

Jeremy snorted. "You were the one who brought it up."

"I was not. I believe it was you who twisted my words into something profane."

"I suppose you're right," Jeremy said with a wry smile.

They spent the rest of the journey speaking of little nothings, and Milo knew Jeremy and Lyra were doing their best to distract him from his impending doom. The carriage ride smoothed as they glided down a damp dirt road. Tall trees flashed past in a dark blur, and droplets of rain raced across the carriage windows.

The carriage soon slowed, and Milo's stomach gave a dreadful lurch. They had arrived. Jeremy and Lyra's expressions shifted—Jeremy's settling into hardened disinterest, Lyra's lighting with pure excitement. Milo suspected his own looked closer to horror.

He sank back into his seat as the carriage came to a stop, the sounds of footmen and servants springing to life outside. Milo wiped his palms on his trousers and reached for his folded coat with trembling fingers. His life would change forever the moment he stepped outside.

"How are you feeling?" Lyra asked, finally noticing his unfortunate state.

Milo glanced at her, taking in her strong jawline and simple yet pretty features. He searched himself for any spark of attraction toward the curves of her body beneath the dress, but found nothing.

"I've felt better," Milo said honestly, and she patted his knee.

"We'll be there with you every step of the way, won't we, Jeremy?" she added, casting her cousin a pointed look.

But Jeremy's attention was fixed outside, his expression taut with restrained anger. Milo knew the reason well—the knowledge that Jeremy was about to spend two months locked away with a family of monsters.

Jeremy met Milo's stare with a faint nod. "Until the very end."

Lyra scoffed. "That is far too dramatic. And where are our coachmen? I am dying to stretch my legs."

As if summoned, the carriage door swung open, manned by a short man with distinctly toad-like features. Jeremy stepped out first, followed by Lyra, who released a dramatic sigh as she swept into the evening air.

Milo drew in a shaky breath and held it until his lungs burned. He could do this. It would be simple. These months could even be enjoyable if he made the effort. He had free time between lessons and engagement obligations, and he would make the most of it. He only had to step out of the carriage.

"Come on, Hale, we haven't got all day," Jeremy called.

Milo cursed his friend under his breath.

Jeremy was right, as usual. He was lingering, stretching the painful seconds into near agony. With one final prayer that his spirit would remain tethered to his body through the onslaught of emotion, Milo stood and stepped into his new reality.

Carriages laden with servants, supplies, and trunks clustered along the parkway adjacent to the manor's grand steps. Milo let his gaze roam across the towering spires and intricate carvings etched into black stone. Arched windows glinted along the upper levels, disappearing into the mist. Something white streaked across one of the windows, and Milo froze, uncertain whether he'd imagined it.

"Matthew, dear, you should get inside before you catch a chill."

Esther's voice came from behind, and Milo turned to find his mother and father approaching in fashionable travel attire. Esther smiled sweetly, and though Duncan mirrored the expression, concern lingered beneath it.

"Are you well?" Duncan asked gently.

Milo shrugged. He felt too much in every moment of his existence—so much that he sometimes feared he might burst. But now, he felt nothing but cold.

"I'm not sure."

"It's natural, my boy. You're likely just nervous." Duncan clapped him on the back, and Milo grimaced.

He followed his father up the steps and into the candlelit foyer. Light danced across his vision, and a strange sense of foreboding crept up his spine as he took in the aged paintings and marble statues lining the walls.

Penn stood near a pillar, bowing deeply as Milo approached. "Come now—let's get ye to yer rooms and freshen ye up before supper."

Milo followed without hesitation. Though curiosity tugged at him, exhaustion settled deep into his bones like a wave crashing hard against the shore. He stumbled a step, shaking his head as a fog crept into his thoughts.

"Please inform my mother that I won't be dining with them tonight," Milo said, feeling the unsettling sensation of his spirit beginning to pull away from his physical form.

It felt as though something were dragging him out of himself, nothing like the sharp snap of astral travel he was accustomed to.

This felt dangerous. Sensual. Foreboding.

"Very well," Penn replied without question, and Milo's

gratitude nearly rivaled the strange fatigue weighing him down.

"Thank you," Milo murmured weakly.

Penn opened a door of dark, polished wood, beckoning him inside.

"I don't blame ye for wantin' a bit of quiet before the insanity begins," Penn said once the door closed, his tone easing into familiarity.

"Insanity indeed," Milo groaned, barely registering the lavish rooms of dark silk and gleaming wood. "My mother has informed me that I am to begin lessons the day after my dreaded wife-to-be arrives."

Penn chuckled. "Never in my five hundred years have I lived with such a cynic. She may not be so bad, lad."

Milo snorted. "I'll be grateful if she doesn't bare her fangs and kill me the moment we meet. I can't imagine she's enthusiastic about the union either."

"I don't doubt her reluctance, but that doesn't mean she's an animalistic murderer," Penn replied, turning away. "I'll be back in a wee bit with yer food."

Milo nodded and waited for Penn to leave before collapsing into a loveseat beside a towering bookshelf. He was exhausted to his core, though the sensation of his spirit retreating eased now that he was alone.

He sighed, thinking of his future wife. Perhaps Penn was right. Perhaps she wasn't a cold-blooded killer, and he was being unfair. But she was a vampire, and Milo did not trust those who took another life in order to live.

"Kings are the slaves of history."

\- Leo Tolstoy, *War and Peace*

Chapter 14

Frances

August 31, 1880

"Are you ready?"

Frances clenched her fists within the folds of her skirts and glanced at Malichi, who stood at her side. He appeared as unimpressed as ever, and she hated him for it. She felt nothing of the sort; in fact, she felt as though she might implode, vomit, or perhaps suffer a heart attack—a feat that would surely make vampiric history.

She returned her attention to the gilded spires and grand entrance of Wisteria Manor, taking in the swaying pines and crashing waves in the distance. The air smelled of mischief and darkness, and an odd, thrilling sense of foreboding slid down her spine.

"We're going to be late if you two keep standing around like dazed idiots," Daithine said as she approached.

Frances rolled her eyes. The queen was dressed in fine navy silk that clung to her curves in the most flattering way, her chestnut hair swept into a neat bun at the nape of her elegant neck. Daithine was beautiful, and Frances often wondered how on Astrum she could possibly be her daughter.

Never mind, she thought. She had a fiancé to meet and a haunted manor to ambush. Standing in the rain would only dampen the experience on all counts.

"I'm ready," Frances said at last. "Let's get this meeting over with."

"As you wish," Malichi replied, pressing his hand against her back and nudging her forward.

Each step up the old stone stairs felt like an eternity. Frances barely registered the double doors as they opened of their own accord, as though stirred by a phantom wind. Her thoughts whirled as she was led through a grand foyer lined with marble pillars and into a sitting room dressed in dark hues and heavy drapes. Everything felt too fast, too sudden. And where were the people?

She felt disconnected, disconcerted, and every other emotion imaginable. Could she truly go through with a marriage to someone she had never met? She supposed it was far too late to decide otherwise.

"You are crushing my arm, Frances," Malichi hissed.

She blinked and snatched her hand away, shooting him a sidelong glare. She hadn't realized she'd grabbed him at all, but now that she bore her own weight, she wasn't convinced her legs would hold.

"It's rather lovely in here," Daithine said brightly, her green eyes sweeping over the satin seating, towering paintings, and expansive windows overlooking the roiling sea.

"It's damp," Frances muttered. "Or perhaps I'm the one who's damp."

Malichi's nose scrunched as he gave her wrist a gentle squeeze. It had been their secret means of comfort in public spaces for as long as she could remember, and she was grateful for it now.

"What's taking them so long? This isn't the greeting I expected," Malichi said.

Daithine waved a dismissive hand. "Oh, they'll come. Don't you fret, my son. It takes humans quite a while to climb all those stairs, I'm sure."

Frances snorted in a thoroughly unladylike fashion, though it earned no attention from her family. She was about to speak when the door creaked open and an elderly servant—more resembling a gnarled tree stump than a man—wobbled in and bowed deeply.

"My apologies for the delay, Your Majesty and Highnesses," the servant croaked.

Malichi and Daithine inclined their heads. Frances managed only a slow blink in acknowledgment.

The servant took two careful steps forward and cleared his throat. "May I present the standing King and Queen of Cathair Liath, Esther and Duncan Hale, and their son, the Prince of Cathair Liath, Matthew Hale."

The moment had come. Her future had finally collided with her present, and Frances stood frozen, numb as it rushed to meet her.

Three figures entered the room, draped in the finest attire. Frances schooled her expression into polite neutrality rather than open surprise. She had never seen humans so impeccably put together—and she had never seen a stardust soul at all.

The king and queen tilted their heads in greeting, and Frances returned the gesture. Both were beautiful—the queen possessing a fair, luminous elegance, the king even more striking. But it was the prince who made her tilt her head slightly as their gazes met.

Piercing silver eyes stared back at her.

He was breathtaking—there was no other word for it.

Frances had never seen anyone like him, magical or otherwise. He was tall and well-built, though leaner than the men she'd favored in the past. A mop of dark brown curls brushed against thick brows, his tanned skin smooth and unmarked. His full lips were pressed into a thin line, his chiseled jaw clenched as though restraining a curse.

She knew it instantly.

He was entirely, irrevocably uninterested.

"May I present Queen Daithine Baudelaire, and her children—Prince Malichi and Princess Frances Baudelaire."

She nearly startled as the servant spoke again, but forced a pleasant curve to her lips as she dipped her head in greeting.

"It's a pleasure to make your acquaintance," Daithine said warmly, though her gaze lingered on the king. "We are most delighted to be here."

"I apologize for the rather improper greeting," Queen Hale replied. "Arranging everything at Wisteria Manor on such short notice was... hurried. It is our least-used vacation residence, as you can imagine."

"Don't fret. We've experienced worse," Daithine said lightly.

The human queen's eyes flashed with something sharp—something Frances didn't like. But it was true, they had experienced worse.

Much worse.

Malichi cleared his throat and stepped forward. "Please don't take my mother's words to heart, we've had a long and taxing journey. It's simply the road speaking."

He ended with a pointed glare toward their mother, though Daithine didn't seem to notice, nor care.

Frances looked again at the prince. His face remained set in anger, his attention fixed somewhere far beyond the conversation unfolding around him. Disgust churned in her stomach, and she turned away.

It seemed they were both being forced into this union, but it would have hurt less if he had pretended to care.

How could she assume he could be interested? She was an undead princess with a dead father and a crumbling kingdom, and he was nothing but a young man wearing the clothes of a king.

"...THE WORLD SEEMS FULL OF GOOD MEN — EVEN IF THERE ARE MONSTERS IN IT."

- Bram Stoker, *Dracula*

Chapter 15

Milo

She was absolutely horrifying.

Milo swallowed bile as he flopped onto the enormous bed, the memory of the girl he was to marry imprinted behind his eyelids like a brand.

She had acted like an animal, tilting her head to the side like that. He had tasted death on his tongue at the sight of her glittering, ice-blue eyes, and he did not like it.

The door burst open, and he let out a groan as the clicks of his mother's heeled boots stormed into his room. A second pair of muffled footsteps followed, and Milo lifted his head at that.

Both his mother and father stood upon the entry, Esther's hands on her hips and Duncan's crossed over his chest. He was in no mood to be berated for not speaking a peep during the meeting, but he supposed he was cornered now.

"Are you all right, dear?" Esther's question surprised Milo nearly as much as his father's rare appearance, and he sat up to face them.

He glanced between his parents and their twin expressions of embarrassment and worry. He was in no way, shape, or form all right, but he had a slight feeling that being honest was not the answer his parents would want to hear.

"I'm magnificent," Milo said, and pressed his lips together, wishing he could have changed the sarcasm oozing from the reply.

Esther's expression hardened, and two clicks of those impossibly high heels brought her closer.

"Don't use that tone with me. We simply want to know why you didn't engage when speaking seems to come quite naturally for you in other instances."

Though her words stung, they were not untrue. Milo tended to speak his mind when he was comfortable and alone, and sometimes it was difficult to keep his mouth shut. The image of the princess's head tilting to the side sent another shiver down his spine, and Milo shook his head. "I believe we made a mistake in bringing them here."

"Why do you say that?" Duncan asked, and Milo met his tired face.

"It's just a feeling. Perhaps it is part of my abilities."

Esther's face paled slightly at this, and the temperature in the air seemed to drop. "Don't say that, dear, you're only nervous. It is a natural *human* reaction to new situations."

"We found a teacher for you," Duncan said in complete disregard of his wife's words.

Real nerves surged through Milo's blood, and he met his father's gaze. "You did?"

"Yes, we brought him to Wisteria Manor so that you may begin lessons at your earliest convenience."

"Who will be teaching me?" Milo asked, the thoughts of his terrifying new betrothed fading from his thoughts.

"He is new to Cathair Liath. The professors brought him in from Elaria after an attack that left him unable to continue mundane life."

"Thank you, father," Milo said, and Duncan gave him a faint smile.

"It's my duty to make you as prepared as possible for when you take the throne."

"This still doesn't excuse you from taking some calming tea and having an early night in," Esther cut in, and Milo couldn't help but lean into her touch as she brushed a lock of hair from his brow.

He wanted to pull away and say that he was more than capable of making his own decisions, but he felt touched by her sudden worry, and an early night to be alone sounded rather nice.

He inclined his head, and Esther seemed satisfied enough with that. "Good, I will have Penn bring you up some dinner, as well."

"Thank you, mother," Milo said with a smile that surprised even himself.

Perhaps it was the attempt on his life that had spurred her into a sudden kindness, and even so, he didn't mind. She had grown cold and distant in the past year, during which Milo had also seen less and less of his father. He sometimes wondered if something had happened to their marriage, yet whenever they were together, he couldn't find a trace of animosity between them.

"Goodnight, Milo," Duncan said.

Milo gulped back the sudden lump in his throat. He hadn't been treated so well by either of his parents in so long that he thought they had perhaps forgotten he was their son at all. He would appreciate it for as long as it lasted, even if it was only for tonight.

"There will be a gathering in the gardens in two days. You can meet your betrothed in a more casual setting, and our courts can begin mingling and getting to know each other," Esther said as Duncan led her away.

Milo gave her a halfhearted nod, not quite liking the thought of being out in the open with a group of vampires. Jeremy would have to attend, Milo realized with a jolt, and he suddenly ached to see his friend. Jeremy had been whisked away with Lyra and Lennora upon their arrival, and Milo hadn't gotten the chance to see them since.

Milo barely registered his parents' departure before he sprang to his feet and began to pace. His rooms were grand and opulent, and he had barely noticed the splendor of the space.

Soft blues and dark reds were the central colors of the bedsheets, the rug, and the large loveseat, placed next to a large bookcase filled with aged volumes. A large mirror faced the bed, and Milo took in his appearance for the first time in an age as far as he was concerned.

He seemed tired, with a pale tinge to his skin; his crisp, silver-embroidered waistcoat wrinkled. He ran shaking fingers through his thick locks and sighed, letting his gaze fall to the large rain-streaked window that was a staggering void in the moonless night.

This was to be life for the next long while, living in a haunted manor by the sea with only a shadowy town as an escape. At least he now had a teacher, no matter if they had come from Elaria. There was no way of knowing how they had come to know stardust souls through their time in a mundane world, but Milo supposed that it was part of the reason they'd been brought to Astrum. He would have to wait and pray to the gods that he would learn how to control the power surging under his skin.

A knock sounded again, and Milo called admittance without much thought. It was likely Penn with a hot meal and a cup of tea.

"I swear, you brood more than you breathe."

Milo whirled around to find Lyra standing in the doorway,

her smirk illuminated through the gloom. She was wearing a silk dress the color of plums, and her hair was braided into a crown.

"What are you doing here?" Milo asked, and Lyra's smirk grew.

"Come on, and you'll find out soon enough," the witch said over her shoulder as she swept out of sight.

Milo huffed and gazed at his bed for one longing heartbeat before cursing and jogging after her.

Candles, set in carved stone grates hung at intervals, flickered through the darkness. Lyra was waiting a few steps down the hall, and he met her mischievous gaze with a frown. "Lyra, where are we going?"

She continued walking, and he cursed under his breath before following. They wound through narrow halls with strange alcoves and doors that seemed to appear for two seconds before disappearing once more, and Milo's head soon began to spin. They crossed through an expansive room with lavish seats and a grand piano, and a fire flickered in a fireplace set into the wall.

Milo jumped as a tall, balding man appeared from thin air, lounging on one of the sofas with a cigar in his mouth. Milo grabbed Lyra's arm to make her stop, and the witch turned with a frown.

"What is it?" she asked loudly, and Milo cringed.

Did she not see the ghost? His frown deepened, and he swiveled her around to face the sofas... but there was no one there. Milo blinked and scanned the room for any signs of the man, but he was nowhere in sight. Lyra sighed and tugged on his sleeve again.

"Come on," she said, and they passed through a small chamber that led into another hall.

"How do you know where you're going?"

"A directional spell," Lyra replied with a heavy note of self-satisfaction.

Milo opened his mouth to reply when a soft giggle emanated on the other side of the walls. Milo staggered at the sound, but Lyra only tugged on his sleeve. The giggle came again, and the flash of something glowing passed in his peripheral vision. There was a nagging sensation of being watched, but there was nothing there when Milo glanced over his shoulder.

"I don't have a very good feeling about this," Milo muttered.

"You never have a good feeling about anything. Trust me, it will be fine."

A heavy crash sounded from the direction of the large room, and the giggle sounded again. Milo cursed thickly and tripped over his own feet.

"What was that?" He asked, his quickened breath echoing against the narrow walls.

"Ghosts," she replied with a grin. "Are you afraid?"

He gulped. Who in their right mind *wasn't* afraid of soul-eating vapors? She took his silence as an answer enough, and her laughter rang out like wind chimes in the darkness.

"Don't worry your little head. They won't hurt you."

"How do you know that?" He hissed, desiring more than anything to get out of this strange place and rid himself of the present moment.

Her voice was still swollen with laughter as she replied, "Because they're harmless. It's only a bit of fun."

"I wouldn't consider what they are doing as a bit of fun," Milo said.

"They truly are very friendly. I met three ghosts just today."

"Sounds absolutely riveting," Milo huffed, and Lyra sighed again.

"Fine, we're here anyway. Jeremy can deal with your insufferable attitude better than I can."

She let go of him, and Milo found himself before a large windowsill overlooking the small town of Baile Sunndach. Milo looked from the warm, glittering lights outside to the gray blanket set with platters of food and dark bottles of drink before him. Jeremy sat with his back against the window, his nose in a book, his legs stretched out and crossed at the ankles. The strange man from the study infiltrated Milo's mind at that moment, with piles of parchment beneath his feet and ink stains on his skin.

"You finally arrived," Jeremy said in a matter of greeting. "I thought you might have gotten lost."

"I can't imagine that would be much of a surprise, given I haven't been here since I was three years old."

Jeremy snorted and placed the book down before gesturing for Milo to join him and Lyra, who had already sat and started picking at the array of food. Milo stepped onto the windowsill and sat, his clenching stomach and need for food betraying the sense of foreboding that still crept at the back of his neck. Perhaps Lyra could brush off ghosts with nothing more than a laugh, but Milo certainly couldn't—the thought of sleeping with a crowd of spirits trailing about made his skin crawl.

"Why did you do all of this?" Milo asked, gesturing toward the platters of grapes, bread, jam, and various meats and pastries.

Jeremy shrugged and popped a grape into his mouth. "It's our last night of freedom before you're forced to court your new lady, and it is my final night of freedom before I have to meet them."

"I'm rather excited to meet them," Lyra chirped. "They all seemed so serious when I passed earlier, though the brother was handsome."

"No vampires," Jeremy said cuttingly, with a glare toward his cousin. "I won't allow it."

Lyra narrowed her stare but said nothing. Silence draped over them, and Milo busied himself with lathering jam upon a thick slice of bread. He wished his parents were as opposed to him communing with the Baudelaire clan as Jeremy was, instead of being the reason he was in this mess.

"How are you feeling?" Jeremy asked.

Milo cut a thin slice of cheese with Jeremy's favorite pocketknife before answering. He was tired of saying too much or the wrong thing, and he didn't wish to cause more uncomfortable silences.

"I feel a bit like a deer caught in a hunter's snare," he said.

"How is that?" Jeremy asked, and Milo could tell it was a question of curiosity, not judgment.

Milo placed the cheese on top of the bread and bit in, the image of the princess dragging in an endless loop through his mind.

"It was the way she looked at me." Milo paused. "It was... feral."

Lyra's bark of laughter made Milo jump and immediately glance over his shoulder, scanning the dark hallway for undead visitors. Jeremy cut her a scathing glare, though Milo noted the slight amusement on his friend's face too.

"Feral, in what way?" Jeremy asked.

"I don't know if I can put it into words..." Milo broke off. He knew they were going to laugh and taunt him for the stupidity of his childlike fear.

When both Jeremy and Lyra stared at him expectantly, Milo cursed the gods and dropped his half-eaten bread on the blanket, the taste suddenly like dust in his mouth. "She smiled at me."

Now it was Jeremy's turn to laugh, and Lyra let out a

dramatic sigh before leaning her elbows on the floor in the most unfashionable way possible.

"No wonder you prefer the company of men, if a girl's smile nearly sent you to the grave," Jeremy chuckled, wiping away a stray tear of mirth.

Milo's cheeks burned, and he looked down at the array of food. "As I said, you needed to have seen it to understand what I mean."

He wouldn't explain himself to the two giggling idiots he chose to call friends.

"Well, I can't wait to meet her, vampire or not," Lyra said with an air of finality. "Anyone who scares Milo shitless is a friend of mine."

"And you aren't my friend?" Milo retorted with a raised eyebrow.

"I am." Lyra smirked. "And I scare you, don't I?"

Milo's lips quirked upward. "Touché."

The energy in their small alcove seemed to lighten at this, and Milo returned to his discarded toast with vigor. He needed this final night of joy and simplicity, for something dark loomed ahead, just out of sight. He wasn't quite sure how he knew this; perhaps it was another ability due to the stars in his veins. But something was coming, and it would shatter their world.

"Let us sacrifice one day to gain perhaps a whole life."

\- Victor Hugo, *Les Miserables*

Chapter 16

Frances

September 2, 1880

They were to spend a day out in the gardens, and it was raining.

Frances gazed at the onslaught of rain that attacked the ground with an intensity she had rarely seen at home. The event hadn't been canceled, only changed to take place in one of the large ballrooms within the manor. She wished not to traipse around a large room and make small talk with strangers; she wished to explore.

She hadn't gotten much of a chance to do it the day before, as Daithine and Malichi had all but locked her inside her rooms to ensure that she did not act foolishly on their first night there. She snorted. It was as if she were a caged animal that they had brought to parade around before being sold to the highest bidder. She wished to be free and to get some fresh air. Frances didn't move at the familiar long strides of her brother entering her rooms.

"You are expected for the festivities."

"I'm not attending." Frances sighed and leaned further into her hand, which was propped upon the tall windowsill.

"You are attending. It was arranged for you," Malichi replied coolly.

"I didn't wish for any of this to be arranged at all." Frances turned to face her twin.

Malichi inhaled deeply, though she knew he did not have to. His lithe body was draped in a closely tailored pantsuit and black coat with golden trim along the cuffs and buttons that fastened at his waist. His hair was swept back, making his sharp features and glacial eyes stand out like a beacon of terrifying beauty.

"I know that you are having difficulties taking this all in," Malichi said. "It was quick and without much communication, but—"

"But I must do what is best for our kingdom, I am aware," Frances snapped and swept for the exit. "Let us go then, I might as well put myself out of my own misery instead of having you do it."

Malichi didn't speak as she walked out of her rooms, and he offered his arm. She had half a mind not to take it, but his pointed glare sent her hand curling around his tight muscles.

They walked to the ballroom in silence, and Frances busied herself with watching the marble walls. Only one flaking red door disappeared into the wall on their journey, but it still gave Frances enough joy that she didn't complain as the sounds of laughter and music drew closer.

Furniture had been removed from the grand room to allow ample space for walking and conversation, and Frances couldn't deny her delight at the splendor of it all. Thick curtains were drawn back to reveal the lashing storm outside, and candles flickered merrily within stone grates. In the corner of the room sat a grand piano, and a young man with blue skin played an intricate piece upon its ivory keys. The room was full as well, and everyone was dressed in perhaps not their finest clothes, but close enough to it. She spotted her mother within the crowd, speaking animatedly to King Duncan, who nodded and added words of encouragement or reply every few moments. Daithine was stunning, and Frances could tell that Duncan was aware of it, his gaze dipping to her bursting décolletage.

Where on Astrum was his wife?

Some stopped and bowed as she and Malichi entered, and others stared. She didn't blame them, for she and her brother were forces to be reckoned with. Both were bathed in darkness, both lethal when needed. Perhaps she was more of a spitfire than her brother, but she could control herself. At least she would try right now.

Her brother leaned into her ear, and she repressed a scowl as he whispered, "I'm going to make my rounds of greeting. Don't leave, or I will find you and drag you back by your petticoats."

She plastered a sickly-sweet smile on her lips, though she prayed that the venom was evident as she glared at Malichi. "Lucky for me, I'm not wearing petticoats today."

Malichi's nose scrunched, and he turned away, clearly not wanting to think about her state of undress beneath the pretty maroon dress that she had put on today. She'd lied about the petticoat, of course, though it wasn't for a lack of trying.

Frances moved past the tables laden with food and bubbling glasses of strong drink to a few seats that were mostly free. Her gaze caught on the prince as he walked in, looking as disgruntled as she felt. Their gazes locked from across the room, and he pressed his lips together in what she assumed was acknowledgment.

Frances huffed and strode over to him. If he wasn't going

to initiate a conversation, then she would do it for both of their sakes.

"Prince Matthew," Frances said as she approached, dipping into a curtsey.

The prince bowed slightly, though she could almost taste the discomfort rolling from his person in a sour wave.

"How are you enjoying the day?" Matthew asked, and she was surprised to hear his low, measured voice.

Frances chuckled, not caring about the prince's raised eyebrow in reply. "I care not for stuffy gatherings. It's only a party if there's music to dance to and enough drink to drown in."

Matthew shrugged. "It's pleasant enough."

Whatever on Astrum that meant.

Frances narrowed her eyes, taking in the clean lines of his coat against his disheveled brown curls. His silver eyes were trained on her, though still just as uninterested as he had been at their first meeting. It was the first time she'd met a man who didn't find her intriguing, which made her all the more annoyed.

"I don't mean to be rude," Frances began slowly. "But why didn't you speak when we first met?"

The prince looked away briefly, a muscle in his jaw feathering.

"I suffer from nerves when meeting new people, though my initial silence is always a disappointment to my family."

She inclined her head, unsure of what to say. Nerves were never something she'd struggled with, so it was hard to imagine what it was like. He met her stare, and they both knew the conversation was over.

"Well, we will have to speak to each other a lot more in the future," Frances curtsied. "So, I will leave you for now."

Matthew bowed and said, "It was a pleasure."

Frances couldn't turn away fast enough. It wasn't that

there was anything wrong with the man; it was only his cold indifference that made it clear he was no more inclined to marry her than she was him. Perhaps that was better than the alternative.

She was halfway across the room when a hard body collided with her.

"*Putain*," Frances muttered as she stumbled back on heels that were slightly too tall for her taste.

A strong hand captured her elbow, and Frances took a step back to both steady herself and peer up at her assailant. It was a struggle to keep her mouth from falling open as she took in the strong jaw and light skin smattered in a blanket of freckles. Dark ginger hair swept in waves around his face, and she looked into eyes of the darkest blue.

Frances opened her mouth and closed it again before taking another step back, his hand falling from her arm. His touch felt like a brand, but somehow, she already wanted it upon her skin once more. He was tall, though perhaps an inch or two shorter than Prince Matthew. But what he lacked in height, he had in a build close to that of a god. She had no words to say for once in her life, and heat rose in her cheeks at the realization of her blatant gawking.

"I apologize for my clumsiness," Frances said finally, and her voice sounded stronger than she felt, *thank the gods*.

The man gave her a short bow. "I was lost in my own thoughts. I believe that I owe you an apology as well."

Frances smiled and found it to be genuine. She dipped her head and curtsied, taking the opportunity to gaze at the barely hidden muscles of his chest and torso. She peered up to find fire in his gaze, and heat rose through her body. He watched her every movement like a cat, and for once, she didn't feel like the predator she was.

"I am Princess Frances Baudelaire of Terre Rouge, pleased to make your acquaintance."

Any signs of interest winked out like a snuffed candle, and he gave her a curt nod. It was as though the temperature in the room became insufferably cold, if only due to the coldness in his expression.

"Jeremy Nightingale, a pleasure, I'm sure," he said coolly. "If you'll excuse me."

Her mouth did fall open now as he swept past in a hurry and headed for the prince, who stood by another corner of the room. Had she said something wrong? Or perhaps she smelled bad? Frances snapped her mouth shut and lifted her chin, not daring to let anyone notice that she had been affected by Mister Nightingale.

Though he wasn't strange, he was beautiful.

Damn her, she needed to come up with better ways to describe handsome men.

No matter, she wouldn't care if he avoided her like the plague. She was sure that he wasn't from her kingdom at any point. She sat upon one of the satin-covered seats with a flourish and looked out at the party, her gaze traveling through the sea of bodies until she found the prince and Mister Nightingale once more. They stood close together and spoke with easy smiles, though Frances could tell that the smile on the prince's face was more for show than out of actual enjoyment. She followed the curve of Jeremy's lips to the hollow of his throat and up again.

The prince let out a laugh and bumped his shoulder against Matthew, and Frances raised her eyebrows. Were they lovers? Perhaps that was the reason why he had suddenly been so cold to her, as well as why Matthew was so uninterested. But she didn't think that was the truth, for when she went to look at Jeremy, he was staring right back.

A vein flickered in his neck, right in the spot where she might have sunk her teeth into, if he let her. But the thought didn't make her hungry, nor did it soothe her. The way he watched her with something between anger and interest confused her beyond what she ever knew possible. *What's wrong with me?* She had met him less than five minutes ago, and he was already driving her mad.

The hairs on her skin raised as his gaze traveled from her face down to the tight bodice that revealed her curves and exaggerated rise of her breasts. She remained like a statue, doing nothing to stop him from dissecting her entire being with a glance. When his attention moved to her lips, she smiled. This seemed to break Jeremy out of his examination, and he met her stare one last time before turning his back on her entirely.

Frances shook herself and dug her nails into her palms, if only to think about something other than the stranger who felt like an old friend, or enemy, she hadn't decided. Curiosity flared inside of her, almost as strong as her desire to explore the manor and read her books. He intrigued her, and that was a dangerous thing indeed.

"FOR NATURALLY A BEAST DESIRES TO FLEE FROM ANY ENEMY THAT HE MAY SEE, THOUGH NEVER YET HE'S CLAPPED ON SUCH HIS EYE."

- Geoffrey Chaucer, *Canterbury Tales*

Chapter 17

Milo

The room was too damned loud. Rain lashed against Wisteria Manor like a beast, casting the candle-lit room in an eerie glow.

There were too many colors— too many people. And that blue man clomping on the ivory was enough to make his ears ache.

Milo pressed himself as close to the corner wall as he dared, though Jeremy's warmth at his side was also quite helpful to keep him tethered to reality. He'd watched the brief exchange between Jeremy and Frances, and a strange sense of protectiveness had washed over him at the sight of their bodies touching.

"I understand what you meant about feeling like a trapped deer," Jeremy said, and Milo turned to look at his friend, only to find that he was watching Frances as she chatted with an older woman on the seats by the wall.

"She seemed to act rather amicable from what I could tell," Milo replied, forcing his voice into an even tenor.

Jeremy snorted. "She's a vampire. There is nothing amicable about that."

Milo leaned into his friend's shoulder for the second time and grinned. "Won't you try to have fun?"

Jeremy rolled his eyes, but Milo felt a slight sense of triumph at his friend's low-chuckled response. "Have we been sent to some sort of alternate universe? I've never heard the ever-melancholic Matthew Hale tell me to cheer up."

Milo laughed as well and shrugged. "There is a first time for everything."

His mother came into view with the queen of Terre Rouge by her side, and Milo stiffened.

"Try to follow your own advice," Jeremy whispered in his ear before striding away as his mother and Daithine arrived.

Bastard.

"Matthew dear, it is wonderful to see you so jovial today," Esther said in greeting, the emerald green dress she wore high-necked as ever, making her pale skin all the more gaunt. Milo dipped his head toward her and the vampire queen. Daithine was striking, though her supple features were decidedly less terrifying than her daughter's.

"I am in good health and within the company of friends, there is much reason to feel jovial," Milo replied, and it felt like his tongue was wading through molasses.

Queen Daithine gave him an approving nod and sipped at the glass of bubbling alcohol held between her delicate fingers. "I am pleased that we were still able to join our families together, no matter the slight hiccup pertaining to the location we were to hold the gathering."

Milo stiffened, remembering Jeremy's warning as they had sat by the lake so many days ago. Someone had attempted to take his life, or at least that was what his mother believed. He wasn't quite sure what he believed, only that something had irrevocably changed that day.

"Indeed," Milo said, unsure if there was anything else that he could say without sounding rude.

Daithine took another healthy sip of alcohol before scanning the party, likely in search of a more entertaining conversation. Esther gave Milo a questioning look, and he prayed his upturned lips gave any sense of contentment. He was all right, truly. He wanted to be left alone so that he could leave this stuffy party and escape back to Rightford Castle.

Perhaps not so all right after all, Prince.

"Oh, there's Miss Devonne," Esther said to the vampire queen. "I must take you to meet her."

Daithine breezed away with a quick goodbye to Milo, who let out a breath of relief once they drifted past. Perhaps this was his chance to slip out of the room and retreat into his rooms before anyone else wrangled him into uncomfortable conversation. A mop of golden hair caught the corner of Milo's eye, and he glanced sharply in the direction of the man who was walking straight toward him.

It was Sage Astaseul.

Milo's heart did a terrible somersault, and he sifted a gasp through his teeth as they locked eyes, and Sage smiled. He was positively ravishing, in a tailored blue waistcoat and crisp white tunic underneath. His dark trousers showed off powerful muscles and long legs that strode closer and closer with every moment.

Milo suddenly had no inclination to leave, or perhaps his feet were stuck to the floor as the man closed in, and then he was standing before him, an image of sunshine held within skin.

"Hello again," Sage said, and sketched a slight bow.

Milo stifled the stupid grin that attempted to fight its way onto his face as he too bowed.

"You're here— I mean, you've come to Wisteria Manor." Milo fumbled over his words, heat rising dangerously hot to his cheeks.

"Yes, I have. I'm just as surprised about it as you are."

"I wasn't aware that you would attend such a stuffy gathering," Milo said, and Sage's laugh sounded like a song.

"I wouldn't attend if I had a choice in the matter, but Professor Binks made clear all of the terrible things that would become of me if I didn't show my face at least once."

"Well, I am glad that you heeded his advice, if it makes you feel any better," Milo said, surprising himself.

Sage blinked in surprise as well, though Milo swore that his face brightened, and he inched a step closer. Milo couldn't breathe, caught between excitement and overwhelming fear. He had never been so forward with anyone before now, but this man made him feel like he was mad, and he didn't know why.

"I'm glad I was able to catch a word before you got swept away again by one of your pretty friends," Sage said, not unkindly, though his words might have indicated some ill-favored emotion.

Milo glanced around the room and spotted Jeremy, who, to his surprise, was standing alone in another corner with a faraway gaze and a forgotten drink in his hand. Milo wondered if it had anything to do with his meeting with a certain vampire princess. Milo returned his attention to Sage, who had followed his look and was inspecting Jeremy with mild intrigue.

"Are you two lovers?" Sage asked, and Milo almost choked on air.

"Not in the slightest," he stammered, and Sage arched an eyebrow.

"Really?"

Never in his twenty years of life had he ever met someone so bold. *Nor so breathtaking.* He bit his tongue before he said something wrong and instead took a steadying breath.

"We are friends," Milo started, scrambling to change the subject. "It is nice to see you again."

Something dangerous yet alluring lit behind Sage's hazel eyes, and the room seemed to heat a few degrees.

"It is good to see you, too. I must admit, I'm not used to being in the presence of royalty."

"Is that so?" Milo asked, feigning nonchalance even though his skin felt as though it had been lit aflame.

Sage shrugged. "I have lived in the city working at my father's bookstore for as long as I can remember. That sort of place doesn't attract these sorts of people."

"It would attract me," Milo said before he could stop himself, and Sage's lips parted before curving upward.

"I would have liked that very much."

Why?

He was nothing.

He was a shadow, a lunatic of a man who couldn't even stay inside his own damned body. And a body that it was anyway, with more sinew than actual meat on his bones. Sage seemed to read every thought in Milo's head, for his gaze darkened a shade as he made a show of reaching up to adjust his cuffs. Milo didn't move as their skin brushed together for a fleeting second.

It was *much* too hot now, and Milo wanted very much to get out of this room and into the torrent of rain beyond if that was what it took to cool down. Yet his feet appeared to be rooted to the floor as he watched Sage's long fingers run along the inside of his smooth cuff and tug at an invisible crease that, in tandem, tugged at a corner of his frazzled heart.

"I'm afraid I must go; our riveting conversation seemed to have gone longer than I expected," Sage said.

Milo fought against the tug his muscles made to reach for Sage, to make him stay there forever if he could. Instead, he dipped his head slightly and curled his hand into a fist, their brief touch still searing the memory of his skin.

"I hope to see you again soon," Milo blurted before he could stop himself.

Sage's smile was more than he needed to forget the sudden embarrassment that crept into his cheeks, and the golden-haired man dipped his head as he said, "I believe that we will, and perhaps for more than a few moments."

Their gazes met one last time, hazel and silver caught together by some strange magnetism. The world froze for a second, or perhaps it was eternity. But the spell was broken too soon as Sage looked away and turned, disappearing into the crowd.

Milo felt utterly alone, all at once. The magic came before he could stop it, and the smell of dew and metal filled the air. His fingers tingled, and he glanced around before backing out of the ballroom and sprinting away. No one would notice his absence, not even Jeremy, who now seemed to see red and had a death wish for Milo's future wife.

He still felt too hot, and the familiar tingling sensation continued creeping through his fingers and toes as he continued his mad dash through identical halls and abandoned rooms. He couldn't lose control, not now. He needed to find a place to be alone and get his thoughts together before returning to the party. He almost snorted at the thought of returning to that horrid ballroom.

No, he most certainly was not going to do that.

A freshly painted black door appeared in a wall, and Milo cursed before lunging for it and stepping inside without a second thought. Dark walls lined with books of varying sizes and shapes surrounded him. The air was thick with dust and the scent of old parchment, and something else that he could not place.

It was metallic and dangerous.

It was the smell of magic.

Milo sank to the floor with his back against the door,

ragged gasps echoing hollowly through the small room. He wanted to cry, to scream, to burst out of his skin. The sudden sensation of lightness flowed through him, and Milo clamped down on his spirit before it could escape.

"Fuck."

Silence was his only answer.

Darkness rippled at the corners of his vision, and a sudden calmness swept over him. It was as though a candle had been snuffed out inside, and the first deep breath in almost three days allowed itself to flow through into his lungs. Milo was able to look about the room more clearly now, taking in the towering bookshelves and ceiling of... Milo's eyebrows shot up.

There was no ceiling.

It was simply a mass of swirling darkness, the four walls around him swallowed by it once they reached the undulating shadows. Milo knew he should feel scared, perhaps bolt out of the room, and do his best to forget this place. Yet the silent darkness felt safe.

Familiar.

Something inside of Milo clicked, and he felt as though all had been rightened in the world. This strange little room, with its aged books and ceiling of darkness, felt like a piece of his very own soul, a slice of himself in physical reality.

He knew he needed to go back out there, needed to get back into the real world and find Jeremy to ensure he hadn't already murdered Princess Frances and ruined the wedding. Not that ruining the wedding would have bothered Milo much. No, it was his still prickling skin and memory of Sage that bothered him, and the silence ringing in his ears was enough of an answer to the dread that was bubbling up in the crevices of his mind.

There was no good deed in coming to this place.

"HIS DESCENT WAS
LIKE NIGHTFALL."

\- Homer, *The Iliad*

Chapter 18

Frances

September 12, 1880

She couldn't stop thinking about him.

He was stuck in her mind, a little prison of annoyance that kept her staring up at the gilded ceiling above her bed. She was doing fine without sleep, since vampires didn't need more than an hour per night to function properly. Yet she hadn't slept at all in almost ten days, and she was angry.

It wasn't that he had aroused her, though she couldn't deny the strange pull of attraction toward his strong features and mysterious reactions. She didn't understand why his dislike of her still clung to her heart, and not in a good way. It wasn't as though she could ask him anyway, for the last time she had seen him passing her down a hall, he'd barely glanced in her direction before speaking to a short, pretty girl with blonde hair and a terribly loud laugh.

Damn him to the gods.

A strangled groan fought its way out of her, and Frances

rolled onto her side, gazing out the moonlit window. Wisteria Manor was louder than anticipated, and yet just as lonely as her own home. No one had spoken to her, though again, she hadn't made much of an effort to change that. It had been that damned Mister Nightingale who'd thrown her off kilter and ruined everything. Perhaps she was just hungry.

Frances lurched up with a laugh. That's what it was! She hadn't eaten since their arrival at Wisteria Manor. She'd never gone longer than five days, and the pangs of hunger and restless fatigue now became a gnawing hole in her stomach.

Frances slid out of bed and padded silently over the large rug to her dresser. A glance out the window showed the sea illuminated by the moon, like lovers in an intimate embrace. Her eye caught on the glittering town beyond, and an idea struck her.

She whirled back to her clothes and pulled out a pair of buckskin breeches, a tunic, and a dark crimson coat before flinging them onto her body without a second thought. As she swept the coat over her shoulders, something clattered to the floor.

Frances stooped to retrieve the gleaming black box, and a shudder swept through her body at the knowledge of what was held within. She didn't remember allowing the servants to bring Anton's dreaded parting gift, and a spark of anger only added heat to the boiling inferno inside. She tossed the box into the chest and turned her back to it, shutting away the memory of Anton as she moved away.

She rummaged through the chest containing her many shoes and pulled out a pair of brand-new boots. She pulled them on and laced them tight. She was down a flight of stairs less than a minute later, and her vision adjusted easily to the thick darkness coating the deserted halls.

A shiver caressed her spine as she turned a corner, and Frances suddenly had the feeling of being watched. It curled around her shoulders and pressed into her mind, and her throat tightened as she shot a glance over her shoulder.

The hall behind her had disappeared. A wall of shadow so pitch black it swallowed the candlelight loomed there, as if encouraging her toward the exit. She gulped and ignored the lurch of her stomach as she turned and hurried forward. The shadow did not follow; it remained.

After some time winding through strange corridors and gliding down steps, the grand foyer came into view. Frances glanced around to ensure that no one was there before she shot for the doors and opened them just enough to slip through. They were heavy, and she let out a small grunt as she shoved them closed again with a strong click.

Cool sea air danced across her face as she made her way through the groomed courtyard and tree-lined road that hopefully led to Baile Sunndach. A faint siren song drifted through the air down the seaside cliffs, and a shiver ran down Frances's spine. She had always loved the stories of sirens as a child, yet listening to them now made her question her childhood obsession.

Frances quickened her stride as she followed the dirt road, and the first buildings in the sleepy town drew near. Dirt turned into cobblestones as she approached the town gates, and soon the song of laughter, drunken shanties, and other assortments of sounds drifted through the night air. Shabby stone buildings of varying states of decay sagged and leaned against each other, and Frances narrowed her gaze down the many alleyways that snaked from the main road. The air smelled of sea and sweat, though the faint scent of alcohol was slowly growing stronger.

A gleaming sign swung in the light breeze, and Frances glanced up at it. *Deadman's Harbor.*

Interesting.

She stepped inside, immediately bombarded with the

scent of incense, alcohol, and sex. Dim gas lamps illuminated long couches draped in red velvet, and a bar sat by the far end of the room. Music of the most ruckus sort filtered through the air, and Frances suddenly felt as though she was on a pirate ship, not inside what seemed to be a bar, and perhaps a brothel, mixed into one.

Frances picked her way through the seats and tables, which were all occupied by one or more people in varying states of undress. Her stomach gave a feral squeeze at the sight of exposed necks and sensual bodies, and she had to force her feet to the bar instead of into the throng.

A drink first always made the blood taste better.

A tall man with one eye and more hair on his body than Frances ever knew to be possible stood behind the scratched counter, and she gave him her most dashing smile. He glanced away and resumed wiping down the countertop.

Rude.

She did her best to ignore the sticky stool underneath as she sat, and another wave of hunger, followed by the vivid image of Mister Nightingale, crashed over her.

"Whiskey on the rocks," she said without looking up, and a glass filled with questionably watery amber liquid slid under her nose.

She sighed and picked it up, tossing the burning stuff down without a second thought.

She swiveled around to watch the room's inhabitants, and a strange lightness pushed away her hunger. No one seemed to mind the blatant lack of modesty and etiquette, nor the lack of personal space. Roaring laughter and moans filled the air, and Frances thought she might be dizzy with the sudden change from the dark manor.

"Who owns this place?" She found herself asking.

"Captain Delarosa founded it," the barkeep grunted in a

wolflike growl. "His ghost still frequents, though no one owns this place anymore."

Frances clutched the edge of the bar until her knuckles turned white. "You mean Captain Archer Delarosa, the pirate who snuck into the Oseti palace in Asura and kidnapped the queen for a day?"

The barkeep nodded. "Very same, though I think if his ghost were near, he would say it was all to steal the palace's wine storage."

Frances frowned, remembering what he said before his previous statement. "No one owns this place? Then how can it stay open?"

"Every man of the law falls dead the moment they cross the threshold, so one could say they stopped trying to shut it down a long time ago."

Frances opened her mouth to reply, but a loud curse and the crash of breaking glass disrupted her confusion. Two men were brawling in the center of the room, and the many bodies had cleared around to form a half-circle around them. Frances leapt out of her seat and moved toward the sound of knuckles cracking against flesh and loud jeers.

One of the voices sounded slightly familiar, however, and Frances's stomach lurched into her throat as the two men came into startling view. A flurry of fists and coats tumbled about the room, and Frances lunged for the one with ginger hair before she could stop herself. Her grip wrapped around a muscled arm tightened with rage and yanked him away with her remaining strength. Frances swung him behind her and glared at the shirtless attacker. He was short and built like a boulder, and madness boiled in his mud-colored glare. Frances smirked, focusing on the small tendrils of magic flowing through her hollow bones.

"I think your business is finished here," Frances chirped, and the attacker took a step closer.

Frances shot her magic at him, and the attacker roared and clutched at his head, falling to the ground like a sack of stones. A few drunken souls rushed toward the fallen body, but Frances paid him no mind as she whirled to face the man still clutched in her grasp. The world halted as she looked up at the ragged face that was terribly familiar.

"Mister Nightingale?" Frances said, and his attention sharpened as he frowned down at her.

"Princess Baudelaire," Jeremy replied, and she hated the rush that surged through her at the sound of her name on his tongue.

"What are you doing here?" he spoke again, and Frances pursed her lips as she let him go.

Of course, the bastard would question instead of thank her.

"I came here for a drink, of course, which I would argue is a fairer excuse than you," Frances replied with enough venom to kill, brushing off her coat.

Jeremy only crossed his arms and glared. "You don't know why I'm here."

Frances raised her eyebrows. "So, not a midnight brawl?"

Jeremy rolled his eyes and sighed. "I don't need to explain myself to you, *princess.*"

She almost recoiled at the way he spat out the title, as if it were medicine that he needed to gulp down out of necessity but loathed otherwise.

"And I don't need to explain myself to you," Frances snapped. "Perhaps my other reasons are too profane for your delicate ears to bear."

Jeremy's gaze hardened at the provocation in her tone and the indication of her words. He knew why she was here, and something close to fear darkened his features.

"I see," he started and took a step back. "It is much too late for this nonsense, don't you get fed your proper... meals, at the manor?"

She hated the way he paused at the word, as though she could change the need to consume blood to survive. He was a prick, so why did her skin burn where she had touched him?

"I don't need to explain my eating habits to you," Frances said, and he took in a rattling breath.

"For once in my life, I wish you would."

She frowned. What in Astrum did that mean? The sounds of the tavern slowly bled back into her ringing ears, and the room lightened back to its red-tinged glow. But there was still the need for blood and hunger pains slamming within her gut. Jeremy's face hardened again, and she realized that she was still staring.

"I need to eat something, or else I might eat you," Frances snapped. "Now, if you will excuse me."

She swept past, but it wasn't before she noticed his clamped jaw and tension rising in his broad shoulders. A hand wrapped around her wrist before she could take another step, and she was tugged back. She swung around to glare at Jeremy, but his expression was unreadable.

"It is much too late for you to be out of the manor alone, Miss Baudelaire. Please, allow me to escort you back, and I will arrange for meals to be brought up to your family from now on."

She gaped, then quickly molded her features into something of annoyance. "I am perfectly capable of taking care of myself. Perhaps the women in your kingdom are afraid of being alone when darkness falls, but I prefer it."

The corner of Jeremy's mouth quirked. "The women in my kingdom are perfectly capable of taking care of themselves, but they are not princesses with a wedding in two months."

She hated the words on his tongue.

"I didn't choose this," she found herself saying, even though he didn't even deserve to hear it.

Time slowed as those lips curved downward, and a sudden sadness swept over her. The room darkened once more, and it was only one beating heart speaking to another stalled in the soft embrace of death forevermore. Sweet nothings and earth-shattering oaths were whispered between the two hearts, though not a sound was made.

The moment rushed to a halt when the touch of skin to skin was broken, and Frances's hand fell to her side with a slight *bump*.

"Let's get you back to the manor, Miss Baudelaire," Jeremy growled and turned around without a second glance.

She stood there, paralyzed and perplexed. Her wrist tingled, and her chest was on fire, yet she was utterly furious with the self-righteous bastard. She had half a mind to ignore him and find her own meal, but he turned to face her and shook his head, as though her thoughts had been written across her forehead in bold lettering.

A huff made its way out of her mouth, and she pushed through the swelling sea of bodies as she followed him, ignoring the tantalizing scent of blood and the elongation of her fangs in primal response to it.

The cool ocean air was a slap to the face as Frances stepped outside onto the cobbled street, knocking the growing blood-lust from her mind.

"Come with me," Jeremy said gruffly and began walking again.

Frances pursed her lips, but her legs began moving, and she trotted to catch up to him. "You are rather rude for someone who constantly chooses to remind me that I am one step shy of a queen."

Those damned lips quirked upward again, and Frances forced her gaze to the towering trees ahead.

"I have never been known to be polite, even with those of royalty," Jeremy replied with a level of confidence that was astounding.

"And you don't fear losing your head over the matter?" Frances asked.

Jeremy chuckled, "Why would I? The crowned prince of Cathair Liath is my closest friend."

"And I'm sure that you are rude to him as well?"

"No." Jeremy's voice softened. "I am rarely rude with Milo."

"Milo?" Frances arched her eyebrow.

They had to be lovers.

Jeremy seemed to notice her exact thoughts once again, and he laughed the laugh that made her legs unsteady.

"I'm not in love with him, if that is what you are thinking. He is simply a close friend."

"That's very sweet," Frances said softly.

She wished she'd experienced that—someone close, not through blood. Malichi had been there, but Frances wasn't all too sure that he would have if they hadn't shared the same womb.

"It is, I suppose," Jeremy agreed. "He is a special man, though many misunderstand his nerves for stupidity."

The faint outline of Wisteria Manor came into view, and Frances suddenly wanted to walk more slowly. Jeremy's long strides didn't waver, however, and she matched her pace to his.

"He is lucky to have you," Frances said, and she meant it.

She only wished that she had the same.

They walked in silence the rest of the journey to the manor, though it wasn't uncomfortable. It was a companionable silence that carried comfort through its song of nothingness.

They walked up the steps in silence, and both stopped a

foot from the grand double doors. Frances turned to Jeremy; the comfort of their silent walk whisked away upon the breeze. Though she knew that he couldn't make out her features, her heightened sight allowed her to see his. And they were shrouded in mystery.

"Why were you fighting that man?" Frances asked, unable to stop the question from tumbling past her lips.

Jeremy's lips quirked, and he shrugged. "It was a long day."

Frances smiled, understanding what he meant perfectly.

"Why did you stop the fight?" His question made her freeze, and for once, Frances didn't know what to say.

"I don't know," She answered truthfully.

It wasn't something she'd thought about, only a primal response to seeing a fist connect with Jeremy's face. She should have let the attacker finish him off, but a strange part of her couldn't let that happen.

"I will have a word with the head cook and ensure your family is properly suited," Jeremy said after the silence had permeated long enough.

"Thank you. I do hope we can be more civil with each other in the future," Frances said, noting the lack of the words *blood* or *meal*. "We might as well be cordial if we will be seeing each other more often."

Something flashed across his eyes but was gone in an instant. He was like a book whose pages constantly fluttered in a strong wind. She wanted to pry the bindings open and read the words hidden inside.

"I think that would be appropriate," Jeremy replied as he slipped inside. "Please do have a good night, Frances."

Frances.

Her name on his lips clung to her very bones the rest of the way to her rooms.

"His Ignorance was as remarkable as his knowledge."

- Arthur Conan Doyle, *A Study in Scarlet*

Chapter 19

Milo

September 13, 1880

"The core principles of the astrological signs..." Professor Binks's voice muddled and blended into white noise as Milo stared out the window, his thoughts still stuck on the day before.

He hadn't returned to the party after his encounter with the dark room; instead, he'd found Jeremy and Lyra and forced them to take him to the sea. They stood there for something close to an hour, perhaps longer, walking along the damp sand and crashing waves in silence. They knew better than to push him for answers when this occurred, for they were answers that not even Milo possessed. The state of chaos inside his body, which at times led him to leave it entirely, was not something to be known or controlled, but rather to be followed and listened to.

He was a dog to the feeling, and the leash was ever tightening.

A soft knock snapped Milo's attention back into the room. The professor paused and glanced at the old wooden clock hanging on the wall, its cracked dark green wallpaper like aged skin.

"Ah, yes, that will be Mister Astaseul," Professor Binks said.

"What?" Milo asked, and his stomach somersaulted as the door opened and Sage crossed the threshold.

"Hello, Mister Astaseul," Professor Binks greeted gruffly, and Sage gave the professor a low bow.

Milo was surprised a face like that was even legal to be shown in public, for the electric shock it sent through his bones was almost enough to kill.

"Am I too early?" Sage asked. "I can return at a later time."

"No, not at all. Matthew has been staring blankly out the window for nearly twenty minutes, so I would say we're quite finished." Professor Binks shook his head, and Milo forced himself not to shrink into his chair.

What on Astrum was he doing here? Sage moved to set a small briefcase onto the table, the tweed jacket pulling against the lines of his shoulders. *How is one even allowed to look like that?* A strange twinkle glinted in the man's stare as he turned to face Milo, and he stepped closer. Professor Binks stooped to collect his books and satchel from the large table on which Milo sat.

"Right then, I will see you next week, Matthew. Remember to do your reading about the planetary alignment of the winter equinox before Monday."

Milo gave a weak nod, fearing his voice would come out as nothing more than a squeak if he tried to say anything. Professor Binks exited, the top of his gray hair brushing the ceiling. For once, Milo didn't want to see him go.

"Hello," Sage said, and Milo slid his gaze to him, his presence seeming to take up every inch of the room.

"Hello," Milo replied, and was surprised, if not slightly relieved, that his voice was steady as words slid off his tongue.

"By the look on your face, it seems that you don't know why I'm here," Sage said, and Milo shook his head. Sage chuckled. "It seemed you didn't know from our interaction at the party either. Well, I'm here to train you. I wasn't sure if you knew, so I thought it best not to say anything at the time."

Milo frowned. Wasn't Sage only a bit older than he was? And how would a simple man be able to train a stardust soul? He couldn't be the tutor that his father had mentioned upon their arrival. Could he? The whisper of their skin touching tingled against Milo's memory, and he took a steadying breath as Sage moved to stand where Professor Binks had just been.

"My apologies, I still seem to be confusing you," Sage spoke again, and Milo did his best to school his features into one of calm neutrality. "I have a lot of experience with stardust souls and their powers, and the scholars thought it was a good chance for you to get some help, and for me to prove myself."

"You passed the sympathy test?" Milo asked, attempting to ignore the flutter of excitement that tickled his insides at the thought of having to spend consistent amounts of time with Sage.

Sage's gaze ducked. "I'm surprised you remembered."

"Of course I remembered."

I remembered everything about you, though I don't know why.

"Well, I did pass," Sage continued. "I did well enough, and the professors decided that this could be a good opportunity to strengthen my standing further."

"And how did a human like you come to know so much about stardust souls and their powers?" Milo asked.

A physical flinch went through Sage's body, and Milo instantly wished he could take his words back. Damn him, he didn't even know the man, and he was already making assumptions. So much for being outside of the discriminating sorts.

"I am not a human," Sage said. "My mother was a stardust soul. She hated life here, so when she came of age, she moved to Elaria, where she met my father, and I was born in London. I've known about Astrum since I can remember, and my mother would sneak my father and me between realms from time to time."

A surge of lightness flooded Milo's chest, yet he forced his tone into a calm tenor. "I see."

The corner of Sage's mouth quirked, and he continued. "I sat with her during many of her practices, so I have a good bearing on how it works and the different reactions of certain emotions."

"Are you stardust then?" Milo asked, and cursed inwardly again. He was asking too many questions too soon.

Sage's grin faded. "I'm a vampire, actually."

Milo's heart stopped for an instant, and both searing anger and fear roared through his ears. He seemed nothing like a vampire and carried none of the characteristics he would have placed with one. But then again, devils always enjoyed wearing the masks of angels.

"I was half stardust, half human, until last year. I tried visiting Astrum on my own. Well, let's say it did not end well. My mother knew of The Study, told me about it, and agreed that it would be best for someone like me to live in Astrum rather than Elaria. I'm good with books and the world of learning, so it seemed like the perfect choice."

Pain flashed behind his hazel eyes, and Milo stood. He didn't want him to feel pain, not on his account.

"Please, it's no trouble," Sage said with a shrug. "I suppose the positive side is I am immortal like a stardust soul now, not only bound to a longer than average life."

Milo inclined his head and, despite himself, took another

step closer. Sage seemed to notice the closing distance at the same moment Milo did, but he didn't flinch. His gaze only darkened, and his attention dipped to Milo's lips.

"You don't smile very often, do you?" he asked, his lowered tone sending a shiver through Milo's body.

"It is a rare sight indeed," Milo agreed, and his lips curved further.

"Well then," Sage said. "I suppose I will be teaching you how to hone your powers *and* teach you all of the reasons to smile."

Milo raised his eyebrows. "That's a difficult task you've assigned yourself."

He didn't move, didn't dare even to blink, as Sage took another step, and they were close to touching. He could see the flecks of gold and green in his irises, along with the sharp line of his cheekbones and demure curve of his lips. Those damned lips swept upward, and Milo's toes curled as Sage spoke. "I think I can manage."

Milo cleared his throat and took a step back. No one had ever gotten under his skin in such a way, and never as quickly as this stranger had. But he wasn't a stranger; he was a cloak of death and light that had always lived inside Milo, but had now come in the shape of a man.

"Well then, what's my first lesson?" Milo made himself speak, and Sage took a step back as well.

"We will cover the basics. I want to see what you can do, and we can build a base from there."

That dreaded fear clawed its way through any lust or longing, and Milo shook his head. "There's too much that I do on accident, but none of it happens when I try on purpose."

Sage ran a hand through his hair, and Milo moved to lean against the table.

"How do your powers come about?" Sage asked. "Do they

burst out randomly, or does something in particular trigger them?"

Milo thought back, recalling how his spirit would withdraw from his body in times of extreme discomfort or fear, and how his magic would surge through his body in moments of anger.

"I believe it's a combination of specific events, though mostly it is the stronger emotions that force tangible magic out of my skin."

"That is not uncommon, though it will make training a bit more difficult to narrow down."

"How do you suggest we begin?" Milo asked.

"You'll have to tell me which particular situations and emotions trigger your magic, then we can simulate them."

Milo let out a shaky sigh. He didn't feel very excited about having his mother's coldness or his anger at not belonging, simulated by a boy who made his heart quicken.

"The portal in The Study was formed because I was angry," Milo said tentatively. "Though stranger things have happened when other emotions become overwhelming."

Sage's face lit up like a ray of light. "I helped close that one; it nearly swallowed the entire room."

Milo let out a shaky laugh. "Not one of my finest moments."

"I do think that this narrows it down at least slightly."

"How so?" Milo asked, dreading the answer.

Sage winked and gave him a dashing grin. "We're going to make you angry."

"THE ROARING SEAS AND MANY A DARK RANGE OF MOUNTAINS LIE BETWEEN US."

- Homer, *the Iliad*

Chapter 20

Frances

September 14, 1880

Sunlight filtered through Frances's window, and she blinked through sleep-soaked eyelids. Faint birdsong filtered outside, and the ever-crashing waves sang their calming lullaby. Frances stretched heavily, letting out a groan of contentment. But then she stopped.

She felt rested.

Frances frowned, recalling the memories of the day before. It had been relatively uneventful, with her mother attending meetings with Matthew's parents all day, and Matthew preoccupied with his studies. She had finished her academic tutoring nearly three years before. However, the hoard of science journals and mystery books that Frances had insisted on bringing to the manor now waited in haphazard stacks throughout her quarters. It had left her schedule moderately free, other than a dress fitting and daily berating from Malichi.

She had spent the rest of her time wandering through the

manor, seeking out hidden rooms rather unsuccessfully and doing her best to avoid any familiar faces.

And, she had been fed.

The older gentleman who had been left in her rooms hadn't been much fun, but he had blood, and it satisfied her. Frances had simply bitten him and drank, and it had been over with in only a few minutes, with him vacating the premises in only a few minutes. But she was sated and had slept for the first time in days.

Jeremy had followed through on his word. The thought of it made her shoot out of bed in an instant, a huff escaping her lips. There were far better things to do with one's time than lie in bed and daydream about nothing.

Mister Nightingale is far from nothing, she thought darkly as she stripped off her nightgown and rummaged through her trunks for a fresh dress. Not having a waiting maid was one of the finer things about being at the manor, as they had decided only to bring a small staff. Besides, Frances hated being dressed by another with all her dark soul.

She did her best to avoid the gleaming black box nestled within the folds of clothing, yet after the third time she brushed over the polished wood, she let out a humph and grabbed it. Frances's nose crinkled at the scent that still clung to it, hating everything that reminded her of Anton.

"Damned demon," She grumbled and tossed the box to the floor, not caring as it skittered and landed with a *thunk* in the corner.

The journey to the sitting room was quick and uninterrupted, the scent of dew and ghosts following her with each step. Frances entered the lavishly furnished space to find Malichi and Daithine standing by an enormous painting of wildflowers, speaking to a rather serious-looking man who made her stop dead in her tracks.

They had to be joking.

"...I really must thank you," Daithine was saying as soon as Frances's world stopped spinning.

Midnight blue eyes slid to her before gliding back to focus on her mother, and Frances forced an expression of nonchalance onto her face before going to stand beside her brother.

"What are you thanking him for?" Frances asked and met Jeremy's gaze with a daring smirk.

He didn't return it, but she swore that his throat bobbed lightly as Malichi replied for their mother. "Only Jeremy's thoughtfulness about our need for sustenance."

Jeremy cringed slightly but dipped his head, sending a lock of flame-red hair sweeping over his forehead.

"It's truly nothing. And we must be on our way if we are to catch the sails in time."

"Of course," Malichi bowed slightly. "Frances, you might want to retrieve your hat."

Frances frowned and glanced sidelong at her brother. "Whatever for?"

"We are joining Jeremy and a few members of the Hale court on a boat ride today," Malichi replied evenly, as though he were talking about the weather.

Frances blinked. "A boat?"

Vampires were made for land, not sea. And most certainly *not* boats. Frances glanced up to find Jeremy watching her, and again the world seemed to fall away from under her feet. He looked away first, and Frances was glad she didn't need to breathe.

"Yes, a boat," Jeremy said after a heartbeat. "We really must be on our way now."

He bowed and muttered a few words about checking on the crew before he turned and strode out of the room.

"You can take mine, dear," Daithine said behind Frances, holding out a wide-brimmed bonnet with pink lace. "I'm afraid the thought of being on a boat makes me ill."

"Then why are you forcing me to go instead?" Frances cried. "I have no desire to go either."

Daithine merely pursed her lips and turned away as she said, "Have fun, and please, don't fall into the ocean."

Frances cursed wildly and whirled on her brother, who, to her surprise, was smiling. There was something dangerous lurking there, a strange knowing gleam that set her on edge.

"Remember why you are here, dear sister," Malichi said as he lifted an arm.

She took it, but cocked her head to the side. "Whatever do you mean?"

Malichi led her into a walk, and she brought her attention to the front. A terrible shiver ran up her spine as her brother's smooth voice crawled up the walls and into her skin.

"You know exactly what I mean. I can smell your desire for him."

Frances gripped the worn wood railing of the boat, which was more like a pirate ship, as they set off into the ocean. Crew members darted here and there, rattling off different commands and affirmations, but they all blurred into the ringing in her ears. The depths of the ocean below were a mesmerizing whirlpool of green and blue, and foam sprayed softly against her face like little mocking kisses, trying to distract her from the hungry beast beneath.

Frances had always enjoyed watching the ocean but had hated being near it. The endless tales of sea monsters were enough to make her skin crawl. The sea was a temptress and a mystery, and Frances hated mysteries that she couldn't solve.

She turned at the clicking heels of boots approaching, and she blinked to find the same pretty blonde woman who had been walking next to Jeremy some days ago. She was as bright as the sun that had decided to make an appearance today, with golden waves of hair and striking features that would have made Frances look twice in the past. But she didn't feel anything but polite curiosity, and perhaps a bit of bitterness. *What is happening to me?* Frances forced a pleasant expression onto her face as the woman stopped at the railing beside her.

"Hello," the woman greeted jovially. "You're the princess of Terre Rouge, is that right?"

"That's correct," Frances nodded. "And you are?"

"Oh, how rude of me. I am Lyra Devonne," the girl replied quickly. "I'm Lennora Devonne's daughter."

Frances blinked, thinking for a moment before remembering the brief introduction to Queen Esther's right-hand woman the day of their arrival. The witch had been kind, if not a bit frightening, with her wild magic radiating from her. She hurried to replace her frown with a smile.

"Very nice to make your acquaintance," Frances murmured, but the stinging in her chest remained. "You're part of the Hale court?"

Lyra shrugged in the most unladylike fashion. "More by name than actuality. My mother is the queen's advisor, and I am merely a pretty pet."

Frances tilted her chin. "And you are betrothed to Mister Nightingale?"

Silence stretched out between them, and Frances had to tighten her grip on the railing as they hit a large wave. Lyra let out a loud snorting cackle at this, and Frances might have felt more confused if not for the terror that lanced through her in tandem with the lurching ship. Lyra, on the other hand, stood as though on dry, unmoving land, her feet planted in a wide and relaxed stance.

"You're truly a delight, My Lady," Lyra choked on another snort. "Forgive my manners."

"Did I say something out of turn?" Frances replied, her nerve slowly returning, along with a sudden spring of lightness in her chest.

It didn't matter if Mister Nightingale was engaged to this pretty, odd girl, nor did it matter if she knew of it. She was to marry the prince, and it was none of her concern. *Liar,* her heart whispered in its dark cage.

Lyra shook her head and chuckled. "I am Jeremy's cousin, not his betrothed."

Frances gaped and then snapped her mouth shut. She was as far from the truth as the bright sky was from raining.

"I apologize, I—"

"I would get away from the railing if I were you."

The deep voice wrapped around her spine, making it stiffen. She turned to find Jeremy approaching. "Sirens live in these waters."

Lyra glared. "You're never any fun."

A soft breeze ruffled Jeremy's hair as he took another step toward his cousin. "I would happily let *you* fall in and fight off a few fish women. I might even enjoy watching it."

"I'm sure you would." Lyra stuck out her tongue before placing her hand into his outstretched one.

Jeremy's gaze slid to Frances once more, and he gestured to the safer main deck. "Come with me."

He took a step away, but not before Lyra halted him with a slight bend of her wrist.

"Cousin, you must take Princess Baudelaire as well. You cannot escort me and not our future queen."

Frances froze at Lyra's statement, and a vein in Jeremy's jaw flickered.

"I won't go with you if you don't escort both of us," Lyra

proclaimed, and Frances tightened her grip on the rails, sure that she might fall if she let go.

"It is quite all right, Miss Devonne, I can walk on my own," Frances said, but Lyra shook her head.

Jeremy gave a resigned sigh and reached for her. She looked into his eyes, only to find a solid wall of steel shuttered behind them. His emotions were impenetrable, and Frances paused before placing her hand into his. It was warm, and she almost gasped. She had expected his skin to be cold, much as his personality was. But it was warm and calloused, and small pinpricks of energy jolted through every place their skin touched.

That steel barrier behind his emotions slid back, if only for one second. It was a flash of not desire, but fear. Surprise jolted through her, and Frances almost retracted before Lyra gripped her cousin's arm.

"That wasn't so hard, now, was it?" the witch sneered, seemingly unbothered or unaware of the tension that passed between her and Jeremy.

The release of their gazes was like a crumbling building, and Frances didn't move until Jeremy's grip tightened slightly, and he led them to the center of the ship. Frances slid her grip to the more proper crook of his elbow, and it was a struggle not to notice the muscle that rippled beneath his cream-colored tunic. His arm stiffened at the movement, and Frances had half a mind to pull away.

Did he hate her so much as to be disgusted by her touch?

A large blanket with cushions and food lay out before them, and the king of Cathair Liath was standing by the captain of the ship, enraptured in conversation, while Malichi reclined upon one of the cushions with his nose in a book. Frances scoffed at the utter disinterest her brother exuded by simply lounging. His head tilted upward, and ice-blue eyes flashed first to Frances and Jeremy's joined arms, and then to

Lyra. Frances didn't miss the fact that his attention lingered on the latter for one second longer than they ought to have.

"Mister Nightingale, how kind of you to retrieve my sister from her impending doom," Malichi said in a manner of greeting.

"It wasn't the first time," Jeremy grumbled under his breath, and the night of their meeting in Baile Sunndach flashed across her memory.

Frances scowled at her brother and promptly slid from Jeremy's grip, moving to sit upon one of the cushions. She didn't wish to be spoken about, especially not when she was in the presence of the conversation. Lyra let go of Jeremy and sat next to Frances with a flourish and a sigh.

"I'm famished. What was packed for lunch?" She asked, not sparing a glance at Malichi, who was now watching her again, the hypocritical bastard.

"I'm afraid I don't know, for I haven't the taste for it," Malichi replied coolly, and Lyra finally met his stare.

Frances stiffened as Jeremy sat on her other side, though not close enough to touch. She dared not look at him, but her mind could hardly concentrate on the conversation at hand.

"That's because you don't eat food," Lyra said, though not unkindly. "Prince Baudelaire, is it?"

Her brother tilted his head in acknowledgment, his gleaming black hair almost blinding against the reflection of the sun.

"And you're Lyra Devonne, I presume."

How on Astrum had he known that? Frances raised an eyebrow, but Malichi paid no mind. His attention was caught by the girl, and Frances was afraid that his eyes might have gotten stuck in their sockets.

"That's my name," Lyra said with a wink, and leaned forward to open one of the baskets before them.

Jeremy was silent at her side, but his presence was deafening as they sat and watched the conversation unfold before them. She still could not comprehend why he stiffened at her touch, or why he was so damned short with her on every exchange.

"I thought we'd agreed to be civil with one another," Frances finally murmured after some time. Lyra had joined the conversation with the king and captain while Malichi returned to his book, once again unbothered and uncaring about anything.

Jeremy shifted at her side, and soon he was lying down, his upper body propped up by a forearm. His face was serious, but his voice was surprisingly kind as he spoke. "I didn't mean to be rude to you about standing by the railing. It's only that I hate open sea and was afraid that I might begin cursing in lieu of actual words."

A grin threatened to appear on Frances's lips, but she smothered it quickly. "I despise boats as well, so I understand."

The corner of his lips twitched, and an odd sense of triumph swelled within her. He tilted his face to the sky, seeming to relish the warmth of the day.

"How is it that you can be out in the sun?"

"Why do you ask?" Frances asked, surprised.

Jeremy shrugged. "It's often told that vampires can only go out in the night, and that daylight burns them."

A laugh made its way out of Frances's throat, but Jeremy watched as she chuckled. She sobered quickly at a glare from Malichi and cleared her throat. "We are perfectly capable of being out in the sun, Mister Nightingale. The stories of our preference for the dark are mere myths created by humans in Elaria."

"Why do they believe it to be true?" Jeremy asked.

"Because it is easier to believe that monsters only come out at night. And we prefer to find our meals in the safety of darkness."

A shadow crossed Jeremy's face, and his jaw clenched in that way that made Frances's blood boil. "I see."

"Don't believe everything that the storybooks tell you, Mister Nightingale," Frances said with a wink.

The boat swayed in silence, Jeremy having drifted off with the captain and King Duncan for a tour of the ship, Malichi still reading his book, and Lyra snoozing on her back. Frances was on her back as well, eyes half closed as the rocking of the ship both calmed and nauseated her at once.

Her mind began slipping from consciousness when it happened.

A cry rang out through the calm sea, and a splash followed suit. Frances's muscles reacted on instinct, and both she and Malichi were on their feet in the blink of an eye. Her legs wobbled slightly at the sway of the waves, but fear of that sound kept her upright.

"The king," Malichi breathed, and they both sprinted to the railing of the ship to peer down at the waves below.

Lyra was at their side in a second, but Frances paid her no mind as cold fear gripped her bones and she scanned the rippling depths. There was nothing-- no sign of struggle, nor a familiar face.

"It might have been a siren playing tricks on us," Lyra suggested, but Frances shook her head.

Something was wrong.

And it was then that she saw it, and the world stopped. Ginger hair tinted dark from the water, and a white tunic like a beacon in the night. She didn't think, barely registered the shout of alarm and gasp at her side as she pressed her palms against the railings of the ship and leapt over the edge.

"NOTHING CAN CURE THE SOUL BUT THE SENSES, JUST AS NOTHING CAN CURE THE SENSES BUT THE SOUL."

- Oscar Wilde, *The Picture of Dorian Gray*

Chapter 21

Milo

Milo was stuck.

He pressed against the darkness, attempting to shove it back so he might see the light. It only thickened with each push, and soon he was suffocating.

This is it.

This is the part where I never return.

The thought should have frightened him, but Milo only felt exhausted acceptance, and perhaps a bit of relief.

The darkness swelled and pulsed, and soon a second heartbeat rang out in the dark. Milo paused, and a whispering voice echoed through the shadows.

I am here.

Pain lashed through bones and flesh, and Milo woke with a gasp. Cold sweat ran down his skin in shimmering rivulets, and the faint scent of metal clung to his nostrils. Milo almost groaned at the sweet relief of oxygen flowing through his lungs and sensation returning to his limbs. This time had been the worst in many months.

Metal and parchment wafted through Milo's senses once again, and he frowned, glancing around his rooms in search of the culprit. He didn't think he had opened any portals in his sleep, but there was always a first time for everything.

Other than faint glimmering specks of stardust in his sweat— a regular occurrence— Milo couldn't place anything out of the ordinary. His sheets were perfectly smooth over his once-paralyzed body, and buttery sunlight warmed the room.

Milo frowned, and that's when his attention landed on the door.

A gleaming brass handle was a beacon through the painted black wood, and a strange pull tugged within Milo at the familiar door that had popped into existence over the bookcase. He knew he'd seen it before, and the memory of his escape into the room of swirling shadows slammed through his vision.

Milo sprang from the bed and crossed the room, already reaching for the handle by some strange magnetism. It felt right, yet so wrong. There was danger behind that door, wrapped in a blanket of allure and familiarity. It was as though a second spirit echoed from behind the polished dark wood, beckoning for him to find it.

He was close now, and the cold bite of metal kissed his fingertips.

A click and groan of old wood sounded from behind, and Milo faltered as he swiveled around to find his mother standing at the threshold of the room.

"Matthew, what are you doing?" Esther asked in a tone of curious concern, and he watched her gaze slide to what lay behind Milo. "What was that?"

Milo stiffened and turned to the door, only to find it had disappeared, leaving shelves of books in its wake.

"Oh— nothing."

Esther frowned. "You look terrible, Matthew. And where are your clothes?"

Milo peered down at his bare chest and legs swathed in

cotton pants, and annoyance flowed through his tired body. "I am half-dressed, Mother."

He wouldn't say a word about his trouble waking. It would send her into a tizzy, and he hated it when his mother was more unbearable than usual.

Esther pursed her lips. "Just get ready, you are going to be late for your lesson with Mister Astaseul."

Milo's heart sputtered at the name, but he shook his head. "It's not for another hour at least."

"I changed your session last night," his mother said. "You are needed later today for a fitting."

Annoyance crept back into Milo's bones, though his heart was still beating uncomfortably fast. He pursed his lips, and Esther's expression softened.

"It will get better. I know it's difficult, but with your lessons and our time here, our lives will become much easier."

She was far from the truth, but it was touching to find her trying to ease his pain. Milo wasn't sure that his life would ever become easier, marriage or not. Perhaps the lessons would help control his outbursts, but that was still a far cry from normalcy.

"Thank you, Mother," Milo said, giving her the best smile he could muster. It seemed to pacify her, and she lifted her chin.

"Get dressed. Penn will be here in ten minutes to take you to your lesson."

"Yes, Mother," Milo said, and Esther bade him farewell.

Milo let out a groan, halfheartedly massaging the cramped muscles in his shoulders. He glanced at the bookcase again, something unknown prickling his mind. There was a reason why the door had appeared. Milo knew it the same way he knew what was up and down.

It had been attracted to his magic, as though his spirit called out to what lay behind it.

"Idiot. There's nothing in that room," Milo grumbled, turning away from the wall.

It was likely nothing, simply the manor going about its odd business. Milo satisfied himself with this thought as the door to his chambers opened yet again, and Penn arrived to help him get ready for the day.

"I HAVE CROSSED OCEANS OF TIME TO FIND YOU."

- Bram Stoker, *Dracula*

Chapter 22

Frances

It was a terrible, horrendous, absolutely idiotic idea to dive overboard to save Jeremy. She didn't even like him, and yet...

And yet she would not let her mind puzzle together her feelings so long as she was in the middle of the ocean with barely the ability to swim.

It wasn't difficult to find him, and Frances kicked her legs with supernatural strength, propelling her forward. Even so, her dress weighed her down, and Frances struggled against the current pushing her away from Jeremy. She was *not* going to get stuck at the bottom of the ocean. She would not die if she ended up drifting down there, only until a sea monster ate her, or she eventually passed away from starvation.

Frances kicked again, her outstretched hands soon meeting soaked linen and smooth skin. He was thrashing and fought against her with a muffled yell as she touched him. Frances had to let go again as his fist swung at her, and she let out a growl of frustration as she reached for him again.

She would have to bite him.

Her canines elongated at her silent command, and Frances didn't hesitate as she grabbed his wrist and bit down.

Be calm.

She retracted her fangs as soon as he relaxed under her magic, not daring to focus on the taste of him as she swallowed; warm and dangerous. Jeremy went limp, and another curse vibrated through her soul as he plummeted, his muscles like rocks in the depths. Frances forced them up, this time toward the glittering surface above. She dared not look down and would not do so until they were back on board. She had no idea how she would get them both up there again, but she would have to try.

Warm air kissed her skin as she broke through the surface, and Frances blinked water from her vision to find blurred figures running about the ship above. Malichi, Lyra, and Duncan peered over the edge, three silhouettes of horrified stillness.

A rope ladder unfolded down the side of the ship, and a male voice rang out for her to take hold of it. Frances grabbed the ladder with her free hand and hoisted Jeremy's limp body flush against her. She did her best to ignore the hard planes of muscle and that damned warmth that emanated from his skin as she held on.

She grit her teeth against the strain of holding Jeremy as the ladder began to rise, pulled up by two sailors with dark gray skin and small horns protruding from their foreheads.

Frances dared not move until worn hands had grabbed her and Jeremy, and they were both on board. She collapsed upon the worn planks, not caring about formalities as the small company rushed around her and Jeremy, who was still unconscious under the magic of her bite. Frances lurched up and leaned over him, and fear nestled its way into her stomach at the sight of his unmoving chest.

"Somebody help him," Frances gasped as the captain, an

older man with the skin texture of gravel, stomped toward them.

"Get out of the way," Lyra demanded and pushed past the grumbling captain to kneel next to Frances.

She immediately went to his wrist, and the two puncture marks that glistened there. Fury creased Lyra's brow as she scowled at Frances. "What did you do?"

"He was thrashing," Frances spluttered. "I— it was the only way to calm him down."

Lyra pursed her lips and looked back down at him. "The bastard never learned how to swim."

The thought might have been funny if the bastard in question wasn't breathing.

"What can I do?" Frances asked, and someone gripped her shoulder from behind.

"Are you all right?" her brother's low voice cracked through any sanity Frances had left, and she shrugged him away.

"I'm fine," Frances bit out.

"I need space to help him," Lyra muttered. "He is all right, or at least he will be once I've had a look at him."

Malichi's hand returned to Frances's shoulder, and she didn't fight this time as she was guided to her feet and turned to face him.

"That was incredibly foolish of you," Malichi admonished, turning her to face him. "And where did you learn to swim?"

Frances wished she could shiver, for she was very cold. She wished she could do many things, like crouch by the sea-drenched man and make sure he awoke. Her fingers tingled with the ghost of his body against hers. His warmth against her ice.

"Frances."

She blinked again and hugged herself at the sight of her brother's stern and worried gaze.

"I said I'm fine," Frances snapped. "I only wish to find a dry dress and get off this boat."

A gagging and sputtering sound from the planks made Frances turn. She sighed in relief at the sight of Jeremy hacking out mouthfuls of saltwater. Lyra stood and darted away from spittle and water with a grimace, but the ghost of relief still shone on her face.

"Princess Baudelaire!"

Frances spun to find King Duncan striding over, strained gratitude on his face. Frances hurried into a curtsy as Malichi left them, grumbling a curse under his breath.

"Please, there's no need for formalities," Duncan said. "Thank you for saving Mister Nightingale's life."

Frances offered a smile and found herself touched by the king's kindness. "It was nothing, truly. Though I am curious to know how he fell."

The king gave her a bashful smile and chuckled. "The poor boy was leaning against the rails, and a rogue wave flipped him straight off the boat."

Frances swept a hand up to her mouth to hide her teeth. Amusement threatened to turn into a laugh, but she schooled herself quickly. "The sea is dangerous if one is not careful."

King Duncan bowed. "I will speak to the captain to turn us back to the manor. I think there's been quite enough excitement for the day."

"Thank you, Your Majesty," Frances replied, and he swept off.

She scanned the boat, but Jeremy and Lyra were gone. She whirled around, though she saw nothing. Frances looked down at her once sky-blue dress, now wrinkled and heavy with saltwater. The breeze clung to her bones, but she shoved the discomfort down as she moved to the back of the ship and found Jeremy alone behind a cluster of wooden crates. Lyra was nowhere to be seen, but still Frances glanced about before approaching.

Her steps faltered as he came into view, the folds of his slightly too large tunic swaying in the breeze. His gaze was faraway, and his skin was pale, but it was the fact that he was breathing that set her at ease.

"You're alive," Frances said in greeting, and Jeremy turned to face her.

"I hear you're the reason for that," Jeremy replied, eyes flashing as Frances moved closer and sat on the crate across from him.

She shrugged, hoping the gesture appeared more relaxed than the chorus of emotions that surged through her. "It was nothing, though you're quite heavy."

Jeremy smirked, but it quickly faded as he regarded his upturned wrist and the puncture marks that still lay there. "Why did you do it?"

She wasn't sure if he meant the bite or saving his life. She decided to answer the first and gave a grim, apologetic expression. "You were thrashing like an eel, and it was difficult to hold onto you. I wish I could have calmed you in any other way, but unfortunately, my bite is both a blessing and a curse. And besides, dying from getting knocked off a boat is not a valiant way to go."

His focus remained upon the puncture wounds as she spoke, and he let out a shaky breath. "Thank you for saving my life."

Relief made her smile. He wasn't angry, and she thought she could even hear a hint of gratitude in his tone.

"It was nothing," she repeated, and Jeremy stared up at her with an intensity that sent heat into her core.

"It was far from nothing, Frances."

She could only stare at him, shock, fear, and something

close to desire melding into one large lump in her chest. He was a mystery, and yet sitting with him on a wretched pirate ship felt like the most natural thing in the world.

"Land ho!"

The captain's call broke the spell between them, and Jeremy jerked his head to the docks that floated next to the boat. He sighed and rose to his feet, and Frances sprang up to grab him as he swayed slightly. He stilled, and she snatched her hands from his shoulders at the tension lining his face.

"That's now the second time I've saved you," Frances said. "I believe that makes us even."

A chuckle rumbled through Jeremy's chest, and he ran a hand through his damp hair. "I believe it does."

They walked side by side to the lowered ramp and started down it, behind the rest of the small group that had been aboard. Malichi strode ahead, stiff-backed, and Lyra's arm was looped through his. Jeremy's shirt brushed against her bare arm, and Frances allowed herself the small moment to seep in his warmth. It was short-lived, however, for the faint outline of someone running from the manor and down the beach made fear crawl its way back into her throat.

"Something's wrong," Frances said.

"What do you mean?" Jeremy asked, and Frances pointed.

The messenger was upon them in seconds. He was a young serving boy with blonde hair and tan skin, and his thin limbs trembled with strain as he skidded to a halt in front of King Duncan and bowed so low his head touched his knees.

"What is it?" Duncan asked.

The world slowed until it halted entirely.

"Your Majesty, there's been a murder in the manor."

"ONE CAN BE THE MASTER OF WHAT ONE DOES, BUT NEVER OF WHAT ONE FEELS."

- Gustave Flaubert, *letter to Louise Colet*
August 14, 1853

Chapter 23

Milo

"There has been a *what*?" Milo exclaimed.

Professor Binks stepped fully into the room where Sage and Milo had just started their lesson, and Milo did his best not to stumble over his own feet as he moved and sat at the long table.

"A murder, Matthew," Professor Binks sighed. "On the second floor."

Milo gulped. The second floor was the one directly below them, and he hadn't heard a sound.

"Who? How?" Sage asked, his usually languid frame now rigid in his seat.

"A nephilim serving girl, and we aren't certain," Professor Binks replied. "Milo, your mother sent me to inform you that you will need to keep her aware of where you go from now on."

Milo blinked. "Why?"

"Because it seems as though the one who tried to kill you at Rightford Castle followed us to Wisteria Manor."

The world stopped, and a terrible sensation of claustrophobia coated the walls. Milo took in a steadying breath, and through his blurring vision, he thought that Sage's hand twitched toward him.

"How must I inform her?" Milo asked.

"She requires a note at this time, but you will also require a bodyguard from now on. She recommended Mister Nightingale with his magic and fighting abilities, as well as Mister Astaseul."

Milo's eyes widened. The fact that someone wanted him dead still felt wrong, and the dread continued its slow descent upon his senses. *Of course it feels wrong, idiot. No one ever believes that it's right to be murdered.*

"I will send her—" the room slid out of focus, and Milo shook his head at the sudden brightness in his vision.

"Are you alright, Matthew?" Professor Binks's concerned question sounded distant in his ears, and Milo's limbs suddenly felt numb.

Oblivion beckoned.

"Milo, stay with us."

Sage's soothing voice and the pressure of a hand against Milo's shoulder instantly snapped him back into the room, though the world still felt much too bright. Milo groaned and rested his forehead upon the table, and a rather indignant huff sounded from Professor Binks's corner of the room.

"I will inform her highness that you are safe, but you must settle on a bodyguard soon. A strange darkness has fallen upon us this day."

The space grew silent as the giant professor left, and Milo let out a shaky breath. Steady pressure on his shoulder eased as Sage slid his hand to Milo's back, where it began to trace idle circles from his shoulders to the waist of his trousers. This might have sent Milo's heartbeat lurching a few moments ago, but now Sage's touch was the only thing tethering him to reality.

"It will be all right," Sage said softly, and it was those words that sent a lash of fury singing through Milo's insides.

His feet acted before his mind did, and Milo suddenly found himself standing over the vampire with sparks of white light dancing across his fingertips. How could he possibly say things would be all right?

Someone had tried to *murder* him, not take him out for a picnic.

Sage took a step back and watched Milo with a bemused expression. "Are you going to do something with that, or just stand there?"

The buzzing energy fizzled like a wet firework, and Milo sagged as the light sputtered from his skin and the world darkened a few shades. Sage leapt to steady him, and Milo's breath caught at the now more present sensation of their bodies this close.

"I'm sorry, this isn't something to be taken lightly," Sage said again, and neither of them moved from where they stood inches away from each other, the vampire's hands still wrapped around Milo's waist.

They seemed frozen like this. Milo's gaze dipped, and his heart skittered at the parting of Sage's lips and the tension in the muscles of his exposed skin. Did Sage want Milo as much as Milo wanted him? Damn him, he *wanted* the golden-haired idiot, and it made the day all the worse for it at the realization.

"You need a bodyguard now," Sage mused.

Milo cringed but nodded. A note wouldn't keep him safe, but perhaps a solid, strong person to watch his back was exactly what he needed. Perhaps a person who couldn't be killed easily.

"Would you do it?" Milo asked before he could stop himself.

Sage blinked, and both embarrassment and the sharp pain of rejection shot through his heart as Sage drew away.

"You want me to be your bodyguard?"

"Well—" Milo stopped. "You're right, it was a foolish thought."

"No," Sage replied. "No, it is actually a good idea."

Really?" Milo looked back up at him.

"Really. I'm skilled with a sword and pistol, and besides, I'm already dead."

A laugh escaped from Milo's chest before he could cage it in, and both relief and a new sort of fear sank within.

"That's exactly what I was thinking," Milo said sheepishly, and Sage let out a chuckle of his own.

"Great minds think alike, I suppose."

They looked at each other, acknowledgment and near-tangible energy crackling between them. Milo was terrified of having a target on his back, but a small part of him was even more afraid of having Sage so close to him out of necessity, in addition to academia.

Sage cleared his throat and looked away first as he glided back to his side of the table. "Right then, I would say the lesson is finished for today."

Milo let out a breath and sat in his chair with an unceremonious thump. "Have you ever been a bodyguard for anyone before?"

The question slipped from his mouth before he could stop it, and Sage paused for a beat before he sat down. "No, but I did learn how to fight and hunt with my father for many years."

"But you died nonetheless," Milo pointed out, and cursed. "I'm such an insensitive bastard, sorry."

Sage only shrugged and ran a finger along the worn leather journal before him. "Don't apologize for being correct. I indeed lost at a moment that mattered the most, and yet, I'm still here, sentient and virtually invincible."

"Vampires are not invincible," Milo replied. "And having

you admit defeat doesn't make me feel very confident in having you protect my life."

The cocky bastard only grinned.

"I may not be invincible, but at least things cannot get any worse for me than they already have." Sage sobered slightly then. "I won't let any harm come to you, Milo. You are far too precious to be taken from this world."

Milo didn't respond, and he found that even breathing was proving to be a difficult task at the strange, backhanded proclamation. He didn't know what to say, didn't know if he could even stomach being in the same room with Sage anymore without wanting to kiss him. *I cannot kiss him,* Milo scowled inwardly at his unruly thoughts. But he did want to kiss Sage, and he wanted to do it badly.

"I think you are progressing quickly," Sage said. "You already have shown a good deal of magic *and* stopped yourself from falling."

"You stopped me," Milo reminded him. "I only responded to your command."

"So?" Sage shrugged.

"So," Milo began, "I didn't do it alone."

Sage smirked and leaned back in his seat. It was impressive to see how casual he was in the face of such darkness mere feet below them.

"You must remember that you won't be alone anymore," Sage said.

Tremors of energy flowed through Milo's skin, and he nodded. No, it seemed as though his days of freedom and being alone were over for good.

"Will you follow me everywhere I go?" Milo asked, and Sage shook his head.

"I don't think my presence will be wanted or needed when you are with the major court and surrounded by trained guards."

"So then I hardly need you at all," Milo said, knowing he was wrong as soon as the words left his mouth.

The curve of Sage's jaw flickered, and his eyes darkened with some unknown emotion, or was it pain?

"If you don't wish for me to protect you, then feel free to say it," Sage said, though his tone was neutral behind the otherwise bitter statement.

Milo shook his head. "No, no. That isn't what I mean. I wouldn't want anyone else to watch my back."

Silence blanketed them. It was the second line that they had crossed in their relationship that day, and energy now crackled like a visible thing between them. Milo felt hot and itchy, and he wanted nothing more than to jump out of the window and fly away. Fingers brushing against his hand made Milo jump back into his skin and look at Sage.

"We will find out who is trying to kill you," Sage promised. "I would be glad to end them myself once we have found out who the culprit is."

Milo gave him a shaky smile and looked back down at their touching skin, differing shades of light and dark. He knew that Sage was serious in his proclamation, even if they'd only met a short time ago. Milo was only afraid that his heart would be shattered in the process as well.

"LISTEN TO MANY,
SPEAK TO FEW."

- William Shakespeare, *Hamlet*

CHAPTER 24

FRANCES

Death clung to Wisteria Manor on gossamer wings. The stench of angel blood held thick in Frances's nostrils as they walked up the steps toward the body. Lyra and Lennora Devonne joined her, their movements stiff and measured as they approached the awaiting scene.

"I really don't think that you should have to see this, Your Highness," Lennora muttered at her side.

Frances lifted her chin and rolled her shoulders back defiantly. "I am a student of Science, Miss Devonne. I daresay I will be more help examining this body than standing by."

"As you wish," Lennora replied slowly. "I heard that you saved my boy today."

Frances almost tripped on a step but quickly regained her composure. Never would she have thought of anyone calling Jeremy '*my boy*'.

"Yes, he fell into the ocean, and I brought him back on board."

"The poor man never learned how to swim."

"That's what I said," Lyra spoke for the first time since entering the manor, and Frances fought back a smile.

"Thank you for saving him," Lennora said. "He would do well to realize that vampires aren't all evil."

Frances blanched, and Lyra chuckled, but Lennora changed the subject before she could ask what in the infinite worlds that meant. "The body is right this way."

The scent grew stronger, and Frances's gums ached as she kept her canines from elongating. They rounded a corner, and a splatter of blood on the floor became visible like an ink stain on paper, more following in a disturbing smear until they found the body.

It was a girl of no more than eighteen, with dark brown hair matted and tangled around her face. Her dress appeared to be fine cotton, and the front had been torn away, her chest ripped wide open. Frances hid her grimace as she knelt at her motionless side. Seeing these sorts of things in drawings and paintings had been one thing, but seeing it before her now was... sickening.

"It looks like the heart has been removed," Frances observed, crinkling her nose as the scent of fresh death rolled through the air.

Scuffling footsteps made her look up to find Lyra slowly backing away, her light skin tinged sickly green.

"I'll go find the queen," she said quickly before turning on her heel and hurrying away.

Lennora knelt at the body's other side, shrugging.

"She claims to be a powerful witch but has never been able to stand the sight of blood."

Frances didn't answer as Lennora drifted a hand over the gaping hole. Her long fingers clenched slightly, and after a moment, she withdrew and sat on her heels. "You are correct. The heart is gone."

"Why in the world would someone want to remove her heart?" Frances asked, and confusion swirled within her disturbed curiosity.

Frances turned her gaze from the body to Lennora and found the witch watching her curiously.

"What?"

Lennora shrugged. "You're not what I expected from a princess."

Frances narrowed her gaze, bristling. "And what *did* you expect? That I would lie around all day and be hand-fed blood whilst someone massaged my feet?"

Lennora frowned and leaned over the body once again. "Not at all, I've just never met someone as curious about the dead as you."

It was neither an insult nor a compliment. Frances pushed the rearing bitterness aside and watched the witch continue prodding within the girl's chest with her magic.

"Who do you think did this?" She asked after a few heartbeats of silence had passed.

"I'm not sure, but whoever did is not very skilled with a blade," Lennora replied with a grimace.

"What do you mean?"

"Miss Devonne!"

Frances and Lennora both whirled as the queen of Cathair Liath swept toward them with Lyra on her heels. Frances and Lennora jumped to their feet and offered swift curtsies at the queen's arrival.

"Do you know what happened to her?" Queen Hale asked, not quite looking down at the body.

"Her heart has been removed," Lennora said conversationally. "Though her entire chest cavity has been hacked to bits."

The queen stiffened, and Frances noticed a sick hue to her fair skin as well. Her gaze slid to Frances and narrowed, but all Frances could do was dip her chin. "Hello, Your Majesty."

"What are you doing here?" The queen admonished. "It is much too dangerous for you to be out and about."

Lennora took a step forward, lightly patting the queen on

the arm. "It's all right, Esther, she's safe with me. Besides, she noticed the missing heart before I did."

The queen's gaze still rested on Frances, but she ducked her chin. "I have no desire to hear how you know such a thing. No matter, we must find servants to clear her out of the way."

"Of course," Lennora agreed.

The queen motioned for Frances and the witches to follow as she turned and clicked through the grand hall.

"Rinnta is only three days away," Esther said as she turned to Lennora. "Would it be wise to postpone it?"

She must be talking about Fete des Étoiles, Frances thought, remembering the approaching holiday. There would be a ball in celebration of their rearranged solar system, but Frances couldn't blame the queen for being uncertain about proceeding with the event.

Lennora shook her head. "I don't think so. It would be too obvious to the killer if we paused everything now. It's best to let them grow cocky and reveal themselves by accident."

Frances walked behind the women in silence, unsure whether she should continue following or sprint to her rooms. She ached to return to the body and continue investigating, but now that the queen had arrived, she knew it was impossible. She was a princess, and princesses were not allowed to put their hands inside dead bodies.

"... The staff to keep a tighter eye on things and ensure that the Baudelaire clan is well protected."

The sound of Frances's family name forced her focus back on the conversation, and she stopped abruptly to keep from slamming into Lennora.

"You and Lyra will find more security for each entry point of the manor, even to the garden," Queen Esther said, and both Lyra and Lennora nodded.

"And what of public areas, such as the ballrooms and dining salons?" Lyra asked.

None of them seemed to notice her existence anymore, so Frances merely curtsied and walked off. None acknowledged her departure, and for once, Frances was grateful for the lack of attention.

A guard stood by her door, and Frances gave him a humorless smile as he opened it for her. She breezed past the man, and the door closed behind her.

Fear was beginning to seep into her bones, starting at the soles of her feet. But Frances was stronger than the fear, and she had prepared herself for the past year to see something like this. And yet the girl's lifeless face still flashed across Frances' vision, and a shudder found its way from her skin.

She shook her head and began undoing the laces of her gown. She hadn't changed from her dive into the ocean, and the once-soft fabric was now gritty with dried ocean salt. Jeremy's face nudged the dead body from her thoughts, and that strange exhilaration and annoyed curiosity mingled with her fear.

Frances let out a strangled curse and flung the ruined dress into a corner. Her day had been a whirlwind, and she had a feeling it was only going to get stranger from there.

"There is something at work in my soul, which I do not understand."

- Mary Shelley, *Frankenstein*

Chapter 25

Milo

September 15, 1880

"Milo, wake. Up."

Milo blasted into consciousness with a lurching gasp. The room blurred in and out of focus and sweat slithered down Milo's spine as he gulped in sweet air. Milo shook his head and glanced around for the voice that called his name, only to find Jeremy leaning against his bedpost.

"Jeremy, what are you doing here?" Milo asked. His dreams had been fitful, full of blood and darkness.

"I came to fetch you. I've been tasked to keep you in shape and able to defend yourself, remember?"

Milo closed his eyes with a groan and leaned back against the pillow. "Do we have to do that today? I have a fitting later and don't wish to be sore for it."

His fitting had been postponed the day before in the wake of the serving girl's death. Milo had been grateful to get the rest of the day off, for he'd barely been able to stand without getting dizzy until dinner time.

It wasn't every day that girls were murdered in one's place of residence.

"Assassins don't wait for fittings to kill people," Jeremy replied. "Now let's go. I already set out your clothes."

Jeremy stalked away to wait for Milo outside his rooms, and Milo closed his eyes for a few more seconds. His body felt charged and out of sorts, like a bucket of ice water had been flung over him on a hot day.

Once he'd readied and cursed his way into the hall, he and Jeremy made their way through the manor in silence. Milo felt his mind fully wake, and the strange news from yesterday filtered through his thoughts. He was about to open his mouth when Jeremy turned sharply through a door that had not been there mere seconds ago. *Damned house,* Milo marveled as he followed his friend.

The room was spacious and well-lit, with dripping candles lit in ornately carved sconces, and large windows overlooking the sprawling cliffside. A large white mat that was springy under Milo's feet spread over the floor, and a rack on the side of the room held a variety of weapons, armor, and other tools that appeared to be exercise equipment.

"How did you know this room would have all of this stuff in it?" Milo asked.

Jeremy walked to the center of the floor and shrugged off his long overcoat. "I found it on the second day of our arrival. It doesn't disappear like the other rooms; it simply changes location within the third floor. It's not hard to spot, but you must enter before it moves again."

"This house is becoming less frightening, more so than odd."

Milo moved closer. He was already without a jacket, so he stood and waited for his friend to get ready. Jeremy's muscles appeared relaxed, but there was an odd, invisible tension around the set of his jaw and the movement of his shoulders as he tossed his jacket rather carelessly to a corner.

"Now," Jeremy said. "Shall we begin with sparring or grappling?"

Milo cringed. He didn't want to do either of those things. His preferred method of fighting was archery or the occasional knife throwing, as it allowed him to stay far away from the action and avoid accidentally making a wrong move, which would inevitably worsen the situation.

"You can pick, it seems as though you are the one with an abundance of energy today," Milo replied.

Jeremy shot him a glare. "You never want to pick."

"Because I never want to fight."

"I don't understand why not," Jeremy replied. "But fine. We can begin with some light hand-to-hand self-defense and then move to the blade."

They went through a few exercises and self-defense tactics, and Milo knew he would be sore after the first twenty minutes. Milo landed on his backside with a pained grunt half an hour later and let out a curse as Jeremy hauled him to his feet.

"You really are bad at fighting," Jeremy mused, completely unruffled and hardly out of breath.

Milo wanted to punch him now, but he knew he was better at dealing blows with his words, not his fists. "What happened with you and Princess Baudelaire yesterday?"

Jeremy coughed and glared at Milo indignantly, though there was an unmistakable flash of nervousness across his features. "Nothing happened yesterday, unless you'd count a rather boring boat ride with stuffy conversation something worth interrogating me about."

"Oh, please, we've known each other far too long for you

to start lying." Milo panted. "Besides, I heard about it all anyway. How on Astrum did you fall into the ocean?"

Jeremy strode to the weapons rack, and a pile of nerves flopped into Milo's stomach. He was terrible with a sword.

"I slipped, if you would believe that. We were on the bottom deck, and the boat lurched to one side, flipping me over the edge."

His tone was on the verge of mortification, which was enough for Milo to know he told the truth. But that hadn't been the part that piqued his interest when he'd heard the story. It was about who had saved him.

"Do you want to tell me about Frances's part in it?" Milo asked, deciding to go straight for the jugular.

Jeremy tossed a sword to Milo, and he scrambled, barely catching it by the hilt. Jeremy approached; his movements like those of a mountain cat. There was a storm in his eyes and clouds over his head, which only made things all the more interesting. It wasn't that seeing these qualities in his friend was a surprise, since Jeremy was Cathair Liath's second-best brooder, but he never brooded *this* much.

Jeremy got into position, his sword angled, ready in a straight stance. Milo mirrored his movements, though he was certain that his own stature was a sloppy rendition of his friend's lethal grace.

"She jumped in and dragged me back on board," Jeremy said, then lunged.

Milo parried the blow with some difficulty, managing to scramble back a few steps. The clang of their weapons vibrated through his arm, making him grimace. Jeremy struck again, and they continued in silence. Milo did his best to dodge and block the onslaught, though he knew the only thing saving him was the naturally quick reflexes in his stardust muscles.

"And did Miss Baudelaire explain why she saved you?"

Milo gasped, then winced as Jeremy caught his unprotected side and the sword ripped a stitch in his tunic.

"No, she didn't," Jeremy said, and Milo leapt forward with his own attack when he noticed that the damned man wasn't even sweating.

"Well then, I suppose that puts her into my good graces," Milo said, and their swords clanged through the open space.

"I suppose so," Jeremy said, and again, a strange feeling tickled at Milo.

"You don't seem to have much of an opinion about the matter," Milo said. "And I thought you, of all people, would have opinions about being saved by a vampire."

The flash of a sword followed by a flurry of movements too quick to catch made Milo freeze, and he found himself lying flat on his back, gasping for air. Jeremy straddled him and pinned his legs, a dagger pressed lightly against his throat.

"You're dead."

Milo sighed and slapped Jeremy's wrist.

"You're doing a fantastic job at avoiding my attempts at conversation," Milo said, though it wasn't beneath him to notice the pressure of Jeremy's hips against his.

Perhaps before, this might have sent a jolt of electricity and fear through him, but now, he felt calm. Jeremy stared down at him, panting slightly now. He swung his leg back and sat on the floor, appearing deflated and younger than his twenty-one years.

"It's difficult to have an idea about how something is going to be, for it to be stripped back and brought forth as something different."

"Meaning, you thought all vampires were bloodthirsty murderers, and now you're confused because one saved your life?" Milo asked, and Jeremy shrugged.

"I don't know, Milo. I suppose my prejudice only goes so

far. I still want revenge, though, and it is a terrible conflict to feel."

Milo sat up and squeezed Jeremy's hand. "I will still help you earn that revenge, Jeremy. No matter if I am married to the same sort of monster that we kill."

Jeremy's eyes darkened again, but it was gone in an instant. "Thank you."

Milo shrugged before scrambling to his feet with a groan. "Gods, I'm already sore."

Jeremy snorted and stood, albeit with a wince, more gracefully than Milo. They placed their swords back on the rack, and Jeremy retrieved his coat from where it lay in a heap by the wall.

"Shit," Milo muttered, remembering with a jolt that Sage was supposed to take him to his fitting.

"What?" Jeremy asked, and Milo quickly told him of the new arrangement to have Sage guard him.

"Oh, that's not an issue," Jeremy said and reached for the door. "He's right outside."

Milo shot his friend a blink of surprise. How in hell did he know that? And yet as the door opened, the vampire with a mop of golden hair and cheerful grin was leaning against the wall, waiting for them.

He was breathtaking, as always. A pair of suspenders held up well-fitting pants, and his shirt was once again unbuttoned four holes down. Milo avoided looking at the smooth skin beneath and instead offered Sage a smile.

"Good morning," Sage greeted jovially.

"Morning," Jeremy said in a less chipper tone. "I don't believe we've met."

Sage bowed. "Sage Astaseul. It is a pleasure to make your acquaintance."

"Pleasure," Jeremy replied with a curt nod.

Milo watched the exchange silently, for a sudden cramp

was beginning to climb up his legs and into his core, making him wince. Sage considered him with raised eyebrows and angled his head back to Jeremy. "What in the gods' names did you do to him?"

Jeremy grinned, and Milo hated his smug satisfaction. "We sparred."

"Ah," Sage said. "A terrible thing, indeed."

"We're going to be late for the fitting," Milo cut in, heat and embarrassment now overwhelming any soreness.

He didn't need his best friend and, well, whatever Sage was to him, poking fun. Both Jeremy and Sage laughed.

Milo hated them.

"Of course, my prince, let's get you to your fitting," Sage replied, still chuckling.

"Thank you." Milo scowled.

"Don't have too much fun without me," Jeremy called over his shoulder from where he was already walking away.

"We will," Milo growled under his breath, and Sage chuckled again.

"I take it you don't enjoy sparring?" the vampire asked as they made their way to the fitting.

Milo shook his head. "I don't. Any fighting in close contact renders me as daft as a brick."

"So, it's a matter of your coordination?"

Milo shook his head again. "I don't like hurting people, not if I can help it."

Smooth skin brushed against skin, and Milo glanced down at their joined pinkies. Sage squeezed his finger before letting go, and noises of high-pitched chatter emanated from a room not fifteen paces away.

"I can hurt people for you," Sage whispered.

A smile bloomed on Milo's lips. He knew that Sage meant it, even if he wasn't sure why. There was only the feeling that this boy would do a lot more for him than he would ever expect. His hand still tingled where their skin had touched as he stepped into the fitting room and was immediately greeted by a high-pitched squeal.

"My Prince!"

Milo could barely think before he was swept up by a woman who appeared to be dressed in the closest representation to a flamingo as possible. Her body was swathed in a dress of varying shades of pink, and a matching hat with an enormous pink feather perched atop her gray tresses. She got to work immediately, and Milo could barely think before his belt was promptly unbuckled and ripped from his pants.

"What in the gods-" Milo broke off and swore, quickly grabbing at his pants that the tailor was beginning to tug from his body.

Her returning glare was pure scathing. "My Prince, I must undress you to get your proper measurements."

"What are you planning on dressing me in?" Milo roared. "A second skin?"

A snort sounded behind him, and Milo remembered that Sage was in the room. *Could this get any bloody worse?*

"I am not going to dress you in any such thing, but to get the most accurate reading, I need these clothes off," The woman said shrilly.

She acted as though she were speaking to a petulant child, not the prince of an entire kingdom. She met Milo's gaze readily and even had the gall to scoff, the small measuring string caught in one of the folds of her vast dress. Seconds stretched out into what felt like an eternity, but still she didn't back down. Milo sighed, cold resignation seeping through his bones. This wasn't the way that he wanted to get naked in front of Sage for the first time, but he had no choice.

Not that he had ever thought about getting naked in front of Sage.

Heat rose through his body as he let the woman take off

his clothing, and soon Milo found himself in nothing but his underthings. Gooseflesh rose to Milo's skin at the woman's feathering touch and the string sliding against his waist.

"You don't look very prince-like," the woman said, almost disappointedly. "Though the placement of your muscles is most lovely."

If the floor were to open and swallow him whole, Milo would have gone down with a prayer of gratitude to the gods.

The woman glanced to the back of the room and narrowed her stare. "You there, give me some aid."

Milo suppressed a groan as Sage came forth on silent footsteps, a strange gleam in his eyes. Milo did his best to avoid the sight of the vampire altogether as the seamstress bustled about the room, muttering to herself. Milo focused his gaze on her movements, but his attention was on the tense body standing before him. *Just look at him*, a voice whispered in the corner of his mind, but Milo fought against it.

Come now, just a peek. Don't be afraid.

Milo lifted his gaze and regretted it instantly. Sage was not looking at his face, but at his body. His gaze trailed up from his legs to his waist, and finally to meet his stare, and Milo couldn't tell what emotions were hidden behind those hazel eyes. He was trapped in that stare, that gaze that was both a promise and a mystery. Sage looked down an inch, settling at his mouth, and Milo had to refrain from biting his lip. The electricity that traveled through Milo's veins was almost painful, and he hoped that Sage couldn't sense the acceleration of his pulse.

"Ah! Here it is. Damned thing was right in front of my nose."

Milo blinked, and the spell was broken as the pink woman returned with a small blue notebook and a pencil. She shoved both book and pencil against Sage's chest and unraveled the string from where it had been draped around her neck.

"What am I to do with these?" Sage asked politely, and the woman didn't so much as glance at him as she grabbed Milo's wrist and wrapped the string around it.

"Take notes of my measurements, of course. This one is twenty-two centimeters."

Sage promptly opened the book and widened his eyes before quickly shutting it again. "Excuse me, Madam, but I'm not entirely sure if you wanted me to see the contents of this journal."

The seamstress waved him off, already moving to Milo's other wrist. "Nonsense, just find a blank page and write the measurements with the concurrent body part like a good lad."

Curiosity over the book's contents tickled at Milo, and he tried to catch Sage's attention to see if he could glean something from even a glance. His wish was granted, and Sage's returning grimace of embarrassment was so intense that it was difficult to refrain from asking what was inside. Sage's attention shot back down at the page and fumbled for a fresh one before jotting down a growing list of numbers that the seamstress rattled off.

At least thirty minutes crept by this way, and Milo soon grew fatigued with both the endless prodding and string wrapping around his body, as well as the frantic beating of his heart whenever Sage looked at him, or any other part of his body. Finally, the seamstress pulled away with a satisfied nod. "I believe you're finished."

Milo let out a sigh and sagged slightly before searching for his clothing. His pants were soon located, and Milo lunged for his modicum of protection.

Sage all but threw the notebook at the woman when she asked for it, and Milo ached to ask what was inside as he buttoned his shirt. Once he was dressed and had pulled on his shoes, the woman bid them farewell and shooed them out of the room so that she could "get to working on the best suit in her career"."

"What was in that notebook?" Milo whispered once Sage followed him down the hall.

Sage shrugged and shoved his hands in his pockets. "Just a few drawings."

Surprise sent Milo's eyebrows up. "Drawings?"

Sage nudged Milo's elbow so that they could continue walking. Milo gulped at the sudden contact, and it wasn't beyond him to notice the pressure of the vampire's touch lingering on his skin.

"I think our resident flamingo has a lover," Sage murmured.

Realization struck, and a cough tore from Milo's lungs. "Drawings of *that*?"

Sage grinned. "They were well done, if not a little bit *avant-garde*."

A chuckle of discomfort bubbled from Milo's lips, and soon the hallway echoed with sounds of their mingled laughter. His skin still hummed with the places that were seen by Sage, and Milo ached to ask him to forget that anything had ever happened.

Sage stopped him before he could open his mouth, the shock of his touch returning to his arm. "I don't want you to take what that woman said to heart," Sage murmured.

"Why not?" Milo asked, if not a bit breathlessly. "She was telling the truth."

Sage shook his head, and a lock of golden hair fell over his brow. "You are prince-like. And besides, I agree with the last thing she said."

Silence blanketed the space between them, rolling to coat the farthest edges of the manor. For once, Milo wished his heart would stop beating, for right now it felt like a fish was caught in the netting of his chest bone. Sage was the one to cough now, and he pulled away sharply.

"We have a study session in thirty minutes," Sage redirected the conversation with neck-breaking speed, and Milo had to remember what the hell he was talking about.

Right, he is *my tutor.*

"We can go there directly if you wish," Milo offered, though he wasn't sure if he could take another heartbeat this close to Sage without doing something he'd regret, or not.

Sage shook his head. "No, I need to prepare a few things first. You can rest a moment and meet me there, though that would break the code of me always guarding you."

Milo gulped. "I think I can manage to keep myself alive for thirty minutes."

Sage was silent, and Milo glanced sidelong at the vampire. His gaze was trained on the floor, his expression distant, and his eyes filled with worry.

"Are you all right?" The question bubbled over before Milo could stop it.

They reached Milo's rooms, and Milo almost thought he wouldn't answer. But Sage spoke just as Milo opened the door. "I hope what I said doesn't make you think of me differently."

Milo paused and turned, a rush of energy bursting through his chest. "Why would I think of you differently?"

Sage shrugged, suddenly seeming uncertain. "I don't know, it's not what one says to a prince."

Milo's heart fell, if only enough to sting a little. He looked at Sage with the most conviction he could muster. "I like you because you don't treat me like a prince."

Milo turned and slipped into his rooms before any foolish words continued falling from his lips, and he sank to the floor with a sigh. He was approaching a cliff of feelings that he knew would lead to his death.

The only problem was that he wanted to jump.

“I WISH I HAD NO HEART, IT ACHES SO...”

- Louisa May Alcott, *Little Women*

Chapter 26

Frances

Frances felt physical pain for the first time in what felt like ages.

"Drop lower, and your upper body must remain upright," said an old woman with gray-streaked black hair and a Liathic-accented voice like a crow.

Frances ground her teeth as she sank deeper into the curtsy, stare trained on her brother, who gave an awfully extravagant bow. The woman made an approving mhm, and Frances straightened her legs with a pained gasp. They had been practicing a dance native to Cathair Liath's court for almost two hours now, and Frances wanted nothing more than to fall into her bed with a vial of blood and a good book. But she wouldn't get her wish, not so long as her brother stood before her, pale fingers outstretched expectantly. She took his hand with more force than necessary, and his grip tightened around her in warning before they got into position and began the dance.

"You seem to be getting worse with each try," Malichi murmured as they took a turn about the room, and Frances shot him a withering glare, though they both knew he spoke the truth.

Though she liked balls and pretty dresses, Frances had never gotten into the flow of dancing, despite her naturally graceful movements.

"It is called fatigue, brother," Frances bit out, and Malichi smirked.

"Vampires are clinically unable to feel fatigue, so your complaint is void. I would assume your distracted mood has to do with the events of our outing yesterday, as well as the death of the maid."

Frances almost missed a step but schooled her scowl in the blink of an eye. Jeremy's warm, wet skin against hers had occupied her mind for longer than she would ever admit. Though she could not lie, a dead body on the premises had sent her into a cold sweat all night, and she had spent most of her waking hours scouring the halls for any clues and reading her forensic papers when nothing of interest showed up within the hallowed walls.

"I have no care for a maid who lost her heart, and I've nearly forgotten about our boat outing yesterday," Frances said coolly, though they could both smell her lie from a mile away.

She forced her muscles to continue the dance, though she wished to stop. She glanced toward the ballroom entrance, where two stony-faced guards stood watch. Dozens of guards had been placed throughout the manor that morning, and now Frances couldn't go anywhere without feeling like she was being watched.

"I should remind you that your heart has already been sold to someone else," Malichi said, grazing over the subject of death, though not without a flash of worry in his eyes. "You cannot give it to another."

Frances froze. "What do you mean?"

Malichi guided her in an ornate spin that granted Frances another mhm of approval from the older woman. Yet, her singular good spin was lost on Malichi as his stony face spun back into view.

"Don't play the fool with me, Frances. You know exactly what I mean," Malichi snarled. "That Nightingale boy is not to be pursued."

Frances almost flinched, and cold fury wound its way through her gut. Who was he to tell her such things? And she did not want to pursue Jeremy in any fashion, proper or otherwise. Liar, a corner of her brain hissed, but she batted it away and settled her most withering glare onto her face.

"You don't have to worry about my pursuits, brother. I'm perfectly aware that my future was signed off without my say in the matter."

His sharp features seemed to pinch slightly, and he swept her into another spin as he replied, "This marriage is for the betterment of the entire continent, as well as our lives. Forgive me if I don't share sympathy for this small inconvenience in the grand schemes of your future."

"Well, I don't forgive you," Frances snapped, her body nearly cracking with the speed at which Malichi caught her spinning body by the waist. "I will live forever, unless I'm murdered, poisoned, or the dark matter of space swallows this entire fucking realm. I am immortal, and so is Matthew, which means that you're forcing me to live a lie forever."

"Perhaps Matthew is kind. You could grow to enjoy each other's company after a few hundred years," Malichi said. "You ought to actually speak to him for once."

Shocks of energy sent hot pricks through Frances's soul, and she quickly blinked away the thought of him.

"The prince is always either studying or sleeping, and I do neither of those things, at least not for as long as he requires. I am convinced this is a sick ploy to give you satisfaction for a place in your life in which you are lacking."

Malichi sighed as they entered the final half of the dance, a slower, more controlled set of movements. "While I am ever grateful for your worry over me, I assure you that I only care about what happens with the wedding, and that this assassin doesn't kill my family."

Frances's hand impulsively tightened at the mention of an assassin, and by the clench of Malichi's jaw, she knew the reaction hadn't gone unnoticed.

"I will not believe that." Frances sighed with a shake of her head. "We're creatures who require pleasure, which is something you are desperately lacking in your life."

"Desire is a temporary feeling that is bereft of stability or opportunity," Malichi replied smoothly, his gaze unflinchingly neutral.

Frances scoffed. "I think that desire is what makes us strive for stability, for the desire of stability is a desire in itself."

He was insufferable, and the only way that she could ever seem to get through his thick skull was by speaking in hypothetical tongue-twisters. Malichi sighed, and they moved through the final sequence in silent, practiced ease. Though no part of Frances felt at ease, nor did she have any inclination to remain silent. He was suffocating her.

"I won't stop until I've succeeded in making you end your own suffering," Frances ground out as she dipped her body into a languid curtsy.

Malichi bowed low, his face void of human emotion. "I'm afraid you will be unsuccessful, my dear sister, for I haven't felt a single thing for some time now."

"Till this moment I never knew myself."

- Jane Austen, *Pride and Prejudice*

Chapter 27

Milo

Milo entered the dim room, his heart racing in preparation for what his mind didn't yet know would come.

Sage was seated at the long table, his nose in a book as he waited for Milo's arrival. His golden hair was lit by the fading sun that filtered through the window at his back. Milo stood and watched for a moment, drinking in every detail of Sage until he was branded in his mind, though it still wasn't enough.

The memory of his attention on Milo's body was still imprinted in his skin, and a small well of confidence had grown in his core over the last thirty minutes. Sage was attracted to him and had admitted it, if indirectly. A boundary had been repeatedly crossed, and they both knew it. But he had wanted it to be crossed the second they'd met in The Study, even if *they* could never be.

Milo forced his feet to move after what he deemed to be an appropriately inappropriate amount of time spent watching someone, and Sage lifted his head. Milo wanted to applaud the vampire for acting surprised, for they both knew Sage had heard his arrival long before.

"You're late," Sage said by means of hello.

Milo glanced at the grandfather clock against the wall. "Only by two minutes."

"Two minutes too late as far as I'm concerned," Sage replied, and Milo's stomach tightened at the indication.

This boy, this man, had wanted to see him even after a short amount of time. Milo wanted to see him every second of every day, though he knew his desires were likely not reciprocated to such an extent.

"How are we setting my powers off today?" Milo asked. "Would you have me burn myself, or perhaps read a book by an old philosopher from Elaria?"

Sage shook his head. "The fact that you compare reading philosophy to causing physical harm to yourself is astounding."

"It feels like physical harm either way."

"I don't intend on causing any sort of harm to you today," Sage said, and Milo bit the inside of his cheek at the flash of something dangerous across Sage's expression.

"Oh?" Milo tried to sound calm. "We haven't found any other methods that seem to work as well as pain."

Those long fingers twitched, perhaps toward his own. Milo did his best not to react, though his breath might have hitched slightly at the provocation of their skin touching.

Again.

"I can think of a few methods we haven't tried yet," Sage said slowly, and heat bloomed on Milo's cheeks.

Milo didn't dare respond for fear of saying something completely, terribly stupid.

"I want to see what happens when you receive the opposite sensation of pain," Sage spoke again, and Milo knew he was stalling.

"And what would be the complete opposite sensation of pain?" Milo whispered, knowing very well what it was.

He wanted to hear that word roll off those lips.

That tongue.

"Pleasure," Sage said.

Milo had to blink to stop his world from spinning. This had never been his reaction to someone who wanted him. His immediate response was always repulsion, flight, to get as far away as he possibly could. Even when he hadn't said no, and had indulged in more primal activities, he'd never felt anything other than a desire to be alone and shrivel up inside. This sensation, this uproar inside of his body, was something entirely different.

And he liked it.

"How do you suppose we go about that?" Milo asked. "It is notoriously difficult to find things that bring me pleasure."

Sage rolled his eyes and leaned forward slightly. "I want to see what your response is to *physical* pleasure. Only if you want to, that is. I would never force that upon anyone, not ever."

Milo was captivated by the sun's glow on his skin. Those lips. Yes, he most certainly did want to experience physical pleasure with those lips.

"If we're both interested in the outcome, then I would deem it a worthy experiment," Milo found himself saying.

It was as close to a yes as he could muster. The word felt like a fish, slippery and potentially carrying a torrent of foolish proclamations after it.

Sage's lips quirked upward, and Milo forced himself not to look down. "Then let us experiment."

Sage slid from his chair and stood. Milo could do nothing but remain rooted to the ground as Sage glided toward him, long legs and powerful muscles rippling beneath his partially unbuttoned tunic.

And then they were standing face to face. One inch more and it would be chests touching, and then...

"Are you sure this will work?" Milo asked, his breath hitching as Sage drew closer.

His heartbeat quickened and nearly sang as skin met skin, and Sage slid his touch up Milo's arm, igniting his skin with desire. Sage's breath was ragged, but his voice was calm.

"I suppose we'll find out."

Milo was still uncertain as to what exactly was going to happen, but he could only guess after one glance into Sage's darkened stare. It was almost too much to see all of the emotion there: desire, interest, and something else that he couldn't quite discern. He could only assume the same emotions were evident upon his own face, as well as a healthy dose of nerves.

Sage's fingers brushed along Milo's collarbone before drifting up to cup Milo's cheek, brushing his bottom lip with his thumb. Milo wanted that thumb to be his lips instead.

"I've never done this before," Milo breathed, and Sage paused.

"You've never kissed anyone before?" Sage asked, and it was again curiosity behind the question, not judgment.

Milo shook his head slightly. "I have done far more than kissing but not like... this. I've never felt anything during or after the act."

Sage's gaze flicked to Milo's lips, and he dipped his head, so they were nearly touching. "And did you kiss boys or girls?"

"Both," Milo admitted, not daring to breathe. "And it never made me feel anything other than a strong desire to get away."

"Well then," Sage murmured. "Let's see if I can do something to change that."

Sage brushed his lips against Milo's, the promise of something greater. An explosion of sensation burst through Milo's skin, and he drew Sage in again, pressing their lips and bodies together in an act of want, need, of whatever this intense feeling was currently swirling through his entire being.

Sage's lips were soft and careful as he kissed him, and Milo opened his mouth slightly in a silent answer to Sage's gentle command. Their tongues slid together, and Milo was almost blinded by the overwhelming desire to get closer, to give and take as much as he could, and leave nothing behind. His skin felt aflame, and every place where their bodies met was like a whirlpool of sensation and pleasure.

Sage's fingers roved through his hair, and Milo gasped against his lips as he brought his hands to explore the muscles and planes of muscle underneath Sage's tunic. He was magnificent, and Milo wanted, *needed* more. He needed their skin to touch, he needed Sage's mouth everywhere on him, he needed to explore and touch and kiss and—

Sage broke away and cursed sharply, and a sudden wave of fear caged around his heart.

"Did I do something wrong?" Milo asked, not daring to open his eyes for fear of what he would see on Sage's face if he did.

"No," Sage breathed. "Look."

Milo didn't want to do that at all, yet the tone in Sage's voice was close to awe, not disgust or regret. And so, he did.

The world felt slightly too bright as he fluttered his eyes open and found Sage staring at him, agape with shock. Milo frowned and blinked against the light, but it didn't dim. It was then that he realized the light was not due to his unadjusted vision, but to himself.

He was glowing.

It wasn't a gaudy shimmering light, for that would have made him laugh and then run from the room in complete mortification. The light was slight, but just enough to brighten his skin and give it an almost god-like glow. He looked slowly from his chest to his arms, and his stomach lurched when he realized that his palms were still flat against Sage's stomach.

Sage followed Milo's gaze, and he felt muscle stiffen beneath his touch. He quickly withdrew, though a glow remained on the vampire's skin. Sage hissed slightly as Milo retracted, and he wanted to touch him again and ask what was wrong. But he would not. His damned hands were glowing too.

"What's wrong?" Milo asked, choosing words instead.

"That stung," Sage said, and began working the buttons of his tunic. "It felt as though I was burned."

It wasn't much of a surprise as to why he had felt that, for two faintly shimmering handprints were like brands against his chiseled torso as Sage removed his shirt. Milo stumbled backward, both confusion and apprehension battling themselves out inside of his already frazzled emotions.

"I am so sorry, that was— I..."

Milo was cut off as Sage grabbed his wrist and squeezed it tightly. Milo nearly staggered at the intensity in those hazel eyes, and the emotion and hidden promise beneath.

"Do not apologize for being who you are, ever," Sage insisted. "You are..."

Milo's breath caught as he waited for the following words.

"You're going to be the death of me."

Well then, not quite the words he was hoping to hear. But he wasn't sure *what* he had wanted to hear. Instead, he took a deep breath and blinked down at the marks on Sage's skin.

"I fear your statement might be more correct than you think."

Sage frowned slightly, and it again felt like a part of him had been torn away, but Milo watched as Sage grazed his fingers against the shimmering marks.

"They don't hurt anymore, and you stopped glowing. It mustn't have been that strong of an activation."

Milo snorted. "Not that strong? I almost singed your skin off."

Sage laughed, and it was music to his ears. Milo glanced at his lips to find them slightly swollen, and a strange sense of satisfaction and crippling desire swept over him. If he could only get a break from all these overwhelming emotions, perhaps then he could begin to sort things out more effectively.

"It wasn't so bad," Sage retorted. "Besides, we succeeded in at least one thing."

"What would that be?" Milo asked, watching Sage's movements as he re-buttoned his shirt.

Sage paused his work, and Milo looked up to find the vampire staring at him with storm clouds in his eyes. "You felt something, did you not?"

It was a dangerous question, and they both knew it. At once, Milo felt as though he was once again standing at the ledge of a cliff, while a pack of wolves closed in and sealed his way back to safety. Yet the chasm at the bottom felt safer than the wolves, and Milo decided to jump.

"What do you think?" Milo asked, and those storm clouds rolled.

"I know what I think," Sage started, then paused before saying, "But I want to hear it from you."

"Yes," Milo said, the word no more than a whisper.

Yes, of course, he'd felt something. He'd felt more than something, and he was unused to the strange animalistic desire that had taken over his senses during the kiss. It was the first time he'd enjoyed the act of kissing and stopped thinking about anything other than the need for more. Damnation, he had more than enjoyed the kiss. He'd loved it. It felt natural, and for once in his life, Milo now understood why so many desired to do it.

But then the worry came. Sage hadn't said what he had thought or felt about the kiss, and Milo had scorched him after all. But he had to know, needed to hear it just as much as Sage seemed to need it.

"And you? Did you feel something?" He asked, almost afraid of the words and the terribly weighted promise held beneath.

Sage didn't answer but instead grabbed the front of Milo's tunic and pulled him against his chest. Milo barely had time to think before Sage kissed him, this time more fiercely than before. Their bodies molded together, moving and exploring in a way that felt like his body, his *being* had been waiting for this man for eternity. Sage's lips pressed promises against his skin, and Milo let out a gasp as Sage's mouth trailed to his jaw, then came back up to his lips before they could go any lower. Milo fought against the tension that came with that realization. Sage was a vampire, and sex was his fuel. But it felt so right, so natural for their bodies to be pressed together and their lips on each other's skin. Milo wouldn't think about it, wouldn't think about anything. Sage's touch spoke more of desire and feelings than any words could, and Milo trusted it more than anything.

Sage's teeth nipped against Milo's lower lip, and he let out another breath as sudden desire and heat welled up in his core. He almost jumped as something clenched, and he suddenly became overly aware of a pressure against his trousers. He wanted Sage, and he wanted him now.

But that couldn't happen.

Sage finally broke away, and Milo found himself glowing again, yet this time a bit brighter than the first time. They watched each other for a few heartbeats, or perhaps it was an eternity.

"Does that answer your question?" Sage panted slightly.

"I'm unaccustomed to physical communication." Milo breathed heavily. "But I think I might have an inkling of what you were trying to say."

Sage huffed, yet Milo's heart sang at the brilliant smile that brightened his face. "Yes, I felt something."

Milo couldn't help it, but his lips curled at the corners. It was a liberating act, and he found he couldn't have stopped himself even if he'd tried. Sage's gaze softened, and he took another step back.

"It's truly a delight to see you smile," he said. "I'm glad it's making a more frequent appearance."

Milo took his own step back, knowing by the darkening sky that he was already late for dinner with his family. He wanted to stay, and it felt as though his heart was attempting to pull itself out of his chest to return to Sage. But he had to leave, had to go back to the slightly bleaker world he called reality.

"I have a feeling that it will make further appearances still, perhaps every day in the future."

"Good," Sage said, grinning widely. "It's the brightest part of my day."

"Dead men don't bite."

\- Robert Louis Stevenson, *Treasure Island*

Chapter 28

Frances

September 29, 1880

Malichi was late.

Frances let out a huff and glared out the window, the swirling colors of fabrics and flowers unnoticed behind her as servants prepared for *Fete des Étoiles,* or Rinnta, as Queen Esther had called the festival. He was supposed to practice with her one last time before she needed to get ready and the evening festivities began, but he was nowhere to be seen, and she didn't feel like waiting anymore.

To hell with him, Frances thought, and spun on her heel. It was time to find some real entertainment before the night began.

Her footsteps echoed along a well-lit corridor as she made her way to nowhere in particular. She felt muddled and foggy, as though her emotions had suddenly drowned out the rest of her senses. It was a terrible thing, and Frances let out another halfhearted sigh as the anticipation of having to dance with Matthew Hale made her stomach churn.

"Lady Frances."

A harsh male voice rang out from behind, making Frances's muscles freeze. She turned slowly to find a middle-aged guard regarding her in a severely neutral manner.

"It's Your Highness, thank you very much," Frances replied. "What do you want?"

The guard gave the slightest nod. "You are needed for questioning. Please, come with me."

Tension lit up the corridor until it almost stung, and Frances shook her head against the onslaught of curses she wished to fling at the disgraceful man. How could she possibly be wanted for questioning? Her family had come here for the very reason of *saving* their lives, not ending them.

"If you have any questions, then you may ask me here," Frances said, lifting her chin as if to look down at the man, though he was at least a head taller than her.

"Your Highness, the topic is of a delicate nature and—"

"And every person within these walls knows exactly what you're questioning about," Frances snapped. "Now ask me, or else I will eat you for lunch."

The guard paled, his Adam's apple bobbing within the constraints of his throat.

"Very well then—"

"Frances! I was wondering where you had gone."

A woman's voice sounded behind them, and Frances whirled around to find none other than Lyra coming up behind. She was an image of beauty today, with a dark green dress cut so close to her body that Frances hardly had to use her imagination to guess what lines lay beneath. Frances shook herself inwardly. She didn't need to be over her head with two Nightingales. One was far more than enough.

Frances schooled her face into pleasant neutrality, giving

the girl a slight dip of her head in acknowledgement. "I've been held for questioning, if you can believe it."

Lyra glared at the guard before giving Frances an apologetic shrug. "It's my fault, I'm afraid. Queen Hale instructed me to dispatch guards. They've been ordered to question nearly everyone in the manor, though I hardly think it fair that they question you."

Frances gave an unladylike shrug and gestured at the guard, who watched them with unbridled apprehension. She could only guess the nerves that would arise with confronting a powerful witch and a vampire.

"Move along, Princess Baudelaire has been helping us with the investigation. There's no need for her to be questioned," Lyra said with a dismissive wave.

The guard bowed low before scurrying off. Lyra revealed a mischievous grin and moved to stand at Frances's side.

"Come with me."

Frances allowed the girl to take her elbow, and together they continued down a flight of stairs that led to the gardens and watery sunlight beyond.

"Has your time here been pleasant?" Frances asked.

Lyra nodded. "It has been adequate, though I must say that it's far more boring than I anticipated. Having the responsibility of issuing guards has offered some relief, I suppose."

"What else would you expect from being locked away in a cliffside manor?"

"I don't know," Lyra said. "I suppose it's still too early in our time here to make conclusions."

They stepped out into the gardens, the scent of roses and rain immediately enveloping Frances's senses. Court members milled amongst the well-trimmed hedges and fountains, idle conversation floating through the misty air.

"What about you?" Lyra asked, and Frances tilted her head toward the girl.

"What about me?"

"Are you enjoying your time?" Lyra spoke again, and Frances's hands coiled into fists on instinct.

"I am doing my best to make light of my current situation, though I cannot say that it's been enjoyable," Frances said, and immediately regretted speaking. "I am sorry. That was far too honest."

Lyra gave her another dazzling smile. "I prefer honesty over lies, no matter how rude. Besides, now I like you more."

Frances's lips tilted upward in turn, suddenly feeling lighter and slightly warmer toward the witch. They rounded a corner and stepped into a shaded gazebo overrun with vines and deep crimson flowers.

Lyra crinkled her nose. "Weeping Roses are much too dramatic in my opinion."

They stepped into the shaded area, and Frances inspected the perfectly manicured brick walkway. Spatters of thick, dark liquid spotted across the ground, and Frances's heart leapt into her throat.

Had someone else been murdered?

"Don't worry, it's only the flowers that are bleeding."

Lyra and Frances both turned at the unfamiliar voice, and Frances found a man with golden hair seated on the single bench within the gazebo, his tunic unbuttoned a few holes down. Hazel eyes met hers, and she gave the man a curious look. "What do you mean?"

He gestured at the dark flowers. "Weeping Roses are rare and hardly planted for domestic use, as they tend to bleed once a week."

"I've never heard of a bleeding flower," Frances said. *It would make my feeding a lot easier, though perhaps a bit less fun.*

He shrugged and stood on long, powerful legs. Frances immediately recognized his kind, as the silent and dangerous grace with which he moved was an echo of her own quiet bones.

"Sage Astaseul, a pleasure." The vampire bowed, and Frances watched the curve of his jaw and the kindness in his eyes as he straightened.

"Princess Frances Baudelaire," Frances said with a curtsy.

"You're Milo's tutor!" Lyra exclaimed. "He forgot to mention how handsome you are."

Sage let out a chuckle, though Frances noted the briefest tension around his shoulders when Lyra mentioned Matthew's name. Interest prickled at her now. She wasn't aware the prince had multiple tutors, and she certainly didn't understand how this *vampire* had come into the Cathair Liath court.

"I thought you were his guard as well," Lyra spoke again, a dangerous amount of interest and arousal emanating from the girl's scent.

"I am." Sage agreed. "But the prince is currently bathing, and his manservant is in his company, so I hardly think I'm needed at the moment."

Lyra let out a rather girlish giggle, and Frances fought the gag that rose in her throat. Sage looked at her again, and Frances met his stare readily.

"You are the mysterious princess," Sage said, and though his expression was pleasant, Frances heard a hint of disappointment behind his words.

"Not so mysterious," Frances replied.

Sage tilted his head to the side. "You aren't what I expected from a Terre Rouge royal."

Frances met his tilt with one of her own. "I've been told that once before already. What did you expect?"

Her silent attack had no effect on him, and she was yet again caught off guard by his complete sense of calm confidence.

"A bit more excitement, I suppose," Sage said. "I've always heard of you southerners being quite boisterous."

I would be a bit more boisterous if I had agreed to be here in the first place, Frances thought, but didn't say. Instead, she pasted on a wicked grin. "That's why you should never believe what you hear from stories."

"Indeed," Sage said.

Gods save her, she liked him. He didn't hate her, nor did he like her, and there was an odd sense of comfort he gave off with his silent confidence. Yes, he might have just insulted her, however slyly, but she appreciated his wit and courage to speak to her as though she wasn't a princess.

It made her feel... Normal.

"Will you be at the ball tonight, Mister Astaseul?" Lyra asked, and Frances had to force herself not to laugh. The gall of this woman was enviable.

"Of course," Sage said. "I will be guarding the prince."

Frances's attention narrowed at Mister Astaseul and the way his mouth caressed the word *prince*. Perhaps she wasn't the only one harboring a secret desire. Though did Matthew feel the same? Lyra gave him another sweet simper, then a rather loud squeak flew from her lips as a droplet of blood landed on her boot.

"I must tell someone to cut down these flowers." Lyra grimaced.

"It won't do you any good," Sage said. "Not unless you want to make them dig six feet into the ground to find the heart."

Frances almost laughed at the way Lyra's face paled, and the witch stepped back. Frances took her arm; afraid Lyra might fall over if not supported.

"We must be going to prepare for the evening," Frances said. "It was a pleasure to make your acquaintance."

Sage gave another dip of his chin toward the women. "A pleasure indeed. I will see you two at the ball."

Frances steered Lyra back inside, their footsteps making soft clicks on the cobbled path. Lyra sagged against Frances and gave a soft sigh. "Mister Astaseul is so handsome."

"And a bit odd."

"Who cares," Lyra almost crooned. "I'm surprised Milo didn't tear his clothes off after their first lesson."

Frances bit her lip, not replying as they made their way past the guards at either side of the entrance and passed into their haunted home. Lyra might have been joking, but Frances had a feeling that the witch spoke more truth than either of them knew.

"AH, LIPS THAT SAY
ONE THING, WHILE THE
HEART THINKS ANOTHER."

\- Alexandre Dumas, *The Count of Monte Cristo*

Chapter 29

Milo

Milo stared blankly at the book in his lap.

He had his first morning to himself since they'd arrived at Wisteria Manor, and he hadn't known what to do. He'd bathed, yet Penn had departed shortly after, leaving him alone. With guards posted at the door, there'd been no need for Sage to visit, and his stomach lurched into his throat at the thought of seeing him again. He'd gone straight to his rooms after their kiss and had been a wreck of nerves and desire all through the night. The thought of seeing him at the ball was enough to make him glow, and Milo took a deep breath, forcing the magic down.

A knock on the door interrupted his thoughts.

There was a pause, and he half considered remaining silent, hoping that whoever wanted to speak to him would go away. *But what if they come in anyway and find that I was ignoring them?*

"Come in," Milo called resignedly.

Penn walked in with a large box wrapped in a silver bow in his grip.

"Penn," Milo sat up slightly. "What's in the box?"

The goblin grunted as he set it on his bed. "Yer attire for the ball tonight."

Oh. Thoughts of the flamboyantly dressed seamstress and her book of drawings made Milo shrink farther into the armchair. Dread crept into his stomach at the thought of what was inside that box, and the memories that would cling to his skin throughout the night.

"Ye cannah disappear into the chair, Lad, we must finish yer groomin' if ye have any hopes of making a good impression tonight."

Milo groaned. "What if I have no desire to do such a thing? Perhaps the Baudelaire's will change their minds and go back home."

"I doubt that will happen, no matter how much I pray different for ye," Penn replied. "Now get up."

Another moment passed, and Penn merely stood by the bed with his arms crossed over his chest. The manservant was as far from proper as one could be, and Milo appreciated it dearly. *Fine*, Milo thought at the unfazed look on the goblin's face, and stood with a sigh, and Penn ushered him to the connecting chamber where a bath waited, full of steaming water.

Another knock sounded after what felt like an eternity of Penn fidgeting with Milo's hair, putting scented oils on his skin, and fitting him into his suit. It was a shock to see the beautiful fabric, a burnt-gold and dark-silver pattern of vines that ran the length of the coat, pooling around his collar and the hems of his sleeves. The pants were black and well-fitted, and Penn was finishing with the polish of a pair of black leather boots.

"Who would that be?" Milo asked.

"Mister Astaseul to escort ye, of course," Penn replied easily and handed the boots over to Milo.

Fear, excitement, and dizzying nerves nearly made Milo stumble backward, and he hurried with his boots as Penn uttered a good evening and welcomed the vampire inside.

"Hello."

It was his usual way of greeting, and yet for some reason it made Milo's heart leap. He had to keep from cursing at the beauty before him. Sage was dressed in a midnight-blue suit, plain in design but perfectly fitted, revealing his strong, elegant stature.

"You're early," Milo commented, and heat warmed his cheeks.

"Only by two minutes."

Milo had to tear his eyes away before Penn had any stray thoughts about their acquaintance, and before Milo did anything foolish. He stood and glanced over at the goblin, who still held the door open for them both.

"Shall we?" Milo asked, and Sage nodded.

"After you, my prince."

They started down the hall, toward the music already filtering through the ballroom located down a flight of stairs. Sage walked at his side, and Milo's breath hitched at the vampire's proximity.

"You look wonderful," Sage whispered, and heat rose to Milo's cheeks.

"As do you," he found himself whispering back.

Milo was about to speak again when something flashed by the corner of his eye. He froze, dread curling in his stomach at the possibility of spotting a rogue ghost. But it was no such thing, and Milo let out a sigh at the sight of Lennora. She was dressed in a modest black gown, though it wasn't too different from her usual attire. She kissed him on the brow, and he thought he noticed the hint of strain in the lines of her mouth as she pulled away.

"Milo, why aren't you at the party yet?" Lennora asked, curtsying to Sage, who bowed in greeting.

Milo gave her a sheepish grin. "Penn got carried away."

Lennora laughed, though the sound was humorless. "Well, you should hurry along now before people begin to miss you."

Milo frowned. There was something slightly off with the witch, though he couldn't quite place what. He knew that both she and Lyra had been given extra duties after the maid's death, but he wouldn't have guessed it would cause Lennora such stress.

"Is anything the matter?" Milo asked.

Lennora gave his cheek a light pat. "No, dear. I'm just a bit worn from all the wards I've had to put up."

Milo gave her an apologetic shrug and took a step back. "I wouldn't blame you for not joining the party. You must be exhausted."

"I'll be there in only a moment; there's just one thing I have to do first."

"I look forward to it." Milo inclined his head and allowed Sage to guide him to the ballroom whilst Lennora swept into the shadows.

They made their way to the party in silence, though their lack of conversation was far louder than the sudden music and ruckus laughter that met them as they stepped into the room. Warm light glittered throughout the high-arched ceilings and marble floors. Tables piled with platters of food and drink were placed throughout the room, and members of both courts walked, laughed, and danced about.

Milo wanted to run away.

"Only thirty minutes and then we can go," Sage murmured behind him, and Milo gulped, though it was as though he were trying to swallow dust with the state of his dry mouth.

Thirty minutes. He could manage that much.

"Matthew, darling!" His mother's shrill voice rattled his skull.

I can manage thirty minutes.

She was draped in folds of silver fabric that revealed little, making her appear ready for battle. Duncan stood at her side, and Milo managed a smile.

"Happy festivities," Milo said, and they both murmured their agreements.

"I do hope you enjoy tonight," Esther said warmly. "There's a dance saved for you and Princess Baudelaire in just a few minutes."

Milo's spirits sank, but he managed a nod. "Thank you, mother."

Esther and Duncan breezed past, and Milo let out a shaky breath. Heaviness settled in his stomach, familiar and unwanted.

"Are you okay?" Sage murmured, and Milo shrugged.

"I will be, though I hope you're counting the minutes."

"Only twenty-eight left to go."

Well then.

Milo glanced around the room, hoping that perhaps Frances had gotten cold feet and decided not to join the party. Yet after a few seconds, his gaze landed on hers, and dread settled into his bones. She was beautiful, draped in a dress of molten gold with pale white stitching coiling around the sleeveless bodice. Her thick hair was loose, tumbling down her back in thick curls, and her full lips were painted a deep blood red. She scanned the room, everything about her screaming *predator.*

A voice echoed through the room, and Sage placed his

hand against Milo's back as he tried to shrink back into the crowd.

"And now, a dance between the future king and queen of Cathair Liath."

No, no, no.

He did not want to dance; he wanted to vomit. Sage leaned in close, his lips brushing Milo's ear as he whispered, "Relax."

Against every overwhelming emotion flooding Milo's body, he did. A strange sense of calm swept over him, though he knew that Sage's small attempt at helping his nerves would only last so long. He needed to get this dance over with as soon as possible, then flee from the party and go to bed.

"Don't watch," Milo grumbled before striding onto the dance floor.

Frances was already waiting, a poised viper ready to strike. He did not smile as he approached, and neither did she. It seemed neither of them was a willing participant in this fight, and Milo was glad of it.

Soft music poured into the air, and Milo swept into a low bow. He'd never been one for fighting, but he was oddly good at dancing, even if he didn't necessarily enjoy it. Frances curtsied, and they both straightened as the music rose and began its journey. Milo forced himself to reach for her, and Frances took his proffered hand with a flourish. He bit back a flinch as her cold skin touched his and guided her close as they began the dance.

"You are more graceful than I expected," Frances said.

"And you are worse at dancing than I expected," Milo replied, instantly regretting the bitter words.

Frances only tilted her head back and laughed, and Milo couldn't help but glance down at the slightly elongated canines. *How can I be so attracted to one vampire, yet repulsed by another?*

"You have wit," Frances said with a grin. "I like you a bit more now."

Milo led her through a spin, and her dress fanned out into a dizzying cascade of gold as she followed the movement and swept back into his arms. They moved in silence for some time, and Milo fought to keep his breath steady as he guided her through another spin.

"I hope you know that I am no more enticed by this union than you," Frances spoke again, and Milo blinked.

"You're not?"

Frances shook her head, and the music leapt in beat, a sign that the dance was nearly over. Milo spun her once again, and energy flowed through his veins at the prospect of ending their little charade.

"I would rather marry a toad," Frances muttered, meeting his gaze with an apologetic tilt of her head. "No offense."

"None taken."

Relief poured through him almost dizzyingly. She didn't want this either.

The music descended into a gentle harmony, and Milo and Frances performed the final steps of the dance. Their spectators suddenly became all too present, however, and nerves crawled their way back down Milo's throat. Frances cocked her head to the side; the same animalistic movement that had made him hate her from the start.

"What is it, afraid of a little crowd?" Frances cooed, and Milo's grasp tightened around her as they performed one last spin, and he caught her, though her skin felt like poison against his skin.

They swept apart, and Milo bowed again, wanting nothing more than to leave this dreadful woman on the dance floor and never see her again. It wasn't that he didn't like her, for there was a strange allure to her personality that made him want to know more. It was simply the fact that she was to be his wife that made his blood curdle.

The music died, and claps erupted from the sidelines. Milo straightened, giving the princess a clipped smile.

"It's not the crowd that frightens me."

With that, Milo turned on his heel and walked away, leaving his future wife behind.

"It was the best of times, it was the worst of times."

- Charles Dickens, *A Tale of Two Cities*

Chapter 30

Frances

Dazzling lights and laughter filtered through the air as the ball pushed on in full force. Frances clutched a sparkling drink as she stood on the outskirts of the dance floor. She couldn't see her brother anywhere, and her mother was conversing with the queen of Cathair Liath across the way. A flash of gold caught her eye, and a strange sense of foreboding crawled across her skin at the sight of Prince Matthew slipping through the crowd with Sage Astaseul behind him. They were out of sight a moment later, and she lifted the drink to her lips, not blinking at the alcohol that scorched her throat.

Her dance with the prince had been very educational, and Frances was still surprised by the lion hiding behind Matthew's unassuming mask. His words had hit her in a way that she had not expected, though she appreciated his bite. It wasn't every day that someone stood up to her. The memory of their touching bodies and his hand on her waist still did nothing to her, however, and Frances knew it never would.

She felt numb, and yet adrenaline pumped through her veins in an almost dizzying frenzy. There was a killer on the loose, and everyone was celebrating as though their lives were in perfect safety.

"You look like you're on the hunt."

The low voice made Frances jump, and she turned. Jeremy Nightingale stood before her, dressed in finery and dripping in that dark confidence that made her knees wobble. Dark velvet, latticed in veins of silver thread, was fitted over broad shoulders and a tapered waist. His hair was combed back, bringing out the sharp planes of his cheekbones and the curve of his jaw. Eyes of the deep sea clashed with those of ice, and friction passed through the air.

"You always think I'm hunting," Frances replied once words found their way back into her mouth.

Jeremy shrugged, and his hand drifted up in an offer. "Would you like to dance?"

The world skittered before pushing forward once more. Frances looked from his hand back to his face, then to the surrounding party. She shouldn't, not after her conversation with Malichi and his razor-sharp warning. But when her twin was still nowhere to be found, she found her fingers drifting upward and folding into Jeremy's hand. His warmth was still shocking, but she ignored it and looked at him again.

"Why do you want to dance with me?"

"Would you rather I didn't?" Jeremy replied, and his eyebrows raised a fraction.

"I didn't say that," Frances shot back, and he simply held her gaze.

He wouldn't tell her anything; she knew that. Perhaps he was feeling generous after she saved his life.

Jeremy tugged slightly, and soon he was leading her to the center of the floor, where a few court members were gathering for the music. She kept her focus on her feet, ensuring they would keep her upright and moving.

The orchestral band in the corner of the room began a

new song, and a haunting waltz filtered through the air. Their gazes were frozen in a silent battle as she bent her knees into a deep curtsy. Jeremy bowed, though his gaze remained firm on hers. They rose, and the other dancers blurred as she stepped toward the man who was both dangerous and utterly intoxicating. Jeremy's free hand slid around her waist, and she shivered at the proximity of their bodies.

"You seem to know this dance well," Jeremy murmured as he led her through a spin and caught her around the waist.

Fingers slid across skin in a skittering dance of fire, and lips parted as eyes met. Frances licked her lips before answering. "It is a common dance."

"Am I not still allowed to compliment you?"

"It would be the first time," Frances shot back, and he smirked.

The music swelled and skirts swooshed by, but she only saw him. Only the touch of his warmth against her cold skin and the press of his touch against her back kept her focused. His gaze darted to her blood-colored lips, and something darkened there, though it wasn't his usual anger. It was intrigue, and perhaps something else. *Don't be an idiot,* Frances thought. Jeremy couldn't possibly think of her in that way; he hated her. So, then, why did his expression convey something different?

Her breath caught as he guided her into a dip, and she tilted her head back to bare her throat. His breath might have caught, too, and she might have smiled slightly as he brought her back up.

"You are a dangerous creature." His voice was like molten honey.

Hot friction returned between their bodies, and Frances pushed down the sudden heat in her abdomen.

"I won't bite, not unless you want me to."

Anger replaced the heat in his gaze, and both confusion and frustration replaced any sensations of desire.

"Did I say something wrong?" Frances asked.

"No," Jeremy shook his head. "No, you did not."

"It's as though my words burned you," Frances said. "It can't have been nothing."

The music swelled into its last chorus, and Jeremy pulled her close to his chest. Her lips parted again, and the world blurred around them as he tilted his head closer. They were almost touching, and the whisper of his lips grazed her ear.

"It's a shame that we're at a formal gathering and you're engaged to my friend, for I'd take you on this very floor, if that's what I'd have to do to get you out of my head."

"What?" Frances gasped.

She must have been dreaming; she *had* to be. For this man who plagued her every waking and at times sleeping hour, was admitting that he wanted her. *If only so that he can forget me.*

The music began its descent into silence, and Jeremy pulled away enough so that they were face-to-face. A storm raged between them, and only a mask of darkness met her as she watched him. He was the image of a god, a prince of shadows and mystery. And she wanted him.

She tightened her grip on his arm, willing him to see the want in her stare, no matter the sting of his words. She leaned forward, and his breath caught. But the music came to a clattering end, and they broke away with a jolt as a scream tore through the air.

"PAIN AND SUFFERING ARE ALWAYS INEVITABLE FOR A LARGE INTELLIGENCE AND A DEEP HEART."

- Fyodor Dostoyevski, *Crime and Punishment*

Chapter 31

Milo

Milo forced back a curse as he stepped off the dance floor. Sage waited with Milo's discarded glass, and Milo grabbed it without a second thought. Sage gave him an amused grin, but Milo only glared, swigging the liquid down in one go.

"Come with me."

The world paused, and Milo's heart sputtered and leapt in an instant reply to Sage's words.

Milo gulped. "Where?"

"Just pretend that you have somewhere to go and leave the room."

Milo's feet started moving before he could think otherwise, and soon they were weaving through bodies, and the exit came into view. The melodious sounds of laughter and music died away as Milo and Sage wound through the darkened halls, shoulders bumping against each other. Electricity buzzed in every place that Sage's skin touched his, and a sudden surge of desire flooded through him.

"Where are we going?" Milo whispered, unable to help a

small giggle from escaping his lips as the drink began to take hold of his senses.

"Somewhere private," Sage replied, lust coating his words in a honey-like tone.

Milo gulped and allowed himself to be led on, anticipation rising in his chest. Sage soon stopped them by an alcove hidden in shadow, facing a large window that overlooked the roiling sea. Milo barely had a second to blink before Sage's lips were upon his own in a tantalizing greeting. Milo's body moved on its own accord, as if it knew the rhythm of Sage's soul.

Skin found skin, and they were soon gasping against each other's lips and tongues. Milo dipped his head to place a trail of kisses and soft nips against Sage's jaw and neck, and satisfaction swelled within as a soft moan escaped Sage's lips, and something hard began to press against his leg.

Fingers tangled in his hair and gently led Milo's face back up, and he almost gasped at the intensity in Sage's eyes. Emotions of desire, darkness, and something deeper and heart-shatteringly intimate whirled there, but Milo couldn't look away.

"Milo, I—"

A scream interrupted his words.

The scent of copper and fear clung to the air in a thick curtain. Another ear-splitting scream tore through the ancient hallways, sending a shiver of apprehension down his spine.

"What was that?" He whispered, but he already knew the answer.

Death had just bestowed its cold embrace upon another victim.

A hand folded into his own, and they pressed farther into the darkness of the alcove, waiting. His heartbeat pounded in his ears and threatened to burst out of his chest as the silence enveloped them.

After what felt like an eternity, a sickening giggle emanated from the silence, making the hairs on his arms stand on end. The scent of blood only grew stronger, and soon it was almost enveloping his senses completely.

"Milo." Sage squeezed gently, and Milo took in a shuddering, grounding breath.

"I'm fine," Milo grunted. "What do we do?"

"I don't know," Sage replied. "The killer could be around the corner for all we know."

Footsteps echoed down the hall, and Milo froze against Sage's chest. He wasn't sure which would be worse, being murdered or getting caught. The swish of crushed gold skirts and polished boots passed by the alcove, and a low-voiced curse emanated from beyond.

"Milo, is that you in there?"

Milo's stomach dropped. It was Jeremy. And Frances? He almost had to shake his head as the pair came to stand before them, and both let out a grunt of surprise when Sage leapt forward and grabbed their arms, dragging them into the alcove.

"What the hell are you doing?" Jeremy hissed.

"I would ask you the same thing," Milo muttered, and Frances tensed against his side.

"Shut up, both of you," Sage whispered. "We can discuss our infidelities after we're positive there isn't a killer on our tails."

Jeremy's impending retort was cut off by another fit of girlish giggles down the hall, and a soft glow passed by them as the ghost of a little girl flounced by.

"I've got another friend, another friend for me," she sang jovially, and bile rose in Milo's throat.

Could the ghosts be the ones killing people?

A loud crash and low hissing curse swept through the

walls, then all was silent. They remained quiet for what felt like an eternity, and finally Frances spoke. "I think we're safe to look."

Milo screwed up his face, wishing beyond everything he held dear that he wouldn't be forced into the presence of a dead body. Yet, as though he had conjured it, Sage grabbed his arm, and he was torn from the shadows.

Jeremy gave him a sidelong look, and Milo retracted his arm from Sage's grasp with a glare at his friend. By the way his and Frances's shoulders brushed, they too had some explaining to do.

"Remind me why we're going to the body instead of calling someone else for help?" Milo whispered, hating that he was the coward in this situation.

But the murderer had come for him, and he was about to see his potential future. It was entirely in his right to be a coward.

"Because maybe the killer is still there," Jeremy whispered back, as if the prospect was as casual as going for a stroll through the gardens.

Sage pressed closer, and a rattling breath passed through his lungs. The corridor was dark, but the large pool of blood that seeped across the sleek floor was like a black stain upon white cloth.

A coppery tang infiltrated Milo's nose, and soon they were standing before the victim. Long red hair matted in the pool of dark blood, and a freckle-smattered face that was all too familiar stared blankly at the ceiling.

Lennora Devonne was dead.

A sob tore through the silence, and Milo distantly heard a low curse and knees cracking against marble as he stared down...

and

fell out
of
his body.

"It is one thing to mortify curiosity, another to conquer it. "

- Robert Louis Stevenson, *Dr. Jekyll and Mr. Hyde*

CHAPTER 32

FRANCES

"Mimmi, no!"

A terrible weight pressed into Frances's stomach as she gaped down at Jeremy, his head bent as he knelt over his mother's fallen body. Lennora's expression was one of cold acceptance, and Frances felt an overwhelming respect for the witch. Miss Devonne hadn't been afraid, not even in the face of death. Her chest was a mess of blood and torn flesh, though it was clear.

This was the work of the same killer.

"I will find who did this," Jeremy growled.

He was on his feet in an instant, and Frances could almost see the fury radiating from him as he clenched his bloody fists.

"Jeremy don't—"

She didn't have time to finish her sentence before he took off, sprinting in the direction from which the curses and crashing sounds had come. She watched him disappear around a corner, footsteps still clanging through her superior hearing as he fruitlessly tracked down the killer.

"What happened to him?" Frances asked as Sage crouched over Matthew's unconscious form.

Blood flecked the toes of her slippers, and Frances looked down at Lennora's body and the fallen prince with a grimace. There was something twisted and profoundly wrong with this place.

"His powers go on overdrive when confronted with powerful emotion," Sage explained, his fingers pressed against Matthew's neck, and he gave a faint nod of approval. "He hasn't learned how to control that much energy, so his body shuts down as a matter of self-preservation."

"I see," Frances murmured, unsure of what else she could say.

Frances met his gaze and was surprised to find worry there. The vampire had already scooped Milo into his arms, and only cold determination molded Sage's features. "I need to take the prince to his rooms."

Frances considered him, a soft smile finding its way to her lips. "You care for him, don't you?"

The question was simple, and Sage didn't look away as he took a step forward, the prince's head lolling against his shoulder. "More than I can say."

She gave him a slight nod, understanding flooding through her as Sage gave a tilt of his head and moved away, fleeing from the sounds of raised voices and wild gossip that drew near. She would be bombarded with questions soon, and that sounded like a terrible occupation of her time.

"Frances."

She whirled around to find that Sage had paused and turned halfway to look at her.

"Yes?" She asked.

"He's more powerful than any of us," Sage said, and Frances knew that it was Matthew of whom he spoke. "Don't let his fear make you think he's worthless."

Sage left Frances with the fallen witch, though her solitude was short-lived. Footsteps and quick breathing made Frances turn, and dread dropped like a block of steel in her stomach as Lyra came into view. She was a vision of fury and wild magic, and Frances had the sudden desire to leave.

"Who did this to her?" Lyra demanded, her voice so cold it nearly sliced the very air. "Why are you here?"

Frances was shocked to find the witch's expression void of any sorrow. There was only anger there, and a promise of hell to whoever had done this.

"I... I don't know," Frances stuttered, seemingly unable to find her usual haughty confidence. "I was with Jeremy, and we found her like this. He ran off to find the attacker, and I could hardly stop him."

Lyra bent over, bracing her hands on her knees. Confusion and concern made Frances reach out to touch the girl's back, but she refrained when a screaming curse flew from Lyra's mouth. Candles blew out in their sconces, and the window-panes shook violently, the woman's pain seeming to rattle the entire world. She straightened and sucked in a deep breath, masking her face back into one of stony malice.

"Stay here. I'm going to find the person who made the mistake of killing my mother."

And with that, Lyra stormed off, leaving Frances standing in a puddle of blood with a dead witch at her feet. She suddenly felt cold and wished to go home.

“Life did not stop,
and one had to live.”

- Leo Tolstoy, *War and Peace*

Chapter 33

Milo

Midnight blue fog and swirling stars gathered and burst across the galaxy, and a boy drifted through them with a smile. It was silent, yet sensation was everywhere. From the bubbling pops of light that danced across his skin, to the swoosh and rolling waves of energy that moved him onward.

It was peaceful in the cosmos, yet a creeping sensation of discomfort built up inside the boy.

This was wrong.

Distantly, a name echoed through existence and shook the stars. The boy paused, knowing that name. It was his name. The voice sounded again, a tether and anchor within the whispering nothingness. That feeling of wrongness carried weight, and it was beginning to pin the boy down, dragging him back to the heart of darkness from which he had fled.

"Milo, for fucks sake, wake up!"

Oxygen that was thick with blood sucked through Milo's lungs, and he sat up with a gasp, his body trembling with the aftershocks of his astral projection. His vision was blurred, but the sensation of something soft beneath him and the distant crackling of a fire was evidence enough that someone had moved him back to his rooms.

That someone let out a loud sigh and sat back, golden hair glinting in the firelight as he bowed his head.

"Sage," Milo croaked, and the vampire blinked up at him.

Milo never knew that pain could mingle with desire, and yet it did. For the pain was blinding him, and Sage sitting on the bed with him still made his heart want to burst. The pain was stronger, though, and hot tears prickled behind Milo's eyelids as he closed them.

"Are you all right?" Sage asked softly, and the rustle of cloth, followed by a cold hand encompassing his own, made the pain and heat swell.

The weight of her absence was unbearable. "She's gone," Milo whispered, his voice barely audible amidst the echoes of his grief.

The image of Lennora's body flashed through his memory, and the thought of leaving this dimension and returning to the next almost became tempting again.

"Stay here, Milo," Sage murmured, as if he knew what Milo was thinking. "I need you to stay."

Milo opened his eyes, but his vision was blurred again, this time by tears. His pain was mirrored on Sage's face, and he crumbled against the hopelessness that dimmed the vampire's light.

"It hurts too much to stay," Milo whispered, falling against Sage's shoulder.

She was really gone, perhaps floating somewhere near the constellations where Milo had danced.

"It will keep hurting even if you go," Sage replied, and strong arms wrapped around Milo's back.

He seeped into the comfort, but no warmth emanated from Sage's already dead body. Milo almost laughed at the injustice. How could some of the dead walk and exist forever, yet for others, it clenched an iron fist and snuffed out life far before one's time was over? But he was grateful that Sage was here, his arms wrapped around Milo and tethering him. It made him want to stay in this reality, no matter how bleak it was.

"You've been called to a meeting," Sage said after Milo's tears stopped, though they had remained in a silent embrace for minutes afterward.

"I don't want to go."

"I tried to tell them that you need rest, but they require your attendance," Sage said and pulled back slightly, just enough so that they could look at each other.

Sage's pain was still evident, and Milo brushed a thumb against his brow as if to smooth it out. Sage smiled softly, and the lines in his forehead eased slightly.

"Sorry," he murmured. "It just hurts to see you like this."

In a past life, Milo would have snapped. But he was so, so tired, and his heart was broken.

"I'd like to see Jeremy," Milo said, remembering the sobs and painful crack against marble before he had astral projected.

Those had been Jeremy's knees colliding against stone.

A new wave of pain sent a spasm through Milo's limbs, and he collapsed into Sage again.

"He will be at the meeting," Sage said against his hair. "He's doing better than his initial reaction; it's mostly anger from him now."

Milo leaned his brow against Sage's neck, savoring the soft scent of eucalyptus and old books that seemed to cling to his very essence. They pulled away, and Sage brushed a finger across Milo's cheek, which sent both a shiver and a pained sigh from his chest. He wanted to stay here forever, in this room and away from the world that seemed to pluck everything good away.

"Are you ready?" Sage asked, and Milo could only shrug.

Sage stood, the crisp lines of his pants crumpled, and the elegant blue coat now missing from his person, though his usual tunic was now buttoned to the collar. He reached out his hand, and Milo took it, allowing himself to be pulled from the bed and guided out of the room.

Moonlight illuminated the world outside, and Milo peered out into the night where the stars still danced and moved despite it all. The rearranging stars had been the reason for the ball, but now the lights in the sky that also ran through Milo's veins felt like a mockery.

They kept their hands intertwined for as long as they could, and Milo felt unsteady again as Sage withdrew and opened the door to the room in which they were to meet. A wave of curious conversation and hushed gossip bombarded Milo's senses, and he froze in the wake of the din.

Vampires, witches, and other magical members of both courts were standing, sitting, and flying in their finery. Milo half-wondered if the entire residence of Wisteria Manor had joined the meeting. Even a ghost watched from the corner, wearing an expression of grim amusement.

The yelling didn't stop, and Milo glanced at Sage desperately, muscles seized and ready to run. Sage gave him an apologetic shake of his head. *This is a special sort of torture.* Milo sucked in a deep breath and glanced around for one person he desperately needed. He found him a moment later and started walking without a second thought.

Jeremy sat alone on a bench near the corner of the room, away from the crowd and half hidden in darkness. His head was bowed, and dark stains covered his clenched fists. Fresh pain bloomed in Milo's chest, and he almost sank to his knees before his friend, but instead, he managed to sit next to him.

Jeremy froze and glanced up to meet Milo's gaze, fury and heartbreaking sorrow as open as a bleeding wound written across his features. His eyes softened slightly, and all response was rendered void from Milo's mind. There were no words of comfort for this; they both knew it.

"Where's Lyra?" Milo asked instead.

"Trying to find Mimmi's ghost, and perhaps the killer too," Jeremy said, though lacking the usual subtle humor that they always shared.

Milo sighed, knowing very well that Lyra wouldn't stop until she did both of those things, mandatory meetings and murderers be damned.

Sage's presence pressed against Milo's shoulder, and he looked up to find him surveying the room, as though the one responsible for Lennora's death would jump out and offer themselves up. Milo wanted to embrace him, but he knew he couldn't, especially with a shaken Frances sitting not ten paces away, staring holes into the large carpet.

A loud ring echoed through the room, and everyone fell silent, though Milo didn't miss the curious glance Jeremy passed between him and Sage before Duncan started speaking.

"Good evening, everyone. I apologize that the ball has been cut short, but there's been another murder within these walls tonight."

Silence blanketed the room, and then a muffled cry sounded from a corner of the room. It was Milo's own mother. She had changed from her ball gown into a more modest dinner dress, but her hair was still coiled into an intricate bun, and her fallen expression was enough to make heat well up behind Milo's eyelids again.

It was as though her cry were a signal— voices crashed through the room, and questions began ringing through the air.

"How did it happen?"

"Who did it?"

"How could someone kill a powerful witch?"

Duncan commanded the room into silence once more, and he suddenly looked like a tired, aging man, not a king. He had removed his waistcoat, a rather inappropriate decision, yet none commented or seemed to take offense.

"We still haven't found the killer, but their movements are still unpredictable, given that a member of both the Baudelaire clan and the Cathair Liath court has become a victim," Duncan said. "We'd assumed that the killer was here to target my son for his abilities; however, now we aren't so sure."

Milo wanted to shrink away as at least two dozen faces turned to him, a mingle of glares and anguished features branding his skin. It was only reasonable for the killer from Cathair Liath to have followed him here, but now he wasn't so sure. Perhaps the killer had been after Lennora all along.

Daithine Baudelaire came into view and stood next to Duncan. "We've spoken briefly and have wondered if it would not be a better idea to hold the wedding sooner, or perhaps to postpone it altogether."

Mottled cries and exclamations passed through the crowd, but Milo found himself looking over to Frances. He was surprised by this, but the prospect of a postponed, or better yet, cancelled wedding, brought a small flicker of hope into his chest. Frances seemed to be thinking the same thing, for her gaze passed from Milo to Jeremy, then flicked back to the floor where it had been before.

Esther cleared her throat. "We decided that neither of these options will be viable, and the wedding will have to continue. However, there will be even further security and questioning throughout the month."

There goes any hope. Milo sighed.

Duncan glanced at his wife and Daithine before nodding. "We've decided to proceed for the safety of both of our kingdoms, as well as the safety of our future. Yet, we believe it will be safest if we all remain inside the manor and gardens, and that we may only exit occasionally through proper inspection until this killer is found."

This time, a "what?" escaped from Milo's own mouth at the order to stay indoors. They would be sharing walls with a potential serial killer for an entire month. It made sense not to let anyone out, but that meant no one was safe.

"What about the safety of the royal court?" A shrill female voice rang out, and murmurs of agreement filtered through the room.

"What about all of our safety?" Another voice cried out, and a louder wave of agreement swept through the room.

"As I said, there will be heightened security throughout the manor by morning, and I have ordered private soldiers to guard every bedroom and major outlet of socialization," Duncan replied. "Lyra Devonne will be entrusted with continuing the build of magical wards throughout the manor and outlying property. We hope these measures will bring the killer to us, leaving no option for them to flee and cause further destruction."

Milo marveled at his father's ability to remain calm in the face of such stress. It was one of the many things *not* passed down the genetic line.

Another outbreak of questions and curses flew, and Milo shut his eyes against the noise. It was too loud, and he just wanted to be alone again.

"Silence!"

Daithine's rich, accented voice cut through the protests like a knife, and soon the room was silent again.

"This isn't a negotiable decision," She began. "We've spoken extensively in these hours with both councils and each other. The wedding will still occur on the thirty-first day of October, and until then, we'll have to work together to find this killer."

Duncan inclined his head toward Daithine with a grateful

smile before regarding the rest of the room. "This is not an ideal situation, I think we're all aware of that. However, I still want our kingdoms to come together in peace, not hostility. Please do your best to relax and enjoy the rest of the month and the coming celebrations."

He gave a final nod before dismissing the group with a curt "thank you."

Both courts filed out of the room in a cacophony of noise and gossip, and Milo clenched his jaw against the clanging in his brain.

"Milo, how are you faring?"

His father's voice sounded before him, and Milo jumped, heart lurching into his throat.

"You should be asking Jeremy that," Milo replied darkly as he gazed into his father's worry-lined face.

He seemed worn, and Milo's gut twisted in regret. Jeremy stiffened at his side but didn't move, and Duncan turned to him.

"I'm sorry for your loss, Mister Nightingale. She was truly a wonderful woman."

Jeremy managed a slight nod but didn't answer, and Milo knew it was the telltale sign of his friend withholding tears.

Duncan turned back to Milo and Sage, who still stood at his side. "Milo, I hope you don't mind, and Mister Astaseul, I do hope you'll agree, but I've ordered the servants to move Mister Astaseul's sleeping arrangements to the room adjacent to yours."

Milo blinked, surprise slicing briefly through his pain. Sage was the one to speak, and Milo was grateful, for the vampire's thoughts seemed to sync with words much faster than Milo's could.

"Of Course, Your Majesty. I would be honored to be of continued service."

A snort emanated from Jeremy, and Milo was prompt in

giving him a quick jab with his elbow. Duncan didn't seem to notice Jeremy's outbreak and gave Sage a gracious nod. "Thank you. And I expect you two to continue training. It would be best to have some knowledge and skill with these stardust powers in case anything should happen."

Milo quickly sobered at this. Something *had* already happened. Lennora was dead, as was the serving girl.

Sage bowed. "Yes, Your Majesty."

Duncan gave Milo one last look before turning away, disappearing into the crowd. Jeremy turned on Milo a split second later, and he found himself enveloped in a bone-crushing embrace. Though he couldn't breathe, he returned the hug with all the remaining strength he had.

Jeremy was alive.

Sage was alive.

He would survive this mess and ensure they all crossed the finish line together. Jeremy pulled away and glanced at Sage with mild distaste. Milo instinctively wanted to touch Jeremy's shoulder and tell him it was all right, but he knew he couldn't.

"We will need to talk," Jeremy said darkly, and Milo clenched his jaw.

"Can't it wait? We're all too harrowed right now to have this conversation."

Jeremy shook his head, and a lock of hair fell over his brow. "If I know anything about Lennora, she wouldn't want us to grieve her for long, if at all. She'd want us to find her killer, and she would want you to be happy."

A lump slipped into Milo's throat, but he forced it down. "Fine, we can talk in the morning, but we're missing a participant in this conversation."

Jeremy frowned. "Who?"

Milo narrowed a glare at his best friend.

"I'm not daft, Jeremy. You know who."

Jeremy froze, but his expression remained impassive. Milo

stood on shaky legs; his arms crossed. "Just meet us at the windowsill for breakfast and make her come too."

Milo passed a glance toward the princess in question before looking down at the shadow of his friend. He was still holding himself together, but Milo feared what might happen if he were to break.

"I miss her already," Milo said softly, and Jeremy glared up at the ceiling.

"Missing her won't reverse her death," Jeremy replied darkly. "But I vow to bring down the wretched soul who made the mistake of killing my mother."

"NO MAN OR WOMAN
BORN, COWARD OR BRAVE,
CAN SHUN HIS DESTINY."

- Homer, *The Iliad*

CHAPTER 34

FRANCES

September 30, 1880

The scrap of parchment was held limply in Frances's grasp as she stared down at it. The words blurred; disbelief muddled with a strange sense of excitement making her curse. The note was written in an elegant scrawl, and a strange corner of her heart wanted to keep the simple note.

Princess Baudelaire,
Prince Matthew and I would like to speak with you tomorrow. Eight in the morning, by the window in the south wing. We will tell you the rest then.
Yours,
-Jeremy

Frances couldn't help pausing on the word *yours* for more than she needed to, along with the name below.

At a glance, the grandfather clock read fifteen minutes till the time she was needed, and Frances didn't hesitate to throw on a thick robe and her best pair of socks before rushing out of her rooms. This was a casual occasion, so she didn't need to be more uncomfortable than she already was.

Hushed voices and a stray chuckle brushed through the air as Frances approached the windowsill. Jeremy, Matthew, and Sage were seated in a small circle. A spread of food was laid out before them, though none ate.

She let herself linger on the light that caressed Jeremy's face and swam in his hair. There was anger etched in his gaze, but he still managed a grin as he spoke to his best friend and the golden-haired vampire. She urged her legs to work again, and Milo stopped speaking as their heads turned to watch her approach. She avoided Jeremy's gaze as she gave her betrothed a smile.

"Good morning. Where is Lyra?"

Jeremy's jaw clenched, and he spoke without looking at her. "She won't be joining us. She isn't feeling well this morning."

A pang of sorrow lashed through Frances, but she forced the smile to remain on her lips. "Well then. What's the reason for this cozy meeting?"

Jeremy moved slightly and indicated for her to sit beside him. A surge of electricity went through her as their eyes met, but he didn't smile, nor did he hold her gaze for longer than appropriate. His warmth still radiated against her leg as she sat, though, and it was an anchor in the raging storm of Matthew and Sage's attention.

"I'm not quite sure," Matthew replied. "Jeremy was adamant about it, though I still think that it's much too soon."

"Don't be daft, we all know why we're here," Jeremy said.

Frances blinked in surprise, and Matthew merely lifted an eyebrow. "Do enlighten us."

Frances glanced at Sage, and he met her gaze. He gave her a small shrug, as if he were saying that the prince and Jeremy were being foolish boys. Silence stretched between them, and Frances shifted against the hard floor. Jeremy was deathly still at her side, and she could almost hear him sifting through his thoughts. "My mother was murdered last night, and I would like to find out why, as well as who did it."

His words sliced through the silence, and a chill whispered down her spine. Matthew's face crumpled slightly, but he nodded. "I think we'd all like to know."

Jeremy shot him a sidelong glare. "And I would like to know what you two were doing in that alcove when the murder happened."

Milo scowled, but she was sure that a heavy blush would have been there if his dark skin didn't hide such things. Sage cocked his head and considered Jeremy. "I think our actions were quite obvious, don't you?"

"Sage," Matthew hissed, but the vampire shrugged again.

"Can we just admit that we caught you two making love last night?" Frances's hushed voice made everyone cringe, as though she had just screamed at the top of her lungs.

"We were *not* making love," Milo grumbled and shrank back against the ceiling frame.

Sage shrugged. "We were about to."

If looks could kill, Milo's glare would have turned Sage to dust. Frances searched inside of herself for any hint of malice toward her fiancé's infidelity, but she only found sadness there, mixed with a healthy dose of relief. She didn't wish to marry him any more than she wished to cut off her big toe. Not a significant inconvenience in the long run, but painful at the beginning, and a complete mess in the process.

"What happened last night is partly why I asked Milo

and Sage to come, as well as the fact that they were closest to the scene of Lennora's—" Jeremy cut off before the last word fell from his lips, and Frances wanted to lean against him or place a comforting touch on his shoulder.

"Why have *I* been asked to be a part of this interesting little meeting?" Frances asked.

"You were with Jeremy when you found us, or rather—well, it doesn't matter," Milo sputtered. "The point is, I don't think it's fair that only Sage and I be interrogated when Jeremy has been brushing shoulders with creatures he swore to take down entirely."

The air seemed to chill at Milo's vague, yet stark, statement. Jeremy stiffened, but his calm expression didn't change as he reached for the pot of tea on the floor.

"I don't think that Mister Nightingale needs to spill his secrets, even if I am technically one of these creatures he wishes to take down," Sage said.

Milo held his friend's glare, and Frances was surprised to see this side of the prince. He'd always seemed introverted and slightly out of it, not haughty and fire-tempered. She wasn't sure whose side she was on, as she did agree with Sage that they shouldn't push, but the curiosity of Jeremy's deadly vow intrigued her immensely.

"Now is not the time for feuds and blood-oaths," Jeremy ground out.

Matthew opened his mouth and then closed it abruptly, not daring to look from his lap. Jeremy was a tornado on the verge of exploding, and Frances did not feel like letting the lashing winds free.

"We were dancing as the screams sounded, and we decided to investigate it together." Frances added, "There was no love-making involved."

She could have sworn Jeremy's cheeks reddened a shade. It

wasn't that she was lying, because she wasn't. She didn't have to divulge his remark about desiring to do so.

If only to get you out of my head.

"But I can see more than either of you can," Milo said. "It's obvious when you look at it, really."

"What do you see?" Frances asked, and she tracked the movements of Sage as he reached for the prince.

"Don't play with them like that," Sage murmured, but Milo shook his head.

"No, I can see when people change, and you have, Jeremy. We hardly spend time together anymore. Besides, we're running in circles with this matter. Frances, do you agree that this marriage is strictly an arrangement, and we have no desire to be with each other?"

It might have been the hundredth time that morning that Matthew surprised her. Frances pursed her lips.

"It's agreed."

"Good, then I think it's perfectly warranted to ask you to keep last night's discovery a secret," Milo paused. "About Sage and me."

Frances considered, thoughts whirling. The discovery was a perfect reason to end the engagement there and then, for matters of propriety, which Astrum royalty took very seriously. Part of her desperately wanted it to be over. But a small corner of her heart pulled at the idea, as if the thought of ending things now would be terrible indeed.

"What would you offer me in exchange?" She asked and shivered slightly at his silver eyes that seemed to pierce through her soul.

"A truce," Milo replied. "If you don't tell anyone of this, then I won't tell anyone about finding you and Jeremy walking unaccompanied through a darkened hall. It would be perfect grounds to end the engagement, but I think finding our killer is more important."

Frances mulled over his words.

"So, if I told anyone of your business, you would tell them of something that didn't even happen?"

Milo shrugged. "I've been told of your knowledge surrounding that of anatomy, and I saw the way that you examined Lennora's body as though it were a puzzle, not a dead woman. I want your help, Frances."

A laugh found its way out of Frances's throat, but Milo remained impassive. *This boy is mad.* He wanted her help even though they desired nothing more than to be rid of each other. The thought of finding the killer awakened a dangerous part of her, but Frances wouldn't admit it. She could find the killer on her own.

"What if I don't want *your* help?" Frances shot back. "As you said yourself, I'm perfectly capable in the art of death."

"Shut up, both of you," Sage sighed. "It's clear that this situation needs a compromise. I believe the perfect one has been offered, and you would be idiots to refuse it."

Is the entire Cathair Liath kingdom so flippant?

She noticed Jeremy was silent throughout their argument, and his presence felt like a dangerous cloud that threatened far more than rain. A pang of regret went through her very bones. Of course, she needed to accept, no matter how stupid it was. Jeremy's mother had died, and she was too worried about her own pride to accept the agreement and find the killer, even if it was with the prince's help.

"Fine." Frances sighed. "I'll do it. But if you're free to fuck who you'd like, then I expect the same benefits out of this agreement."

Milo shrugged. "It was part of the reason why I asked you here."

Jeremy's low curse sent a shiver through Frances's body, but she dared not look at him. She could play this game, as long as both sex and bringing down their enemy were certain.

Nothing is certain, not even the thing you want so much that you dream about it. Frances bit down the thought.

"Good, I think we've settled it then," Sage said lightly, as though they were going over dinner arrangements. "Whatever information is found should be brought forth to everyone, ensuring there are no holes in this investigation."

“Do you want to help us?" Jeremy asked, his sudden outbreak of sound making Frances jump.

The golden vampire met his gaze.

"I was murdered in the dark with no knowledge of who killed me. The vampire who took pity on my dying soul is the only reason why I'm sitting with you three now. No one deserves to die in such a way, and no one deserves to live with an unknown target on their back."

"Very well then," Jeremy cleared his throat. "Let us begin."

"You pierce my soul. I am half agony, half hope...I have loved none but you."

- Jane Austen, *Persuasion*

Chapter 35

Milo

October 14, 1880

Milo kicked off his boots with a groan and made for his bed as the day caught up with him. Two weeks had passed since Lennora's death and the formation of their strange little agreement with Frances and Jeremy.

There had been no new deaths, nor had there been any new leads. There was no possible motive for anyone in the manor to kill both a Nephilim servant and a witch, unless there were two different culprits. They had taken up the time after Milo and Sage's training sessions to discuss things and share any new revelations or news, but even after only two weeks, the conversation was running dry.

The door opened, and Milo spun around, his heart lurching into his throat, but it was only Sage. Milo blew out a sigh and tried his best to ignore the flutter in his abdomen that occurred every time he saw the vampire. Indeed, they had spent a good amount of their allotted training time doing other forms of exercise, though it had never gone as far as Milo was sure both wanted. It was too great a risk to engage in such activities in public, no matter how much they both wanted to do so.

Milo moved to the armoire and began tugging at the buttons of his coat. He was aware of Sage's attention on him, and a shiver passed over his skin that was not only due to the chill night air.

"Your bedroom is the next one over, in case you had forgotten," Milo said finally, and tucked his coat away.

"I didn't forget," Sage answered with laughter in his voice, along with something else that sent dangerous excitement shooting through Milo's toes.

Milo turned.

"Oh? Then what's the occasion of this untimely visit?"

Sage had drifted closer and was now leaning against the wall adjacent to the bed. Milo couldn't help but stare at the curve of skin that always seemed to beckon him through the unbuttoned fabric of Sage's tunic, and it was an effort to look up again.

"What if I only desired to be in your presence?" Sage asked. "I'm rather enjoying this saucy version of Milo."

Milo ducked his head, heat surging through his bones. Not even he was sure what had taken over him that morning with Frances, nor was he sure why the heated quips were becoming a larger part of his everyday vocabulary. There was still the dull ache in his chest from Lennora's death and the anxiety of his fast-approaching marriage, but all of it seemed less important now for some reason.

"Did you not like the quieter and emotionally unstable Milo?" He asked and took a step closer.

Sage's gaze darkened, and he closed the space between them in less than a heartbeat. Milo almost gasped as strong hands swept around his waist, and he could feel the planes of muscle shift beneath Sage's tunic.

"I like you in whichever form you choose," Sage murmured, and his hazel eyes shone like diamonds in the firelight. "I like Milo, not only the variants or certain stages in which he lives."

"Oh," Milo breathed, and looked down.

Stupid, stupid, stupid. This perfect man professes his near love to you, and the only thing you can think of saying is "oh"? Pathetic, Matthew Rose Hale.

A finger notched underneath Milo's chin, and he couldn't help the small gasp from escaping his mouth.

"Milo."

The name sounded like a blessing on the vampire's tongue instead of a simple name. *A simple name for a helpless man.* Though perhaps he wasn't helpless, not anymore. Perhaps it was this sudden strength that he felt through Sage that gave him the courage to confront the day, instead of simply letting it toss him around.

It was Milo who closed the space between them, and he could taste Sage's smile on his lips as they drew closer. Everything was falling apart around him, but not Sage. Not Sage, who had appeared in the strangest, yet most perfect way. And though the vampire kept him from drowning, the entanglement of their hearts most certainly was a problem. But with Sage's tongue against his and his fingers against his back, Milo couldn't bring himself to stop.

The room swelled with light, and Milo broke away, panting as both the light that illuminated his skin, and a strange, almost dizzying sensation swept into his soul. Sage still discovered the skin beneath his tunic, and Milo shivered as the vampire's attention drifted to the buttons of his shirt.

"Does it not embarrass you? My light?" Milo asked, unable to speak in more than a whisper.

Sage met Milo's stare, though his touches did not stop. The light grew brighter as Milo's skin was exposed, and cool air caressed his skin as the tunic fell to the floor.

"You do not embarrass me," Sage replied. "I cannot hate the light that cuts through my darkness."

Milo blinked, a lump rising in his throat.

"I suppose that's where we're different. I am afraid of the light, I'm afraid of living, and I am afraid of how much I feel for you. You make me feel alive, Sage. You make me feel like days are worth living, and you make me *feel*. And it terrifies me."

Sage's hands were kisses of snow as they drifted from his chest to his cheeks, and Milo closed his eyes as Sage kissed him again. This time it was soft and sweet, and his touch told Milo more than words ever could.

"I will not break your heart, Milo," Sage said, pressing his forehead against his. "I will not break something that I love."

The world tilted, and Milo instinctively clutched the front of Sage's shirt. He waited for the familiar tingling that meant he was about to fall, but nothing came. Instead, only a smirk graced his lips, and he tugged Sage closer by his fisted tunic. It was quickly thrown off between kisses, and a deep hunger welled inside of Milo at the sight of his chiseled olive skin. Milo's attention landed on a small dark mark about the size of a coin resting on Sage's left ribcage.

"It's a birthmark."

"I like it," Milo said, and was surprised by the husky tenor his voice took.

They stood there, watching each other, and Milo almost couldn't take the bursting emotion that sent his frayed heart thumping through his chest. Sage took a tentative step forward, a dark hunger clouding his eyes. Fingers grazed the line of Milo's trousers, and his breath caught. The pressure against his pants sent a soft sound falling from his lips.

"Sage," he breathed as the vampire's fingers played at the edge of his waistline.

"Milo?" Sage replied, and he knew there were two questions within that name.

Yes, he did. He wanted Sage in every way that he could possibly, selfishly, have him.

"Please," Milo said, hoping that he, too, would understand the meaning behind his words.

A flicker of sadness crossed his expression, but Sage still smiled, and his hand slipped beneath Milo's waistband. A gasp tore from his lips at the sensation of Sage's grip around him, the soft yet deliciously firm movement making him shudder already. Their mouths found each other once more, and Milo couldn't stop the frequent gasps of ecstasy that escaped his lips as Sage worked him into a dizzying sense of lightness.

They broke away panting as Sage withdrew his hand, but only just enough to start at the buttons of Milo's pants. Milo let him do it, though not without some trepidation. He had gone this far with others before, but not in this way, not with someone that he...

His pants fell to his ankles, and a whoosh of sensation rushed through Milo as he was freed. Sage's gaze drifted downward, and dark clouds of desire settled over its depths.

"You are magnificent," Sage murmured as his eyes painted their way over Milo's skin.

Milo had never felt more exposed in his life, though it was both liberating and mortifying.

"I don't know how to respond to that," Milo breathed, and the corners of Sage's mouth twitched.

"You don't have to say anything at all."

They returned to a kiss, and hot tendrils of desire twisted around Milo's being. A gasp pressed against Milo's lips as the vampire took him in his hand and began moving with each press and sweep of their lips. Milo found Sage's waist, and he drew him closer, too close. Sage stopped his idle torture, and they broke away panting.

"Milo, I won't be able to do much like this. Though we could do other things," Sage murmured against Milo's jaw, where he now feathered butterfly kisses.

"I want to see you too," Milo gasped against the still pulsating desperation that made his skin glow brighter.

Sage paused and pulled away enough to look at Milo. His pupils had dilated, almost swallowing up the swirls of hazel and green. Yet Milo could only see how beautiful this was, how attractive *he* was. Sage seemed to struggle to gather himself, removing his hands from Milo's skin.

"Do you want to stop?"

Milo bit his lip and prepared himself for the mortification he was about to put himself through.

"No, not ever. But I want to do the same for you. And it feels strange to be stark naked with you clothed and touching me like that."

Sage's chuckle was like warm honey, and Milo thought he might explode by the sound of his voice alone, and the soft teasing touches against his skin.

"Very well, I think we can arrange that, though I am technically half-naked."

Sage stepped back, but Milo took another step forward before he could think twice. Indeed, he was half naked and already making him come undone, but it wasn't enough.

"I want to do it," Milo said, and Sage gaped. Milo's fingers brushed his waistline.

Before he could think, Milo was pressing kisses against Sage's neck and chest as his hands found their way to the buttons at his waist. They were opened in his haste, and Milo didn't think of anything other than the vampire in front of him and the squeezing pain of his heart at the pure emotion and desire he held for him.

A noise, something between a whimper and a gasp, escaped from Sage's lips as Milo painted his way down his chest with kisses and licks. Then he was on his knees and doing what they had both wanted for so long. Milo's heart leapt into his throat at the pure size of him, but also at his own daring. He had never done this before, as willingly as he was now. *You've never wanted to do it before at all, you idiot.* Milo pushed down that thought and looked up to find Sage watching him.

"You don't have to do this," Sage growled, an animalistic sound that sent that heat tightening its coils around Milo's skin.

"I want to," Milo replied, and began without a second thought.

It was the strangest sensation, to be doing an action that once held little to no fulfillment but now made Milo's vision blur with desire. Sage gasped from his touch, his tongue, and brushed a lock of hair from Milo's brow. He paused at this, and Sage's hand moved lower to guide him back to his feet.

"What was that for?" Milo asked, still inwardly cursing himself for currently being the human equivalent of a candle.

"What was what for?" Sage asked. "I don't want you to finish things before they've even started, and a second longer with your mouth on me would have done just that."

His toes curled at his words, and he ached to touch and kiss him in any way he could. But he still paused.

"Not that. Why were you so gentle with me?"

Sage's finger hooked under Milo's chin to guide their gazes back together. A dangerous promise curved his lips, and Milo became utterly aware of the predator that hid beneath his skin. And yet it didn't scare him one bit.

"I don't have to be gentle." There was only love there as he whispered a kiss against Milo's lips. "I *want* to be gentle, Milo.

You deserve to be given the world, not to be treated as something miles below your true nature."

Heat prickled behind Milo's eyelids, and he quickly closed them, pressing another kiss against Sage's jaw. Never in his life had he been seen or cherished in this way. It was... unfamiliar. And yet it touched his soul in more ways than he would ever be able to put into words. Not even the words that hovered on his lips as he gazed at the monster hiding in the image of a man who had captured his heart.

"Sage—"

"It's okay," Sage cut him off gently, and yet there was sadness there as he took Milo's hand and led him toward the bed.

Warm sheets and cool skin caressed him as Sage guided him down against the mattress, pressing their bodies together. The sensation of Sage's body, his *everything* on top of him, sent a tremor through Milo's body, and the room pulsed with his light. Their bodies moved in a dance of tongue and teeth, and a moan escaped his lips as Sage slid his hand lower once again. He reached up instinctively to rove through Sage's silken hair as pleasure exploded through his very bones, and Milo brought his other hand around the hard pressure against his stomach.

"Milo," Sage groaned, and Milo sighed against his lips as he too began moving up and down.

"Your skin..." Sage breathed. "It's hot."

Milo instantly pressed his arms against his chest as worry shot through him.

"Am I hurting you?"

Sage shook his head and guided Milo back to where he needed his attention most.

"Your light could never hurt me, Milo."

"THERE'S ROSEMARY, THAT'S FOR REMEMBRANCE. PRAY YOU, LOVE, REMEMBER."

- William Shakespeare, *Hamlet*

Chapter 36

Frances

October 18, 1880

Midnight pooled through the open windows, but Frances paid the swallowing void no mind as it followed her down the hall toward her rooms. She was tired and hadn't eaten for some days again, though her hunger was the least of her concerns now.

There was a killer on the loose. And she had feelings for Jeremy fucking Nightingale. She shook her head, as though the image of his face would fly out of her mind. It did not.

Of course.

The strange dread for her safety mingled dizzyingly with a newfound excitement, or perhaps she was only in need of some dinner.

A low chuckle drew her attention to a room on her left, and curiosity tugged at her. She walked more slowly, and again the chuckle sounded, followed by... Was that her mother speaking?

A frown tugged at her lips, and she kept walking when a muffled thump, followed by what was undoubtedly her mother crying out, made her pause. Silence ensued, and Frances's mind went blank as she turned and sprinted for the sound. She wouldn't lose another parent to death.

Not now, not again.

The door separating her and the muffled thumps came down with a crash under Frances's foot, and she didn't even flinch as the entire thing cracked off the hinges and slid in a splintered mass across the marble floor. Someone was trying to hurt her mother, and she would rip their heads off before they got the chance.

"*Merde! qui-* Frances?"

The world tilted dangerously before righting itself, and Frances staggered at the sight of her mother held in the arms of none other than the father of her betrothed.

"What in the gods is going on?" Frances cried and cringed as her attention dipped to where their clothes bunched to the side and their hips met.

"Oh my—" Frances spun around and held back convulsions at a sight she never wished on any child to witness. "What the hell are you two doing?"

"What does it look like?" Daithine cried, and Frances thought she might be sick.

She turned slowly after a few seconds to find them both completely clothed and separated, though by the slight grimace on Duncan's face, it was clear that they'd only just started before she had barged in.

They stared at each other for what felt like a painstaking eternity, and Frances wanted nothing more than to retrace her steps and pretend as if nothing had happened. Yet it had, and new possibilities bloomed with this knowledge. It could change everything, including her impending marriage. The tension rose and fell, and Frances's legs began moving before she could stop herself.

"Frances, wait!"

But she was already marching away, unaware and uncaring about where she was going. An inferno of hurt and rage boiled inside, and Frances cursed loudly at the image of her mother in such a position printed behind her eyelids.

"Frances?" A low voice rang out, and Frances's stomach did an odd lurch as she turned to find Jeremy approaching, a frown on his face. "Are you all right?"

"Why wouldn't I be?" Frances snapped, though she waited for him to approach.

He stopped a foot away, and something close to concern flashed across his chiseled features. She yearned to step away and come closer at the same time. *What's wrong with me?*

"You look like you've just seen a ghost," Jeremy replied. "Which wouldn't be surprising, so I take back what I said. It looks like you've seen something much worse."

The sound of heels clicking against marble made the hairs on Frances's arms rise, and she took a healthy step away from him. "You need to leave, now."

His brow furrowed.

"Why?"

"Because the horror that I just saw is coming," Frances said and shoved him behind a heavy velvet curtain. "Hide then, if you won't leave."

She hated the way her body hummed as he gave her a confused frown, but she obeyed, and soon the swishing of her mother's skirts and the livid look on her mother's face came into view. Duncan was nowhere to be seen, and Frances was grateful for it. She could only handle one uncomfortable conversation at a time.

"Frances, why in the gods' names did you do that?" Daithine roared, and she swore the windows vibrated.

"Trust me, I wish I hadn't." Frances grimaced.

Daithine crossed her arms, and suddenly Frances was a small child again. A fragile thing. Nothing. She bit back the pain and met her mother's stare.

"Who else knows of this?"

"No one else knows," Daithine replied. "And I would prefer if it remained that way."

"Why?" Frances snapped. "So that you can fuck the king of Cathair Liath in peace while I have to suffer the consequences?"

A muffled curse sounded from the curtain, and Frances stiffened as Daithine's attention perked. "What was that?"

Frances waved dismissively.

"A ghost, likely."

Daithine looked at Frances again, and there was pain marring the planes of her smooth face.

"I didn't mean for it to happen, I swear."

"You don't have to give me excuses, mother," Frances snapped. "You've placed me in the strangest position possible, and you know very well how I might choose to use it."

"Do *not*," Daithine stepped forward. "You can't tell a soul about this."

Frances scoffed. *The gall of this woman is unbelievable.*

"And why not? There is no good reason to withhold this from the court. I don't wish to marry the prince, and this would be a perfect way to stop our marriage. I do believe Queen Hale would demand your head."

"You can't do that. I am your queen above all else, and you will do as I say."

Frances almost staggered at the blow her words dealt. *A queen before a mother.* As she always had and always would be. Daithine's harsh mask cracked slightly, and she took a step forward.

"Forgive me, Frances, I didn't mean that."

But whatever cracks that had formed around the wall in her heart were sealing at a remarkable speed, and cold numbness spread over every muscle and fibre.

"I won't tell them, but you must," Frances said, raising her chin. "It isn't my job to tell those who deserve to know of your mistakes, but it is also not my job to be a mascot for you to find your own pleasure behind."

Daithine's mouth opened, but Frances held a hand up to stop her again.

"You might think of yourself as my queen above all else, but I don't. Am I not your daughter, your *child*, above all else? Have we not gone through hell and back together?"

"Frances," Daithine began. "When I was pregnant with you, I was lost and abused. Your biological father was not a good man. When Cesaire offered me a way out, we never expected to fall in love. But he did love me, and I wanted a better future for you and Malichi."

Frances scoffed, though fresh pain bloomed in her heart. She had vague memories of her life before being rescued by Cesaire's men on a stormy night. The pain from his belt, her mother's cries as he hurt her in more ways than she ever cared to remember. She had chosen to forget that life the second Cesaire, the only father that mattered, had taken them in. She'd only been nine years old, but the gratitude and freedom she'd felt would never be something Frances would forget.

Which was why her mother's proclamation stung so badly.

"So, you didn't care for Papa at all? You only wanted his crown to save your own neck," Frances spat, clenching her fists.

"Don't you *dare* say such a thing," Daithine snapped. "I loved Cesaire with all of my heart. I thought my life was over before him. It's true, I didn't at first, but I was a scared peasant with no money or pride to her name. I only knew Gustave and his terrible ways, so forgive me if I wasn't quick to trust a new man."

A strange inkling of understanding eased the pain, but it still wasn't enough. Daithine had sacrificed much for her and Malichi, yes, but her involvement with King Duncan had all but crumbled any forgiveness Frances had left. Cesaire had been a good man, but her mother's actions were a spit on his grave.

Her mother's expression fell.

"Frances, I—"

Frances didn't wait for her to finish. She turned on her heel and strode for her rooms, barely acknowledging the fact that their conversation had been overheard, and she was leaving him behind without so much as an explanation that everything had changed.

The door to her room threatened to crack as she slammed it shut, and a curse fell from her lips. She didn't need to break two doors in one evening. Fury melted through every part of her, threatening to consume her fully. Her mother had made a mistake, and yet she was still too cowardly to accept her actions and the harshness of reality. Her back pressed against the cold oak, and a soft sob flew from her mouth.

"Fuck," Frances groaned, burying her face in her hands.

"Be careful with your language, the manor is sensitive."

Frances snapped her head up as a little girl's whisper filtered through her ears. She was standing by the bed, pale skin almost translucent in the dim light. Her long black hair wrapped around her head in a braided crown, and the simple shift she wore brushed against the tops of her little bare feet.

"Who are you?" Frances asked, and the girl tilted her head.

"Mary Edmunds," she said in that twinkling voice. "I'm a ghost."

"I know that. But why are you here?"

Mary giggled. "You are very grumpy. I watch you all the time, and you aren't usually this sour."

That wasn't a very comforting thought. Frances gave the girl her best smile, though she was certain it wasn’t convincing. The girl cocked her head again, a dangerous thing that made even Frances unsettled.

"You are very sad," the girl said. "Why?"

Frances sighed. Explaining her emotional turmoil to a ghost had not been on her agenda for the evening, but she supposed life was full of surprises.

"I'm merely confused, and there's a killer in the manor, which doesn't make me feel any better."

Mary giggled, though it was not an endearing sound. "I've been watching your little group of friends try to solve the case. You aren't doing a very good job."

"How would you know?"

"Because I can go everywhere, and I can talk to the people who have died under the killer's blade before they cross worlds."

Something strange fluttered against Frances's chest, and she straightened.

"Do you know who's doing this?"

Mary shook her head, and the world dimmed.

"I don't, I'm afraid. The newly dead have nothing much to say other than that they are in pain and wish to go home."

Frances shuddered. She wondered if there was such a place as home for a ghost.

The little girl took a step closer, and Frances stiffened, the cold tendrils of her body whispering against her toes.

"Do you know anything at all?" Frances asked, and the girl's soft features hardened slightly.

"Just because I'm dead doesn't mean that I don't know anything."

Frances held her dead stare, and a laugh bubbled from her lips. "Well, I'm dead too, and I know less than most."

"Touché." Mary smirked.

They both giggled now, and Frances let her shoulders relax.

"I'm sorry for being rude. It's important to find out who is killing these innocent people."

"Why?" the girl asked again. "As you said, you're dead yourself. It isn't as bad a fate as one might think."

"It's worse than other fates," Frances said. "And I don't want to sit by while the lives of others are cut short."

"You care too much. But I will play your game if you wish it."

Frances waited, and they watched each other. Frances wanted to look away from the gaunt lines of her cheeks and the hollow swirls of her eyes. But she didn't, and the girl's faint smirk broke out into a full grin.

"Very well. The first girl's death was a test, though done by the same hand that took the life of the witch."

Frances frowned, unsure how any death done on purpose could be an accident.

"The witch's murder was on purpose, though she was in a right fury upon her death, and I could hardly get a word from her."

"But did Lennora say anything?" Frances asked, and her chest burned for Jeremy and his pain.

"Yes," Mary paused. "Though it was unsettling at best."

The world seemed to freeze, and Frances waited with bated breath. Mary Edmunds shook her head and glanced over her shoulder.

"You would be wise to keep this information to yourself; it's dangerous, and knowing will put your existence in danger."

Frances stood on surprisingly steady legs and peered down

at the girl. A strange desire to comfort the little ghost swept through her, but Frances merely nodded kindly.

"If it helps protect the ones I care about, then I am willing to be at risk."

Mary let out a girlish giggle, though there was something like fear behind her swirling gaze.

"Very well. The killer is attempting to find something, something very important."

"I declare after all there is no enjoyment like reading! How much sooner one tires of any thing than of a book! — When I have a house of my own, I shall be miserable if I have not an excellent library."

- Jane Austen, *Pride and Prejudice*

Chapter 37

Milo

October 20, 1880

"I like your hair," Sage murmured, fingers traveling paths through Milo's unruly curls.

Milo scrunched his nose, though the sensation of Sage's touch sent calming shivers down his spine.

"Why is that? It's a mess half the time."

Sage's lips curved upward, and Milo bent to kiss them without a second thought. They were still in bed, though the sun had already risen hours ago. Milo was sure he was late to whatever fitting or stuffy gathering his mother had scheduled for that day. He knew the stakes of being discovered were higher than either of them could afford, but time felt like it had come to a stop in their small corner of the manor.

Milo broke away, and Sage smiled up at him, brushing another kiss against the corner of his mouth before speaking. "I like that it's a mess, and I like it because it's you."

Heat that might as well belong in hell's inferno rose to Milo's cheeks, and he hid his face in the crook of Sage's neck.

"You're just saying that."

Sage scoffed and drew away. "I am not. I'm telling the truth."

"I got it from my father's side," Milo said quietly, taking one of the messy ringlets on his head and pulling at it.

It wasn't the same as his father's halo of lavish, tight curls, as his fair-skinned, light-eyed mother had mixed his genes to create the mop on his head and his light brown skin. Sage reached for him, and a warm pool of contentment rose to Milo's chest at the sight of their joined fingers. He peered out the window, and a groan found its way from his mouth at the sight of watered-down sunshine fighting its way inside. "Penn will likely be coming to wake me soon."

"Well, as they say, all good things must come to an end," Sage sighed, releasing Milo's hand.

"This won't end, though, right?" Milo couldn't stop the words before they fell.

Sage paused and turned back to face him. A strange fear pressed itself within the insides of Milo's throat, and Sage's returning look of intensity only made it tighten.

"You're everything, Milo, and I might be selfish saying I'll never let you go, even if it means that I break because of it."

Heat prickled behind Milo's eyelids as the sensation in his throat tightened, and he sat up. The glow from the night was washing away dangerously fast, and he wanted to hang onto it for as long as he could. Reality always had a sick way of reminding one it was in charge of things. But for now, he would ignore the harshness of the world and hang onto his daydream one moment longer.

"I'll never forgive myself if you break because of me," Milo said, and reached up to sweep a lock of golden hair from Sage's forehead.

They gazed at each other, a conversation a thousand words passing through their eyes, even though Milo registered not even a single word. It was only his frantic heartbeat and more emotion than Milo could have ever guessed he could possess for a single person. Sage leaned forward, and Milo almost cursed at the sudden tears that threatened to spill to his cheeks from the tender touch of their lips. He didn't want to pull away, both their bodies and souls desiring something that they could not have.

"I will find you in every lifetime, even if we can't be together in any of them. I will always find you," Sage murmured, and shiver caressed its way down Milo's spine.

Their gazes locked again, and though Milo knew that vampires couldn't cry, a strange glimmer cast across Sage's eyes. The pain of longing in his chest spasmed, but he couldn't act on it before a soft knock pressed against the door.

"Reality awaits," Sage murmured, and was off the bed before Milo could blink.

The vampire threw a pile of clothes onto the bed, and Milo lunged for them, glancing over to find Sage already tugging on his trousers with his shirt flung loosely over his arms.

"One moment!" Milo called as another knock reverberated through the room.

Confusion swam in harmony with his fear as to whom it might be. Penn only knocked once before entering, if he even knocked at all. Milo quickly buttoned his shirt and tossed the bedsheets into place as Sage moved to sit on the reading chair, his hair already smoothed out and his general appearance as though he might have just gone for a stroll in the park, not... other things.

Milo didn't even bother touching his hair as he straightened his cuffs and moved to sit on the end of the bed, grabbing a random book from the shelf before he did so. He snuck a glance and found amusement playing at Sage's lips. Milo couldn't help his own faint smile before he flung the book open to a random page and spoke.

"Come in."

Duncan entered, and the book almost slipped from Milo's grasp. He quickly tightened his grip on the leather binding and snapped the tome shut as his father gave them both a slight nod.

Sage stood languidly and gave the king a deep bow.

"Your Majesty."

"Hello, Mister Astaseul. I see you two have had an early start to the day," Duncan replied, his gaze sliding to Milo.

Milo repressed a gulp and ignored his hammering pulse.

"We decided to do an extra training session before breakfast."

Duncan glanced down at the closed book in Milo's lap and frowned.

"Jane Austin? I didn't realize reading romance novels from Elaria was part of the curriculum."

Milo's smile faltered, but Sage's grew as he said, "I've been experimenting with the best ways to activate Milo's powers, and it seems as though certain pieces of literature can trigger strong emotions for him."

"Is that so? And what sort of strong emotions have you felt from reading *Pride and Prejudice*?"

"Mortification," Milo grumbled as Sage shot him a grin.

"Very well then," Duncan said. "I can return later if you are in the middle of your training."

"No, it's all right," Sage said before the king could turn away. "We were just finishing up. I have to meet Professor Binks in the gardens in a few minutes, actually, so I must be going to get through the guards in time."

Duncan bowed slightly, and Sage turned. Milo sent a silent prayer to the gods that his face didn't betray the rush of emotions that swept through him as they looked at each other. But Sage only bowed.

"I look forward to our next training session."

Bastard, Milo thought as he watched the door close behind Sage with a final click.

Duncan moved to sit in the chair once occupied by Sage, and Milo met his gaze. His father had never come to visit him for the sake of it.

"I haven't seen a story from Elaria in many years," Duncan mused, observing the book held within Milo's grasp.

Milo had heard of Jane Austen in his studies of human literature with Professor Binks, but he'd never once bore a desire to read any of her books. He set the tome on the floor and glanced back up at his father, who now gazed out of the window with a pensive expression on his face.

"Do you miss Elaria?" The question flew from Milo's mouth before he could stop it, and Duncan blinked in mild surprise.

"I haven't allowed myself to think about it all too much," Duncan admitted. "But I suppose that I do at times. Things are much harder for people like me, and many of the societal customs in my dimension mirror the ones of Astrum. Yet I do miss the simplicity of it all."

"The simplicity?" Milo asked, and Duncan nodded.

"Yes. I wasn't a king, and your mother was still herself. I didn't have to care for an entire nation, only for my family. I admit there are some days I wish I could change things back to the way they once were."

He had never heard his father voice his desires before, and especially not to this extent. It was suddenly very apparent how old he seemed, and how utterly human he was. Milo shook his head and peered out at the now drizzling day. He wanted to get out of the manor and explore Baile Sunndach and the cliffs by the sea.

"Did you have something to tell me?" Milo asked after a few minutes of strangled silence.

He waited for his father to say something, or perhaps to tell him that things with the wedding had changed. Yet his father remained silent, and Milo kept his gaze fixed outside. Now he made himself look at Duncan and was surprised to find an expression of utmost guilt painted across the king's face.

"Milo, I am so sorry."

Pain flashed through Milo's cheek as he bit into the side of it. Had something happened? Had he and Sage been discovered? Or worse... *Does he know something of the killer?*

"What's the matter?"

"It won't be easy to explain, but I hope that you will do your best to understand," Duncan said. "I have made some grave mistakes as of late."

"What do you mean?"

The question was barely a whisper, and Milo took a deep breath to combat the already light feeling ebbing its way under his skin. Duncan reached to place a hand over his, and Milo jumped. The touch grounded him, though, if only just enough to stay in the room.

"Milo, you must promise that this will remain a secret, and you will not judge me too harshly. And your mother cannot find out."

His father's plea was edged with something dangerous, and another, sneaking fear crawled into his bones. Did his father have something to do with the murders? His sudden kindness, the odd behavior... But it wasn't possible. His father couldn't possibly be a killer.

Anything is possible.

Milo forced his lungs to expand, pushing down the fear as deep as he could. He had to be strong for this, even if it meant finding out something he did not wish to find out. *But you do want to find out*, a voice whispered in his head.

"Just tell me, Father," Milo said.

A sad smile touched Duncan's lips.

"You're far stronger than most I've met, and I believe you are destined for great things."

Milo swallowed the rising fear again, but didn't reply as he waited for his father to say whatever blasted secret it was that he needed to tell. Duncan took in a shaky sip of air and cursed under his breath.

"Milo, I—"

The door flew open with a bang, and both Milo and Duncan yelled out a curse as Penn burst into the room. Worry lined his wrinkled face, though it went slightly blank at the sight of his king.

He sketched a sloppy bow. "My Lords, I apologize for my rather hasty entrance."

"What's the matter, Penn?" Milo asked, alarm bells ringing through his ears at the sight of the frazzled goblin.

"My Lords," Penn panted. "There has been another murder."

Milo and Duncan cursed again, and Milo gulped down air as a wave of lightheadedness swept over him.

"Where?" Duncan asked.

Penn glanced at Milo, his expression one that Milo had never seen from him in his many years of service. Something was terribly wrong, and he suddenly wished that he would leave this dimension before things crumbled around him even further.

"The murder happened in the gardens, Sir."

"He hated all this,
and somehow he
couldn't get away."

- Joseph Conrad, *Heart of Darkness*

Chapter 38

Frances

The scent of roses clung thick to Frances's nose, and she stifled a sneeze as she strolled through the wild gardens. She had decided to confront the guards and spend time outside the moment the sun rose, and now, the soft give of grass beneath her bare feet and the scent of rain-coated greenery, mingled with roses, settled her frazzled senses.

Things were moving too fast, and she hadn't realized how suffocated she'd felt being in the manor for so many days. It had been over a month since her small rendezvous at the strange tavern in Baille Sunndach, and she found an odd desire to return to the shoddy place. She knew it would be no use, though, as it took her nearly twenty minutes to convince the guards at the garden gates to let her through.

She was trapped here.

Her conversation with the ghost girl hadn't helped her feelings of confinement either, not with her creepy laughter and swirling, vacant eyes. She had popped out of view when Frances had asked what the "important thing" was that the killer was trying to find, and frustration had clawed at her ever since.

A few council members milled here and there, though they all seemed to be from the Liath court, and none seemed too inclined to make her acquaintance. Frances didn't mind; however, the thought of idle chit chat was far more suffocating than the flowers.

A yell followed by a muffled thump crashed through the silence, and the scent of copper that Frances knew too well fluttered through the air. Fear latched onto her skin, and Frances was moving before she could think, and the scratches of roses against her cheeks were left unnoticed. There was only one thought, one terrible thought that repeated itself through her mind.

The killer was in the gardens.

She saw the pool of blood before the body, and her fangs already slid out slightly as her stomach gave a cramp of hunger. But she pressed forward and soon came upon the sight of the dead man.

He was tall yet seemed frail in constitution, his pale skin slowly turning grey. His blonde hair was matted with blood, and hazel eyes stared lifelessly up at the sky. Frances's stomach gave a strange lurch at the sight. He seemed young, though the gaping hole in his chest and blood flecking his entire face made it difficult to tell just how young.

She took another step forward, warm liquid seeping between her bare toes as she crouched by the victim. A strange sense of loss swept into her heart, though she wasn't sure why. She didn't know him, but he looked oddly familiar.

More rustling sounded from behind, and Frances whirled, only to make out the sight of booted feet and a dark coat sweeping into the orchard tree line.

Once again, her legs began moving before her mind could catch up, and Frances took off after the figure. She crashed through a rose bush, pain shooting through her palms as a thorn sliced deep into her skin. Frances let out a growl and shoved away the prickly branches, but they wouldn't give. She cursed and turned, forced to go the long way around.

She wouldn't lose the killer, not now.

The figure was moving quickly, and their long coat went out of sight with a flick as Frances escaped from the grip of the roses. Her muscles coiled in preparation to sprint, when something stopped her. Strong fingers swept around Frances's wrist, and panic surged through her chest. She spun, ready for a fight. *I should have brought those damned daggers.* She raised her free hand in a fist, but when she turned, a familiar face made her use all her might to stop her fist from colliding with Jeremy Nightingale's expertly chiseled jaw.

"Jeremy," Frances gasped, surprise now doing an odd dance with the fear still clinging to her gut.

"Frances," Jeremy replied. "What is going on?"

She opened her mouth to reply, to say something flippant or sarcastic, but she couldn't. Because for the first time in her life, she couldn't bring herself to lie.

"I—" Frances shook her head, trying to find the words to start over.

"Frances," Jeremy repeated, and she barely registered him turning her palms upward to reveal the deep gashes across them. She blinked, not realizing how badly she'd been hurt. "Who did this to you?"

His question was a snarl, but Frances knew that his anger was not toward her. *He's concerned for my safety.* Frances shook her head again, blinking down at the blood splattered across her bodice and still coated between her toes.

There was so much blood.

"Answer me, please," Jeremy insisted, and she made herself look up to find his eyes roving across the blood and her hands with a cloud of anger shrouding his expression.

"No one did this to me," Frances said.

"Frances," Jeremy said for the third time, and Frances shivered.

Her name sounded like a prayer on his lips, and she wanted to hear it forevermore. His broad shoulders were tense beneath his coat, and there was a slight tremble in his fingers as he gingerly brushed Frances's palms. She let out a hiss as pain still pulsed there, yet the cuts were already healing.

"It was the roses," Frances shook her head, fury in her failure making her muscles tense. "I tried to take a shortcut through the bushes, and it didn't go well. I lost the killer; they were right there."

"Damnit, woman, I don't care about that right now," Jeremy growled. "You were going to make me hurt people, and no one wants that."

"Jeremy," Frances now said his name, and he finally met her gaze.

It was a collision of emotions, and Frances almost gasped at the pain and rage that roared there. He took a step closer, and she froze as his arms encircled her waist, pressing her close against his chest.

"I said it was the bushes," Frances repeated. "And it was. I'm completely unharmed, and my wounds will heal by nightfall."

She wished she could do something to ease his rage as his grip tightened around her waist. She wanted so badly to be closer, but their bodies were already pressed together.

"Frances," Jeremy whispered, and Frances's spine tingled at her name on his tongue.

She stepped back to see him better, and the emotion that lay in the lines of his face was too much to bear. She wasn't sure who moved first, but it was soon too late. Their lips crashed together in a frenzy, and Frances reached up to cup his cheeks on instinct as he drew her closer. Pain sliced through the contact of his skin against her wounds, but Frances paid them no mind as she opened her mouth against his. He swept her closer, and the pain of her hands and the pleasure of his tongue was almost dizzying.

He broke away with a low curse, and Frances bit her bottom lip with the taste of him still on her tongue. The rage on his face softened and turned into something so incredibly tender and broken that it made her chest burn.

"What have you done to me?" Jeremy breathed. "I hated you the second we crossed paths, and yet I think it was because I was already afraid of losing you."

"I'm still here," Frances whispered.

He took a shuddering breath, and she yearned to brush his hair back from his brow.

"I will never leave your side again, even if it kills me to watch you be bound to another."

The words were a slap of reality, and as though his proclamation was also a spell, Matthew Hale sprinted into view from the bushes. Frances leapt back from Jeremy, and twin smears of blood streaked across his freckled cheeks.

The man appeared as though he had just come from a fight, though perhaps it had just been his attempts to get through the rose bushes, or maybe the guards. Milo skidded to a halt, pausing before them with a slight widening of his silver eyes. Frances froze, taking another step away from Jeremy. But the moment was gone, and Milo looked away, scanning their surroundings.

"Where's the body?"

Frances led him and Jeremy, her mind now going strangely blank. It was as though the onslaught of events had overwhelmed her, numbing her, perhaps as Milo's spirit had escaped his body to preserve its fortitude. They reached the body, and Frances cringed at the scent of death that now danced with the very substance she needed to survive.

An expression of heartbreaking worry creased Milo's brow

as he knelt beside the body, muttering under his breath. Jeremy and Frances exchanged a glance, and another shock ran through her skin at the storm still brewing behind his stare. The spell was broken too soon, however, and Milo's muttered curses were slowly beginning to push away the haze of need that had shrouded Frances' bones.

"No, no, no," Milo hissed. "You can't die for me, please don't have fucking died because of me."

A frown found its way to Frances's lips as she stared down at her fiancé, who was attempting to strip the dead man of his shirt. The scent of metal and blood clung to Frances's nostrils, and her muscles seized in alarm as sparks of shimmering light flew from Matthew's fingers and landed onto the dead man's shirt. The fabric smoked where the magic touched it, and soon the cloth was disintegrating right in front of her.

"What are you doing?" Frances asked, and Milo's fervent attempts only turned into a frenzy.

"Please, you bastard," Milo croaked, ignoring Jeremy, who now crouched at his side.

"Milo," Jeremy began, and reached to take Milo's hand.

The movement made Frances's heart sting. Jeremy's touch was tender as he tried to pry Milo away, but the prince only yanked away and continued fighting with the endless buttons, which were now melting beneath his touch.

"Milo, you have to leave the body," Jeremy murmured, speaking as though he were consoling a frightened kitten.

But Milo was no kitten. No, right now, he was a tornado.

"Not until I know," Milo snapped.

"Know what?" Jeremy asked, frowning.

"The birthmark—" Milo broke off and hung his head, fingers becoming limp at the torn buttons.

Milo collapsed, and Jeremy caught him with ease. Frances's feet began moving before she realized it, and soon the sticky warmth of blood was seeping between her toes again as she knelt at Milo's side.

He looked like he was dead.

Fear roared its ugly head inside of her once again, and the memory of her father's limp body flashed across her mind. The claws in her stomach tightened, and Frances forced herself to blink and return her attention to the garden and the dead blonde man lying at her side.

"We need to call a guard," Frances said, then paused as she focused on Milo's crumpled form. "Did he do that thing again?"

"He projected," Jeremy affirmed, brushing a lock of hair from the prince's smooth forehead.

"That's what he does?"

Jeremy opened his mouth to reply, but the whisper of two people running through the bushes made them both freeze. Frances sprang to her feet in the blink of an eye, and the world went red.

No one was going to touch her or her friends.

A man and a woman, both with hair of gold, sprinted into the clearing. Frances cursed in relief at the sight of Sage, as well as Lyra. The vampire's muscles were taut, and his hazel eyes were tinged red as his gaze first rested on the bloodied corpse, and then on Milo. Jeremy's hold tightened around his friend, and Frances's damned heart gave another pained squeeze. Perhaps it was jealousy, but there was no time to think about that right now.

"What happened?" Sage demanded.

"Did one of you spot the killer?" Lyra demanded, hurrying to the dead body.

The vampire followed Lyra, moving like the predator he was, honed and ready to kill if the opportunity presented itself.

"Only a glimpse," Frances admitted. "They got away."

"They *what*?" Lyra spat, fury lining each of her rigid movements as she inspected the hole in the man's chest.

Frances bit her tongue, not responding. Guilt thrashed at her insides, ruthless and stinging. If she had just kept running, she might have caught them. But then what? She hadn't thought that far ahead and knew her skills in fighting were not up to scratch, especially not against a killer.

Sage stopped at the head of the dead man, gazing down in mild interest. Any interest faded when he looked down at Milo, and he almost lunged for the prince, abandoning Lyra's side.

"Did he project again?" Sage asked, and Jeremy nodded.

The vampire reached for Milo, but Jeremy's grip tightened even more. Only pain remained on Sage's face now.

"Please, I know how to bring him back."

"NOTHING IS SO NECESSARY FOR A YOUNG MAN AS THE COMPANY OF INTELLIGENT WOMEN."

\- Leo Tolstoy, *War and Peace*

Chapter 39

Milo

Oxygen surged through Milo's lungs, and he lurched back into his body with a painful crack of muscle and bone. Strong arms caressed his damp skin, and Milo blinked at the vampire holding him.

"Sage?"

"You can't keep fainting if I'm not there to catch you," Sage murmured, and embarrassment flooded Milo's cheeks.

"I didn't faint," he protested, but then the fear came clawing back. "I thought it had been you."

Sage's mask of calm cracked, and something like love flooded his gaze. Milo had a sudden urge to kiss him, but his body still felt like it had been torn apart and put back together with rusted nails. Another face came into view, and Milo was glad that he hadn't tried to kiss Sage at the sight of Jeremy's worried face.

"Good to see that you've come back, that was only ten minutes this time," Jeremy said, and Milo managed a weak smile.

The sound of tearing cloth made Milo turn to the dead body, only to find Frances and Lyra kneeling by the corpse, removing the last scraps of his shirt. His fiancée was covered in blood, while Lyra watched the princess work in mild disgust, mingled with rage. Frances's mouth was pursed, and her brow was furrowed as she peeled away the man's stiff shirt, which was somehow nothing more than burnt ribbons. Any normal person would have grimaced at the sight of a gaping hole in a dead man's chest, but Frances only leaned in closer with a frown.

"Interesting."

"You find the insides of a body interesting?" Milo asked, and his voice cracked.

Frances hardly noticed but instead touched along the jagged lines of raised flesh and pulled slightly to get a better look.

"Yes, actually," she said absentmindedly, though she grimaced slightly. "If I hadn't been so distracted as of late, I would have already solved this case."

Milo glanced up to meet Sage's stare, but the vampire was watching his fiancée intently. She leaned in closer, and a gag threatened at Milo's throat as she stuck her hand inside the jagged hole.

"What is it?" Lyra asked at the sight of Frances's eyes widening.

"His heart has been removed," Frances announced. "And part of his lung, though I think that it was a mistake on the killer's behalf. It was the same procedure as the Nephilim girl."

Milo scrambled to sit up on his own, though the comfort of Sage's lap made it slightly difficult. He glanced at Jeremy, the sight of him and Frances locked in a kiss flashing across his memory. Perhaps her reaching inside a dead man would make Jeremy change his mind. By the respect and surprise on his friend's face, Milo knew his silent hopes were meaningless.

"What do you think the killer would want with a vampire's

heart?" Milo asked, though he wasn't quite sure he wanted to know the answer.

"I'm not sure," Frances shook her head.

"Lennora's heart was also missing," Lyra replied, her voice thick with emotion, though her expression betrayed no such thing.

A slice of pain jabbed at Milo's gut. But it was true. Her chest had been opened in the same fashion, and he could only guess what had been taken from her.

"How did that much blood come out of him?" Milo asked. "I thought that vampires didn't bleed."

"We bleed," Sage said. "Extra blood not needed for energy is distributed through our organs and veins like a regular living being. It's why all our other body parts function like those of a human. It's why we can bear children."

Lyra grimaced, but Frances only hummed in agreement.

"This man must have had a large meal too, or perhaps he had just fed," Frances said absentmindedly, and her fingers were coated in crimson as she retracted her hand and wiped it on her skirts.

"What do we do?" Jeremy asked. "The killer is clearly after something by removing the heart from each victim."

"I'm not sure if there's anything we can do," Milo grumbled.

Someone wanted to rip his heart out of his chest. Simple as that.

Sage shook his head, a sudden gleam lighting his eyes. Milo frowned, and he met the vampire's stare.

"There might be someone who would know more about this," Sage said.

Who in the hell would know about the frequent removal of hearts? Milo shook his head.

"Who?" Jeremy asked, tension rippling beneath his blood-smeared coat.

His friend appeared disheveled and tired, and Milo yearned to reach out and comfort him. He didn't.

"Professor Binks," Sage explained, and Milo let out a groan.

Of course, he would suggest going to the tall, wiry man. Sage cocked his head, and Milo sighed.

"Fine, we can go to Professor Binks."

"He's not all that bad," Jeremy chuckled, and only then did Milo find twin smears of blood on his cheeks.

Frances stood and wiped her hands on her skirts, as though the gore on her skin were paint, or perhaps crumbs from a meal. Milo fought back a gag and focused on his trembling fingers and the faint sheen of crimson that coated the nail beds. Cold air caressed his cheeks, sending a breath of calm through his senses.

It hadn't been Sage. He was safe. Everyone he loved was safe.

Someone loved that man, too.

"Milo," Jeremy's low voice anchored him back to reality, and Milo exhaled before nodding that he was okay.

"Well," Frances said. "I don't know who this professor is, but if he has answers, then I would like to meet with him."

"I'd like to go with you all as well," Lyra said. "I have to get this mess cleaned up first, however."

"I will arrange the meeting now," Sage said with a nod and started to his feet.

Fear pounded in Milo's veins, and he sprang up in tandem with the vampire.

He's alive. He's safe.

"I can walk to the manor with you," Milo said, hating how breathless his voice sounded in his ears.

Sage gave him a grateful look, and that same tired concern returned. Jeremy stood and moved toward Frances, perhaps out of instinct. The five of them stood in a strange, understanding silence. Both Jeremy and Sage were safe, and he was in more danger than he wanted to admit. Jeremy met his stare, and Milo considered his friend.

He was still just as handsome as before, and the appearance of his desire for Frances in such a transparent way had startled Milo at first. Yet now he found that it suited Jeremy, and he was glad that his friend was allowing himself to feel something other than mild contentment or moodiness at all times.

Yet something had still changed, as if a shimmering veil had been pulled from Milo's eyes and he could truly see Jeremy for the first time. The flicker of his jaw and the linger of his gaze no longer made Milo dizzy with feeling, at least not as intensely as before. It was oddly relieving to realize this, and Milo found himself smiling at his friend.

"I'm glad you're okay," Milo said, and reached for Jeremy.

Jeremy took Milo's hand without hesitation. Milo squeezed it, and all became right in the world once more.

Aside from the fact that a dead body lay at their feet.

"I will take Princess Baudelaire to her rooms so that she can change before our meeting." Jeremy then angled his head toward the vampire. "If you wish that I escort you, that is."

Frances considered him, and her head tilted to the side in that terrifyingly animalistic way as her gaze drifted down to Jeremy and Milo's joined hands. Milo had the sudden urge to pull away, but he didn't, as Jeremy didn't seem too inclined to let go just yet. If Milo were being honest, he wasn't ready either.

Frances lifted her gaze and rightened her head, then gave a small nod. "An escort would be much appreciated, thank you."

Jeremy pursed his lips, and their forced formality clung to the air in an almost strangulating hold. Milo gave Jeremy's hand one last squeeze, and Jeremy returned the gesture. Their gazes met, and a small whisper of sadness caressed Milo's heart at the sight of pain lingering on his friend's face. It was pain for the victim at their feet, for Lennora, and the serving girl. Yet it was also sadness of a different kind that Milo could not place.

They drifted apart, and Milo took a single step back, careful not to look down. It had been the second dead body to make him project, and an odd sense of embarrassment threatened to heat his cheeks. It was maddening to be flung into the galaxy every time tangible life became too surprising.

Jeremy shot Sage a pointed look. "Take care of him."

"And who will take care of me?" Lyra asked, flinging her arms in the air with a huff.

Jeremy turned to her with a sigh.

"Lyra, you've never needed anyone to take care of you. It is your gift."

The witch gave him a half smile and shrugged, though her usual light had significantly diminished since their time at Wisteria Manor. Milo's heart ached for the girl, who was as much a sister to him as she was to Jeremy. But Jeremy was right. Lyra had never truly needed anyone in her life, not even the men whom she claimed to love.

"You're right," Lyra said with a nod. "It's nice to be reminded of my greatness every now and then."

Jeremy chuckled at that, and a small corner of Milo's heart sighed in relief. It was a glimpse of what they used to be before this mess began.

A family.

"Don't let him leave your sight," Jeremy said, turning to Sage again.

"Do you really think that I'm unable to stay alive on my own?" Milo's tone was exasperated, yet there was an odd sense of foreboding that crept down his neck all the same.

Jeremy's faint smile faded.

"I think that you dying is more probable than any of us may think."

The foreboding darkness crawled down Milo's throat, and he fought off a shiver at the inclination of his friend's words. A solid body brushed against his back, and the darkness retreated slightly at Sage's presence.

He's alive. He's safe.

Sage swept a hand up to brush against Milo's back as he said, "Milo is far stronger than any of us, but I swear we won't be separated until the meeting."

"Well then, I suppose we'd better be off before you dampen the mood any further," Milo said, and Jeremy's haunted expression faded slightly.

"We'll wait to hear about meeting with Professor Binks," Jeremy said with one last lingering look in Milo's direction, and Milo's jaw clenched on its own volition as he watched him escort Frances and Lyra back inside.

Sage nudged his back, and Milo turned the dark, towering walls of his lavish prison. Wisteria Manor looked almost enticing from the outside, with its gilded walls and pointed spires. The groomed hedges and scent of flowers in the strengthening rain sent a sudden prickle of heat behind Milo's eyelids. It smelled like home, and a time before Lennora was gone—a time before he knew that his life was about to change forever.

"Milo." Sage's voice cut through the pain like a knife, and Milo tilted his head to find the vampire watching him.

"Yes?"

"You don't have to be okay, you know," Sage said, and the brush of his touch against Milo's arm sent a tremor through his body.

Silence enveloped them, save for the soft crunch of dead leaves over cobblestones and the gentle patter of drizzle against the greenery. The words tossed through Milo's mind like waves crashing against jagged rocks.

The brush of skin turned into a soft pressure, and Milo allowed Sage to intertwine their fingers. Milo leaned into his shoulder, the heaviness suddenly becoming too much to bear. Heat prickled behind his eyelids again, and Milo sniffed.

"Is the world always so hopeless and dark?"

He wasn't sure why he asked it, because he already knew the answer.

Yes Milo. The world is a hopeless and dark place, as it has always been.

"No, it isn't always like that," Sage said, and Milo blinked back both his tears and his surprise.

Sage took a step closer, and soon Milo was wrapped in his arms. He leaned into Sage's chest, taking in his faint scent of eucalyptus and parchment. "The world can be quite bright and lovely, actually. I think we choose to remember the sad parts more than the happy ones."

Milo bit against the memory of Lennora's bloodied chest and lifeless face.

She's never coming back.

A sob cracked through Milo's ribs, and the pain was almost overwhelming again. He distantly felt himself sagging to the ground, but he didn't fade away; he simply crumbled. Sage sank to the ground with him, arms still wrapped around his shoulders as he let out his anguish. Hot tears streaked down his cheeks, but Milo didn't care. He grabbed fistfuls of Sage's shirt as if it were an anchor, and Sage only held him, silent and yet more comforting than any words could say.

Lennora was gone. He was engaged to a girl who frightened him more than she enticed him, and he felt as though he hadn't seen Jeremy and Lyra since they'd arrived at the manor. The only constant was the vampire holding him now, stroking his back in idle circles that were tiny kisses against his skin.

Sage had been there through it all, and Milo had done nothing to deserve it.

"I don't understand," Milo croaked as the final wave of tears subsided and they sat in the rain, held in each other's arms.

"Don't understand what?" Sage murmured.

"Why are you doing any of this?" Milo whispered. "Why do you treat me with such kindness?"

Sage's muscles stiffened against him.

"Milo, look at me."

Milo obeyed, pushing away just enough to look at Sage. His hazel eyes were molten in their fury, though it wasn't anger at Milo, he realized. He realized how puffy his face felt, and that snot had likely gotten on Sage's shirt. For some reason, it wasn't as mortifying as it surely should have felt.

Sage's voice was low and growling as he spoke. "I have never done anything in my life that I didn't want to do, and I *never* let myself feel without good reason."

Milo wanted to look away, but he couldn't. He just couldn't. An emotion so foreign and yet so familiar bloomed in his heart, curling and entwining with the stardust in his blood. It was an odd sensation, both intoxicating and clarifying. Painful, yet blissful.

"You keep saying that you love me without saying it," Milo said, and laughter danced on his tongue despite the stone of pain that still lingered in his gut.

Sage glanced away, and there was a sudden glint of embarrassment in the vampire's expression.

"Perhaps it's because I'm still afraid of saying it directly, just as you are afraid of committing to what you feel."

"That stung," Milo retorted, but knew Sage was right.

Sage's gaze dipped to Milo's lips, and an expression that was like discovering the sun after a lifetime of darkness spread across his face. Milo wanted to bite his lip, but he refrained, and Sage's attention glided back up, his expression growing solemn.

"Things are only likely to get worse, you know that, right?" He asked, and Milo nodded as the stone rolled in his stomach. "You're free to feel pain, anger, sadness, and joy. But don't ever lose your will to fight."

The words cut through something within that almost made Milo gasp, but he only held Sage's stare.

"Please," Sage whispered, and his face fell slightly.

The sight was unbearable. Milo leaned forward and kissed him, hoping that the touch would say what he couldn't put into words. It was soft yet firm, and Sage lifted a hand to cup Milo's cheek, so tenderly it made the cracks in his heart splinter.

They separated, and their foreheads came to rest against each other. Milo cared for this man more than he could have ever imagined. The stranger seated on the floor of the study with papers littered around his legs ran through Milo's memory, and he had the sudden desire to smile again.

"I won't stop fighting. Not when I have so much to live for."

“VENGEANCE AND RETRIBUTION REQUIRE A LONG TIME; IT IS THE RULE.”

- Charles Dickens, *A Tale of Two Cities*

Chapter 40

Frances

Cold, sticky blood blanketed Frances's skin as she and Jeremy walked to her rooms.

They had alerted a passing guard about the murder, and Jeremy had led her away before too large a crowd had congregated around the fallen body. Lyra had stayed behind with the guards, saying that she would be back in the manor shortly and wouldn't miss the meeting.

Frances felt nothing as they moved through endless halls of moving doors and whispering ghosts. She felt like she was floating, and Jeremy's warmth was the anchor keeping her feet tethered to the ground. They remained silent during the walk to her rooms, though it wasn't an uncomfortable silence. Frances wasn't sure if she would be able to say much of anything after what she had seen and done.

I put my hand inside a dead man.

The thought should have curdled like spoiled milk in her mind, yet it didn't. The thought passed by, and only dried blood under her fingernails and on her dress remained. They reached her rooms, and Jeremy halted. A guard stood by, motionless as they approached. She glanced at him expectantly, though a faint rush of nerves managed to seep through the numbness.

"I think it would be best if I waited here," Jeremy said, clearing his throat.

Frances considered him. His shoulders were still tense, and his expression was stony, though she could still see the flicker of anger and worry behind it.

"I wouldn't mind the company," Frances said finally, stepping inside.

"But—"

"You can stay in the sitting room and talk to me if the prospect of seeing me naked is so unthinkable," Frances cut him off, and Jeremy tensed further, stepping inside and slamming the door shut.

He spun her around so that they were face-to-face. His expression was unreadable, but the sheer intensity of his stance made Frances want to bite her lip.

"I have thought of you far more than naked," Jeremy growled. "It's what the thought does to me, that I am worried about."

Frances did bite her lip now, despite the numbness. It was thawing ever so slowly, the well of heat that Jeremy always seemed to ignite with even the briefest of glances rearing its head. The memory of his lips on hers made her body shiver, and arousal purred deep in her stomach. She gritted her teeth, closing her eyes and schooling her desire.

"I'm covered in blood, Jeremy. I reached inside of a corpse, and yet you are less repulsed by me now than when we first met?" Frances asked, moving deeper inside, hating the feeling of her sticky feet against the thick blue rug.

She swept to her bathing chamber, straight for the wash basin, and the sight of clean water made her bloodied skin itch. It was her sustenance, her life-force.

Yet at this moment, it was nothing but disgusting.

She cringed, remembering how just this morning she had still wanted nothing more than to be one of those detectives, dissecting and discovering the secrets behind murders. She suddenly wished that she hadn't cared about her father at all.

She wished she could be more like Malichi.

Footsteps padded closer, and Frances bit her lip as she heard Jeremy enter the sitting room without a word. She dipped her hands into the warm water and grabbed a washcloth to scrub at her skin.

A curse sounded from the sitting room, followed by the crash of a falling stack of books. Frances cringed slightly, but smirked nonetheless.

"Please watch your step."

Jeremy cursed again.

"You certainly have an interesting choice in reading material."

Frances scrubbed harder at her skin, and blood bloomed like roses in the water before turning it crimson. She turned her palm up, noting the cut from the rose was already healing. *Good.*

"It wasn't much of a choice," she muttered, though it was still loud enough for Jeremy to hear.

"Someone's forcing you to read these?" Jeremy asked, and Frances shook her head, even though she knew he wouldn't see the movement.

The memory of Cesaire's smiling face as thunder cracked through the sky branded itself behind her eyelids, and Frances tasted blood as her fangs punctured her lower lip. She let out a curse and retracted them. *I can tell him about my father, can't I?*

"My father was murdered a year ago. No one investigated it further than necessary. They say it was a hunting accident, but it wasn't. A rogue vampire killed him." Jeremy remained silent, and Frances continued. "I couldn't live with the knowledge that, if I had known more about causes of death and the signs of struggle, I could have helped. And so, I began reading, though it hasn't done me any good thus far."

"That's not true," Jeremy countered, and Frances tensed, surprised by his statement.

Hands now clean, Frances dried them off with a fresh washcloth and started for a spare dresser next to the bathtub. She let the question slip from her lips as she opened it and rifled through silk and velvet.

"How so?"

"You were able to distinguish the victim's cause of death just now," Jeremy said. "I couldn't have done that, even if there was a sign in bold letters saying that his heart was missing."

Frances snorted and pulled out a pair of soft trousers and a blouse, deciding against a dress for a change.

"It was quite obvious; I don't think that a trained eye was needed to come to that conclusion."

Frances removed her ruined dress and pulled on the trousers. Blood still coated her feet, and Frances shivered, running back to the wash basin after she was fully dressed.

"Thank you."

Frances jumped and turned to find Jeremy leaning against a wall, watching her. She was glad to be clothed, but even still, she'd never felt more naked in her entire existence.

"Why are you thanking me?" She asked, the washcloth paused above a bloodied foot.

He simply stood there, flame-colored hair disheveled and swept slightly over his forehead. His clothes hadn't been spared by their embrace, and there were still twin smudges of crimson on his cheeks. Yet he seemed uncaring of his state, nor the fact that Frances was now working a dead man's gore from between her toes.

"Thank you for telling me about your father."

Frances paused, her chest seizing slightly.

"Everyone in Astrum knows of his passing. He was one of the oldest rulers in the realm."

"I know," Jeremy murmured. "But I didn't know you or anyone from the Baudelaire clan then. I didn't care, nor did I know a rogue vampire killed him."

"And you care now?" Frances asked, raising an eyebrow as she continued her scrubbing.

"Yes, even though I shouldn't," Jeremy replied.

Frances bit her lip but kept scrubbing, hating the sound of *shouldn't* on his tongue. The silence was brief, and then Jeremy was speaking again.

"Lennora is not—" he paused. "Was not, my real mother. She found me when I was six, after a group of rogue vampires slaughtered my family.

"It happened in the dead of night, and my real mother told me to hide under my bed and not to make a sound until they left. I heard the screams of my parents and siblings for hours. I still hear them now."

Frances looked up from her now clean feet, but didn't say anything. Jeremy's expression was still unreadable even though her own body felt like it might cave in.

"How did you survive?" she asked.

"I almost didn't," Jeremy admitted. "One of the vampires found me and dragged me into the main room so that I could see what they had done to the rest of my family. They hadn't only drunk them dry; they had torn them apart. The vampire who'd grabbed me was about to bite when Lennora appeared and killed them all before, they could fight back."

Frances opened her mouth, then closed it again. She knew that story. It was famous amongst vampires, and a significant reason why every single rogue group had been hunted down for years after the incident. She remembered being afraid for her own family when it had happened, knowing rogue vampires killed anything, *anyone*, for sport. It had made her loathe the idea of growing soft, of *caring*. The monsters couldn't get you if you were one too.

Yet the fact that the poor boy who had witnessed the attack, who had been tossed against the dead bodies of his family and nearly killed, was the man standing before her now. It was almost unbelievable.

"Jeremy," Frances breathed, and realized that she had moved closer to him.

He stared at the floor now, stare blazing with hatred and pain.

"I didn't sleep for weeks afterward, and Lennora had to give me potions to knock me unconscious for a few hours at a time so my body could have even a little bit of rest. I've hated vampires every single day after that and wished that Lennora hadn't killed them so that I could have done it myself."

Frances yearned to take another step forward, but the fury in Jeremy's eyes suggested that it was not a wise idea. So, she moved back to the dresser and pulled out a pair of thick socks, even though she didn't need them.

"It's why you hated me," Frances said, more as a fact than a question.

It made so much sense, and a sudden crash of guilt punctured her heart at the annoyance she'd felt by his animosity.

Jeremy dipped his head.

"It is why I've been so confused by you, and by Sage."

Frances blinked. "You fancy Sage?"

"No!" Jeremy exclaimed. "No, I don't. I simply don't mind him. He has made Milo smile almost as many times as I have."

"An impressive feat indeed."

Jeremy's expression turned wistful for a moment, and Frances knew he was thinking about Milo. Their relationship wasn't romantic; she had realized this fact after some time, although she wasn't so sure if either of them had felt something more.

"You frightened me the first time we met," Jeremy said.

"I did?" Frances snorted. "I thought you hated me."

"I did hate you," Jeremy said easily, and though his words stung, she now understood. "Yet you were also the first vampire I'd spoken to since that night, and it scared me that you were so kind."

He wasn't looking at her while he spoke, yet she could still see the guilt and confusion radiating from him. She knew that they needed to find Milo and Sage, yet it was the farthest thing from her mind as she took another step closer. Frances reached out and brushed the sleeve of his coat. It was not a good idea to touch him right now, but she wanted to.

"It's maddening in here sometimes," Jeremy murmured, and Frances knew he wasn't speaking about the manor.

"It's a constant state of mild madness inside my head," Frances shrugged. "We get used to pain if it's handed to us every day. It simply turns into noise in the background."

Jeremy looked up, seemingly surprised by her words. Frances grinned back, and her skin felt like it was prickling with electricity again. He moved, and soon his arms were around her. She welcomed the embrace, not caring about the faint smell of death that clung to his coat.

"Thank you," Frances whispered, and his arms squeezed slightly. The muscles in his chest tensed, and Frances pulled away slightly. "What's the matter?"

"I forgot about the other night, with everything that has happened," Jeremy growled.

Daithine and Duncan, wrapped in each other's arms, punched through Frances's mind, and she shuddered. Jeremy pulled away slightly, and Frances stepped out of his embrace completely.

"We can't tell Milo."

"Why not?" Jeremy frowned, though his expression was, once again, on the verge of rage.

"Because no matter how much I believe in my strength to convince my court that something happened, I cannot convince my brother," Frances huffed. "Malichi will find some sort of loophole to ensure that Milo and I are wed, no matter if our parents..."

She couldn't even speak the words out loud, and Jeremy grimaced. After brief consideration, he nodded, and his features softened again.

"It's best Milo doesn't know unless entirely necessary."

Frances let out a sigh of relief. If either the king or her mother spoke to the court, something of real change could be obtained. Yet for now, she and Jeremy would have the secret looming over their heads.

"We should find the others," Jeremy murmured.

Frances turned away, unable to hide the strange medley of emotions racing through her tired soul. Her conversation with Jeremy pushed aside the less-than-favorable one of her mother, and her shoulders relaxed. It was as though a layer of Jeremy's armor had been peeled back, and she could see his soul a bit clearer. Frances pulled on a pair of worn boots before leading to her bed chambers, the memory of his touch still on her skin. She was about to turn away when the gleam of light against polished wood caught her eye. Anton's knives had been placed on a shelf in the dresser, waiting patiently for her to do with them what she pleased.

"Fine," She grumbled under her breath, snatching up the box.

It would be smart to have some protection that went beyond her teeth and faint magical powers. Jeremy raised an eyebrow as she opened the box and withdrew the daggers, tucking them into her belt without a second glance.

"Those are beautiful," Jeremy commented. "Where did you get them?"

Frances snorted and started for the door.

"No one important."

JEREMY SUGGESTED THEY TRY PROFESSOR BINKS'S office once they'd left Frances's rooms, and they spent much of the trip in companionable silence. A balding ghost wearing a sheet around the waist in place of clothes passed by at one point, and Frances thought she saw the flash of Mary Edmunds cross her peripheral vision. The ghosts didn't bother Frances in the slightest, and by the relaxed grace in Jeremy's movements, he wasn't disturbed by them either.

Frances was about to open her mouth to speak when an all too familiar French curse echoed through one of the adjoining hallways. Shouts and yells followed suit, and it was now Jeremy's turn to freeze.

"That's Lyra yelling."

"And that's my mother cursing her to hell in French," Frances frowned.

They glanced at each other in confusion and turned down the hall. The yelling approached them, however, and soon the flustered image of Lyra came storming toward them. Frances's frown deepened. *Why was she yelling at my mother?* The image of Daithine and Duncan wrapped in each other's arms sent another wave of disgust through her body, and Frances shook her head slightly to find Jeremy catching Lyra by the wrist before she could slip past them.

"Lyra, what in the gods' teeth is going on?" Jeremy demanded, and Lyra wriggled her wrist from his grip.

"Nothing is the matter. I only needed to have a chat with the queen."

"You were yelling, not chatting," Jeremy said, and Frances angled her head toward a small black door that appeared at the end of the hall.

Her mother was nowhere to be seen, which was odd.

"I really must be on my way," Lyra insisted, taking a step away.

"We're on our way to Professor Binks's office," Jeremy replied. "I thought you were going to join."

She glanced between Jeremy and Frances, scowling. Frances only pressed her lips together, unsure whether to be kind to the witch or reprimand her for cursing at her mother. *But what if she had a good reason?*

Lyra shook her head.

"I have other business to attend to now."

Jeremy's expression hardened, and Frances watched as he and Lyra engaged in a silent battle. After a moment, Lyra still hadn't budged, and Jeremy crossed his arms with a sigh.

"Fine," Jeremy said. "Keep your secrets."

"We all have secrets, Cousin," Lyra said, though her skin was rather pale as she spoke.

Lyra turned and stalked off without another word, leaving both Frances and Jeremy standing in the hall watching her retreat. Frances shook her head and again wondered where in the hell her mother had gone.

"Well, that was odd," Jeremy muttered.

"Just a bit," Frances agreed, and they continued on their way, though an odd sensation that something terrible was about to happen followed Frances all the way to their destination.

"A HUNDRED SUSPICIONS DON'T MAKE A PROOF."

- Fyodor Dostoyevsky, *Crime and Punishment*

Chapter 41

Milo

Sweat ran down Milo's back as he entered Professor Binks's office.

Once he and Sage had reached the manor, they went straight to the office, where they had previously discovered a great many things about each other. He only prayed that the giant man didn't have some power that detected past lust or other passionate activities.

"It will be fine. I promise," Sage murmured.

Milo glanced at him sidelong and sighed.

"I suppose there's only one way to find out."

Sage knocked on the door. The sensation of being watched prickled Milo's neck, and he whirled around to find Frances and Jeremy approaching. Both appeared slightly confused and disgruntled.

"You two took a while to get to the professor," Jeremy commented, and Milo glared.

"Shut up."

Sage paused. "Where's Lyra?"

Jeremy's expression hardened slightly, and he shook his head. "No longer joining."

Milo frowned. It wasn't like Lyra to miss out on essential conversations, even if only to stay informed about everything going on in the world. Her behavior had changed since Lennora's death, however, and Milo could hardly blame her for being less inclined to be around others. He thought that Jeremy would have also turned into a recluse, but it seemed as though his assumptions were incorrect.

Sage shrugged and cracked the door open, poking his head through before opening it further and gesturing for Milo and the others to come inside.

Professor Binks sat at his desk, rifling through a pile of parchment as they entered, and Milo gave his teacher a slight nod as the man lifted his head to watch the four of them file inside.

"Is this all of you?" Professor Binks asked.

Sage took a step forward, and Milo silently thanked the gods for Sage's confidence. It was also painfully attractive, but that was beside the point.

"Yes, Professor," Sage began. "We had a few questions about the recent murders, and we thought you might know more about what's going on."

Professor Binks studied each one of them in succession, though his eyes lingered on Milo and Frances a bit longer than what made Milo comfortable.

"I'm afraid I don't know very much about what has happened. I only know there was a third victim this morning," Professor Binks said.

Milo's hope sank like a ship in the sea, yet it was Frances who stepped forward and spoke.

"*Bonjour,* Sir," She began, and Professor Binks inclined his head.

"Your Highness."

Frances's smile tensed, but she continued, "I felt inside the last victim's chest, and it appeared that his heart was missing."

Professor Binks's expression turned blank at her casual proclamation, but she didn't seem to notice.

"The previous victim's chests were open as well," Jeremy added. "If that helps."

Silence enveloped the room, and Milo could do nothing but focus on breathing. Professor Binks considered them again, and his impassive expression was almost maddening.

"I will start by saying that you all must work on easing into heavy conversations," Professor Binks began. "However, I believe that your gruesome discoveries do change a few things."

Frances didn't appear to feel abashed in the slightest, though Jeremy had the good grace to look down.

"I have been doing my best to investigate and find out who is behind these attacks, though with my limited time, I have not been very successful." Professor Binks admitted.

"Have you come up with any theories?" Sage asked, and Professor Binks nodded slowly.

"I have, and I'm afraid that this information about removed hearts has only deepened the belief that my fears might be correct."

"Well, what is it?" Frances asked impatiently.

Professor Binks looked at her, then sighed.

"I have reason to believe that someone is trying to find and use *The Book of Silver*."

Cold seeped into Milo's chest, and he had to blink away the darkness and bite his own tongue to stay grounded in his body. Frances cursed and grumbled something about a little girl speaking in riddles, but Milo didn't have the mind to focus on her words.

"Why?" Sage asked. "And what do the hearts of vampires and witches have to do with it?"

"Please sit down before I explain. I feel slightly cornered with the four of you staring down at me like vultures."

Professor Binks waved them to sit at the long table, upon which Milo had been taught a great deal of things, which unfortunately had little to do with his powers.

They all sat, and Milo forced himself not to glance at Sage to see if he was affected at all by where they had sat down.

"Much better." Professor Binks grunted. "Now, to answer your question, we must first remember the origins of the book's creation."

"I think we're all aware of the book's creation," Jeremy was the one to speak now. "The gods each removed one of their fingers and put them inside of a comet, which then turned into a book bearing the knowledge of everything."

"Correct, yet that's not that part of the origin to which I am referring. It is the part when they gave the book to the angels and demons on Astrum."

"The gods made it so that only the mix of blood from both heaven and hell could open the book," Sage said. "That, or a stardust soul could do it, since they have the Infinite Galaxy inside of them."

"Also correct," Professor Binks said.

"So, what does that have to do with people's hearts getting ripped out of their chests?" Milo asked, speaking for the first time since entering the room. Everyone's attention turned to him, and Milo sank deeper into his seat. "It's an obvious question."

"I have heard of a tracking enchantment found amongst dark magic practitioners that uses three hearts from hell and one from heaven to find rare, enchanted objects," Professor Binks muttered.

"I've never heard of a spell like that before." Jeremy frowned.

"That is because it is very illegal, and only found among the worst sorts of people," Professor Binks replied.

"So what then? I am not actually being hunted?" Milo asked, and tentative relief tickled his spine.

"You could very well be a target," Professor Binks said gravely. "Remember, your blood on its own can find, open, and use *The Book of Silver* with as little as a drop. Not to mention, any stardust soul who has used the book has died instantly."

Terror swallowed the relief, and Milo bit back a loud curse. He wasn't safe. In fact, he was as far away from being safe as he was from Elaria. Milo jolted slightly as Sage reached under the table and took hold of his hand, the cold touch both comforting and frightening.

"What do you mean they died?" Milo asked, his voice trembling.

"It is an overcharging of like-to-like energy. The contact of a stardust soul with the book is like lighting a dry forest on fire. It eats everything up and only stops once every tree is destroyed."

"So, if I were to use the book, I would die?" Milo asked.

"The likelihood of you surviving would be very slim," Professor Binks replied.

"If I'm understanding correctly, Milo is both a target and not?" Jeremy asked.

"And someone's attempting to find *The Book of Silver*," Frances finished for him, then cursed. "That little ghost girl had warned me about the killer wanting to find something important."

Jeremy and Professor Binks gave her a look that verged on concern.

Milo didn't say anything, and Professor Binks leaned his elbows upon his heavy oak desk. "I'm afraid that both of your guesses, of Milo and the book, are likely true."

"What would someone want to do with *The Book of Silver*?" Jeremy asked. "It's used to create dimensions."

"And destroy them," Milo muttered.

Silence swept over the room once again, and a sudden realization dawned upon Milo. Someone was trying to find the book to destroy Astrum. Panic welled inside his chest, and soon black splotches were dancing across his vision. Milo shut his eyes and squeezed Sage's hand, focusing on his cold skin and the sensation of a slight breeze on his cheeks.

He would be of no use in saving the world if he were to leave it.

"Why would someone want to destroy Astrum?" Sage asked, voicing the exact thoughts that swam in Milo's fuzzy brain.

"I can't be sure, but I don't think anyone who seeks to destroy an entire dimension has their head correctly placed on their shoulders," Professor Binks said.

Milo opened his eyes to find the splotches had subsided slightly. *I will be safe. My friends will be unharmed.*

But what if Astrum is destroyed?

Milo shook his head, and Jeremy gave him a concerned glance. Warm fingers found Milo's other hand. Sudden heat prickled behind Milo's eyes, but he wouldn't let himself cry in front of the professor. The two people who had been there for him more than anyone had, perhaps aside from Penn, were there. They were at his side, and Milo knew that they would not leave him even if the gods themselves tried to take him away.

"Wait," Frances uttered, and any inkling of warmth that had seeped back into Milo's bones vanished.

"You said the spell to find lost things required *four* hearts," she finished.

"I did."

"What does that have to do with—" Milo cut off, and a horrible realization struck him.

There had only been three victims thus far.

As if they had rehearsed it, all five occupants of the room let out a spirited *fuck!* And jumped from their seats. Milo didn't care that his hands were still interlaced with Jeremy's and Sage's, nor that the impropriety was in plain sight. Neither Professor Binks nor Frances seemed to notice or care, even when Jeremy let out a secondary curse. They all let go, though Professor Binks was now hunched over his desk, scribbling madly.

"One of you, please deliver this to the king as soon as you can. I don't care if one of the highnesses must do it; this is a great emergency," Professor Binks babbled, and stood to his full gigantesque height with a small paper folded in his outstretched hand.

Sage strode forward. "I'll take it."

"Hurry," Professor Binks demanded. "If what we have discovered is true, then we must find *The Book of Silver* before the killer does."

"ANGRY PEOPLE ARE NOT ALWAYS WISE."

- Jane Austen, *Pride and Prejudice*

Chapter 42

Frances

Frances smelled the blood before she heard the screams.

It was a terrible sound, like that of a stag uttering its final cry of defeat before the wolf ended its life.

It was the sound of death.

The world fell into slow motion as Milo's face paled, and Jeremy let out a roar of fury that rattled the windows and sent cracks splintering through the marble floors. Frances only watched them sprint down the hall, toward the sound that still echoed through the walls, though it never came again.

She barely felt the cold as she rounded a corner, and a pool of blood seeped over the floor. It barely hit her as something terrible, something odd even. For it was the second murder she had seen today, and killing became meaningless after one saw it enough times.

Though it was not the girl with light hair coughing up blood, nor Jeremy's cries and curses of anguish as he knelt at her side and placed his glowing hands over the hole in her chest. It wasn't Milo falling to his knees or Sage catching him just before they crashed upon the ground.

It was Malichi kneeling on the girl's other side with *The*

Book of Silver clutched against his chest. Frances's legs moved before she could think, and soon she was clutching her brother's shaking shoulders and guiding him to his feet, pulling him away from the dead body and Jeremy's glowing hands.

They walked quickly, and Malichi didn't speak, nor could Frances hear past the pounding in her ears as she led them through a door that popped into existence before their eyes.

Frances let go of Malichi as soon as they stepped inside the lavish room bathed in silks, paintings, and white marble statues. But Frances didn't take any of these things in, for all she could do was stare at her brother and the book in his bloodied grasp.

"What did you do?" Frances asked, her voice calm and steady.

Malichi's gaze was bound to the book, and a lock of dark hair fell over his brow as he shook his head. "I don't know."

"How could you not know how you murdered Lyra Devonne?" Frances replied evenly, coolly.

Malichi's gaze raised now, and there was fire within the icy blue of his stare. "I didn't kill Lyra Devonne."

"Then why is she lying on the floor with a hole in her chest?" Frances asked, crossing her arms. "And why are you holding *The Book of Silver* in your arms like it's a life raft?"

The sense of nothing that blanketed over Frances's body might have been alarming. *It should be alarming*. And yet she felt nothing, so she thought nothing of it.

"I. Didn't. Kill. Her." Malichi ground out, and his tone was like the sharpest of knives.

"Then how did you end up here?" Frances asked and spared a glance at one of the paintings, a rather realistic depiction of a woman with snakes for hair.

"I was taking a walk when I heard her screams," Malichi said, and his voice shook for the first time in a very long time.

"I yelled and ran toward the sound, though she was already dying when I arrived."

"And the book?" Frances asked, glancing down at the very thing that kept the walls around them from collapsing.

"The killer dropped it as I arrived. There was a black door that had appeared in the wall, and it disappeared after the book fell to the floor."

Frances nodded slowly, and though the story wasn't entirely clear, she believed him. Her brother had always been an excellent liar, yet now, with his slightly trembling shoulders and wild eyes, Frances knew that what she saw was no act.

"You should take that book to Professor Binks. He would know how to protect it."

The tremble in Malichi's muscles increased slightly. His jaw clenched, and a small sound fell from his lips.

"Are you all right?" Frances asked.

"I-I'm not sure," Malichi stammered. "I feel hot, and I feel the ardent desire to cry."

Like a drape had been lifted, the numbness that coated Frances's heart was wiped away and replaced with a feeling she could only describe as anguish. His expression cracked, and Malichi's chin trembled slightly.

"I'm afraid, Frances."

Frances stepped forward and swept her brother into a firm hug, *The Book of Silver* held between their chests. Heat prickled at her skin, and Frances gasped as a wave of emotion flooded into her body.

"It's the book," Frances breathed. "It's making you feel."

Malichi pushed away and looked ready to drop the tome, but Frances placed her hand over his, ignoring the jolt of overwhelming emotion that flowed through her skin.

"Don't drop it."

Malichi's lips pressed into a grim line. "I will keep the

book for now. It's much too dangerous to have everyone knowing where it is."

Frances took a step back, understanding his slightly emotional, yet sensible reasoning. The killer would be desperate to find it again and placing it in the possession of someone who couldn't protect themselves was more dangerous than keeping it with someone who was created to kill.

"I need to find Jeremy," Frances said, realizing that she'd left him alone in front of his dying cousin.

Malichi's gaze hardened, though only just enough for Frances to tell. She didn't give a damn about what he thought, however, especially not now.

"It's okay to feel; it makes eternal existence a bit more interesting."

He shuddered in reply, and Frances took off, back to the crime scene.

Jeremy was no longer there when Frances returned to the site, though neither was Lyra's body. Only a large smear of blood, deep cracks in the marble, and two bloodied handprints were left to give evidence that anything had happened at all.

Frances closed her eyes and opened her senses, seeking past the overwhelming scent of copper in the air. She found it in only a few seconds and began following the scent of cinnamon and frankincense.

The occasional splatter of crimson upon the floors might have been enough to lead Frances to Jeremy's location, but she couldn't trust that he had been allowed to follow his cousin's body. She landed in front of a door much like that of her own rooms, and Frances knocked on the dark wood twice.

When no one answered, Frances pushed it open and stepped inside.

Jeremy was curled on the floor, eyes closed, chest rising

and falling rapidly. Frances rushed forward and sank by his back, the muscles rippling with unleashed tension beneath his shirt.

"I should have never allowed myself to love." His voice came out in barely a croak, hollow and lifeless.

The fibers in Frances's bones cracked at the sound, and she placed a hand over his shoulder. She yearned to do more, to wrap him in her arms and hold him until it all went away, but she stopped herself. She knew how hard it was to be touched when your heart hurt so badly.

"It wasn't your love that killed Lyra," Frances murmured, but the words still rang like a broken promise through the air.

Jeremy's shoulders shuddered, and he didn't respond as a sob cracked through his body. Frances sat, hand on his shoulder as he yelled and screamed his pain. She knew what it was to hurt, yet she had a sinking feeling that what she had experienced was only a drop in the bucket of Jeremy's ill-fortune.

Minutes passed, perhaps hours. Yet when Jeremy's cries ceased, only silence remained for some time. Eventually, he sat, and Frances again wished she could hold him.

"I need you to leave," Jeremy said, and Frances almost recoiled at the cold anger in his voice.

"Why?"

Jeremy shook his head, and she could almost feel the icy rage radiating from him.

"Go, now."

"What have I done?" Frances asked, and a strange sense of anger coiled in her stomach.

"Don't force me to explain myself," Jeremy muttered. "I can't stand the sight of you right now."

It was like a blow to the head, and Frances climbed to her feet before she had a chance to think.

"Fine," Frances snapped. "But I hope you know that

pushing away the ones who care for you won't make life any easier."

Frances wrenched the door open, not caring about the questionable crack that splintered through the wood from her sudden movement.

She didn't know where she was going as she started down the hall, and she didn't care. The only thing she knew was that the world was falling apart, and even her impending marriage was the last thing on her mind. The anger simmered and turned into something worse, making the inability to cry excruciating, and something between a growl and a scream tore from her throat.

Everything had gone horribly wrong, and a terrible, sneaking suspicion crawled its way down Frances's throat. The last time she'd seen Lyra was no more than an hour before her death, and the girl had been in a downright rage. Pain twisted and curdled in Frances's stomach, and he wished she could vomit as the possibility swelled and burst across her consciousness.

Had her mother killed Lyra?

Was Daithine trying to destroy Astrum?

"When sorrows come, they come not single spies. But in battalions!"

- William Shakespeare, *Hamlet*

Chapter 43

Milo

October 29, 1880

The nearly full moon streamed down upon the bed, its silvery glow wrapping the room in a calm sense of serenity. Yet it was far from calm or serenity that lived inside of Milo.

A shaky sigh escaped his lips, and Milo watched the sleeping form of Sage at his side, moonlight turning his hair silver. They had decided to go to hell with the rules and spend the past few nights together, though it was mainly due to Milo's fragile grip on his consciousness and Sage's concern that he might not come back.

His projection this night had been the worst of them all, and a residual shudder of the sensation of being stuck between two realities ran through Milo's limbs. With another huff, Milo swept the blankets from his body and stepped from the bed. A strict curfew had been placed over the manor following Lyra's death, declaring all inhabitants, both living and undead, were required to remain in their rooms after sundown. But Milo needed to get outside, consequences or danger be damned. He felt suffocated, and another moment, trapped within the haunted walls of Wisteria Manor, sounded impossible.

Milo shrugged into a heavy coat over his tunic and soft pants, then pulled on thick socks and boots. Sage remained asleep, and Milo had half the mind to wake him so they could go together. Yet the exhaustion had been evident on Sage's face before they'd gone to bed, and Milo slipped out of the room without a sound. The manor was empty as Milo crept down to the front entrance, and he sent a silent prayer of gratitude to the gods for it.

A flash of silver swept across the hall, and Milo let out a silent groan as the young ghost, Mary Edmunds, appeared not two feet away.

"Hello," she said brightly, and Milo cringed at the loud echo her voice gave.

"Keep your voice down," Milo hissed.

The girl shrugged.

"Are you trying to get outside?"

Milo paused, crossing his arms across his chest. "Perhaps."

"You won't get outside through the front doors; there are big boulders with warts all over guarding them." Mary giggled again.

Milo sighed. "They're called trolls."

"Oh." Mary shrugged. "I don't like them."

This conversation was going nowhere, and the loud bounce her high-pitched voice gave through the walls was making Milo's body seize. He would get caught if he stayed another minute in this corridor.

"I suppose I'll go back to bed then," Milo said and turned away.

"Okay." Mary giggled. "Though I could show you the secret way that leads to the beach."

Hope leapt into Milo's throat, and he spun around to face the little girl again. She wore a knowing smile, revealing her teeth, and gave him a beckoning wave.

"Come with me. I like helping people do dangerous things."

Perhaps that's the reason why you're a ghost now. Milo shook his head, deciding not to utter his thoughts out loud.

He followed the shimmering girl down a flight of stairs to a small iron door. The girl stopped and tittered. "This is it."

"That was quick."

"It opens into a tunnel, but the journey is not very long," Mary said, ignoring him.

"And where does this tunnel go?" Milo asked, the thought of having to find his way alone through a dark tunnel making his heartbeat quicken, and not in a good way.

"It goes through the cliff and leads you to the bottom of it. There's a bunch of rocks there, but it's a short walk to get to the sand."

Milo sifted a breath between closed teeth. He could do it. The prospect of a sea breeze and some freedom made the thought of walking through stone manageable. Mary stepped aside and gestured for Milo to open the door. The iron was icy against his touch, but it swung open silently as he pushed it.

"Why isn't it locked?"

Mary shrugged. "It has been locked many times, but we don't like it that way."

By *we* she likely meant the other ghosts who lived within Wisteria Manor. Milo narrowed his eyes but couldn't help a small sense of gratitude from blooming in his chest. Perhaps ghosts weren't so bad after all.

"Thank you," Milo said, and Mary Edmunds giggled once more.

"You're welcome. Try not to slip."

And with that, the ghost disappeared.

Milo let out a huff and shook his head. Children were terrible, but ghost children were something else entirely.

The dark tunnel gaped at him like an open mouth, and he had the sudden urge to turn back and slip into bed with Sage. But the walls still felt like they were pressing too close, and the smell of blood seemed to be imprinted within his nostrils. He needed to get outside.

The first step sent darkness crawling over his boots, and the second made Milo understand why Mary told him not to slip. The tunnel was damp, and after a few steps, Milo realized it was a long, narrow flight of stairs that led through the stone.

"Wonderful," Milo grumbled, and let the darkness embrace him.

The slippery trek went much faster than Milo anticipated, and soon the crash of waves and gleaming moon lit his way out onto sand smattered with dark boulders. The soft breeze caressed Milo's cheeks and bruised heart, easing the pain slightly. He let out a shaky sigh and began picking his way across the rocks to where the spotless beach lay just in sight.

Each step further from the manor brought lightness to his feet, and it was already easier to breathe as Milo reached the shore and crashing waves. The deep sand made movement difficult, and short pants escaped his parted lips as he finally sat.

Moonlight glinted off the dark water, and the waves were gentle at this hour, like a warm embrace and sensual retreat. The soft sound of singing floated through the air, and Milo stiffened. But it was not a siren's song, as the crash of glass and curses that followed made it evident that it was some maiden from Baille Sunndach, not a mile away.

Sorrow tiptoed its way into Milo's heart, and he leaned back onto his elbows to watch the beauty around him. Lyra's lifeless face replaced the ocean, and Milo let out a pained moan. The tears came next, and Milo let them flow freely as he rested his head on the sand and closed his eyes. Stars blurred across his vision as he wept, and soon nothing could be seen past his tears.

First Lennora, then Lyra. The past few weeks had been nothing short of torture, and so Milo let out the emotions that had long since gathered and turned into a stone weighing down his heart. He let himself cry about those who'd perished because of him, the ones whom he'd never known, yet to whom he now owed his life. He let himself weep about Jeremy, and the strange void that had grown between them since their arrival. He missed his best friend dearly, painfully.

And then there was Sage. His entire body ached with the thought of him and the love that he had given Milo so freely. Milo had smiled more times since meeting Sage than he could remember, even throughout these dreary times. But it was more than that. Milo cared for him, liked him, lo—

"What are ye doing crying on my beach?"

Milo's stomach dropped, and he spun around, groaning inwardly at the prospect of fighting off a drunk sailor from the town or any other unsavory characters. Yet the slightly glowing man with straps and buckles keeping his coat secured over his bulging stomach, and the ridiculously plumed hat atop his head, was evidence enough that this was no ordinary man.

The pirate ghost grinned at Milo's confused expression and sketched a bow.

"Apologies, allow me to introduce me-self. I am Captain Archer Delarosa, esteemed pirate and owner of *Deadman's Harbor*."

"Okay," Milo replied, the information meaning nothing.

"I might've stopped breathing a few years ago, but I ain't've forgotten me manners," Archer said with that grin still plastered to his face. "Yer supposed to tell me yer name, boy."

"Matthew," Milo said dully.

"Are ye that prince boy that people have been talking about?"

Milo sighed and nodded, deciding that it wouldn't be all that dangerous to tell a dead pirate who he truly was. Captain Delarosa gave him a knowing nod and put a finger to his hat.

"Very pleased to make yer acquaintance. And if ye don't mind me prying, why in the gods and goddesses' teeth are ye crying?"

Anger, sharp and palpable, made its way through Milo, and he wondered what ill fortune had made him so popular with the likes of ghosts. He wiped at his puffy eyes.

"Does a man need a reason to cry?"

Captain Delarosa considered him. "Well, no, I suppose he don't. But yer awfully loud, it sounded almost like ye were calling out for help. It's why I came."

"I appreciate the sentiment, but I'm fine," Milo said, then mumbled more quietly, "I was just trying to get away from dead people for a little while."

"Though that may be," the captain said. "I was sorrow's best customer back when I was still breathing, and it was right exhausting."

"I'm sorry to hear that," Milo said, though he didn't really mean it.

Captain Delarosa nodded solemnly and let his gaze travel to the sea.

"It was the only thing I never learned, yet the only thing that I wish I *had* learned. Life be of choices, boy, and not all lead to sorrow. I've found that it's right easy to fall into the darkness, but it's also a bottle of brandy to see the good things in life."

"A bottle of brandy?" Milo echoed, utterly confused.

Captain Delarosa waved, as though his question were a bug whirring in his ear.

"My point is, when things seem like there's no way out and yer backed into a corner, just know that the walls surrounding ye ain't that sturdy. Break the walls down, get yerself out of that corner. It's easier than ye might think."

"I've never been good with riddles," Milo grumbled.

Captain Delarosa didn't seem to hear him, or perhaps he chose not to, as he gave a hearty laugh and adjusted his enormous hat.

"I could've been a proper scholar instead of a pirate. Might've lived longer then."

Milo didn't answer, as there weren't any polite words left in his brain, it seemed. The crash of waves was calming him, if ever so slowly, and Milo found that he did feel slightly better, even with this strange ghost and his useless words.

"Looks like ye've got company, and I'm missing more cheerful faces," Captain Delarosa said, tipping his hat again.

Fear sank its claws into Milo's chest, and he glanced around wildly.

"Who's coming?"

Captain Delarosa shrugged and turned back toward the glowing town beyond. "I'm sure ye will find out soon enough."

"Fucking pirates," Milo grumbled and scrambled to his feet.

He scanned the horizon from which Captain Delarosa had disappeared, but found nothing. Fear tightened its grip, and Milo turned slowly to face the outcropping of rocks that hid the opening he'd come through. If the person had come from the manor, that could mean he'd been followed.

Milo took a step back. Perhaps he could run to the town and go through the front door of the manor instead. *Do you want mother to bite your head off?* Milo cursed and shook his head. But it was too late to make any other decisions now, because a tall man came into view moments later.

It was Jeremy.

Milo let out a breath of relief and sat down again. His friend remained silent as he approached, appearing almost as tired and beaten as Milo felt. Jeremy sat at Milo's side and let out a sigh.

"Gods, I missed fresh air," he murmured, and Milo hmphed in agreement.

"How did you find me?" Milo asked, sinking his fingers into the fine grains of sand.

"The little ghost girl found me when I was wandering through the halls trying to find an alternate way outside. She told me that you'd gone outside too and looked grumpy."

Milo snorted. "I was more than grumpy."

"I know," Jeremy said, his tone softer now. "I'm a bit more than grumpy as well."

Sorrow hung thick in the air, and Milo found Jeremy's hand, squeezing it gently. Jeremy squeezed it back and let out a shaky breath.

"They're both gone, Milo."

"I know," Milo whispered. "It almost doesn't feel real."

"It feels a bit *too* real for my taste," Jeremy muttered.

"I'm sorry."

It was the only thing that he could think of saying, as there didn't seem to be enough words to tell Jeremy how bad he felt. Lennora had been something like a mother to Milo, and Lyra the sister he never had. They shared the same pain, the same hopelessness that had made its nest inside their hearts.

"I'm the one who should be sorry," Jeremy said after a moment, and Milo frowned.

"Why?"

"I've hardly been there for you these past few weeks. I've been too tangled in my own problems that I lost track of us."

Jeremy's voice was hushed, and shivers ran down Milo's arms at his proclamation. Jeremy did nothing as Milo rested his head against his friend's shoulder.

"I'm not angry with you, even if you have fallen in love with my fiancée."

Jeremy stiffened but didn't move, and Milo couldn't help but smile. He said nothing; instead, he waited for Jeremy to digest the words and allow them to mingle with the pain.

"It wasn't intentional," Jeremy said finally. "And I don't want to love her."

Milo fought down a laugh, allowing Jeremy's comforting warmth and the sound of the sea to calm his whirling emotions.

"No one ever *intends* to fall in love, and we can hardly choose who we fall in love with."

"Since when did you become such a wise man?" Jeremy asked, and Milo shrugged, thinking of Captain Delarosa and his ridiculous hat.

"I just finished speaking to a rather scholarly individual. It inspired me."

"Clearly," Jeremy chuckled, then fell silent.

"Are you afraid?" Milo asked silently, and again damned his lack of timing.

Jeremy nodded, however, and let out another strangled sigh. "I'm terrified, Milo. And I feel guilty for it."

"Why? You know that I'm as attracted to her as I am to becoming the king."

"No, not because of that, no offense, of course," Jeremy said quickly. "Because... because I don't feel like I should have allowed myself to feel that way for another when two people that I love so dearly are dead."

"Jeremy," Milo whispered as his heart gave a terrible squeeze.

"I know," Jeremy said. "But it doesn't help that the ones that I did love are now gone."

Suddenly, they were walking through the field between Cathair Liath and Black Wood again, hands intertwined as drizzle dampened their hair but lifted their spirits. Milo leaned against his friend and hoped that it would be enough in place of the many words he couldn't say.

"I'm still here. And I'm not planning on leaving any time soon."

"Aside from when you faint," Jeremy chuckled. "I swear, it's been more times on this trip than I've seen from you my entire life."

Heat rose through Milos's body, and he lifted his head from Jeremy's shoulder. "It's been a stressful time, and it's not like I can help it at any point."

"You could, if you and Sage had actually trained your skills instead of other things," Jeremy replied, and Milo was sure he would light on fire with the heat coursing to his cheeks.

"Shut up," Milo shot back, but couldn't stop his laugh. "Besides, I've learned enough to protect myself."

Jeremy met his stare, and Milo dipped his gaze to watch the faint smile bloom on his friend's lips. A corner of his heart clenched. It was the corner that only Jeremy would ever occupy, and it was the safest part of his soul. A strange lightness overtook Milo's limbs, and he pressed his lips together, gaze dropping to the sand.

"Jeremy, I—"

"I know," Jeremy cut Milo off, his tone strained. "I feel it too. I always will."

Milo swallowed hard, unsure of what to say. His heart still beat for Sage, as he knew it would forevermore, yet it wasn't his entire heart.

Jeremy cursed, and Milo looked up to find him staring out toward the sea, his expression pained. "We're in a right mess, aren't we?"

Milo laughed. "Which part is messy? The part where I'm supposed to get married in two days, or the part where everyone is dying, and someone is attempting to find *The Book of Silver*?"

"Malichi has the book," Jeremy spat, his expression changing into something dark and foreboding. "I would think he's the killer if not for the way he cares for his family and country. Frances swept him away as soon as we found Lyra, and he hasn't left his room since, other than to meet with Professor Binks."

"Professor Binks hasn't asked him for the book?"

Jeremy shook his head. "I met with him yesterday. He said he is trying to find the best containment spell and location to hide the book. Somewhere that a tracking spell like that can't be used to find it again."

Milo mulled over his words. It was odd that the killings had stopped since Lyra's death. It had been nine long days of waiting, unable to speak with Malichi and too afraid to bring it up with his parents.

"Can you ask Frances if we can meet with Malichi?"

Jeremy's jaw clenched, and he shook his head. "I don't think that's a very good idea."

"Why not?" Milo frowned.

It was the perfect solution. If Malichi had the book and hadn't used it to destroy the world yet, then it was clear he wasn't the killer. Which additionally meant they had the advantage. They would be able to stop the killings and give the book to Professor Binks so that he and the other scholars from Cathair Liath could hide it properly again.

"I don't think Frances will want to see me any time soon, if ever," Jeremy mumbled.

Stupid, idiotic boy. Milo sighed and scrubbed at his face, then cursed as granules of sand showered across his skin. “What did you tell her? Actually— don’t tell me, I don’t want to know.”

Jeremy pursed his lips, and Milo pressed on, an idea forming in his mind.

“Whatever it is that you said, it can’t have been so bad that she would never speak to you again. She loves you, too. I can see it in the way she looks at you. Besides, we need to put an end to this mess, for Lyra and Mimmi if nothing else.”

A moment passed in silence, when Jeremy hung his head and let out a groan. “I can talk to her.”

“Wonderful,” Milo nodded. “I’ve grown rather tired of seeing those that I love die.”

“Me too,” Jeremy said and looked up, his eyes glistening with unshed tears. “I do love you, Milo. I know I don’t say it enough.”

Milo opened his mouth and then closed it, the swell in his chest slowly melding his crushing sadness into steely resolve, almost overwhelming him. Instead, he leaned forward, pressing their foreheads together.

“I love you too, Jeremy.”

They pulled away enough to watch each other, and Milo marveled in the emotions that waxed and waned from his friend’s beautiful face. He did love him, and it was the only thing that mattered. Love was the only thing holding the broken pieces of Milo’s soul together, and it would be the only thing that got them out of this mess.

“We should get back inside. You’ve got a lady to woo back into your good graces,” Milo said, and Jeremy rose to his feet.

They started toward the rocky meadow that led to the secret tunnel. Jeremy glanced sidelong at Milo with a dubious expression, though Milo couldn’t manage much of anything in response due to the exciting and equally terrible resolve rising in his chest.

"You have a plan, don't you?" Jeremy asked, and Milo shrugged.

"I might, but you won't like it."

"I LOVED HER AGAINST REASON, AGAINST PROMISE, AGAINST PEACE, AGAINST HOPE, AGAINST HAPPINESS, AGAINST ALL DISCOURAGEMENT THAT COULD BE."

- Charles Dickens, *Great Expectations*

Chapter 44

Frances

Frances stared at the words of her book, *The Woman in White,* yet she read nothing.

It was her favorite book of all, one stolen from Elaria, and she thought that getting into her favorite silk chemise and curling in bed with good literature would soothe her aching soul. But it did not, and she only stared, the words blurring on the page.

Dread had clung to her insides for hours now, what with Jeremy and her horrible presumption. She should have immediately told someone about the possibility that her mother might be the one behind all of this, yet she couldn't.

She could not lose another parent.

Instead, she kept her thoughts to herself and would soon learn if doing so would be to the realm's detriment.

A knock made her jump, and Frances swept from the bed, concern filling her for whom might be waiting on the other side. There was a curfew after all, and no one had been allowed to leave their rooms for hours. Yet when she opened the door, she let out a curse and nearly closed it again.

It was Jeremy standing at the threshold.

"What are you doing here?" she asked instead, crossing her arms over her chest.

Jeremy's cheeks were flushed, and his hair was ruffled, as though he had just been outside in the breeze.

"I came to speak with you."

Frances raised her eyebrows. "That's a surprise. I thought that you couldn't stand the sight of me."

Pain flashed across his gaze, and both hurt and terrible satisfaction spread through Frances's bones. She knew it was wrong to say hurtful things to him, especially now. Yet what he said had stung, and she couldn't stop hearing the words that he'd spoken inside her head.

I just can't stand the sight of you right now.

"You know I didn't mean it like that," Jeremy murmured.

She wanted to believe him badly. Yet she couldn't, not when his words struck such a deep chord. She was tired of men saying hurtful things. Her teeth found her lower lip as she contemplated ripping his head off, but decided against it. He was much too pretty, and besides, she did care about him. Perhaps a little bit too much.

"What do you want?" Frances asked, and Jeremy dragged his gaze from her lips to her eyes.

"I came to apologize, and to tell you that I've been a complete ass since we met."

Heat rose to Frances's core, but she dampened it down.

"Apology denied, I'll see you tomorrow."

Jeremy shot a hand out to stop her from slamming the door in his face, and Frances sighed. She knew she was being a complete bitch, but she cared little about that fact presently.

"Frances, please let me try," Jeremy said, and Frances hated how his low tenor made her toes curl.

"Fine," she relented. "But make it quick."

She stepped aside, and Jeremy walked to the shelf where she had stuffed more of her books. Frances closed the door and nearly ran to stop his perusal. He had seen quite enough of her reading material the first time he'd been to her rooms, and she didn't want him to look any further.

"It continues to surprise me that you are such an avid reader," Jeremy mused, running a single finger along the spine of a rather gruesome crime journal that Frances hadn't been able to finish.

"I prefer the company of books over that of people," Frances replied coolly, and Jeremy turned to face her, a smirk on his face.

Oh, she hated him passionately now.

"I see," Jeremy mused, though his grin faded slightly. "Milo likes reading too, though I don't think you two would be able to exchange recommendations."

Frances stalked closer; arms still crossed.

"I swear you two were lovers at one point. You know him better than I think you know yourself."

Jeremy tensed slightly, then shrugged. "We were never lovers. And I didn't come here to talk about Milo, I came to talk to you, about us."

About us. Had such a thing ever existed between them? Frances kept her mouth shut, and Jeremy turned to face her fully.

"I've never been good at expressing myself. It was something I closed off from at a young age, and I think you know why."

Frances blinked and nodded weakly, unsure if she could manage to say anything.

"I've fucked and laughed and cried, but I never truly let myself *feel*," Jeremy almost spat. "That's why you terrify me, Frances, and it's why I told you to leave earlier. Your unwavering presence scared me, and I didn't know what to do with how it made me feel, especially not then."

Understanding bloomed through Frances, and guilt nearly

crushed her shoulders inward. Yet she stood firm and took a step forward. She had expected him to welcome her with open arms, but how could he when his very world had crumbled?

"And how are you feeling now?" Frances asked.

Jeremy shrugged, though tension rippled beneath the casual movement. "I feel angry, mostly. Ever since I started living at Rightford Castle two years ago to teach Milo combat, my time with Lennora and Lyra has decreased greatly. It became easier to build walls around my heart, keeping them at bay, though they will always be family. I'm sad, though I feel anger more. I want to end this mess, and I want to find a way to keep you from marrying Milo."

Frances balked. "You want to do what?"

Jeremy stepped closer. "You don't want to marry him, and he most certainly doesn't want to marry you."

Frances blinked. This was all too sudden, and her mind was still reeling from his sudden proclamation to reply. Jeremy cursed and clenched his hair in his fists.

"Gods, I'm such a fool."

"Don't say such things about yourself, even if it's partly true."

The corner of his mouth quirked, and she took another step closer. He watched her movements like a predator, his stare burning with pain and something more lethal. Small prickles of energy began dancing through Frances' core, and she allowed for the strength of his gaze to warm her as she stopped before him.

"I don't want to fight you, Jeremy. I never have."

Her knees buckled slightly from the intensity of his dark gaze; shadows etched over his angular cheekbones. His muscles were strained beneath his tunic, and she couldn't help but let her gaze flicker down at the sheer power of him, and bite her lip again.

"What do you want from me, Frances?" His voice came

out hushed and gravelly, sending sparks skittering down her spine and through her legs.

"I—" she faltered, and bit her lip again.

This action sent a growl rumbling through Jeremy's throat, and she looked into his smoldering eyes, though they had flicked down to her lip clenched between her teeth.

"I can't give you what you want," he spoke again, though he came closer still.

Frances stretched out, his rough calluses and warm fingers against her skin sending a spark that drew her closer, ever closer. She brought his palm to her lips and brushed against it softly. A satisfied rush went through her at the sight of Jeremy's sharp intake of breath. His grip tightened against hers, and he dragged her closer so that their bodies were pressed flush against each other.

"You've already given me what I want," Frances breathed, and couldn't help but lean harder into his taught body.

Planes of strong, male muscle shifted against her dress, and Frances had to fight the sudden urge to rip off everything standing in the way of their bare skin. Jeremy was a roiling storm as he tilted his head to regard her. She felt weak in the face of his overwhelming power and lowered her gaze. His free hand came to press under her chin, the movement making her tilt her head back up to look at him.

"What have I ever given you?"

His breath was a ghost's touch against her cheek as he bent down closer. He let go of her, only for his touch to travel up her side before coming to rest on her hip, the sensation positively maddening.

Frances took his hand from her chin, guiding it to press against her chest, right in the place where her heart might have been beating rapidly, if only it could. She tried to ignore the fact that his expression did not change, and he did not recoil in disgust when he found no pulse beneath his touch—tried to ignore the flutter of hope at his lack of fear. Frances brought her face closer to his, taking in the freckles that smattered his fair skin in a perfect constellation.

"You've given me life, Jeremy."

His touch against her skin was maddening, and biting her lip was all she could do not to lean in and ravish him at that very moment. *Gods, first you want to kill him, and now you want to...* His eyes dipped down to watch her mouth, and another low curse rumbled against her body.

"I've decided that it drives me mad when you do that," he murmured, and she released her lip to open her mouth slightly.

"Are you going to kiss me or not?" She challenged, the inside of her chest feeling like a swarm of butterflies had taken flight within.

Before she could take it back, before she could do anything, his lips were crashing down upon hers. She immediately melted into the heat of him, opening her mouth to his and angling her head for better access.

He tasted of cinnamon and cloves against her tongue, and she was soon dizzy with him. Jeremy broke away first, his breath ragged against hers, but he didn't stop. His lips pressed against her jawline and to her neck, each kiss like a smoldering coal against her cold skin. It gave her life, and she couldn't stop the gasp of delight and pleasure from escaping her mouth as his tongue grazed her skin and he nipped the sensitive area between her jaw and ear.

"Jeremy," she breathed, both a question and a command.

He lifted his gaze to meet hers, and their lips connected once more, this time more feral and desperate. Her palms pressed against his chest, and she let them travel down to the hem of his tunic. She needed to feel his skin under hers, feel him against her. Her touch dipped underneath the cloth, and he let out an animalistic sound of pleasure against her lips as their bare skin met, and she let her hands travel up his muscled torso.

His lips continued their exploration across her skin, and they dipped lower to press nips and kisses against the topmost area of her breasts. Frances tightened her grip around his sides as he lifted his head and met her gaze.

"Do you want me?" His words were gruff and sounded almost as though it were an effort to speak.

Yes, she wanted him. She needed all of him, and she had a feeling that he might feel the same. Frances let her attention slide from his waist down to the bulge against his trousers.

"Do *you* want *me*, Jeremy Nightingale?" she breathed, and the replying growl was answer enough.

"I will always want you, Frances Baudelaire."

He brought his hand to the opening of her chemise and tugged it open. Cool air brushed soft kisses against her bare skin, but she wanted Jeremy's lips to be kissing her there instead. His eyes darkened with desire at the sight of her breasts, and he dipped his head down once more. The connection of his lips against her sensitive skin sent a gasp through her body, and her grip tightened instinctively. Another growl emanated from his lips and vibrated against her, and she almost cursed her heightened senses to the devil for the mind-shattering sensation that roved through her core. His lips left her skin, and he looked up at her.

"I want to please you first."

She knew what he was asking, and she would comply, though her body ached to touch him. She let her fingers fall from his trousers and slip underneath his shirt once more. He continued his exploration of her skin almost immediately, and she let out a sigh of satisfaction and need as he sucked on her skin.

His left palm worshipped her other breast, and she was close to gasping at the overwhelming sensations. She had never known the singular stimulation to feel so good, so earth-shattering as it felt now. Perhaps it was because their hearts were entwined, no matter that one pumped blood and the other consumed it.

Jeremy's touch drifted downward to trail along her stomach, just as his head rose once more to watch her. She needed him, needed to feel the emotion on her skin. And so she widened her stance slightly as he continued to trail down to the hem of her nightgown. Her eyes did not waver from his as he lifted the dress slightly, tucking his hand beneath to glide up her thigh.

She bit her lip as his fingers trailed her skin, and his eyes darkened into a storm as his thumb met its mark. He growled with pleasure at the wetness that pooled between her legs, and a small gasp escaped her lips as he idly ran a finger up and down. He teased her skin; a slight pressure that made her want to beg him to go harder.

"Jeremy," she gasped.

It was a demand, and a plea.

A grin curved at his lips, and Frances took a step back, closer to the bed behind them. He followed her, an animal on the prowl. She stopped when the backs of her knees bumped the mattress, and Jeremy's hand slid around her full waist as he guided her to lie down.

Her skin felt hot and cold at once, and she wanted nothing more than to guide Jeremy on top of her, to press his body against hers and mold their spirits together. But Jeremy did not lean over her; instead, he lowered to his knees, calloused hands wrapping around her ankles with a pressure that sent her senses reeling.

"I want all of you, Frances," Jeremy breathed, his hands trailing upward slowly to her calves, then her thighs.

When his hands nearly reached her apex, Frances let out a

shaky curse. She did not want him to ravish her; she wanted him to take her and consume her entirely.

"You would do best to begin then."

A growling chuckle flew from his lips, and Frances lifted her head to watch him as he slowly lifted the hem of her gown, baring her to him. His mouth met her skin, and her vision exploded into a symphony of color. His tongue was the devil whispering sweet nothings into her very soul. The pressure was maddening, and she fisted her fingers in his hair as he dealt her sweet torture.

"Stop," Frances almost cursed, and Jeremy froze.

"Am I hurting you?" his voice was laced with concern, and it made the rising pressure building in her core threaten to burst.

"No, it takes more than that to hurt me," Frances purred. "But I like to keep things interesting."

Jeremy raised his eyebrows, but that heat remained, and he allowed her to lead him back to kiss her. She tasted herself on his tongue, and it nearly did her in. His hands traveled down her body once again, but she stopped him before he could trail too far.

Quick as lightning, Frances hooked her leg beneath him and turned, flipping them both so that he was on his back, and she was straddling him. He let out a surprised chuckle, and she gave him a wicked grin in return.

"I am certainly intrigued now," Jeremy breathed, and Frances let her fingers trail against the hem of her chemise.

He gripped her full thighs as she swept the cloth over her head, slowly dragging it up and revealing her skin beneath. She tossed the fabric to the floor, and a strange sense of uncertainty clawed its way into her stomach. She had never done this with someone she cared about so deeply. Not even Anton had touched her in the way Jeremy did, and it was unfamiliar. She felt naked, and even more than just her skin.

Jeremy's gaze traveled across her curves, and his fingers softened against her legs.

"Gods, you're beautiful."

The heat from his touch traveled to her core, and Frances gave him a shy smile, though she remained focused on his chest.

"What's wrong?" Jeremy asked, noting her hesitancy.

Frances shook her head. "Nothing's wrong, in fact, it's the exact opposite of wrong."

Jeremy sat up, and Frances almost moaned at the hardness that rolled against her and their joined hips. His eyes were pools of the night sky, and the pure emotion behind them sent her arms instinctively wrapping around his shoulders.

"We don't have to fear this," Jeremy murmured, and Frances shook her head.

"No, I don't think we do."

Their lips collided, and articles of Jeremy's clothing went flying to the floor until he had nothing on but his trousers. Frances slid from his lap, and they both fumbled with the buttons before nearly tearing the pants from his legs. And then he was lying at her side, and the sight of his chiseled muscles and smooth skin made a strangled, breathless sound fall from her lips. She let her gaze travel down to his length and bit her lip. She wanted him, *now.*

"I should be the one biting that lip," Jeremy growled, and Frances looked up at him again, warmth clawing at her core.

"By all means."

And then he was on top of her, her lips between his teeth, and his hand stroking her, teasing her. Frances let out another moan against his lips and raised her hips, aching to bridge the gap between them. He complied, though his thumb remained at the apex of her, worshipping her most sensitive spot as he eased inside. They both let out a small gasp in unison, their gazes locked as he pushed in further, his hand not stopping.

The pure, open emotion on his face made frozen tears threaten to spill, and she hated that she couldn't cry for the millionth time.

"Thank you," Frances murmured, her voice calm even though her nails dug into his back as he began to move within her, the sensation in combination with his fingers breathtaking.

"What for, Frances?" Jeremy breathed, and her name on his tongue sent the rising energy inside of her bubbling toward its breaking point.

"For not running away from me completely when I gave you love, and for allowing yourself to begin loving me back."

The words fell from her lips before she could stop them, but Jeremy did not withdraw, nor did his face contort with disgust. Only overwhelming softness fell over his expression, and he lowered his head to brush a kiss against her lips.

"I am yours, Frances."

"Brevity is the soul of wit."

- William Shakespeare, *Hamlet*

Chapter 45

Milo

October 30, 1880

"I don't think they're going to come."

Milo and Sage had been waiting in the barren office for some time now, and restlessness began to settle under his skin. He'd slept well for the rest of the night, if not only slightly fitful with strange dreams about the world turning silver.

Sage stepped closer. "They'll come, just relax."

The hand on his arm pulled slightly, and Milo let Sage turn him so that they were face to face.

"They will be here."

Milo nodded dully, unable to stop the pit of worry from dragging deeper through his body. His conversation with Jeremy had been nothing short of vulnerable, and Milo realized how much he truly missed his friend as they had cursed and inched their way up the slippery tunnel into the manor.

He hoped Jeremy would succeed in winning Frances over, even if the thought of her still made his skin crawl.

Sage leaned closer, brushing a soft kiss against his lips before pulling away. "Did that help?"

Milo glanced up at the ceiling as if in deep contemplation and shook his head. "A bit, but you might want to do it again just to make sure."

Sage chuckled, and he leaned in. "With pleasure."

The door opened before their lips could meet, and Milo let out a curse as Frances and Jeremy strolled in, Malichi following behind.

Jeremy looked between the two of them before giving Milo a faint smile. Milo returned it and glanced between him and Frances with a raised eyebrow. Jeremy shrugged, though his cheeks turned red as Sage broke the silence.

"Thank you for coming. Milo was convinced you weren't going to make an appearance."

Jeremy scoffed. "You have so little faith in my communication skills."

Milo raised his eyebrows at his friend. "You would be correct."

Frances sighed and leaned against Professor Binks' desk.

"I still don't understand why we are all here, aside from you wanting to berate my brother about something he didn't do."

Thick heaviness draped over Milo's heart at the memory of Lyra's death-stricken face, and he shook his head. "With good reason, since I've barely spoken three words to him."

"You do not need to speak of me in third person, I'm standing right here," Malichi replied coolly. "And no, I did not kill your friend."

"How can we know that?" Sage asked, and Milo could almost kiss him again for speaking when his own tongue felt like a puddle of molasses.

Malichi licked his lips. "I have no way of proving it, but you are more than welcome to give me truth serum if that would make you all sleep better."

Jeremy shook his head and leaned against the desk next to Frances. She didn't shy away; in fact, Milo noted the hint of a smile on her lips as their shoulders brushed.

"I think we're all clear on what happened, though you might want to tell Milo and Sage for yourself."

Malichi explained that he'd been wandering through the halls when he'd heard the screams, and the killer, draped in a heavy black cloak, had dropped the book as soon as they saw Malichi come into view. The mention of the black door made Milo perk up. It couldn't have been the same one that had appeared in his rooms, could it?

"We must give the book back to this professor Frances mentioned," Malichi said once he was finished explaining. "This entire situation has paused the wedding long enough."

Icy tendrils wrapped around Milo's skin, and both he and Frances shook their heads in tandem. Frances crossed her arms and looked pointedly at her brother.

"You do realize that the only one who wants this marriage to happen at all is you?"

Malichi crossed his arms. "So does the entirety of both of our kingdoms."

"That doesn't count."

"I think it's more important to find the killer and stop them before thinking about a wedding," Jeremy said.

"I agree." Milo nodded, though he didn't miss the slight tension in Frances's shoulders as he continued. "Giving the book to the scholars won't solve anything. The killer will continue killing until they find it again. They followed us here, and I'm certain they will follow us anywhere we go with the book until they're found and apprehended."

Frances smirked. "This is the most confident I've seen you since we met."

Milo shot her a scowl, but it was Jeremy who spoke. "He's one of the most confident people I've met when he has strong opinions and is comfortable in his environment."

"You're like a cat," Frances chuckled.

Her expression reminded him of the first time they'd met, and she had tilted her head in that predatory way. He shivered and shook his head. "Hardly a cat, just a fool with a loose tongue."

"And how do you suppose we catch this killer?" Malichi asked, his voice cutting through the air. "No one has been successful this far."

"That was before we had the book," Sage said.

Milo pursed his lips together, and his slowly forming plan whirled in his head. Malichi looked between Sage and Milo before his gaze dropped to their interlaced fingers. Milo stiffened but didn't let go, and Malichi's expression remained a steely mask of neutrality.

"You do still have the book, don't you?" Frances asked.

Malichi dragged his gaze away and looked at his sister, nodding once.

"Good," Frances said. "We can use it as bait."

"No," both Malichi and Sage protested, and Milo stiffened at the vehemence in Sage's voice.

"It's the only way," Milo was the one to speak. "No trap that we set will be successful unless we use the book."

"And what if this trap turns against us?" Sage asked. "We would be reduced to nothing. The entire planet could be destroyed, along with every dimension that exists within it."

"I agree with the scholar," Malichi growled.

Frances opened her mouth to say something that would have likely made Milo's cheeks warm, but Jeremy waved a silencing hand through the air. "Stop, please."

Everyone stilled, and sweet pain bloomed in Milo's chest as Jeremy spoke, his tone low and broken. "Lyra and Lennora both died at the blade of this killer, so please forgive me if I agree with Milo and Frances."

The room fell silent, and Milo yearned to give his friend a comforting touch or say something to ease the pain. Yet it would not go away so quickly; anyone who had experienced loss knew that. It would remain forevermore, lingering until oblivion greeted him in a few hundred years.

"Okay," Sage said. "If we can do this in a way that doesn't harm the book, nor any of us, then I agree to using it."

"And as long as it is returned to the proper safekeeping after this mess is cleaned up," Malichi said. "Professor Binks said he is close to finding a solution for its keeping."

"Are you going to work with us on this?" Frances asked.

Malichi scowled at her, and a slight shiver went through Milo's bones at the intensity shared between them. They were weapons set into the bodies of monsters.

"My duty is to my family and my realm, and if that means I have to work with you four, then so be it."

Frances's jaw clenched, and something like guilt swept across her face. Milo hadn't the slightest idea why she might feel that way, but he supposed that it wasn't only he who had a dramatic family life.

"We will make a plan for tonight, then," Sage said. "The sooner we do this, the better."

Everyone murmured in agreement, and Jeremy let out a shaky sigh.

"I am truly sorry for your loss," Malichi murmured, and Jeremy looked up with mild surprise. "No one deserves to lose their family."

"Thank you," Jeremy said gruffly.

Resolve settled into Milo's bones, and he took in a steadying breath. He would ensure this killer was brought to justice, and no other soul that he loved would be torn away. What was the point of having stardust in his veins if he didn't use it?

"Okay," he said in a tone so calm it betrayed his thundering heartbeat. "Where should we start?"

"There is prodigious strength in sorrow and despair."

- Charles Dickens, *A Tale of Two Cities*

Chapter 46

Frances

Frances's mind raced as she glanced out at the bleeding gardens.

She and Jeremy walked in silence to her rooms, where they would stay until they met Milo, Sage, and Malichi, and followed the plan. It still clanged inside her head, and she wished that it were already nightfall.

Or do I?

Frances bit her lip. She'd remained silent about her suspicions about her mother, as getting Malichi to meet with the others had been a feat. It was better to say nothing and be correct than to say something and be wrong.

"You are being silent," Jeremy murmured, and Frances almost jumped.

"I was thinking."

"About what?"

She yearned to come closer, but she refrained. It would put them both in more danger if they showed their attraction now than if they waited for this mess to be over.

"I don't think you would be thrilled to know what I'm

thinking," Frances admitted, and Jeremy opened the door to her rooms. "Thank you."

He followed her inside, and the memories of the night instantly swept from the corners of the room to bombard her mind. Jeremy seemed to have the same thoughts; his eyes darted from the bed to the floor.

"I have no way of knowing if your thoughts make me glad or not unless you speak to them," Jeremy said finally.

Frances glided to the overstuffed bookshelf and grazed her fingers across the medley of aged and pristine book spines. Perhaps holding one of her friends would make her next words more bearable.

"Are you still mourning Lennora and Lyra?" Frances blurted, her back still turned to him. "As in, is doing this all too much?"

Silence pooled over the floorboards and coated the walls until it suffocated her completely. *Stupid girl, you shouldn't have said anything.* It wasn't her place to ask, especially not when both murders had been so recent. Loss was a strange thing, and it affected people in strange ways.

"Why are you curious about this?" Jeremy asked, his voice as rough as a cart rolling over sharp stones.

Frances shrugged, vaguely registering just how human the movement was. She turned to face him, only to be met with a guarded expression of curiosity.

"I don't know," Frances admitted. "I suppose the last two months have felt overwhelming for me, so I could imagine it might be even harder for you."

Jeremy's throat bobbed, and his pain nearly radiated from his chest. They watched each other, and Frances wasn't sure if she wanted to jump out of the window or comfort him. Jumping out of a window sounded too similar to something Milo would do. And yet, comforting Jeremy when he was as closed off as the gates of hell sounded equally unsavory.

"It is not too much," Jeremy began slowly. "It is best for me to mourn them this way."

"It is?"

Jeremy nodded. "It has all been very overwhelming; too much happening too fast for my mind to catch up. There are times when I forget they're gone, and it feels like I'm so occupied that I haven't seen them for a few days."

It was a feeling she knew all too well. Her father's death had affected her in the same manner, and it had only been after the whirlwind of the aftermath and Malichi's instatement as standing ruler that her body and soul had truly realized what had happened.

"It's the worst kind of torture," Frances murmured, "knowing that they are gone, yet part of you can't fully believe it."

Jeremy took a step closer. "It doesn't feel like torture, at least not yet. It is odd to be in a state of such sorrow and yet so much hope at once."

Frances froze. "You feel hope?"

In this bleak manor, where only the dead keep you company?

"Yes," Jeremy said softly, and suddenly he was standing before her, much like the way they had started the night before.

Shivers ran straight to Frances's core as Jeremy brushed her arms with his palms. She felt trapped by his presence. Yet she didn't wish to be anywhere else.

"I feel the pain of loss, yet there is still so much to live for."

The emotion in his gaze nearly broke her, as did his words. Frances stepped closer, wrapping her arms around his waist. Jeremy dipped his head lower, and she could feel the whisper of his breath as their lips gravitated closer.

"You are worth living for, one thousand times over."

"But I'm not alive," Frances whispered, and her heart cracked slightly at its stillness.

"You do not breathe, but that doesn't mean you are truly dead," Jeremy whispered. "You have given me life, too, Frances, and it is the scariest damn thing I have ever experienced."

Frances couldn't fight the smile that tugged on her lips, and she ached to break the space between them. Yet she only pressed herself closer, as though it would mold their bodies into one.

"You make me feel mortal, and it scares me beyond anything I've ever experienced," Frances admitted.

It was the other thing that plagued her thoughts, though she wasn't sure if she was ready to admit it to herself. She would exist for all eternity, unless they didn't make it through the night. Yet Jeremy was mortal, though he would live up to hundreds of years old before being swept into the beyond. Their time was limited, making their delicate situation more terrifying. Her smile remained, however. It was something to think about later, after this mess was resolved and she somehow convinced Malichi to end the marriage agreement.

It would all be okay; it had to be.

A smile that mirrored her own bloomed on Jeremy's lips, and it nearly shattered the world. "Well then, it appears as though we might be good for each other after all."

"Or incredibly bad," Frances retorted, and Jeremy chuckled softly.

"I'm willing to take my chances."

And then he was kissing her, and time turned into an insignificant thing as his lips scorched her skin in delicious torture. Her grip tightened around him on instinct, and the sudden mad hunger, yet not for his blood, pooled into her core. She opened her mouth to him, and a soft sound escaped her throat as his tongue swept against hers.

She let him take everything as they felt each other and dragged pleasure from skin and heart. It was strange to feel loved entirely for being who she was and nothing more. It wasn't an act of trying with Jeremy, and that alone made the graze of his teeth against her neck ease a moan from her lips. Their clothing fell to the floor between kisses and soft bites, and soon they were on the floor, the scratchy rug hardly registering through the overwhelming desire coursing through her body.

The planes of muscle beneath smooth skin rippled as he knelt above her, and she trailed her palms along his shoulders and torso, then lower. A soft gasp pressed against her lips, and Jeremy broke away as her hand wrapped around him. Fire crackled behind his gaze, and the intensity in the small act was enough to make her feel insane.

"I don't think gentle lovemaking is our style," Frances purred, and used her nails to run down the length of him softly.

Jeremy let out a ragged breath, and the grin that graced his swollen lips was a dangerous thing indeed. It was a promise, and Frances wasn't quite sure if she was prepared for what that grin promised.

"No," Jeremy said, his tone low and rough. "I don't think that we're very gentle people."

"Thank the gods," Frances smirked, and tightened her grip slightly.

He let out a surprised gasp, and the fire roared behind his pools of midnight. "You're entirely unprepared for the position you have put yourself into."

"I hope many positions," Frances said, and dizzying pleasure swept across her skin as his body vibrated against her with laughter.

His lips pressed against her jaw, followed by teeth, then tongue. Gods, it was intoxicating. She let her hand move steadily, and it was all she could do not to guide him inside of her immediately. He seemed to read her thoughts, for one of the hands that was braced by her head moved to catch her wrist, the pressure of his grip sending more pleasure through her than imaginable.

"We have a few hours until we need to meet the others," Jeremy purred. "I'm in no rush."

"I'm expecting great things from you, Mister Nightingale," Frances replied, and for once in her life, she sounded breathless.

He let go of her wrist, and his fingers brushed against her apex, sending a tremor through her legs. A wicked grin grew on his lips, and Frances felt as though he were the animal, not she. Yet the heat and torturous slowness with which he kissed and touched her, combined with his darkness, made her heart swell, and she almost thought it would give one faint beat.

“The Devil hath power to assume a pleasing shape.”

- William Shakespeare, *Hamlet*

Chapter 47

Milo

It was time.

Moonlight cast a merry glow over the candlelit bedroom. Yet Milo felt nothing remotely close to merriment. He felt terror, thick and sticky, against his insides.

Sage tucked the last knife into his boot, and Milo watched this with the pressure of his own dagger pressed against his leg. It had been Jeremy's idea to be at least slightly armed, though Milo had a sneaking suspicion a meager blade would do little against someone who had sliced hearts out of chests.

"Do you think that it's going to work?" Milo asked, unable to take watching Sage's silent preparations any longer.

Sage straightened, meeting Milo's stare. "I think that you're more capable than you think."

Milo frowned. "That wasn't a very good answer."

Sage crossed the room, and soon they were held in each other's embrace. Milo let Sage's cold touch trail lazily across his own flaming skin, calming and soothing the parts of him that felt like they were on the verge of exploding. The worst part was that he wouldn't put it past the stardust in his veins to do such a thing.

Long fingers curled beneath Milo's chin, and his breath hitched as Sage guided him to look up. The complete trust on Sage's face did nothing to help his guilt, the secret that he was keeping. They had come up with a plan to find the killer, but they'd decided to rely on brute strength and brains to corner them and force them to confess. The knowledge that it wouldn't be enough whispered through Milo's bones, and the stardust answered.

They would truly hate him for this.

"We will succeed, and even if one of us dies, I know that we will be bound forever," Sage said. "I have to believe that."

Heat prickled behind Milo's eyelids, and he squeezed Sage's fingers. Gods, he felt so much for this man it hurt. A deep aching thing that both brought pleasure and more pain than he'd ever thought possible.

"How can you be so sure? How can you trust me like this?" Milo asked, unable to keep the question down any longer.

Sage smiled, though it was not one of humor. It was one of sadness, and of something that Milo could not put into words.

"Because I love you, Milo."

I love you.

The words sank into his skin, burrowing into the crevices of his heart. *I love you.* Was that the odd sensation that Milo was experiencing day after day? Such calm yet such concern that wasn't only for himself?

Sadness stretched beyond that something else, and Sage's palm drifted to Milo's thundering chest. "I'm not asking you to say it back, or even to return the sentiment. I only want you to know it, to know that you are loved even when it feels like the entire world is trying to crush you to the ground. I love you, Matthew Hale, no matter what comes of tonight, and no matter if you marry Frances in the morning. My heart belongs to you."

Lightning sizzled in Milo's veins, and sparks danced across his skin. Surprise crossed over Sage's face, but he didn't step back. Emotion, unlike anything else, swept through Milo's body, and the heat behind his eyelids threatened to burst. But he pushed it back, and it was easy to push down the magic, too. He was loved, and not only by someone who was forced to love him through blood or duty. It was everything, and yet he didn't know how to feel it. He didn't know how to receive it. And so, he stood, and scrambled for any tether of calm that was left in his frazzled heart.

Sage watched him, and only sadness remained. It was not disappointment nor fear, only sadness, and Milo had a feeling that it had been there long before they'd ever met. The knowledge tugged at him, and he cupped Sage's face on instinct, kissing him. It was not a soft kiss, nor one of passion and pleasure. It was a promise that this was not the end of them, even if it would be the end of him. Sage's hands bunched the fabric of Milo's shirt, and he allowed him to press their bodies closer as their skin spoke in a way no words ever could.

Milo pulled away first, and his voice was calm. "Let's end this, once and for all."

Frances and Jeremy were already waiting for them in the ballroom when Milo and Sage arrived. They stood close together, and the waves of both worry and happiness nearly radiated from both of them.

"You two were late," Jeremy mused, and Milo narrowed his eyes at their disheveled states.

"We were on time, actually. You were early."

"Which is surprising," Sage muttered.

"Come now," Jeremy sighed. "We don't want to be talking about such profane things when Malichi comes."

"Speaking of Malichi." Frances frowned. "He *is* late."

Unease swept through Milo's toes and curled around his stomach, making it clench uncomfortably. It had been risky enough to let him keep the book, let alone allow him to walk from his rooms to meet them alone. There was a killer on the loose after all.

"Are you sure he didn't return the book to Professor Binks?" Jeremy asked, and Frances shook her head.

"No, he is a man of his word, to his own detriment."

"We can wait a few minutes," Sage said. "He's a bit late, that's all."

His tone betrayed his casual words, and Milo knew that no one trusted the prince was simply late. Milo's skin suddenly felt like ants were crawling across it, and he adjusted the collar of his shirt. Silence enveloped them, which terrified Milo even further. Wisteria Manor was rarely silent, but now not even a ghost swept by.

"We should get into our places and hope that he comes soon," Jeremy said after a few minutes had come and gone with no sign of him.

Frances shook her head. "There is no plan if we don't have the book."

A strange tingling sensation crept up the back of Milo's neck, and his muscles stiffened on instinct. Now was not the time to lose his grip on reality, though he would be dreadfully unsurprised if the stardust decided to take him now. Yet after a moment, the tingling did not cease or grow stronger, and Milo frowned.

"What is it?" Jeremy and Sage asked in tandem.

The tingling spread across the back of his head, and Milo swore he heard whispers.

"Something's wrong," he said, as though it were the stardust speaking for him.

Frances huffed in a rather unimpressed manner, but Jeremy and Sage both narrowed their eyes, and Sage stepped closer. Milo barely registered it, but he was still utterly present.

"What is wrong?" Jeremy asked, and Milo shook his head.

"I don't—"

The sound of splintering wood and a male shout rattled through Milo's ears. Thumping and the sound of struggle followed the crash, and Milo watched numbly as Frances pivoted and sprinted toward the sound, her supernatural gifts making her look almost angelic as she tore out of sight.

"We should go after her," Jeremy said, and Milo didn't struggle against Sage as he took off behind Jeremy, dragging Milo behind.

Panting and low spitting curses that sounded all too similar to the voice of Malichi Baudelaire ricocheted off the narrow walls, and Milo squeezed his eyes shut as the tingling sensation strengthened against his head. It was as though the tingling were warning him, but of what, he didn't know.

Terror, sickly sweet, poured down Milo's throat as he staggered to a stop before the scene. Malichi cursed and growled in his native tongue from where he lay on the floor, a wooden stake punctured through his chest. The book was not on the floor, nor was it in the vampire's grasp.

Reality seemed to ripple and bend as Milo dragged his gaze upward to the person who held the book, her beautiful face now grotesque and far different from what Milo had known his entire life.

It was his mother.

"In a word, I was too cowardly to do what I knew to be right, as I had been too cowardly to avoid doing what I knew to be wrong."

- Charles Dickens, *Great Expectations*

Chapter 48

Frances

It wasn't her mother.

Relief, intense and almost overwhelming, heated Frances's worried heart, yet fear gripped it even stronger at the sight of her brother dying on the ground, as well as the queen of Cathair Liath clutching *The Book of Silver* in her bloody hands. It was Malichi's blood.

The queen stood frozen before them, and Frances could almost feel the confusion and anger radiating from both men standing at her side. Strands of straw-colored hair framed the queen's face in what would have perhaps been a complimenting manner, but now it only made her seem out of her mind.

"Mother?"

Milo's voice was a cracking whisper, and Frances felt a tug of sympathy for the man. Queen Esther straightened slightly, and the smile that was painted onto her crimson lips was almost believable. "Milo, what are you doing here?"

"We could ask you the same thing," Jeremy ground out. "Your *Majesty.*"

Malichi let out a choking sound, and fear dragged Frances

down to her brother's side. She reached out to him, but he let out a sputtering noise that could have been a *non* if he weren't spitting up blood. She knew that he wouldn't die if the stake hadn't touched his heart, yet it was likely still painful, and did appear awfully close to its intended mark.

"His death will come slowly," The queen said almost calmly. "It's only touching a corner of his heart."

Frances was surprised that Milo was still standing.

"It was you all along," Milo whispered, a feeble sound that barely escaped his mouth.

Frances tore her gaze from her brother's wound to rest on the queen, though she looked more like a demon. Her lips curled into a grimace, and she and Milo locked in a battle of stares.

"Everything I have done was for you, my darling," Esther said, her voice thick with unshed tears.

"How could cutting the hearts out of the people I love ever help me?" Milo cried. "You've hurt me more than you could have ever helped me."

Esther tightened her grip on the book, and Frances noticed that crimson smears stained her nails. Malichi let out another choke, and fear gripped her chest as she glanced back down at him. Anton's daggers pressed against her side in a silent command, and Frances hoped that her aim would be accurate enough if she had to use them.

"I'm going to get this out of you," Frances whispered, and Malichi shook his head.

"I wouldn't recommend that if I were you," Esther shot back. "The stake was carved from a torr tree."

Frances blanched, and she faltered mere inches from the stake. Torr trees were incredibly rare and known for their grotesquely humanlike limbs. When properly carved and honed, they were one of the only stakes that could kill vampires and most any creature with hellish blood. The tree was frequently harvested to create torture devices for the sickliest of sorts, and it burned vampires simply by touching it.

"I'll take it out," Jeremy said gruffly, and his entire body vibrated as though he were holding himself back from lunging at the queen.

"No," Frances snapped. "It will burn you too."

"I wouldn't go anywhere if I were you," Sage said calmly, and Frances looked up again to find Esther's back slightly turned to stare at Mister Astaseul.

Esther narrowed a glare at him, and her tone was close to hissing as she asked, "Why are you here?"

"To protect your son. A job *you* hired me to do," Sage replied with a tone so sharp it could cut.

Esther's lips almost disappeared as she pursed them, and her expression filled with distaste. "Step away from my son. I have no desire for your rudeness to tarnish his mind."

"I am an adult, Mother," Milo snapped. "And we're getting further from the point. Why have you done this?"

It was the most demanding he'd ever been in Frances's presence, as though the title of prince suited him perfectly. Power radiated from his skin, and the queen took a step back, her eyes widening.

"My dear boy, it has only ever been for you!" Esther cried, her grip tightening further around the book. "This place, this dirty realm, took us the night you were born. It tore us away from everything that could have been. A life of normalcy, where we could be a happy family."

Frances looked down at her brother, and fear made her stomach cramp. His skin had taken on a grayish tone, and his eyes were beginning to close. Gods be damned if she let him die because she was afraid of getting burned.

"What do you mean?" Milo asked in a hushed tone.

Esther took in a rattling breath, and Frances inched her shaking fingers toward the stake protruding from his chest.

"You don't understand what it was like, life on Earth," Esther began. "It was good, it was simple. Your father and I were young, and the circumstances of our union were less than ideal, but we were happy. We had little, but we could afford our own cottage in the countryside, and your father worked with one of the astronomers near Edinburgh.

We were both elated to welcome you into this world, though the pregnancy was less than smooth. I knew something was wrong the moment I was pregnant with you, like a strange itch at the back of my mind that would never go away."

"Why are you telling me this?" Milo blurted; his expression drawn.

Esther's attention was entirely on her son now, and Frances clenched her jaw as she wrapped her hand around the stake. Malichi's mouth gaped as pain bloomed across Frances's skin, but she clamped down on a whimper as she yanked the stake out. Malichi shut his eyes and doubled over, yet he didn't make a sound. Frances remained silent as well and carefully set the stake upon the blood-spattered floor. He straightened slowly and gave her a nod of thanks, though pain still cracked across his features. Jeremy's presence was taught behind her as she turned wrist to find a blistering burn across her palm, marring her smooth skin. She prayed that he wouldn't say anything, and she glanced up at him, ready to shut him down. But he only watched her with an intensity that she could only place as respect. Esther was speaking again, and Frances offered him a strained smile before they turned their attention back to the mad queen.

"You must understand, Milo," Esther began. "We weren't meant to live this life. We were never meant to mingle in a world with magic and creatures that belong in storybooks and nightmares." Her cutting glance at Sage made Milo stiffen visibly, but she continued.

"All I have ever wanted was to keep you safe and happy, Matthew. However, your father was always more interested in the planets than in our family, and we had no choice but to follow Lennora when she found us. We were forced into this world, Milo, not given it. Astrum should not exist at all. It is unnatural and feral, and I am tired of it."

"You could have left." Milo shrugged. "Though I don't understand how you dislike the title of queen stamped in front of your name."

"Matthew Rose Hale, you take that back!" Esther hissed. "I have stepped into the role that I was handed. I would have never done this if it weren't for you."

Milo shook his head, and Frances was impressed by the amount of nonchalance held in the simple movement.

How is he so collected when his world has just been shattered?

"Why were you so adamant about the union between Frances and me if you hate it here so much?" Milo asked. "Why didn't you force us all to leave Astrum in the night?"

Esther ran a hand down *The Book of Silver* as though she were stroking a cat, and the strange feral air about her returned in full force. "Because I realized this would be my chance to end things once and for all."

"How?" Milo asked, though Frances wasn't sure if she wanted to know the answer.

"Ever since we moved to Astrum, your father and I have grown apart," Esther began, and Frances fought the urge to look at Jeremy. She knew all too well how accurate the statement was.

"It is the worst feeling in the world, to love someone so dearly and watch them slowly fall out of love with you," Esther said softly. "I grew desperate, knowing our problems only began when we were brought here and handed an entire kingdom. You were growing older, and we both knew that you would become king the day the council deemed you fit to rule."

"But I would never have to become king if I weren't in Astrum," Milo finished, and Esther nodded.

"I began doing research and asked Lennora about the creation of this place, at first only wanting to find a way to get back to Earth. However, when she told me of the hidden doors within every city that led between realms, I decided that a more permanent solution was needed. I knew that both you and your father would want to come back, which is something I cannot have. That is when I learned about *The Book of Silver*. I learned of its power, and I discovered where it was hidden."

"That doesn't explain why you wanted our union," Milo said, confusion and hurt thick in his voice.

"You were never meant to marry her, not truly. I needed a way to get our family away from Rightford Castle, and a simple holiday with our current political climate was not something that I could believably do. We needed something larger, something that would grant the ability to change locations."

"So, it was you who went into my rooms that day?" Milo whispered. "You were the one who forced us to leave home."

"I had no intention of harming you, and Cathair Liath is *not* your home," Esther snapped, and Milo flinched as though he'd been struck across the face. She took in a steadying breath. "I knew you were doing your studies, but I needed to create a reason for us to move here, where the book was hidden."

"But why Frances?" Milo asked, and Frances wanted to know the answer as much as he did.

"Because they were born from demons, and any blood that flows through their veins inherently becomes hellish," Esther replied. "I had already decided to kill Lennora and Lyra to find the book, but I needed more blood from hell to activate it."

"You wicked *bitch*," Jeremy snarled, and Esther turned to him without an inch of remorse.

"Your mother was the reason my family was thrown into this disgusting place," Esther snapped. "And your cousin was always getting into more trouble than she was worth. She had discovered my secret and was about to tell the entire Baudelaire clan before I stopped her. Permanently."

"I will never-"

"Be quiet!" Esther snapped with a stomp of her foot.

Frances's blood boiled, and it was all she could do not to rip off the queen's head. Esther and Jeremy stared each other down for a few moments, but Jeremy remained silent, and Esther continued.

"Those two were thorns in my side from the beginning, and since the only thing they ever wanted to do was help, they got their wish. The other two were simple sacrifices, though I do feel sorry for their families. However, if we, a family with most of our court containing heavenly blood, were to mingle with a family of vampires, it would be easy to find one last sacrifice for the book."

"So, you only wished for us to be around the Baudelaire clan so that you could pick them off one by one?" Milo asked in repulsion.

Frances felt sick.

"When you are a queen, you have power, and I wielded mine. The Baudelaires are an ancient bloodline, which means the power that transfers into their blood is more than that of a regular hellborn. I need that power to do what I must."

"And what exactly must you do?"

It was Malichi who spoke now, and he stood with no more than a wince. Esther's eyes widened, but only for a second before her haughty composure returned.

"I told you not to do that," Esther said, attention flicking onto Frances.

"I've never been one to follow the rules." Frances retorted with a wicked grin that she hoped hid her terror.

Her hand slid to the leather belt at her sides, and the blades sheathed there. Hot stinging pain bloomed on her skin as blisters connected with the leather-bound hilt of *tormenta,* but she kept her pain to herself.

"What are you planning, mother?" Milo demanded.

This seemed to shake Esther from her disappointment, and she clutched the book in her arms tighter. "I'm going to destroy Astrum."

The world fell from under Frances's feet, but she managed to remain standing. If the book that had created their very existence wasn't held in Esther's grasp, Frances might have laughed. Yet the hatred that radiated from her being only made Frances gulp and tighten her grip on the dagger.

"What?" Jeremy and Malichi bellowed in tandem.

What indeed.

"No."

Milo's voice was so loud that it reverberated through the walls and crashed through Frances's ears. She thought she might have stumbled back again, and briefly registered Jeremy's hand wrapping around her waist for support or comfort, she didn't know.

"It's the only way, Matthew," Esther said, her tone holding no sadness. "And you cannot stop me anyhow."

"Yes, I can, and I will," Milo ground out, but Esther shook her head.

"No, my dear, for it is already done."

Before anyone could react, Esther lifted an arm and brought it to her mouth. The sound of skin tearing between teeth made Frances shudder, but the queen didn't do so much as grunt slightly as she lifted her arm, now dripping in blood. Horror froze Frances's bones as her gaze fell to the queen's fingers and her brother's blood that remained on them.

Human blood was considered heavenly in ancient texts, and the combination of her blood and Malichi's was all that was needed to destroy Astrum.

Before she could think twice, Frances ripped the dagger from her belt and threw it, though rather clumsily. Anton's proclamations were correct, however, and the blade rightened itself before connecting with its target. The queen's scream shook the very air, and for a moment, Frances thought they might be safe.

She was wrong to doubt a furious woman.

Blood dripped to the floor from the open wound in Esther's side, but the queen stood again on shaking legs, pained determination etched in her angular features. Frances glanced at Milo, though it seemed that he wasn't terribly put out by the fact that she had just stabbed his mother. Faint lines of tension marked his body in a silent desire to run to her, but Frances knew he would do no such thing.

Esther glared at Frances, and her teeth shone red with her own blood.

"Foolish girl."

"Mother, don't do this!" Milo yelled and started forward.

"Don't move a muscle," Malichi growled to Frances. "We must wait until we're needed."

"What does that even mean?" Frances asked, but Malichi only shook his head.

"It is the only way, Milo," Esther gasped. "The entire body must be burned for the virus to be cleansed away. Astrum must be destroyed for things to go back to normal."

Esther muttered a word in a language Frances didn't know and wiped her bloodied arm across the silver binding of *The Book of Silver*. "Only then will our family be happy."

She muttered another word and switched the book to her other hand, muttering a different word as she wiped Malichi's blood over hers.

Nothing happened.

A relieved laugh escaped from Frances's lips, and she sagged against Jeremy slightly. It hadn't worked. They were safe.

Malichi took a step forward. "Your lunatics are over, Your Majesty."

"They are far from over, Your *Highness*," Esther spat and opened the tome.

The air exploded into a wall of light and wind, and Frances gasped. The force sent her flying onto her back, her bones slamming to the marble floor. She gasped, pain lighting through her bones, and the sting of icy heat coiled around her face. She blinked rapidly, and soon the light dimmed slightly so that she could see, if only slightly. Esther gave out a wild cry of laughter, and Frances scrambled onto her hands and knees.

"We need to stop her, *now!*"

Jeremy groaned from a few feet away, and Frances opened her eyes as wide as she could to see him. His outline was beginning to grow clearer, though even her extended sight was struggling against the blinding light.

"Mother!"

It was Milo's voice through the humming silence, and Frances whipped her head around to see the faint sight of the queen lying in a heap a few feet away from the book, now lying open on the floor.

Esther sprang up as though she woke from a nap and lunged for the book. Yet Milo's unruly curls were visible as he, too, sprang for it, and soon mother and son were locked onto either end of the world's salvation, and its end.

"Milo, don't."

It was Sage's calm voice that rang out now, and Frances gritted her teeth against the strange thickness that seeped into the air. It must have been from Milo's touch against *The Book of Silver*, as everything suddenly felt slower, as though she were attempting to move through honey.

"You would be wise to listen to your friend," Esther panted. "Let me end this, Milo, let me save our family."

Milo let out a pained sound, and the light pulsed around them before dimming just enough for Frances to see clearly. The air still felt thick, however, and she was beginning to feel the familiar panic of being trapped.

"I can't let you do this," Milo gasped. "Everything that I love is here. *Everyone.*"

Esther's face twisted. "You should only need your father and me. I know you never wished to marry the girl, and you don't have any friends."

Jeremy spat a curse at the queen then, and Frances wished she could move closer. But she couldn't, and it was the worst sort of torture.

"You murdered my friends!" Milo shouted. "You know nothing of love, and you know nothing of me, it seems."

"Matthew," Esther admonished, her features stricken with shock.

"No!" Milo snapped. "You know *nothing* of my desires, my life, nothing. Did you not stop to consider if Father and I would *want* to leave Astrum? Did you ever consider the fact that for the first time in my life, I'm *happy?*"

He let out a wild laugh, and Frances felt a tug in her chest for Milo that surprised her.

"I'm happy, mother, throughout the loss and pain that you have created. I can now feel joy in things, and I *genuinely care* for these people. I care for this place, for all the innocent creatures you deem unnatural. They are worthy of life; they are worthy of protection. And I will *not* stand by and let you destroy everything that I love simply because you are unhappy with your own life."

Esther's face slowly drained of all emotion as he spoke, and

Frances felt the danger before it came. The queen lifted her hand even through the thick air, a droplet of blood hovering from her skin, a second from dropping.

"I'm sorry," was her only reply before the blood dropped, and she uttered a single word. "*Bhás.*"

The world exploded again, and this time Frances felt it in her soul. It was the sensation of a thousand splinters embedding into her bones and pulling outward again, yet this time carrying her skin with it. A scream tore from her lips, and the pain was dizzying. She blinked quickly as the cries of her brother, Sage, and Jeremy echoed through the air in a horrifying song. Esther crumbled against the floor, her matted blonde hair shrouding her face.

Milo did not scream, however. Even through the cracks in the air lined with molten silver and the slow crumbling of the walls, Milo did not say a word. His lips quirked upward, and Frances knew what he was going to do.

"Milo, don't!" She screamed in tandem with Sage and Jeremy.

But their calls went unanswered by the prince. He moved through the breaking air with the ease of a skilled dancer and withdrew a small dagger from his belt. A dry sob tore through Frances's chest, though not only from the pain of the crumbling realm and her own body.

The blade made contact with Milo's skin, and he didn't even blink as the top of his hand welled with shimmering blood. The crimson pulsed with light as it slowly rolled toward the silver pages below.

"Milo, please," Sage sobbed. "Please don't do this."

Milo only turned to face the vampire, smiling. "I love you, Sage."

And then his blood rolled onto the page.

The pain was gone. In fact, everything was gone, the light, the silver cracks, the strange thickness in the air.

Gone.

Frances scrambled to her feet and scrambled to Malichi, as Jeremy and Sage were already surrounding Milo and the now closed book. Her brother lay on the floor, blinking as though he were waking from a restful sleep. The wound in his chest was gone, and the gray sheen had also left his skin.

"Are you all right?" Frances asked breathlessly, and Malichi shuddered.

"I thought it was going to be the end."

"I did too."

Malichi opened his mouth, and the guilt and relief in his expression made Frances reach for him. She knew what he wanted to say, as their minds were tethered, no matter how much both hated it.

"Later," Frances said, and Malichi dipped his chin.

She turned back to the hunched figures of Jeremy and Sage, and the queen's limp body. Frances stood and approached, though worry crawled down her throat at the silence in the air.

The queen's pale arm was draped over *The Book of Silver*. There was no longer a bite mark on her arm, nor the blade or wound in her side, but she didn't move at all. The familiar scent of death wafted through Frances's nose, and she shivered slightly. She felt no triumph for the queen's death, surprisingly, only pity and sadness.

Frances tore her gaze away from the fallen queen and went to stand by Jeremy, who held Milo's limp body in his arms. Milo's eyes were closed, and his hand that was now held in Sage's was free of any wound or blood.

The prince looked peaceful.

Too peaceful.

"What's wrong?" Frances asked, looking down at Jeremy.

Only then did she realize his shoulders were trembling with silent sobs.

Sage looked up at her, and heart-wrenching clarity filled his face. His expression was not clouded with pain, no. It was the worst kind of clarity, the most excruciating sense of presence that one could experience.

Jeremy did not respond, though Frances almost didn't want to hear the words that floated from Sage's mouth as the vampire blinked down at the man who had loved him.

"Milo is dead."

"Our souls sing together. Not one over the other, and not one sings louder or quieter. They are the same, your soul and mine. Both cracked and frayed around the edges, though strong and ready to fight through life. Yet we do not have to fight through life when we are together. No, my love, when we are together our souls dance."

- Matthew Rose Hale, *The Infinite Galaxy*

Chapter 49

The stardust boy opened his eyes, and the galaxy said hello.

Winking lights danced and glittered against his skin, placing soft kisses over his bruised and battered heart. Yet, as the boy took in a breath of starlight, he noticed that his heart hurt no longer.

He felt at peace, but something was missing.

The boy could not put a finger on the strange sense of lacking in this place of dancing lights, and so he stood from his bed of sunset.

The boy walked, though he didn't know where he was going, and the stars followed him. The boy passed by planets and meteors and swam through oceans of black holes and darkness. Yet he did not stop, though he did not know where he was going.

There was only a pull in his chest, and he followed it.

Time passed, though it was nothing to the stardust boy, as he felt nothing but peace and that strange sense of lacking. Eventually, he came across an ocean of glittering stones, which turned into a city. The boy walked through the silent city, filled with beings that made no sound.

In fact, it seemed as though they didn't know he existed at all.

A field of silver soon stretched out as far as he could see, and the boy walked. A voice rang out through the silence after some time, which made the boy stop. For he knew nothing but silence, but now there was sound.

Come.

The stardust boy followed it, and through the fields of silver stood a figure bathed in moonlight. Another figure appeared in one blink, though this one was swathed in flowers made of shadows and starlight. They beckoned him forth, and so the boy went.

The two figures smiled when the boy stopped before them, but he did not smile back. Both figures were taller than he by many feet, and both bore a sense of power that made something tickle the back of the boy's memory, though he didn't remember these two beings.

The one swathed in moonlight was a woman, with hair as sleek as water and skin glowing from within. The one bathed in flowers was male, his dark skin glowing and laced in mesmerizing patterns. They were both beautiful, and the boy recognized them, though he did not know how.

"Am I dead?" the boy asked, and the gods smiled.

"You are, dear child," the woman replied, and her voice was the sound of love and rippling water.

The boy knew he should be sad by this news, frightened even. Yet he felt nothing other than a pulse of that strange lack. The god in starlit flowers stepped forward now, and the smile that painted his dark lips made Milo want to do the same.

"You have saved an entire dimension, dear boy," the god said, and his voice was like honey and wine. "For this, we shall grant you a blessing."

"Who are you?" the boy asked, unable to take the strange sense of familiarity he felt for them.

The moonlit woman spoke. "I am Odona, goddess of moonlight and love, and this is my brother, Akiru, god of luck and miracles.

"I thought the gods were gone," the boy said, and he thought it might be appropriate to feel something by saying this, but still, there was nothing.

The gods shook their heads, and Akiru spoke. "Sleeping, not gone. Odona and I are the only ones who have woken. We have you to thank for that."

"I woke you?" the stardust boy asked, and the gods nodded.

"Your blood against the book woke us," Odona replied. "We suppose it is because you placed your blood on a page with both of our names upon it."

"The book has not been wielded by a stardust soul in millennia," Akiru said, and though his voice was sugary sweet, it sliced through the galaxy with such strength that the boy shivered. "Your touch was a blessing, yet you must be careful."

"Why must I be careful if I'm already dead?" the boy asked.

"Because you will not be dead for long," Odona said. "You feel a sense of lacking, do you not?"

The stardust boy paused, then nodded once. The goddess spread her arms out as if in an embrace.

"It is love missing from your heart that you sense, dear one," Odona said. "You are still far too loved down there to stay here. For some, it doesn't matter that many love them, yet I sense incompletion in the love you have left to give."

The boy didn't know what to say, so he didn't answer with words. Yet the strange sense of a lack in his chest pulsed, and he seemed to remember eyes of swirling hazel and ones of darkest blue. The goddess gave him a knowing nod.

"For this, I will grant you a miracle, and luck will follow as long as you stay on the crooked path," Akiru spoke now.

"I need no luck," the boy said. "For I am already forgetting what it is to be alive."

"Which is why I must act quickly," Akiru said. "We must begin our search for our brothers and sisters soon, and you must return to the ones who carry your heart."

The boy took a step toward the gods. The sense of familiarity swam through his soul, and the boy spoke. "Why do I know you without knowing you?"

Odona stepped closer to the boy and leaned over him. Her body moved like water, and her lips were soft as silk as she placed a kiss upon his forehead. A tingling sensation worked its way down the boy's body, and he began to feel the sense of lacking grow into something different, something sweeter.

"You know us because you are our son," Odona said, stepping back. "Though we slept, we chose to put our essence in your soul, which made you one of us by nature."

Akiru stepped forward now, and the boy felt a jolt of something familiar. Something human that made him blink. Akiru reached out a hand, and the boy took it.

"You will always be different; it is as evident as the change from day to night. Yet this is not something to be ashamed of. You have gifts to share, things to say, and do that will rattle the infinite galaxy. And if you ever feel alone as you return to life, remember that we are watching you, guiding you."

The boy blinked his understanding.

"Very well then," Akiru said and stepped away from the boy.

Two presences appeared at his sides, and that sense of lacking pulsed as the boy looked upon two familiar faces. Even in death, they were vibrant, and the boy took a step toward the fallen witches. The older witch smiled, flaming hair sweeping behind her back like a waterfall. The younger witch took her mother's hand and winked at the boy.

"I'm sorry," the boy said, though he couldn't remember why.

The older witch shook her head. "Do not apologize. Our deaths were not your fault."

"But you are dead," the boy said. "And there are those who still love you far too much in the living world."

The younger girl laughed now, and it sounded like wind chimes in a light breeze. "We know that we are loved, yet we have no desire to return to the mortal world."

"You do, however," the older witch said to the boy. "And you must go soon before it's too late."

The boy looked between Akiru and Odona, and they took a step back in unison. The witches stepped closer, and something heavy settled in the boy's chest, though he did not know why. These two women had been important to him. He loved them. Yet he could feel no such thing, and the strange heaviness grew.

"Tell my boy that we love him," the older witch said, her voice soft and warm. "We will watch over the two of you forever. Tell him he must live, that he must choose life above all else."

The boy nodded, and the lacking pulsed. This boy that she spoke of needed him to return, and the knowledge of this was almost overwhelming in this place of infinite nothing. "I will tell him."

The girl gave him a knowing look and stepped closer to her mother. "And you, you must choose your heart above all else."

The boy nodded again, and Akiru stepped forward. "It is time."

The older witch moved to embrace the boy. He let her come close, and the heaviness grew still. He felt the faint sensation of her lips brushing over his forehead, in the same spot where Odona had kissed him. The world shattered, and the boy distantly heard the woman's whisper as he fell into oblivion.

"I love you, Milo."

"ONLY TO LIVE, TO
LIVE AND LIVE! LIFE,
WHATEVER IT MAY BE!"

- Fyodor Dostoyevsky, *Crime and Punishment*

Chapter 50

Milo

October 31, 1880

Oxygen trickled through broken lungs, and Milo took his first breath.

Dull pain pulsed through his chest, and it was a struggle to peel his eyelids open. Dusk bathed the room in a soft glow, and he found himself lying on his bed. A single pillow caressed his head, and silk sheets nestled over his legs. Another pained breath pushed through his body, and Milo grimaced.

But he was alive, and that was all that mattered.

He glanced around to find that he wasn't alone; in fact, the room was filled with familiar faces that made his chest ache. Penn sat in a chair, his chest rising and falling with the even tenor of sleep. His father was seated on a stool, his head resting against the wall. His dark skin was ashen, and his thick, coiled hair was ruffled.

Jeremy and Frances stood in an embrace, the vampire's

head resting heavily upon Jeremy's chest. Their eyes were both closed, and tears stained Jeremy's cheeks as he swayed slightly.

Even Malichi and Daithine were present, Malichi perusing a thick book by the far wall, and Daithine sitting at his father's feet in a rather unfashionable way, her cheek resting on his knee.

The ache in Milo's chest grew as he watched them in silence. He'd never fully realized how many people cared about him, and seeing everyone now made heat prickle behind his eyes.

But something was missing, or rather someone.

Where was Sage?

Milo glanced about once more, but there was no sign of him. Panic bloomed in his chest, and Milo forgot about the fact that he'd been dead less than five minutes ago. He began to move, but a weight was draped across his chest. With a wince of effort, Milo tilted his head down to see what was stopping him, and relief made a gasp tear through his dry throat.

It was Sage, his head resting against Milo's chest. He seemed to have fallen asleep. Milo didn't know how he hadn't realized this sooner, yet the god was so still that it had been as though he were a statue.

Milo gulped and lifted a shaking hand to brush the hair from Sage's forehead, and the locks were silky smooth against his shaking fingers. The ache pulsed and grew, and the heat behind Milo's eyelids came close to bursting.

"Milo?"

The gruff voice sounded from beyond the stone table, and Milo looked up to find Jeremy watching him in wide-eyed amazement. The world blurred, and only his friend remained. Milo's lips curled upward, though even that was an effort. His heart pulsed rapidly, and Sage shifted.

"Don't tell me you were worried," Milo said, and Jeremy let out a cry of relief that made Milo laugh with true joy.

Frances uncoiled from Jeremy's arms and stared at Milo in disbelief. "*Putain*, Milo, you were dead!"

"Sorry to disappoint." Milo croaked, and Jeremy tightened as though he were keeping himself from rushing to the table.

Sage stirred again, and the weight left Milo's chest. Milo dropped his gaze, and the tears fell to his cheeks as he met Sage's stare. It was like taking his first breath all over again, yet this time with the soft caress of sunlight greeting him awake. Lines of worry and pain washed away from Sage's face like the tide, and only the open expression of relief and love remained.

"Sage," Milo whispered, and the name felt like a prayer on his lips.

Sage moved like lightning, and Milo felt his strength return as Sage kissed him, and Milo wrapped his arms around him. Their bodies pressed together, and both arms and lips held each other as they met again. Sage's lips were like a breath of life, and his embrace was the only home that Milo would ever need. Tears flowed down Milo's cheeks, and he tasted his own joy on his lips as he and Sage broke apart.

"You were dead," Sage said softly. "I heard your heart stop beating."

Milo could only stare, and it was his father who tore through the silence.

"Thank the gods, how are you feeling, son?"

Malichi had closed his book, and Daithine rose to stand by Duncan's seat, though the king seemed like he was about to jump out of it.

Milo met his father's gaze, grimacing against the ache in his bones. "I feel some pain."

Sage tensed at his side, and Milo took the boy's hand, squeezing it. He almost gasped at their touching skin, and the love in his heart galloped wildly. Jeremy walked over now and sat on the other side of the bed.

"You saved our lives," Jeremy said.

But his mother had died in the crossfire. Sorrow pelted against Milo's insides, and he didn't stop the tears from falling. He looked at his father again, and Duncan seemed to read his thoughts as though he were reading a book.

"I'm sorry, Father," Milo said quietly.

Duncan gave him a sad smile. "Don't apologize for doing the right thing, Milo."

"But Mother is gone because of me," Milo choked, and another warm hand enveloped his free one.

Jeremy squeezed gently. They'd both lost their mothers in such a short amount of time, and it was a loss only they would share. Neither death had been a heroic one, and both had died out of blindness and misunderstanding.

"Your mother was gone for a long time before that," Duncan replied. "The real Esther left many years ago, and only a mind full of mad 'what ifs' remained."

But she was still his mother, and he missed her. Even through her madness, he would never see her again. Yet Milo understood his father's feelings of acceptance just as much as he understood his mother's mad desires.

"You saved Astrum, and for that, we are all forever indebted to you," Duncan spoke again. "I have always been proud of you, Milo. What you did was more than admirable."

"You aren't angry?" Milo asked, and he looked at each person in the room.

Penn, who now stood trembling in the doorway. Malichi, with his arms crossed, and Frances, Jeremy, and Sage all standing around what would have remained his resting place before he was laid in the ground. Yet as he asked this, there was no anger on their faces, not a flake of animosity.

"I was furious," Jeremy said, and the truth in his words

was nearly palpable. "But I understood why you did it, which only made me sad that I couldn't mock you for your sudden heroics."

Milo chuckled. His friend returned the gesture, and relief, pain, and something that Milo could now see was love, molded his face into something beautiful.

"I wasn't angry," Sage said, and Milo turned his head, surprise trickling through his chest. But Sage was smiling, and Milo wanted so very badly to be in his arms again. "I was happy knowing that you learned the greatest thing of all, and that you chose your heart and the love you felt for this place above anything or anyone else."

The words hit him like a blow, and Milo was speechless again. He had so much to say, but he could not find the words. And so, he smiled, and Sage's face lit up like a brilliant sun.

"I do love you," Milo said softly. "More than I can say, I love you."

Sage's throat bobbed, and he bent down again to brush a kiss against Milo's lips. *I love you*, the touch said, and they needed no words for Milo to understand.

The realization that Duncan and Daithine were still in the room made Milo freeze as Sage straightened again, but there was no frown or anger on his father's face, only understanding.

"Father, I—"

"There is no need to explain, Milo," Duncan said. "I have known for some time now, which is why I must tell you that your mother and I stopped being faithful to each other for many years."

He knew this in his heart already, yet hearing it still stung. "Will the wedding still happen?"

Duncan and Daithine exchanged a glance, and Milo frowned at the weight held between their gazes. Frances and

Jeremy stiffened, but they remained silent as everyone watched the king and queen's silent conversation.

"Yes, there will still be a wedding," Duncan said finally, and the room seemed to darken further.

"However, it will not be today," Daithine spoke now. "And you are not marrying my daughter."

"What?" Malichi spoke now, his tone tired, not angry.

Daithine looked at Malichi, then Frances. Embarrassment painted her face as her gaze landed on her daughter, and Frances raised her eyebrows expectantly. Milo only felt confusion now, and he waited with bated breath.

"Queen Daithine and I have grown closer during this time," Duncan said slowly.

"That's an understatement," Frances muttered, and her mother said something in French that Milo could only guess was vulgar.

Duncan tensed slightly before saying, "We have discussed this extensively, and if I had known the depth of Esther's discontent, I would have offered her a legal separation. And as sad as today might be, I think we could all use a bit of celebration."

"Are you saying that you wish to marry my mother?" Malichi asked, and it was the first time that Milo had ever seen the steely man look shocked.

Daithine placed a hand on Duncan's shoulder, the touch tender.

"Our countries are still in political strain with the rest of Astrum, and the joining of our families would help both of our standings greatly. I have known what it is to wish for a life that is just out of reach, while marriage dragged me back. Cesaire granted me the life I wanted, and it is my duty to give my children the same opportunity."

"Are you serious about this?" Malichi asked, and some of his dangerous brooding returned.

"We are," Duncan said, and Milo shivered at the earnestness in his voice. "I wish to marry Daithine, and I wish for our courts to join forces and help each other. After all, it would be no use in going through this mess without an actual marriage at the end."

Daithine scowled at him, and Duncan offered her a bashful smile. She couldn't hide the upturn of her lips, though, and the energy between them was clear enough to see. Daithine turned to Malichi then, but the prince was no longer angry.

"It would still give us the union and strength that we need," Malichi began slowly. "And I suppose that it doesn't matter if you two are joined, as you are both widowed."

"Thank you, dear," Daithine said, and Duncan nodded.

"It will be put in legal binding that once my time is over and my spirit leaves this earthly plane, Milo will still become the king of Cathair Liath."

Relief, unlike anything else, swept through Milo's bones, and he thought he might fly. He was free to love whom he wanted, though not entirely free to be *who* he wanted. He would still be a prince, and eventually a king. But the freedom of his heart was enough for now, and life felt just a bit less bleak than before.

"You look tired, my son," Duncan said finally and stood from his seat. "We should let you rest."

Milo realized that he was, in fact, exhausted. Who would have thought that being briefly dead could make one tired? Daithine and Duncan filed out of the room, and Milo nodded as they murmured something about the wedding the next day. But he didn't care, not right now. He was safe, and he was free.

Malichi peeled himself from the wall and took a single step forward. Milo stiffened, prepared for a rebuke from the prince. Yet instead, Malichi bowed.

"Thank you for saving my family," Malichi said, and turned away before Milo could say anything, though he wasn't sure that anything other than a surprised laugh would have come out.

Now only Frances, Jeremy, and Sage remained, and Milo felt like he could finally breathe again.

"So, I suppose this means that we're no longer required to tolerate each other," Frances said, though a mischievous gleam shone in her eyes.

"I suppose." Milo sighed. "Pity, though. I was beginning to like you."

Frances snorted, but her gaze softened, and her smile became genuine. "I won't say thank you because the word has turned into mush in my ears, but I'm glad that you came back. It's not every day that your fiancé turns into a friend instead."

Milo blinked in surprise, but he found that what she said was true. She had become his friend through it all, even if she still scared him.

Milo looked at Jeremy, and the memory of Lennora and Lyra in the Infinite Galaxy prickled at his heart. But it wasn't time to tell him yet, not when the first inklings of joy were beginning to return to his friend's weary body.

"So, now that you're free, will you two finally admit that you're in love with each other?" Milo asked instead, and Jeremy laughed.

"I don't think you have any right to ask that question," Jeremy said, glancing pointedly between Milo and Sage.

Sage's grip tightened slightly against Milo, and he spoke. "We already told each other, if you haven't forgotten."

"True," Jeremy grinned and squeezed Milo's hand once again before letting it go and getting to his feet. "That's not to say we haven't either."

He angled his head toward Frances, and she was watching him with something like nervousness, as well as something rather innocent and girlish, which made Milo want to snort at how unnatural it looked.

"We should let you be," Jeremy said and placed his palm at the small of Frances's back. "We'll see you at the wedding."

Milo smiled at Jeremy, and a knowing weight passed between them. They were each other's rocks, their shields against the harshest of storms. They needed no words to speak of the love between them, and their simple nods were enough.

The door clicked shut behind them, and Milo let out a sigh. *I'm alive. I'm free.* Yet the thought of freedom suddenly felt daunting, and fear threatened to clamp down on him all too soon.

"Master Milo," Penn said in a wobbling voice once everyone had cleared the room. "Is there anything ye need, anything at all?"

Milo shook his head. "Only rest for now, thank you, Penn."

His manservant bowed deep enough for the tips of his wispy hair to brush against the floor, and he scurried away in seconds.

Milo turned to Sage and found the vampire watching him. They stared at each other, and Milo's chest nearly burst.

"Stay with me?"

The words were barely a whisper, but he knew Sage heard them nonetheless. Milo's skin felt like it was on fire as the vampire curled next to him, and they turned on their sides to watch each other.

"You're free," Sage said, and Milo shook his head.

"*We're* free."

Sage's gaze flashed in surprise, and Milo grinned. "I don't wish to be free on this planet without you by my side. It would be like living without my left leg, doable, yet clearly missing something."

Sage raised his eyebrows. "You're comparing me to your left leg?"

"I was just dead a few minutes ago, give my swagger a moment to return," Milo shrugged, though he couldn't contain his small chuckle.

Sage leaned forward and brushed his lips against Milo's, and shivers rushed through every cell in his body. Milo pressed closer, wrapping his arms around Sage's waist and bringing their bodies flush together. The feeling in his chest vibrated, and soon, a blinding light burst across his vision, though he didn't care. For he was alive, and he was free. They broke apart, and the light dimmed, though it didn't entirely disappear.

"I was freed the second you became mine," Sage whispered, and Milo understood without knowing.

Their hearts danced as their bodies rested, and even the ghosts slept as peace fell over Wisteria Manor once more.

"ONCE AGAIN... WELCOME TO MY HOUSE. COME FREELY. GO SAFELY; AND LEAVE SOMETHING OF THE HAPPINESS YOU BRING."

- Bram Stoker, *Dracula*

Chapter 51

Frances

November 1, 1880

Sunshine smiled down upon Wisteria Manor, seeping light into the bones of weary souls.

Frances couldn't help the sense of giddiness that swept through her skin as she sat before her vanity, putting the final touches on her hair and face. There was to be a wedding after all; she had never been one to pass up the opportunity to look good. Well, now that she knew *she* was not the one getting married.

Exhaustion still left her body slightly sluggish, but her vision was clear and her mind sharp. The events of the night before had only confirmed how badly she wanted to live her truth, and it proved how little everything she'd thought to be so important truly mattered.

Milo had sacrificed himself for them, and Frances couldn't explain the strange medley of emotions that had ravaged her soul. She had been terrified of the end; of everything she knew disappearing and turning to ash. It was not a heroic thing to feel, not like those in ancient storybooks, though Frances didn't care. She was not some gallant savior who was utterly selfless and cared not for their own life. She'd never had the chance to try living, and the realization had caused her more horror than even the end of the world.

She shook herself as the door to her rooms opened and Malichi entered. Frances considered her brother, noting the slight changes in his movements and the set of his jaw. There was a lightness about her brother that made Frances want to hug him.

"I thought I'd be the one in a wedding gown today," Frances said as a matter of greeting.

"As did I," Malichi agreed. "But our mother has always been full of surprises."

Frances snorted and stood from the vanity to give her midnight-blue dress a twirl. "What do you think?"

"It's different from your usual red," Malichi said and lifted his arm for her to take.

"I think we've all had enough red for a while," Frances said with a shiver, and Malichi gave a throaty *hmm* in reply.

"How are you feeling?" Frances asked.

Alas, he'd been stabbed in the chest not a day ago.

"Good as new. It appears that *The Book of Silver* thought I needed mending."

"Whatever happened to it?" Frances asked, and worry prickled at her insides.

She'd left with Sage and Milo immediately after the prince had died, and Malichi had met them a few minutes later, appearing relieved but too tired to speak.

"The book is safe," he said slowly. "Professor Binks and I found it another room for the time being, though we had the help of a young ghost girl who wouldn't stop talking."

Frances let out a chuckle and squeezed her brother's arm. "I might have met her once or twice."

They walked to the grand ballroom in silence, though the sounds of excited chatter and lilting music filtered in as they entered. Nerves sang through Frances's veins as she scanned the space, hoping to catch a glimpse of familiar red hair or a clenched jaw.

White flowers were strung across the walls and over the windows, and council members from each court stood on both sides of the green velvet aisle, waiting for the procession to begin. It was odd to be in this room again in such a different state, as her life had been all too different the first time she'd entered it.

Jeremy had hated her for one, but now, as she spotted him through the crowd, standing next to Milo, his blooming smile made Frances feel like she might fly. Malichi seemed to notice where her gaze landed, and he patted her hand twice before stepping away.

"I will make sure our mother is ready," he said and took a step back.

Frances caught her brother before he could escape and flung her arms around his neck. She rested her cheek on his shoulder, and eventually, his arms wrapped around her back.

"Thank you," she whispered, and she hoped that he understood the weight behind her words.

Malichi squeezed her lightly and drew away, and a new light gleamed behind his eyes. He pressed his lips together and stepped away again. "Go now, before anyone begins to think we Baudelaire's are sentimental."

Frances grinned, and Malichi disappeared through the crowd. She stiffened at the presence behind her back, and she turned to find Jeremy walking toward her.

"Should I stumble into you for old time's sake?" Frances asked, and Jeremy's expression widened into a wicked grin.

"Only if you curse in French again," he said and leaned down to brush a kiss against her cheek. "I found it oddly attractive."

Frances gave him a wink, hoping it would make her toes uncurl. Just the sight of him made her stomach pool with desire, but she shoved it down. But how could she not want him, in his crisp midnight blue coat that fit perfectly over his broad shoulders and tapered waist?

"We're matching," Frances noted, and Jeremy's eyes perused her body as though she were his next meal.

She would arrange just that later in the night.

"Good," Jeremy said when he finally looked up at her again. "Everyone will know we're here together."

Frances couldn't hide the surprise on her face, and Jeremy laughed. He offered his arm to her, and she took it, though they didn't move.

"Are you certain?" Frances asked, and she sounded more unsure and tentative than she had in her entire life.

It wasn't a question of her wants. No, she knew what her own heart felt. His and Malichi's well-being had been the two other things on her mind before Milo had saved them.

They watched each other now, predator and darkness held in a silent conversation. He drew her closer and dipped his head down so that his lips brushed her ear. "I was sure the moment we met."

Frances shivered but laughed and continued to do so as Jeremy straightened and led her toward Milo and Sage.

"You wanted to murder me when we met, not bed me," she said, and Jeremy chuckled.

Sage's attention perked as they neared, and an easy curiosity washed over his face. "I think there's been quite enough murder in these walls as of late, though not enough bedding."

Milo whirled on him, his dark skin flushing. "Sage, shut up."

But Sage only laughed, and the warmth of Jeremy's arm traveled to her heart at the sight of Milo and Sage standing together with such ease. It was clear they belonged together, shadow and light in perfect harmony. Milo appeared healthy and fed, and she had to admit he cut a striking figure in his silver and dark green coat. Sage, too, was quite dapper in the customary black jacket and pants of those who worked in The Study.

"You look well," Frances said to Milo, and he met her stare with a nonchalant shrug.

"I feel well."

"I was trying to be polite." Frances sighed, and Milo raised his eyebrows.

"That would be the first time."

They both laughed now, and Frances squeezed his shoulder. "Oh, Milo, I think I do actually like you."

"Hopefully not too much," Jeremy said easily, and Frances nudged him playfully with her shoulder.

Milo cleared his throat and stepped closer to Sage, who wound their fingers together in an almost unconscious way. But Frances only felt soaring joy, so much so that it was as though her heart would burst.

The music quieted, and Sage ushered Jeremy and Frances to stand next to them as the crowd hushed and the sweet sound of Terre Rouge's customary matrimony song filtered through the room, and the wedding began.

Fairies soared and twinkled through the candle-lit room, and the celebration for the union of Terre Rouge and Cathair Liath had begun in earnest.

Frances tilted her head back and laughed as both alcohol and joy made her feet move to the music. She and Jeremy had been dancing for over an hour now, and though she felt no strain, a steady gleam of sweat shone on Jeremy's forehead.

Yet he laughed with her, and she let out a girlish squeal as he pressed a kiss against her neck. She sighed as his teeth grazed her skin, and her fingers clenched around his shoulders.

"Careful now, Mister Nightingale," Frances purred. "Or we'll have to cut this celebration short in search of some privacy."

Jeremy chuckled and straightened, though his attention remained fixed on her as the music slowed and he bowed. The aggravatingly low curtsy was nothing to Frances now, though, and she batted her lashes at him with feigned innocence as he led her away from the moving bodies.

It was easy to spot Duncan and Daithine, both dripping in finery and bathed in smiles. They sat on their thrones and spoke in low tones, though their gazes watched the crowd with pride, and perhaps a hint of relief.

There was still a touch of grief on the king's face, but Frances could hardly blame him. She couldn't imagine the strange muddle of confusion, sadness, and glee that must be roiling about inside of him, and she was delighted that she wasn't in his place.

She hadn't asked Milo about his feelings on the matter, but she supposed they were siblings now, and she would pester him about it for the rest of their immortal lives. But she understood the pain of losing a parent, and by the strained happiness on the prince's face, she knew he was just as confused as the king.

"I'll get us refreshments," Jeremy murmured in her ear, and Frances nodded before making her way to sit on the low couches that surrounded the outer wall.

There was still a clear view of the dance floor and the

newly joined couple, and Frances allowed herself to watch. Malichi was in the throng of people for once, a tentatively kind expression on his face as he spoke to a pretty woman with chestnut-colored hair. Frances raised her eyebrows as she watched, and he seemed to notice her stare. He gave her a slight scowl, and Frances gave him a mocking salute and a wink in turn. He shook his head slightly and turned back to the woman, offering his arm so they could take a turn about the room and disappear from Frances's view.

Jeremy returned shortly with two flutes of bubbling pink drinks and handed her one with a slight bow. "My lady."

Frances sat up and took the drink. "How gracious of you."

Jeremy sat down beside her and offered his free hand. His warmth never ceased to make her shiver and now was no exception. She took a sip of the sweet alcohol and leaned her head back.

"How are you feeling?" she asked, and Jeremy sighed as he leaned his head against the back of the couch.

"Would you think less of me if I said I don't know what to feel?" he asked.

Frances shook her head. "I could never judge someone for how they feel. You've been through so much, and we're all grieving even through such a happy occasion."

Jeremy took a sip of his drink before answering. "I can't help but think that this is all a dream at times, and that I'll wake up to find Lennora and Lyra still here. That Esther wasn't the one to put us in this mess."

"I'm Milo's sister now," Frances said around her glass. "How ironic."

Jeremy snorted into his drink, and they glanced at each other sideways. "I'm just glad you didn't marry him."

Frances looked at him fully now, and it was a wondrous thing indeed. Every time she did, it was like the first time, and she felt like a puddle of emotion all over again.

He watched her with half-lidded eyes, his throat bared from the uptilt of his head against the couch. She wanted to bury her teeth in that throat, in the most loving way possible, of course. Frances found herself leaning closer, her body aching to kiss him. Crippling desire crossed over his face, but he remained still as she brushed her lips against his.

Someone cleared their throat behind them, and Frances let out a groan before separating herself from Jeremy. Sage and Milo stood there, both drunk off each other's company, as well as from the drinks in their hands.

"Are we interrupting something?" Sage asked, and Frances shot him a withering glare.

"Not at all," Jeremy said, and Frances took another sip of her drink before any insults flew from her mouth.

"Good." Sage led Milo to sit on the couch across from theirs.

"You two look rather dashing tonight," Frances said, glancing between Milo and Sage, who had changed into attire more suitable for dancing, which was to say they only wore billowing tunics and dark trousers.

"Thank you," Sage said, and Milo only sank deeper into his seat.

"Oh, come now, you've saved the entire realm, yet you still can't take a compliment?"

"They're two very different things," Milo replied and sipped at his drink.

"It's okay, Milo, I'll continue to solely insult you," Jeremy said, and Milo shot him a grin.

"That would be much appreciated."

Jeremy winked. "I do what I can."

"What are you kittens mewling about now?"

Frances peered up to find Malichi standing before them, a fresh glass of bubbling liquid held in his grip.

"Mewling kittens?" Frances raised her eyebrows. "Brother,

are you all right, or have you been possessed with the spirit of someone who's actually joyful?"

Malichi gave her a noncommittal shrug. "Only the possession of liquid spirits, I'm afraid."

Frances only watched in mild surprise as her twin strolled to the couch and sat next to her, his usually perfect hair slightly skewed in the most dashing of ways.

"So, now that you have escaped my clutches, what are you planning to do with your eternity as a princess?" Malichi asked. "Well, unless something happens to mother or me."

Excitement and nerves made Frances reach for another sip, and she cleared her throat. "Well, I was thinking perhaps I might travel for some time and learn about investigative practices around the world."

"I would've thought you'd gotten your fill of investigative practices by now," Malichi mused.

Frances had thought so too, yet she had to admit their experience had been rather exhilarating, even through the loss and fear.

"We will also be traveling to find an old witch in Asura," Jeremy said. "I'm hoping that she'll be able to help train me more. I am skilled with a blade, but not as much with my magic."

Frances swiveled to gape at Jeremy, and he gave her a shy tilt of his head.

"If you'll let me join you."

Words in both French and the common tongue couldn't explain the bubbling sensation that swept through Frances's chest, and so she kissed him, swift and hard.

"Yes," she whispered against his lips before turning back to her brother. "What about you, dear brother? Now that we have a king on our throne again, you're as free as I am."

Malichi glanced at the raised dais where their mother sat and shook his head. "I will return to Terre Rouge and continue as regent. I haven't seen our mother this happy in a long time, and I have no desire to force her back to the place that causes her such pain."

Frances gulped. "That is very selfless of you, brother."

Malichi gave her a worn smile, one more like the old version of him. "Not so selfless. I will only act as her advisor and make sure the laws they pass are carried out at home. There will be a lot of free time, and an entire castle at my disposal until you return."

If I return, she had to admit the time away from home had done much to help ease the pain of her father's passing, and she wasn't sure what would happen if she went home just yet.

"You must get into as much trouble as possible," Frances said, and Malichi rolled his eyes.

"No trouble, just some light fun."

"I'm still proud of you." Frances nudged his arm.

It was true, though. This new light that emanated from him made her more grateful than she could say, and she only wished that it wouldn't dim when he returned home.

"What about you?" Frances turned to Milo and Sage, who had been leaning against each other, watching Frances and Malichi's bickering in amusement.

"I wouldn't mind a bit of adventure and fresh air," Milo said, and Jeremy choked on his drink.

Milo narrowed a glare at his friend. "What? Everyone is turning over a new leaf; why can't I?"

"You want to travel around the world with us?" Jeremy asked, and Milo wrinkled his nose.

"Gods no, not the entire world. I can do that in my sleep. No, perhaps just a short trip to Asura to learn more about the first stardust soul. Then, I want to go back home and stay there for a good long while, perhaps lose myself in The Study for a few months and learn more about the gods."

Frances frowned. "You want to learn more about the gods?"

Milo's gaze flashed toward Jeremy, and something like guilt flickered across his face. It was gone in an instant, however, and Frances wasn't sure if she had imagined it.

"Very well, I think we have enough space for you to come with us for a short trip," Frances said, then looked at Sage. "And you?"

Sage blinked, as though surprised that he was part of the conversation.

"I'm to be a professor," Sage shrugged. "I assume that I'll return to The Study upon our return to Rightford Castle and continue my training."

Milo stiffened slightly, and Frances's spirits dropped for him. She understood what it was like to want someone who had to live a life different from what she wanted, and was glad it was no longer something she had to endure. Anton's dark features filtered through her mind for the first time in weeks, and she jolted.

Thank the gods that part of her life was over.

"You must join us in Asura," Jeremy said quickly. "I think Professor Binks can spare you a few weeks of travel before you return to your studies."

Uncertainty and hope washed over the vampire's face, and he glanced at Milo. The prince was fidgeting nervously with the hem of his tunic, and Sage placed a hand over his.

"A small trip could be nice, if you'd like that," Sage said, and Milo met his question with shy excitement.

"I would like that very much."

"Good," Jeremy clapped his hands upon his thighs. "I wasn't ready to give up our little band of idiots quite yet anyway. We were just getting started."

He stood from the couch and drained the last of his drink. "Now, who wants to dance?"

Acknowledgments

I would first like to thank myself from 2020 for writing this book. Everyone remembers that year, and I turned the solitude into a story. *Stardust Souls* is unlike anything I've written, and my desire was for it to feel like a stroll through the woods, rather than a grand epic rollercoaster. I had read a few books with the same flavor, and I yearned to create something like that for myself. We all know that saying, "write the story you would want to read," and I believe I did that with this book. So, thank you, past Gabriela, for writing and then forgetting about *Stardust Souls* for so long, allowing me to find it again.

Thank you to my dear friend, Cathrine Swift, for supporting me not only with this book but with my entire author journey. I couldn't have done this without your support, cover-making genius, and guidance to help me find my footing again. You are a light, and anyone who knows you is lucky.

Thank you to my parents. You have always told me to do what I love, and the rest will follow. This is what I love.

To Raven, my dog, for keeping me company during the many hours of drafting this book, and for reminding me to go outside and stretch my legs.

And most of all, thank you, reader, for being patient as I return to the world of publishing, and for believing in me and my art. It is a dream come true to share these stories with you.

About the Author

Gabriela has been writing and telling stories since she was a young girl. Perhaps it was inevitable that she would call grappling with words and making writing-related videos on YouTube a career—and love every moment.

When not writing or filming, you can find Gabriela reading, cuddling her dog Raven (better known as "Raisin", dubbed by her doggy grandparents), or riding and training horses.

Get in touch through Gabriela's social media to discover more about her work, writing process, and future endeavors.

www.ingramcontent.com/pod-product-compliance
Lightning Source LLC
LaVergne TN
LVHW010627110826
845149LV00014B/2799

* 9 7 9 8 9 9 3 1 5 0 1 2 3 *